PhDeath

THE PUZZLER MURDERS

JAMES P. CARSE

PhDeath: The Puzzler Murders
by James P. Carse
An OPUS Trade Paperback Original

ISBN: 978-1-62316-066-1

LCSH: Puzzles--Fiction. | Ciphers--Fiction. | Distributive justice--Fiction. | Social justice--Economic aspects--Fiction. | Plato--Fiction. | Universities and colleges--Economic aspects--United States. | Universities and colleges--Political aspects--United States. | Education, Higher--Philosophy. | Academic-industrial collaboration--United States--Fiction. | Military-industrial complex--United States--Fiction. | Christianity--Fiction. | Socialism--Fiction. | Celebrities--Fiction. | College students--United States--Political activity. |College students--United States--Social life and customs. | LCGFT: Detective and mystery fiction. | Thrillers (Fiction)

LCC: PS3603.A7753 P43 2017 | DDC: 813/.6--dc23

E-BOOK EDITIONS ALSO AVAILABLE.

Publisher's Cataloguing-in-Publication Data to come.

www.opusbookpublishers.com

A Division of Subtext Inc., **A Glenn Young Company**
P.O. BOX 725
Tuxedo Park, NY 10987

OPUS is distributed to the trade by The Hal Leonard Publishing Group
Toll Free Sales: 800-524-4425
www.halleonard.com

FIRST EDITION

10 9 8 7 6 5 4 3 2

Printed in the United States of America.

PRAISE FOR JAMES P. CARSE

"James Carse reveals that we don't have to go to India to have a mystical experience, and transcendence can and does occur in our own backyard. His fresh new book shows us how."
— DAN WAKEFIELD

"Beguilingly beautiful, hauntingly evocative, and serenely successful."
— JOHN DOMINIC CROSSON,
AUTHOR OF *THE HISTORICAL JESUS*

"Once in a while a book comes along that adds a new pattern of knowledge to existing facts. The result is striking. Old dull things you've known for years suddenly stand up in a whole new dimension."
— ROBERT M. PIRSIG, AUTHOR OF
ZEN AND THE ART OF MOTORCYCLE MAINTENANCE

"Carse is a kind of agile provocateur, eager to prise us out of our set positions, to get us thinking ... He contrives to make the thrashing out of essential issues both urgent and enjoyable."
— PICO IYER, *THE NEW YORK REVIEW OF BOOKS*

"The engaging and insightful stories explain why Carse has gained an almost cult-like following at NYU and beyond."
— *PUBLISHERS WEEKLY*

JAMES P. CARSE is Professor Emeritus of History and Literature of Religion at New York University, where he was also Director of the Religious Studies Program. Carse is the winner of numerous awards including New York University's Great Teacher Award, New York University Distinguished Teaching Award, and Doctor of Humane Letters from Georgetown University. He is the author of eight non-fiction books, including *Finite and Infinite Games, Breakfast at the Victory: The Mysticism of Ordinary Experience,* and *The Religous Case Against Belief.* He was host of *The Way to Go,* a CBS Sunday morning program for eight years that focused on religious, artistic and intellectual figures. He lives in New York and Massachusetts.

for Frank Peters

ACKNOWLEDGMENTS

If writing a novel is rarely a solo performance, *PhDeath* has been nothing less than an orchestral project. To list all of the contributing players would double the size of the volume. It would have to include five decades of students, scores of academic colleagues, and many close friends. Some names cannot be omitted. Kristen Olsson gave the manuscript a first and critically perceptive reading. Carol Mack generously ushered it to the stage by directing it to Opus Books. Alfredand Sally Alcorn, Will and Sam Blattner were invaluably instrumental in its overall design. Stephani Cook and Robert Walsh heroically blue- penciled the text's multiple blunders, both trivial and grave. Having dared to accept an unconventional composition, Publisher and Editor, Glenn Young, hovered over it as a masterful conductor, identifying its flat notes and disharmonies, and patiently working toward a unified production of its many parts.

PhDeath

THE PUZZLER MURDERS

REGISTRATION
FALL SEMESTER

ONE

His body, when it was discovered at the entrance to the University's Administration Building, lay partly on the sidewalk and partly in the street. Most of his head, or what was left of it, was about a car's width from the curb, too shattered for positive identification.

Although it was not immediately known to whom the body belonged, it seemed to have fallen from an upper floor of the ten-story building. Campus Security was on site minutes after it was reported at 8:13 A.M. by a taxi driver in his strong Urdu accent.

Campus police immediately made a cordon around the unknown man's remains, holding back students and passersby to avoid trampling on the fragments of skull extending out to the yellow line at the street's median. The face had the rough appearance of a stained sandwich wrapper with teeth and hair. The body evidently had hit the pavement headfirst.

Two city police cruisers blared their way to the scene followed by an ambulance from the University hospital. The EMTs, springing from their ambulance and pushing through to the victim with their stretcher, stopped short when they got a full view of the body. Even to an experienced emergency worker, the sight was disturbing. They covered the remains with a blue plastic sheet. Only a pair of men's expensive cordovan shoes protruded from beneath. There would be no immediate need for the stretcher. Nothing could be disturbed until the Coroner arrived.

Overnight denizens of the Square were the first onlookers to appear. Bleary-eyed students began to emerge from the subway on the far side of the park. Dormitory residents wandered out dazed and curious in bathrobes and flip-flops. It was as if a signal had gone out, calling a chorus of citizens to view the mysterious shattered remains. Newcomers whispered among themselves, analyzing, speculating, buzzing in solemn communion about the fate of the human body at their feet.

The quiet was shattered by a woman's scream from an open window at the top floor of the Administration Building. The woman's face briefly appeared over the sill, then vanished. Moments later, she burst through the glass doors of the building's entrance and rushed in panic and horror toward the covered body. She was recognized at once by the growing mass of students and professors as Lucille Morrowitz, the Executive Administrative Assistant to the Dean of Arts and Sciences. Her whispered name could be heard circling through the crowd.

Through convulsive sobs, Lucille affirmed the identity of the body as that of her boss, Dean Oliver Ridley. When the officers began to lift the heavy-gauge plastic, she held up a hand to stop them. As she later testified, she needed only to see his feet. The Bettanin & Venturi shoes had been purchased a few weeks earlier for the Dean's first day in office. It was Lucille who had advised him on the purchase, introducing him to one of her most valued shoe saleswomen on trendy Spring Street.

TWO

It was about an hour and a half later that I left Café Rossetti and headed for my office across the Square. Two large white vans ominously flashed their blue lights; yellow tape marked out a misshapen rectangle at the entrance to the Administration Building.

I stopped a young man leaving the scene.

"What's going on?"

His response was immediate. "The Dean. He did himself."

"The Dean did what?"

"The Dean, man. He used a window. He shoulda used the door."

"Dean? Which Dean?"

"How am I supposed to know?" he said over his shoulder. "That's all they say: it's the Dean."

Still twenty yards from the site, I could just make out through the trees an open window on the top floor of Oliver Ridley's office. The dark emptiness of that rectangle threw a macabre cast over the entire building. As with most shocks, the initial reaction was one of incredulity. How could he? Why would he? He, of all people?

When I reached the yellow tape, I fought with myself not to look for the stain. The police were looking off in several directions, repeating the familiar chant:

"Move along. There's nothing to see."

Strangely, although there was nothing much to see, I, like the others, resisted leaving. We stood there as if our mere presence would give the spot a vague spiritual weight.

It had not been twenty-four hours since I was myself in that very tenth floor office. I remember seeing not only a live Oliver Ridley, but also a man riding the high edge of his enthusiasm for assuming a new challenge. He had been installed as Dean of the College of Arts and Sciences not three weeks earlier, and I had gone to congratulate him. There was a delicate matter involved. Ridley was named Dean at the same meeting of Trustees that elevated me the rank of University Professor, a somewhat greater honor. I wanted to head off any feelings of envy or resentment.

THREE

I had arrived at Ridley's office a little after 8:00, early enough not to disturb a morning meeting. I entered with care, knowing that Lucille might well be there as well. Ridley, I was sure, knew nothing of the complicated relationship I'd had with his executive assistant over the past year. Her door was partly ajar. What I saw stopped me. It was no more than an extended foot, oddly positioned because of the way she must have been sitting at her desk. Hanging from her toe was one of the three-inch spike heels she favored, in scarlet patent leather. A quick movement of her leg would have catapulted this fashionably dangerous missile skyward, for me an unsubtle reminder of my own precarious status with Lucille. I skirted by her office and went directly into Ridley's chamber.

He was on the phone, leaning back in his new Aeron Chair, his gaze fixed on something immovable in the atmosphere above the Square, while mumbling with obvious annoyance into the mouthpiece. His desk was a model of the proficient administrator. The fresh green blotter at the center was still unstained and empty, except for the large uncapped Mont Blanc lying at its center. Surrounding it were three or four tidy stacks of papers, flattened and stapled, and a gold-framed photo of his wife and their two daughters. There was also, I was amused but not surprised to see, a pair of binoculars. I recognized both the brand and the size: Fujinons, 8 X 24's.

He suddenly noted my presence and without taking the phone from his ear, gave me a sweeping signal to enter.

I walked over to the bank of grand nineteenth-century windows, open to the warm early September air, and looked out, waiting for him to end his phone conversation. Of course he would have his binoculars. It was the height of the fall migrating season. It was typical of Ridley that he had joined the official Audubon bird count, tallying the most recent arrivals, now refueling after their long nighttime migratory flights, in the giant sycamores and oaks that shade most of the Square.

Looking over this urban forest, I was reminded that because of the University's location at the center of the city, and because of its intimate collaboration with powerful cultural and corporate institutions, President Jack Lister had decided it needed a new tagline. For his predecessor, it had been the "International University." Under Lister we had become the "Enterprise University." How much further from migrating golden-crowned kinglets and evening grosbeaks can we get?

The Dean's mumbling had gotten louder and more impatient. I could make out a few words: "Yes, Nat. Sure, Nat. I got it. I don't know about that. You're right. I agree, Nat." Of course, I thought to myself, it's Nathanael Holmers, Professor and Chair of Anthropology, in his characteristic alpha-wolf mode, assailing the new Dean for a series of past decanal blunders Ridley had nothing to do with. It made sense that Holmers, having been passed over for the position, was undergoing a severe onset of jealousy.

I heard the phone slam and turned to find Ridley coming around the corner of his desk, fastening the center button on his summer tweed.

"Carmody! Welcome! And congrats, friend."

"The same, happily returned."

Oliver Ridley was a slight man, carefully tailored, who moved in staccato jerks like a small animal whose muscles seem to have one speed. This trait gave him the appearance of one capable of focused purpose and swift decision. In fact, he was such a man. His intelligence was absent of blurred edges. When his signature was found at the bottom of the page, the reader knew the subject had been fully covered and aptly resolved. Second guesses were not part of his intellectual armory.

As the new Dean of the Faculty of Liberal Arts, Ridley's mandate was imposing. The President of the University had long since tired of the professorial fondness for endless qualification which regularly greeted his struggle to bring coherence and focus to the College of Arts and Science faculty. The other colleges — especially the Medical, Dental, Commerce, Social Work, Nursing, Education, Engineering, and Law Schools — were models of academic order, their curricula revolving smoothly around the natural divisions of each profession. The School of the Arts, at the other extreme, was a school of artists and other creative types, and therefore lay beyond any hope of civilized order. The Arts faculty's explosive disagreements, endangered egos, and shared personal dislikes erased all but the most superficial shows of collegiality.

The College of Arts and Science, the school that bore the largest responsibility for the University's public reputation, was serenely oblivious to administrative influence. Worse, of all the University's colleges it was the most indignant about having to seek independent financial support on its own, acting instead like a teenager with an enormous trust fund. It was therefore ignored by donors more interested in attaching their names to a hospital clinic or a wing of the School of Commerce than to an endowed professorship for research in the civilizations of the ancient Middle East. Ridley was chosen for the honor over a half dozen other ambitious nominees.

"Setophaga castanea!" he announced with an amused grin. "I saw it this morning in the red oak at this corner of the Square. Beat that if you will."

I had to mouth the familiar Greek words a couple times before they clicked in. "Bay-breasted! Nice work, Ridley." This tiny warbler is devilishly difficult to identify in the fall. "I got a black-throated blue myself, in the London planetree by the fountain."

"Setophaga caerulescens." He was right, of course.

Ridley had for years served on the board of the National Audubon Society. Even in that crowd he was an accomplished life-lister. He was only forty-seven species short of identifying every one of the 914 birds that are officially recognized as native to North America, a prodigious achievement. Birding is an interest we shared, although with a life list hovering around 150, I'm strictly farm team.

"Oh, Professor Carmody! Good morning." Lucille was standing in the door with what appeared to be the Dean's mail, feigning surprise at my presence. She presented herself in a tailored Evelyn and Diane deClercqs suit, winter white with cuffed pants, one of the many I had seen in her closet.

Ridley's immediate shift of attention to Lucille was the signal that his business with me was concluded. After a few empty final exchanges concerning his plans for the College and my responsibilities and privileges as the newly minted University Professor of Rhetoric, I left his office.

I had observed nothing in that brief meeting with the Dean that hinted at self-destruction or any emotionally precarious state. On the contrary, he was a man celebrating his own finest hour.

FOUR

As the elevator door opened on the third floor of the building where most of the faculty of Arts and Sciences had their offices, my first view was that of the ample posterior of the distinguished Professor of Classics, Alfred O'Malley. He was leaning over, giving close attention to a document on the desk of the third floor secretary, Iolinda Thompson. O'Malley was known to have an active fascination with all forms of popular culture. It was not uncommon to find him in extended conversation with Iolinda about Eartha's final appearance in the city, or a new release featuring Tina, with the subject shifting to Lena, then to Marian and on to Mahalia, even Nina and Ella.

O'Malley, chewing on the stem of his glasses, his face inches above the document in question, could have been translating a text of an ancient language, Ugaritic or Linear B, say (two of his specialties).

"Professor Carmody! Thank the Lord Jesus you're here!"

Iolinda Thompson jumped to her feet and threw her hands out as soon as she saw me. Her evocation of the Lord was as original and unexpected as any greeting I've received at her desk. That a declared ex-Catholic would evoke that celebrated fellow to thank was a clue to a sense of alarm she seemed to share with O'Malley.

Alfie looked up at me like he was waking from a dream. "Oh, Carmody. I suppose you've heard the news."

"I have just come from the Square."

"Carmody," Alfie said, "look here." He leaned back to give me a view of the desk, and pointed at the single sheet of paper he had been examining.

PUZZLE ALERT!

1. THE FIRST ARTICLE IN THE DECLARATION OF INDEPENDENCE.

2. WHITHER THE RIGHT-HANDER SPED FOR FAME. *

3. AN ALSO WITHOUT AN O.

4. IN THE MIDST OF GREEK CONFLICT.

5. GUATEMALAN'S AFFIRMATIVE REVERSED.

6. THE FIRST A SECOND TIME.

7. STORM, SMOTE, STOMP, STOMA, MOIST, STORM: ~~REPAIR~~.

8. THE CENTER RE-CENTERED.

9. THE FIRST PREPOSITION IN THE DECLARATION OF INDEPENDENCE.

10. OGLER'S HIGHEST VALUE.

"γνφθι ςεαυτον"

"Iolinda, tell Carmody what you think."

"Well, this thing came by email, the date stamp reads 7:32 a.m."

I gave it a closer look. I recognized it as something that appeared in my email as well, but without comment or signature. I had deleted it as spam. Somebody had also taped it to the rear wall of the elevator I had just exited.

"It was so quiet this morning, nobody here yet, I started playing around with it. *The Times* crossword I finished on the subway. I think I got numbers one, six, eight, and nine."

"If you don't mind, Iolinda, I'm not exactly in a mental state suitable for solving puzzles. If you'll excuse me …"

"Hold your horses, Carmody," Alfie said. "What if I told you this might have to do with Ridley?"

"Suicide note?" I looked at it more closely. "All right, I'll play along for two minutes then I must get to my office. What have you got, Iolinda?"

"Well, for number one, I guessed *The*."

"She's right," Alfie said. "There are no articles in *The Declaration of Independence*. It's just five paragraphs and a tiresome list of the King's injustices. So the clue's reference has to be to the title itself."

"And then for six," Iolinda continued, "that seemed to mean another *The*. Then nine. I figured they meant just the title, like in number one, not what's actually in the *Declaration*. Since, we already have *The* twice, I suppose it has to be *of*."

"Has to be," Alfie said.

"I didn't know what they could mean by re-centering unless it was re-spelling. The only thing I could get from **center** was *recent*."

"Brilliant," Alfie said, "brilliant."

"That's all I got," she said.

"Don't worry, sweetheart," Alfie assured her, "we have the University Professor of Rhetoric right in front of us."

"That's not much of a suicide note so far," I suggested.

"Makes sense, though," Alfie said. "It gets sent out to the whole faculty, and probably the entire student body, only a couple of hours or so before he leaps tens stories to the street."

I gave him a doubtful stare. "Okay, let's solve it and see."

"And because it's a *puzzle*," Alfie added, "he clearly wants us to *get* something. As the puzzle is titled, it's an 'Alert.'"

Iolinda took out a clean sheet and wrote four words. *The, The, recent,* and *of.*

Alfie pulled a chair over and sat across the corner from Iolinda. I leaned on the desk, facing them.

"I'll take a shot at seven." I read out the line:

Storm,

smote,

stomp,

stoma,

moist,

storm:

~~repair.~~

I thought I found the trick at once. "You notice there is one word with a strikethrough, repair, and six without. You can also read, repair, as six separate letters — r, e, p, a, i, and r — to find that each letter occurs in one of the six preceding words. If we then strike through those individual letters, we get, let's see: stom, smot, stom, stom, most, stom. As you see at once, the four remaining letters all spell one word and one word only: *most.* Agreed?"

"Agreed."

"Agreed."

"What does **'ogler's highest value'** mean? The tenth clue." Iolinda asked.

Alfie looked at Iolinda and with an exaggerated expression, wiggled his eyebrows.

"What's an **'ogler,'** anyway?" she asked, ignoring Alfie's indelicacy.

"You're a ten, sweetheart, that's all you need to know." He gave me a quick glance. "Did I just commit a sexist innuendo?"

"Need you ask?"

"Add *ten*," he said, nodding at the list. "What do we have so far?"

"*The, The, recent, of, most,* and, *ten*."

I took out my pen and wrote at the bottom of the page, the Greek letters, αγον, as a hint to Alfie.

"Ha!" he responded. "Carmody's being a little cute," he said to Iolinda. That's *a-g-o-n*," he explained. "It translates as 'conflict.' You know, basis of *agony*. So we can read the fourth clue, **In the midst of Greek conflict**, as 'In the midst of the Greek word for conflict, that is, agon. And the middle of *a-g-o-n* is …?" He gave Iolinda the eye treatment again.

"*G* and *O*?"

"Right. And that spells?"

Without answering, she added a seventh answer: *go*.

There was a digital ding as the elevator opened and Professor Raimundo Guttierez emerged, heading in our direction as if propelled. Acknowledging neither Alfie nor me, he tossed a crumpled piece of paper onto Iolinda's desk as he marched by.

"Throw this out," he told her. I recognized it at once as the puzzle. "Somebody stuck it up in the elevator."

"I did." Iolinda said, and gave him a withering smile.

"Too goddam much clutter around here," he responded.

The manner of his sudden and aggressive presence, whether physical or intellectual, was what we had come to expect from Guttierez. With the official title, Lecturer in Catalan Studies, he had been appointed to the faculty several years earlier by an executive act of the President, Jack Lister. His status in the University was unique. Because his salary was paid by an unnamed foundation independent of the University, he was not subject to the usual tenure proceedings, and, as far as we knew, was hired for life.

The anger he displayed in this little scene was typical of the way he viewed the world through an unforgiving lens. He seemed to have come late to the academic profession. I guessed that he was in his early or middle fifties, and though still at the beginning of his career, he was on his rapid way to becoming a respected scholar.

"Raimundo," Iolinda called to his retreating figure without losing her put-down expression of amusement, "there's a question here for you, *en Español*, sort of." She flattened out the piece he had thrown at her, and pointed at clue number five — **Guatemalan's affirmative reversed** — with a fingernail sharpened like a weapon. "Solve this one for us."

His look of outrage softening before a woman's challenge, he returned, stuttered a bit then said with unnecessary emphasis, "Si, si. Si!"

"**Reversed**," she prompted.

"No. That's the answer. No." He turned and started off again, then stopped and looked back. "No, not no. *Is. Is!*"

A slamming door soon followed this last exclamation. For a moment the three of us just stared at the empty corridor. Iolinda added Guttierez's contribution.

"Let's see what we have," Alfie said, leaning over her.

She read off the list. "*The, The, recent, of, most, ten, go,* and *is.*"

"Sorry, Io," Alfie said, "I don't yet see what this has to do with the Ridley's suicide."

"There are only two clues left," I noted. "Let's stay with it."

Iolinda read number three out loud. "**An also without an O.**"

"**An also,**" I repeated. "Strange formulation. If there is **an**, or one also, maybe there is another. What's a synonym for the word?"

"And," Alfie suggested, with a shrug.

"Too," Iolinda added.

"Touché, Iolinda!" Alfie said. "Drop an O and you get — ?

She wrote a *to* on to the end of the list.

We looked at the second clue,

Whither the right-hander sped for fame.*

I gave Alfie a poke with my pointed elbow. "Hey, you're the sports guy here."

"I'm thinking. I'm thinking." He held up the puzzle as if it needed closer attention. "*Aha!* Simple. Once you connect a righty with 'fame' plus an attached asterisk, the answer comes up on the mental screen before you can say Armando Galarraga, June 2, 2011. Galarraga would have had a perfect game, but the umpire made a disastrously wrong call. As to 'whither,' it's gotta be first base. Armando made the catch and had an easy tag out at first base. He got there a full step before the runner. That's when the umpire made one of the most famous calls in baseball history. Would have been the first perfect game in Detroit's entire franchise."

Alfie was obviously warmed up.

"Now had it been a left-hander, you've got one even more famous. Harvey Haddix, May 26, 1959. Pittsburgh Pirates. Completes nine innings without a hit or walk. Twenty-seven batters. But the game is tied. The eleventh inning, three more batters, game still tied. Now it's the thirteenth. The thirteenth! Thirty-six batters, thirty-six outs in a row. Raimundo Mantilla gets a hit. Hank Aaron, believe it or not, yeah him, Hank Aaron, draws an intentional walk. Joe Adcock, another great, gets a hit. Indians win."

"Alfie, what's the answer?"

"*First*, of course."

"Iolinda?" Alfie pointed at the list.

"Here's what we have: "*The, The, recent, of, most, ten, go, to, is,* and *first.*"

"Makes no sense." I spoke for all of us.

"Put them in their original sequence," Alfie proposed.

Iolinda took a minute to rearrange the words and write them out in the order in which they occur in the puzzle: *The first to go is the most recent of ten.*

"Holy *shit*!" Alfie jumped to his feet. "'The most recent of ten.' There are ten deans, remember? Ridley is the last to be named. This could very well have to do with him. If so this is big, guys, *big!*"

"Iolinda," I said, "get me the President's office."

She punched in a few numbers and handed me the phone.

"What?" was all the President said when I was connected.

I quoted the solution to the puzzle. "Get your ass over here. Sprint." He hung up. The whole conversation wasn't 15 seconds.

I hit the down button on the elevator. "Alfie, we forgot something."

"Yeah?"

"The 'γνφθι ϛεαυτον' at the bottom of the puzzle. You realize the killer put quotes on it like it is something he's saying to us. Think about it."

25

The elevator opened. As I stepped in, I realized that for the first time I had used the word *killer*.

FIVE

"Professor Carmody."

Jack Lister spoke my name as I entered his office like he was presenting me to an audience. He was sitting at the head of the large antique table that dominated the center of the room. Built of teak stripped from a wrecked nineteenth century schooner off Perth Amboy, New Jersey, he referred to this remarkable piece of furniture as his pirate's desk. Whether intended or not, it was a clue to his personality. He was the University's thirteenth President.

Demands for immediate action, dawn phone calls, repeated tweets, a breathless torrent of emails were the very signatures of Jack's administrative style. He was a trustee's dream, and a professor's headache — a man of little deliberation and fast resolution. But smart. And, as no one knew better than I, a demon genius on the squash court.

He pointed to the chair next to his.

"Now, Carmody, let me get this straight," he said, looking at me over the rim of his glasses, "you're telling me that you think Oliver Ridley's not a suicide, that the poor bastard's been offed? Make your case, please."

I placed the puzzle on the desk between us. "This puzzle was sent by email to the student body and the entire faculty."

"Word puzzles, Carmody? I'm stuck here with real puzzles. The ones I have to deal with are called students and professors. In fact, according to my latest info, I got — " He leaned over and looked at a handwritten note on his desk. " — 43,739 of them."

"At about 8:00 this morning, Jack, not four hours ago, that became 43,738."

"Right," he said and with a pencil drew a slash mark across the note. "Go on. So, you got this puzzle. Was it you that solved it?"

"Not alone. Alfie O'Malley along with Iolinda Thompson, the third floor secretary — "

"And you all decided the solution to the puzzle said what?"

"*The first to go is the most recent of ten.*"

"Okay, Carmody. You're our newly crowned master rhetorician. Does this maniac mean ten Deans?"

"*The most recent of ten* is strictly adjectival and refers to *the first to go.* No one is specifically implied."

"To me," he said, tossing the pencil across the full length of the huge desk, "*the first to go* sounds like a threat."

"It may be. But it is too vague to interpret closely."

"What's this Greek doodle at the bottom?" He turned the page around. "You can probably read that stuff. Please."

"Pronounced, *gnothi seauton.* It's usually translated, 'Know thyself.'"

"To wit, Socrates," Lister responded at once.

"Exactly, Socrates' most quoted remark."

"The point being — ?"

"My guess is no better than yours, Jack. Unless 'know thyself' means that we are all somehow complicit? Who knows how a madman thinks?"

"And so he kills a Dean I installed not three weeks ago? Carmody, this fucker's crazy. None of this makes any sense."

"Crazy, Jack, yes. But also clever. His modus is not uzis and pressure cooker bombs. He's planting bombs right where we live: in our minds."

"Then let's get our best minds on his trail. Here's what you do. Pick out some high-octane mental cases from Arts and Sciences. Give it a classy name. 'The Presidential Commission on Something or Other.' Puff up a few bastards, promise them anything, money, I don't give a shit. We gotta catch this guy. In the meantime, I've already got the top cops involved."

"Frankly, Jack, I'm not your best choice for raising the most effective committee. What about —?"

"Too late. You're already appointed. Now get cracking." He stood to signal that the meeting was over.

SIX

I went straight to Alfie O'Malley's office to report on my meeting with Jack Lister and his demand that I set up a committee at once. His raised eyebrows said: Of course, what else would you expect?

O'Malley's office always impressed me as a mirror image of his larger life, inner and outer. On the one hand, it felt like a grotto carved out of a mountain of books. Many of the shelves were double-stacked, and in how many languages, it was hard to say. Some of the titles were so obscure they made no more sense than a Scrabble tray of random letters. Alfie was a scholar of surpassing talents and the author of a small library of his own volumes. I recognized his renowned *From Osiris to Orestes: the Alexandrian Deconstruction of Pharaonic Wisdom,* and his classic, *Torah, Gospel, and Sharia: a Study in Misprision.* On the other hand, taped to the back of his door was an enormous poster of Aretha's last performance at Madison Square Garden. As noted earlier, he was also a fan of all things popular, not only music of a dozen genres but also sports, politics, and, of course, crime.

"And," he said, looking away from me, "you probably have me on your list."

"You're the first."

"Look, Carmody," he began in an unconvincingly confident voice, "we can do it, the two of us. Hey, you and Iolinda and me, we got it in, what, an hour?"

"Not so simple, Alfie. You realize that even if we had solved the puzzle *before* Ridley was killed, it would not have been obvious that it was targeting him. It made sense only *after* the fact."

"*Post hoc, ergo propter hoc.*" I heard him mumble to himself.

"What we need is a panel of brainiacs who can think their way into the head of the Puzzler and catch him before he kills another."

He was silent for a few seconds. "All right," he groused, "we'll just hustle a few guys and gals from a different disciplines, wordy types, good at useless knowledge. Plenty of them around."

"Alfie, as for words, stop using that expression, 'guys and gals.'"

"Sorry. Gals and guys." He paused to study Aretha's commercial portrait as though it might produce the ideal roster.

Our cells rang at the same time. I noticed the text was sent from the President's office. It wasn't half an hour since I had left him. Typical.

To: Full teaching staff.
From: President Lister
Re: Dean Oliver Ridley. It has been brought to our attention that the Dean's death may not have been a suicide. In this era of mass murders at

academic institutions, it is not possible to be too cautious. I have alerted the metropolitan police. They have assigned their top detective to the case. He agreed to meet with the faculty at once.

Tyverson Lecture Hall.

Today, Four o'clock.

Attendance mandatory.

I looked at my watch. 2:15. O'Malley and I exchanged glances.

"Right after," he said. "Let's meet right here and get going on this committee."

SEVEN

Tyverson Hall was a small auditorium where I frequently lectured. I was, I must admit, fascinated. My colleagues were displaying an excitement and attentiveness I had never observed in department and faculty meetings, much less at the presentation of learned papers. There was such a rush of animated conversation that no one noticed we had been there nearly half an hour without the appearance of an administrator, much less a police investigator. When the door opened, the talk ended as if it had an on-off switch.

President Jack Lister entered first, followed by a tall, gentleman, nearly up to Jack's six-feet-five inches.

Jack stepped to the lectern, loosened then tightened his tie, and gazed over the room with the look of a commander taking charge.

"Good afternoon, colleagues," he began, using a term I had never heard him utter. I knew he was thinking, "staff," or, more likely, "employees."

He unfolded an index card, and read:

"I will not add to your weighted reflection in the aftermath of this infortuitous tragedy." (He meant *unfortunate*.) "I will say only what you all know, that we are a close community with a dedication to caring about the well-being of our fellow seekers after truth. That someone shatters this comradeship with an act so vile as to be unique in the one hundred and forty-nine years of our University's history sends a message to our friends in the larger society, as well as to prospective students and to our loyal and faithful contributors, that distorts our humane commitment to the world. We are correctly known as the 'Enterprise University' because of our undying desire to advance the prosperity of all human beings whoever and wherever they are."

In the pause that followed, I sensed his relief at having unloaded this verbiage in no more than a few breaths. It was doubtless a practice run for what he knew would be a frequent test of his PR skills over the coming weeks.

"Look, guys," he resumed, quite as if we were a different audience, and tucked the index card in his jacket pocket. "We got two issues here. One's your safety. You gotta believe me that what we're doing is an all-out protection of the faculty. You're going to see a lotta cops around here. Be grateful. They've got your back. On the other hand, if, on the outside chance, the perp's one of you — ? And while it is revolting to entertain the notion, would you like us to ignore the possibility?"

He looked around the room.

"On that note, let me get to the main act on our program this afternoon. Gentlemen," he said with a grand sweep of the arm, "may I present decorated hero, Lieutenant Thomas Roche, among the finest of the city's finest." He turned to the officer and said, "Our distin-

31

guished faculty, Lieutenant," then added in a dismissive tone, "They're all yours, Tom."

Roche removed his hat and tucked it under his arm in the manner of a military commander reviewing his troops. He looked over our heads without responding, and seemed so interested in what was happening in a far corner of the ceiling that several rotated on their chairs to discern what was underway there. A camera? A recording device?

"Good afternoon, professors," he said in a slow-paced greeting that seemed at once respectful and bored. There was Bronx/Irish music in his voice.

"I want to thank each and every one of you for taking the trouble. We've got a circumstance here that requires fast and professional action."

There were frequent pauses in his speech that suggested he wanted every word to be remembered. He could have been talking to a grade school class about good citizenship. But there was also a mild elegance to his language, as if he were mindful of addressing an assembly of the higher learned.

"There's a perpetrator afoot, as you have divined, and he must be collared before something else transpires. I am," he said with careful emphasis, "the official in charge of the investigation. All inquiries and pertinent information are to be directed to me via this telephone."

He turned to the white board and wrote it out in large numerals.

"The line is exclusively for this case. We also have a secure email connection devised for this happenstance."

He wrote the email address directly below the number, and waited to see that we had all made a note of it. He then erased both addresses with such vigor I thought the board would show a scar. We got the point. It was a privileged access to the authorities reserved for faculty use only.

"Of course," he added, "you can also communicate through Jack here," he added, nodding at the President.

With these remarks out of the way, the Lieutenant abruptly shifted into an interrogatory mode. The transformation from genial Bronx Irishman to professional cop was complete. The questions came fast.

Seeing that there were no eyewitnesses on the outside, did any of us observe suspicious persons in the halls of the top two floors? Or in the classrooms that filled most of the building below the Dean's office? Do we know anyone with whom the Dean had been in dispute? Was there an aggrieved member of the faculty or student body who might have taken revenge or be driven to irrational rage? Indeed, was there anyone physically able to carry off the murder since it did require genuine physical force? Whom do we know who could compose a puzzle of such subtlety? Who would be so daring as to signal in advance a determination to commit a crime of this nature? Does the content of the puzzle point in the direction of a certain academic field? Is there any reason to think a student might have committed this crime?

The Lieutenant sped through these queries as if he were merely planting them in our memory, with the hint that there would be a later occasion when complete answers would be expected. He waited for no responses and none were provided.

Then he paused, looking at us over his rimless glasses. It was a clear signal that he was not finished. There was a matter that needed deeper examination. I quickly realized that he had been primed by President Lister to bring up the one controversy in which Oliver Ridley had been involved. I was not surprised and I could guess Lister's motives.

"The Night School," the Lieutenant said, without elaborating. "I understand there were strong feelings."

Everyone in the room knew the terms of the controversy, and most had taken positions on one side or the other. Roche waited. No one reacted. No one spoke. We all knew these "feelings" hadn't receded.

Over the previous year, Ridley had surged to the leadership of a rebelling faction of senior faculty demanding an end to the College's historic Night School. Resembling nothing so much as a classic revolutionary colonel, Ridley deftly raised and delivered a fatal majority on the final vote. The Night School faculty and staff were dismissed.

The Night School served those students unable to pay the College's high tuition and fees who were therefore forced to fit their education around full-time jobs. They commuted from their homes in and around the city and were typically either first generation or foreign born, comprising a full range of ethnicities. Many had young families.

Ridley's campaign was striking for its on-target exclamations: "We are an *international* not a *community* college!" "Our campus isn't the city but the nation! No, the world!" And then there were the embarrassing cries of genuine outrage, oft heard repeated among senior professors: "Does Harvard have a night school?" "Can you even imagine Yale stooping to such an institution?" To no one's surprise, Ridley's cause had the supporting *huzzahs* of the University President and the Board of Trustees. It was as if he were ripping a shroud of mediocrity, even shame, from the University's academic reputation. They no doubt thought it a heroic act with certifiable intellectual distinction. A Deanship was the least they could bestow in gratitude.

Ridley was Lister's hero through this messy affair, and no doubt Lister felt the Dean's murder was somehow directed at him. I knew from my own long history with Jack that an appetite for getting even was no small part of the man's personality. Of course, he would assume that it was a vengeful member of his own faculty behind this crime and, of course, he would draw a prominent lawman like Lieutenant Roche into the matter.

Having made his point, Roche seemed to ease off. He sat on a corner of the desk at the head of the room. "We have a few more minutes," he said. "Are there any questions? Any questions at all?"

The silence that greeted his request revealed how unacquainted we were with this mode of thought. Check the footnotes in a graduate student's dissertation? Yes. Skewer bloated writing in term papers, or deep flaws in a colleague's published work? A matter of course. But our advanced academic credentials were little help in finding a killer who could, after all, be one of us.

"Sir! I ask you a question!" The commanding voice, only a decibel below a shout, came from the back of the room. Half of the entire gathering turned to look. I didn't bother. From the hint of Spanish in it and its full-throated timbre, not to mention a whiff of rage, I recognized Raimundo Guttierez's voice at once. Lieutenant Roche stared at him without expression, the classic non-response response.

"Sir!" Guttierez repeated. "I ask you. Are we now secret agents of espionage? We are, what, to do snooping on our colleagues? Be *espias* on our students?"

The Lieutenant's gaze could have been directed at a squashed insect. I could almost feel Guttierez taking a deep breath for another verbal explosion. But the officer's granite visage must have silenced him. This imperturbable Irishman, I thought to myself, must be terrifying in an individual interrogation. Nothing more was heard from Raimundo.

Another hand went up.

"Are you assuming we all have investigating skills — which we have never been trained for?" This from an economist. No reaction from the Lieutenant.

"Isn't this what we have cops for?" An angry music historian. Silence.

Professor Justine Secour, chair of the Physics Department (no doubt pissed at Jack's hammy boy style and his overlooking the fact that a number of women professors were present) asked in her severest voice, "You have nothing to say to Professor Guttierez?" No answer.

"What's the University's policy on concealed weapons?" Leonard Gold, Professor of Political Economy, demonstrating his predilection for side railing.

The Lieutenant did not so much as honor Gold with one of his interrogator's squints. Instead, he waited like an impatient teacher until the classroom returned to quiet.

"There is a murderer who has come amongst you," he said at last. "And as President Lister has intimated, he may be an individual who calls this University home, be he professor, student, or staff." He paused, as if for emphasis. "And we will do what is necessary to catch him." The final terse remark had the feel of a conclusion to the discussion.

When it was obvious nothing more was to be asked or answered, President Lister stepped forward and in a voice that had faint military resonance said, "Thanks, Tom, and gave the Lieutenant an approving slap on the shoulder. "Any of you geniuses detect anything suspicious, you know whom to call."

EIGHT

I went straight from Tyverson Hall to Alfie's office. He was already there, evidently having left the meeting early. He was staring at a single sheet of paper on his desk. I could see that he had scribbled down names.

"Whom do you have?" I asked.

"I like that guy from English, Winston, the deconstructionist." He tapped at one of the names on the paper. "Or is he in queer theory? He'd be perfect. Nothing he says makes any sense. At least he talks a lot."

He looked up at me. "How about Lucille, she's a smart broad, knows everybody. Oops, probably shouldn't have mentioned her. I know you — well, never mind. And, I'm sure you'll love this. That great, self-acclaimed scholar of European philosophy, Percival Calkins."

I didn't respond to his mentioning Lucille. I also made no reference to Calkins's tiresome obsession with the scientific and philosophical fraudulence of psychoanalysis, not to mention his claim to be one of the few professionals in the field who actually understands the late Heidegger.

"Okay, Bobo Winston, Percival Calkins. Go on."

"There's one guy I'm x-ing out at the beginning, and if you want him, I resign."

"Let me guess. Nat Holmers." It wasn't a tough guess. It was a phone conversation with Holmers that I interrupted when I visited Ridley on the penultimate day of the Dean's life. I remembered Ridley's relief at having an excuse to end the call.

"That jerk," Alfie said with an exasperated sigh. "Okay, he's a so-called recognized scholar, but as we both know that's no guarantee

37

against extreme obnoxiousness. There are so many topics that make him go *off*, you gotta wonder what he's *on*."

"We need a scientist," I said.

"They can't talk," Alfie said, "but they're good on formulas. What does that chemist, Armand Chernovsky, do for you? Now that he is now an associate of yours as one of the ten University Professors."

I corrected him. "Chernovsky is not a chemist, but a physicist doing research in chemistry, and as for talking, just try to stop him. And sometimes it's in English."

"Let me float this name," he said. "Evgeny Klonska."

At first, I thought he was joking. Klonska was certifiably brilliant. Among colleagues in the field of physics, he had star status. Moreover, his name was recognized in the world at large. That very year he was number forty-seven on the list of Time Magazine's "The Hundred Most Influential People in the World."

My objection to Klonska had nothing to do with his thinking, right or wrong, but with his personality. On the rare occasions I encountered him, passing into the library or across the Square, he did not disregard me or turn his gaze aside but looked straight into my face. I should say straight through my face, as if he were focused on something behind me, far behind me. I have heard others describe a similar experience. In contrast to those rare teachers of whom it is said that they never saw a student they didn't like, Evgeny never saw a student, period.

Legends grew up around him. He was once lecturing on the effect of entropy on the cosmos, executing a two dimensional design of arrows, numbers, and symbols on the whiteboard. The students watched the performance with a combination of amusement and panic. Only a few were taking notes. In his enthusiasm, Klonska continued the elaborate construct off the edge of the board and along the wall until it ended at the doorway. There stood the popular professor of religion, patiently waiting for the scientist to discover that he was in the wrong classroom, where the subject was not the steady decay of the universe but the origin of Chan Buddhism in China.

I nixed Klonska.

Before we were finished nominating members for the committee, the names Marguerite Gardolini from French, Samantha Gupta from South Asian Studies, Harvey Rilling from Math, and Nkwame Smith from African Studies were added to the list.

"You all right with Darius Pennybacker?"

I couldn't tell from his expression how seriously Alfie had made this suggestion. I admitted it would be useful to have someone from Art History, specializing in Greek and Roman references. But Pennybacker had an odd status in the faculty. His scholarship was competent, even if routine and conventional. It was not just that he was aloof and removed from his colleagues — nothing unusual about that — or that he gave the annoying impression of being somehow culturally and morally superior. But Pennybacker took aloofness to a new level.

He is the only professor I have ever known to have his office designed and furnished by one of the city's hotshot interior decorators. I can report a wall-to-wall Persian carpet, probably antique, a massive mahogany desk, bookcases with leaded windows, and a scattering of spirit lamps. No huge surprise there, I suppose. Darius was one of the wealthiest members of the faculty — a sizable distinction since many of our colleagues arrive with inherited endowments or very rich spouses, especially in the College of Arts and Science and the School of Commerce. The catty rumor was that Pennybacker's fortune derived from the coal fields of Montana, the forests of Madagascar, and

Zimbabwean diamond mines.

A memo from the Dean had come to my desk a week earlier — one of Ridley's last acts — announcing that Darius had been appointed Chair of the Faculty Committee on Sexual Harassment. No surprise there. He was the very model of professorial morality, known for his frequent dissertating on the delicate line between mentoring and intimacy. His own memo shortly followed the Dean's, reminding us that exploitation ran in several directions. His committee, he assured us, would also be alert to the sexual manipulation of faculty by students. He added, rather unnecessarily I thought, that sexual impropriety knows no gender distinctions, and that we should not be restricted by the image of male professors aggressing on their female students.

"Pennybacker?" I said, unable to decide.

"Hey, we're not putting together a dinner party here." He responded as I had expected. He is not as sensitive to gender issues as I. "It's smarts we need. Remember, Carmody, people are being murdered, for Christ's sake."

"Not people, Alfie. A person."

"Thus far, Carmody. Thus far."

We scanned the list to make sure we hit all the proper ethnic, gender, and age categories. "Oh, shit, you know what?" Alfie said in a tone of mild alarm.

"What?"

"Count the names. Include yours and mine."

I did. "Ten. So what?"

"Seems like we're locked into that number. Ten Deans. Ridley's tenth floor office. Ten clues to the first puzzle. A committee of ten chaired by whom? By the newest member of the University's Gang of Ten!"

"If this were a paperback murder mystery," I offered, "it would be titillating. As it is —."

"There could be as many as ten deaths before he's finished."

"He?"

"The murderer. The Puzzler, if he's the same guy."

"Or the same woman?"

"Get off it, Carmody."

We agreed that each of us would call four on this list. Three of my four answered at once and responded with yesses so quickly I had the impression they were waiting for the call. The fourth, Professor of French Marguerite Gardolini, was not in her office and when I called her home, I got her answering machine: *"L'homme est né libre, et partout il est dan les fers. Nom et nombre, s'il tu plait."* She called back in several hours with an emphatic *"Mais oui!"*

We had our committee.

NINE

In the meantime, Lister and Lieutenant Roche were hardly idle. By the morning of that second day, scarcely twenty-four hours after Ridley's murder, the police had already organized themselves into an aggressive investigative phalanx.

It was before noon when I was privileged to be called upon by a sergeant, apparently placing me high on the list of the well-informed. After a few awkward introductory remarks, showing his discomfort at finding himself in an academic office and surrounded by several thousand books, he asked me, "You're the Professor of, what do you call it,

41

Rhetorics? Doesn't that mean you're good with words and such?"

"You surprise me," I answered, not without a touch of condescension. "Most people have no idea what 'rhetoric' means."

He opened a spiral notebook, thumbed through several pages as if looking for the spot pertaining to me.

"You got no ideas who might be behind this crime?"

"Yes."

"Yes?" His surprise was visible.

"I was just answering your question. Yes, I have no ideas who might be behind this crime."

Nothing moved in his face but his eyebrows. Thereafter his queries grew briefer and vaguer. Finally, he thanked me, sort of, and left without having made a single mark in his notebook. I was not interrogated again.

TEN

The press, especially the tabloids, did their best to get heart-tugging shots of Ridley's wife and their daughters. Their grief was intense which, sadly, meant photographic gold for the paparazzi. Because he had successfully sheltered his family from the tug and tumble of University affairs, their pain had little effect on the faculty beyond their distaste for the media's heartlessness.

Ridley was an admired but not particularly loved professor; there were few signs of genuine personal mourning. Yet there was a communal sense of vulnerability that no one would have thought possible a week ago. How could something so dreadful occur in an institution based on the rational and civil discourse of ideas?

On the other hand, in a university of this size, the murder was for many something equivalent to a news event on an anonymous campus at another place and time with little relevance to the concrete reality of one's own life. On Thursday morning — two days after Ridley's death — I had several encounters that nicely illustrate the extremes of these two dispositions.

I had just left the Café Rossetti and was headed across the Square to my office. Preoccupied with details of the work ahead of the Committee, I was slow to be aware that somebody was calling my name. I looked up to find two students walking alongside trying to get my attention.

"Professor Carmody!"

"Yes? Yes?"

One was dressed in a suit and tie and had short, neatly combed hair — a virtually obligatory uniform for students in the School of Commerce. His companion looked like she had just emerged from the shower, skipping the nuisance of drying her hair. Even wet, its colors, all unnatural, were quite vivid. The array of rings on her ears, lips, and even her tongue hinted at enrollment in the School of the Arts.

"Me and him," the girl nodded at her friend, "Shlomo, we read in the student paper that you're like the Chair of the Committee and are crazy busy, but we have these questions. May we — ?"

"By all means. So far we don't know a great deal, but I am pleased to tell you what we have. What is your name?"

"Oh, it's Jeannie."

"Yes, Jeannie?"

"We live in like the Dorms. Me, I'm a junior and Shlomo, he's in his last year. In the Dorms, a lot of kids are scared. They're all locking

43

their doors and some won't even open when someone like knocks. There are stories that there's this killer, or killers, roaming the halls, that they can come in whenever, because they've got IDs like they're faculty or a graduate student. I know it's just rumors. Still."

"Professor Carmody." Her friend spoke up, not waiting for my response. "I took your course, the Rhetoric of Commerce, end of sophomore year. It was really cool, what I understood anyway."

"Yes, Shlomo?"

"I have a question. So the killer just walks into the Dean's office. He's like he belongs there. Can't this happen in like a classroom? Or the student center? Like Jeannie says, a lotta students are freaked. This guy could just come in and shoot up the place. With no one to stop him. I mean, if they can do it in like grammar schools. I've been here three years and I have yet to see a campus cop with a gun."

"President Lister has asked the city police for round-the-clock protection of all students and faculty. The officers will be armed and many of them will be under cover. The classrooms and dormitories are quite safe."

"I'm not thinking just safety, Professor Carmody," Jeannie said. "It's like the whole mood of the place has changed. I've heard kids talk about dropping out until they catch the killer. Or going to another college."

"I share your misgivings, Jeannie. The University is facing a rare challenge. But you needn't worry about lone gunmen creeping through hallways and hiding in closets." I added with what I knew was weak comfort, "The killer was quite obviously focused on the administrative and teaching elements of the University, and not on student life."

They stared at me showing scant signs of reassurance. "I guess," Jeannie shrugged.

"Carmody!"

Leonard Gold made a sliding stop next to the three of us, his chest heaving. He was still in his running suit, which was no more than shorts, sock-less shoes, and a tee shirt with the face of Karl Marx on it. Gold was the Professor of Political Economy who confronted Lieutenant Roche with the issue of concealed firearms. He was a voluble sage on a range of issues, mostly political. The tee shirt was a mockery, an ironic expression of his radical views. A frequently interviewed expert on conservative talk radio, he was one of the most publicly identifiable members of the faculty. He was renowned for his statistical proof of the theories of Friedrich von Hayek and for his own solution to the current financial crisis he called, not without a telling smirk, the "Gold Standard." From the way his pile of hair, normally wild as Marx's own, was soaked and partly glued to his forehead, I could see that he was on at least his tenth sprint around the Square, on its half mile outer sidewalk of crumbling asphalt.

"I think I've got it!" he announced, as if addressing the entire Square.

"Yes?" I turned from the students and waited for Lenny to catch his breath and to announce the name of the killer.

"The reason ecology is a meaningless concept …" he said, his chest still heaving.

"Ecology!" I said, as close to a shout as I ever come. "Lenny, where have you been the last couple days. The Dean …"

"Yeah, I know the Dean got it. But, Carmody, I'm talking big death, so-called global extinction, not the little death of a faceless administrator. I was saying, the reason ecology is a meaningless concept is that its basic reference is to permanence. You know, preserving the present content of the physical and animal world."

45

Gold was the only member of the faculty — the only one I was aware of — who thought the environment, especially global warming and the exhaustion of natural resources, was a waste of a serious thinker's time.

"If Ridley was ever faceless, Lenny, he's not faceless now. He looks at you from every TV news broadcast in the country."

"Give it a week, Carmody, and nobody will know him from Daffy Duck," he said, brushing my shoulder with his sweaty hand. And ignoring the students. "Look, by virtue of being human, we live in an environment of change. Between human beings everything evolves and expands at the same time. So, on the one side you have permanence, on the other change."

"You don't think his family misses him?"

"Who? Christ, no! Ridley's kids may miss his paycheck — when that's replaced, he will be totally forgotten. Don't be such a ridiculous sentimentalist. You see, our connection to permanence has to be exploitation. Everything has a capital value whether we like it or not, even death, and I know you lefty dudes do not like to talk capital value. The emphasis, Carmody, has to be on the nonpermanent, because capital increases as it finds possibility in the new."

"Lenny, what you're leaving out of your analysis is the odd character of money. The important fact of money is always its quantity, but quantity does not vary according to its connection to the permanent, it varies only in our relations with each other. Remember that the association between the object and its price, or value, doesn't always balance, not for reasons of available resource but because it is psychologically determined and therefore will adjust only as we revalue our importance to one another."

"Well, then you don't get my point. What a pity! Go on with your

Victorian melodrama then. Find the dyspeptic graduate student who whacked the dean."

"Why do you say graduate student?"

"Why not say graduate student? No matter what I say the sum value of Ridley's loss is a big fat zero."

"Some of us are interested in protecting the rest of the community."

"Yeah, Carmody, I saw you were one of the geniuses on the committee that got the puzzle. It took me more time to print it than to solve it."

"A lot of people solved it, Lenny. But, as the world knows, we were all too late."

"It read like a corporate board report." He looked off to the side as if to get a mental picture in focus. "The first article in The Declaration of Independence," he quoted as though reading it off the page.

"With one word," he went on, "Jefferson gave you liberals an open barn door to sloppy thought. Locke said nothing about happiness! 'Life, liberty, and the pursuit of estate.' *Second Treatise of Government.* Property, man, property! Only sponge-for-brains think they can count the degrees of happiness. How much glee makes a dollar? Are you miserable at a dime? Commit suicide for a penny?"

Before I could decide how to pull the curtain on this act, he went straight to the fifth clue, again citing it from memory.

"Guatemalan's affirmative reversed. That goddamned liberal hero of yours, Daniel Ortega. His so-called revolution reversed nothing. He only wanted to be another ruler like Guatemala's Óscar Mejía, just richer and more violent. But with zero statecraft. Bananas, man! That's what made Guatemala a real state. Bananas!"

Gold was dancing from one foot to the other, taking deep breaths and exhaling with a forced grunt. "I'm off, friend," he said. "Maybe I should say, comrade. Ha ha." He turned and looked back at the students. "Talk is cheap, bunnies. Stick with bananas!"

As I resumed my walk across the Square, I cringed at Gold's utter indifference to the event that was tearing at the University's understanding of itself.

ELEVEN

Not ten minutes later, I looked up from my desk to find Alfie leaning against the doorframe.

"Carmody, sorry to mention her name again. But, Lucille."

"What about her?"

"She was the only one in the building at the time of the murder. By her own admission."

I nodded. "Except for the janitor, remember."

"I don't mean to claim she's in on it ... but to sit behind an open door and not see someone come in?"

"How would you know her door was open?"

"Have you ever seen Lucille's door closed? That's the source of her power. And then not to hear a tussle that couldn't have been twenty feet away?"

"She wasn't listening for murder, Alfie."

"She's smart. She basically runs this goddam institution."

"That doesn't make her Miss Marple, snooping around doorways."

"What if Oliver didn't want to be pushed around. What if he wanted his own independent assistant? He tells her she's through, and..."

"Who's Monsieur Poirot now, Alf?"

Lucille had occupied the position of Executive Assistant to the

Dean through several of Ridley's predecessors. There was a mystery about her age. When she told me she was forty-three, I realized that more than a year earlier she had given me the same number. Whatever her age, she was remarkably fit, with the body of an athlete, and to all appearances a regular at the gym. (Oh, those thighs.) She spoke a polished faux English accent, aristocratic but thankfully free of Oxbridge grunts and stutters. Her tone of voice, translated into her native New Jersey, said, "Look, Pal, it's me that runs this joint." When she made her appearance during my visit with the Dean, I knew to translate her cheery greeting as, "What exactly are you up to, Bozo, coming here at this hour?"

Lucille's skillful manipulation of the language was a clue to her true character. The flow of words was as assured as, say, George Eliot's. However, to a trained ear (if I may, as the University Professor of Rhetoric) every now and then there would be a slight mistake, usually a word that was subtly misused — but said so fluidly it could be overlooked. I came to understand that it was a kind of joke she played on the learned professorial culture. Each small slip was a reminder that within the Stratford-on-Avon there was always a Hoboken-on-Hudson. To the attentive listener, in other words, she was truly *performing* her job. It was a show. The honesty in this brazen masque was startling. How could I not have been seduced?

"At least, we can be sure," Alfie continued, "that it wasn't her who threw the bastard out the windows. I mean physically speaking, she's, well, okay she's a ten, but Ridley was a tough, wiry little fucker. She had no evident bruises or torn clothing. You see what I'm getting at? "

"Someone in on it with her?"

"Now you get my point."

"That would be the killer, is what you are saying."

"The killer. You got it. Such a genius."

"No one was seen in the building," I reminded him.

"Nobody was reported as being seen. Doesn't mean he wasn't there."

THE FALL
SEMESTER

TWELVE

In spite of the shocking loss of its Dean, a strange quiet had fallen over the College of Arts and Sciences. The usual confusions and distractions of a new semester were preoccupying in themselves: students changing classes, professors searching files for old syllabi, registrars shifting room assignments, assistant deans correcting the overlap of class schedules, chairmen cushioning the resentment of young faculty having to teach introductory courses, fraternities and sororities amping up their rushing efforts. At the same time, beneath these superficial distractions a deeper order held, a comforting and smooth functioning of the College's essential systems — budgets, promotions, grant supervision, alumni relations, fundraising, new- student and-faculty recruitment — all controlled from the Dean's office ... that is to say, by a certain person in that office.

It was commonly assumed, though rarely said, that without Lucille the College of Liberal Arts would be treading the lip of chaos. Some extended this implied managerial talent to the University as a whole. Because of the rational operation of the Dean's office under Lucille, she was in an administrative category of her own. She was expected to report to the Dean and through the Dean to the President. She waved off this clause in her job description. She reported to no one and was essentially without supervision. She could set her own hours, vacation when she wished — and how long she wished — and no doubt she ignored any limitation on her salary. In sum, as long as Lucille occupied that office there was no need for a dean. His death had no *real* effect on any of us.

THIRTEEN

In the false calm that had settled on the University, there developed an odd game: naming possible suspects. Lucille was a common designee, though generally cited without conviction. Most of the candidates were more subjects for a wish-list than genuinely imagined criminals.

What's more, there was a renewed suspicion that Ridley might have been a suicide after all. It would have been helpful if someone had heard a cry or seen how the body exited the window, whether it sailed out in a sleek dive or fell in a desperate swimming motion — that is, whether he jumped or was pushed. The puzzle we were all obsessing over might prove, after all, to have been Ridley's idea of a suicide note.

The murder scenario was increasingly less likely since nobody had been spotted anywhere near Ridley's office around the time of the death. One of the custodians, Jose Ramirez, had spent an hour — spanning the time of the event — operating the mop-and-wax machine on the tenth floor, all in clear view of the entrance to the Dean's office. Anyone approaching it would have had to walk haltingly on the wet and very slippery floor and then to step over the equipment before entering the reception area to the Dean's office.

Though a small man, Ridley was no pushover; he was fit and capable of furious resistance, as Alfie correctly noted. It would have required someone with exceptional brute strength to lift him to the sill of the window with one hand, open it with another, and then push him out with both, while he kicked, scratched, and clubbed his assailant. At the very least, it had to be a maneuver of a practiced and determined attacker. Such a figure would have been too conspicuous to escape notice.

The advocates for suicide pressed their case. One of them was Nathaniel Holmers, the prominent anthropologist. I had the misfortune of being at lunch with half a dozen colleagues in the faculty club when Holmers joined us at the large table in the center of the room. It was not odd that he would do so. It was the manner of his eating that was odd.

In fact, his ritual appearance at the faculty club, every day at 1:15, was something of a spectacle. He always chose the buffet option, returning to his table with a plate dangerously overloaded. How he went through this mounded provender in a matter of minutes without breaking a single sentence, but also without a flaw in his table manners, was a cause of considerable professorial admiration.

Somewhere between the turkey stuffing and french beans almandine, he began with the declaration, "There was no murder, you understand."

That none of us at the table responded, knowing what was coming, had no deterent effect.

"The man landed head first, you recall," he said addressing each of us. "It's a known fact that anyone who's been thrown will complete his journey feet first in the illusory hope that he can land on them."

It was Holmer's direct gaze that held you. His wildly hirsute eyebrows provided a kind of protective shield that only magnified the manic gleam behind them. This, combined with the unique gesture of pointing at your face, sometimes only inches away, and screwing his index finger as though drilling into your defenses, had the result that you dared not look elsewhere.

"A conscious adult in free fall for 138 feet, the distance from Ridley's window to the pavement, has five and a half seconds, enough time to adjust himself to his illusions. Ridley was a rational man, not possessed of illusions. No?"

With scarcely a glance at the food, his fork and knife seemed to be doing the work of consumption by algorithm, the effort greatly facilitated by a mouth with large reddish lips so able to contort themselves they seemed living things by themselves, larval perhaps. In fact, the variety of his facial expressions in these encounters reminded me, perversely I admit, of his famed, museum-quality collection of masks from primitive cultures.

"Some of you psychologizers may argue that Ridley was too addled by the reputed push to alter the disposition of his body in those five seconds. I tell you, being strictly scientific about it, that the man didn't lose his head after being pushed, he leapt to destroy his head!"

Holmers's recruitment to the University was memorable. He was persuaded — bribed may be the better term — to give up an endowed professorship at Chapel Hill, a position any academic would have considered the triumphant peak of a career. The heart of the inducement was the promised control over a handsomely outfitted and funded laboratory where he could conduct empirical studies of genetic and anatomical issues currently troubling the field of anthropology. The University hadn't make a mistake. Dozens of refereed articles under his signature, whether by him or his graduate students, announced his discoveries to the world.

"Some of you might object," Holmers continued, "assuming the gentleman had no known reasons for committing such a singular act."

He paused here to look at each of us singly, the twisting finger at eye level.

"*Who*? I repeat, *who* dares to claim to be on such intimate terms with the demons that haunt a great man's heart?"

His voice had risen to a near roar. I even thought I heard a trace of ululation. I had to ask myself which "great man" he was referring to.

As he continued his classic rave, I observed for the first time a trembling in his hands and arms. It caught my attention when a large mass of creamed spinach slipped off his fork. After a few more deliveries, I noticed that the garbanzo beans, too, were causing him difficulty. The more he chased them around on his plate, the more determined they seemed on escape. Another datum: his coffee had spilled over into its saucer. In fact, there was altogether a slight mess around his plate. Suddenly, his riveting stare came to mean something other than intellectual intensity.

FOURTEEN

The University's Institute for Applied Mathematics, a body of solid international renown, had for some years conducted research on projects for what is in fact the world's largest single employer, the United States Department of Defense. Although the Institute tried to shift attention away from what had become their most ambitious, and most secret, project ever, the constant presence of armed and uniformed soldiers on campus was difficult to conceal or justify. Access to the top floor, the tenth, of the Institute's handsome building was restricted by the silent presence of military representatives of the special forces — Army Green Berets and Navy Seals — at the central bank of elevators and at each end of the corridor.

The director of the project, though not officially identified as such, was Aleksander Krauss. Like me, Krauss had been appointed by the Board of Trustees to the position of University Professor. In spite of his arrogance and social rudeness, there was no doubting his wizardry as a computer scientist. Face to face with this severe genius, no one dared use any appellation but "Professor." However, among his colleagues he was referred to (out of his hearing) by a growing number of nicknames, among them Al, Ex, Sandy, Aleks, with a few anagrams thrown in: Akser, Laser, Leaky and so on. To his wife, I've heard, he is just "him."

There were only a few indisputable facts about Professor Krauss's D.o.D. enterprise, but each had its significance. For one, it had been initiated a few years earlier by the Armed Services Committee of a Republican Congress, known to have an enduring affection for the fantasy of building an electronic missile defense umbrella over the North American continent. For another curious fact, there was neither a laboratory nor a weapons testing capacity on the tenth floor, the conclusion being that it was all a matter of computational research. A proper missile defense shield is a challenge of maddeningly detailed mathematic calculation and model building.

The Green Berets, Army Rangers, and Navy Seals, standing erect and mostly silent at the floor's entrance apparently annoyed the police detectives on the Puzzler case. They not only refused to answer any questions, they didn't even acknowledge the presence of the uniformed blue. There were no proper suspicions of a connection between the murderer and what might be happening on the tenth floor of the Institute, but the police claimed to have the privilege of access to every part of the University.

Lieutenant Tom Roche was called to the scene. He and a decorated Marine colonel faced off against each other in the lobby of the building. The exchange was correct and orderly until Krauss appeared and stepped between the two. Practically pressing his chin against the Lieutenant's medals, Krauss challenged the officer's patriotism and questioned his intelligence for failing to comprehend the delicacy and magnitude of research required to protect the American population from enemy missiles. In his passion, he made the tactical mistake of naming North Korea, Iran, and Russia as rogue nuclear aggressors whose dearest wish was to vaporize the U.S. and its people from one end of the continent to the other.

This interaction might have gone unnoticed by the world except for the attendance of a student with an iPhone who dutifully taped the scene and minutes later transferred it on YouTube and thusto the nation and to the world. The student got a clear side view of Krauss as he screamed with a raised arm, "What are you, some kind of fucking leftie?" As he had previously, Lieutenant Tom Roche responded only with his squashed-insect-on-the-wall stare. The famed scientist, his chest heaving, found himself in a rare state of wordlessness.

The next morning there was a news conference in the West Wing of the White House, during which the White House press secretary made a brief apology to the Russians. (There was none to the Islamic Republic of Iran and The Democratic People's Republic of Korea.) *The Times* actually printed the text of the President's statement in the International section, complete with a photograph of Krauss, his arm stretched up and outward in a disturbingly suggestive pose.

FIFTEEN

The result of the media noise caused the University to be slow in noticing that a second puzzle had been posted. It was sent as before, in the form of an email to the entire university community and the press. For the most part, in the lull following. The beginning of the fall semester,

PUZZLE # 2

1. ONE LETTER AFTER A LIBERAL ARTS DEGREE.

2. ENTIRE ENTIRELY RE-LETTERED.

3. NET THE WRONG WAY.

4, PAS D'UN, MAIS IL Y A SEPT.

5. LEADS CONFUSED.

6. HALF A LAUGH OF A LAUGH.

7. SCATTERED HITS.

8. MIXING FEET WITH A FIN.

9. THAT'S TWISTED OPPOSITE.

10. REMOVE THE BEGINNING OF ONE,

AND REMOVE ONE AT THE END OF ONE?

the University community realized they had consciously press. For the most part, in the lull following. The beginning of the fall semester, the University community realized they had consciously repressed the fear that more horror would lay ahead. It was a classic instance of collective denial. Speculation that the Dean might have been a suicide ended at once.

I asked Iolinda to alert the Committee: meet at twelve sharp, tomorrow, Wednesday, Graduate Seminar Room, third floor.

By Tuesday evening, Alfie had circulated a memo to the entire University community inviting possible solutions to the clues, regardless of how bizarre or remote they may seem.

I got to the office early Wednesday to look over the responses to O'Malley's memo. A number were bizarre, silly even:

Letter after a Liberal Arts degree got only two: "Sorry, we're not hiring," and "You just spent a hundred thou, sucker, for a worthless resumé." The second clue, **Entire entirely re-lettered**, inspired the silliest proposals. "Complete completely repeated is completely complete," for example. Or: "Wholly, holy, wooly, Lord God All Flighty." The most popular of the clues was Scattered hits. It was definitely a favorite among students. One envelope contained as its answer to the clue a parking ticket smeared with the very substance, which one hopes, is of canine provenance. The final clue, **Remove the beginning of one, and remove one at the end of one**, got mostly dismissive comments, indicating that it was so obvious as not to be a clue at all. The Puzzler must be an idiot to think anyone couldn't read the answer straight off the page. Although no one actually provided the correct answer.

I set these aside and looked over the more thoughtful answers, also disappointing. The phone rang.

SIXTEEN

Because I was the Committee chair, I was irresistible prey for the hungry media. But, at President Lister's request, I forwarded all enquiries to his office. Deborah Waterson came from a different angle, somehow persuading Iolinda to put her straight through by phone.

"Professor Carmody, you probably don't remember me but I was in your class, 'Idioms, Slang and Profanity,' god, thirteen years ago I suppose. I was a journalism major. Never forgot it. Really helped when I started looking for work in media. And here I am at *The Times*. I don't suppose you have time for a chat."

I did not recall her name but aware that students are more likely to remember their professors than the opposite, I agreed to meet briefly for coffee at the faculty club before the noon meeting of the Committee.

Deborah Waterson was an unprepossessing figure who had the reporter's indispensable gift of convincing you she was looking at the affair from your own point of view. She talked as if she and I were a two-person team, collaborators working privately on our own solution. I admired the strategy, even as it was a pose. I knew that behind this seductive persona, she was after every possible newsy detail, the more sensational and embarrassing the better. I was slow to realize why I was so attracted to this manipulative little woman. I saw that it was what first drew me to Lucille. Although Deborah Waterson had nothing of Lucille's elegance, not to mention, allure. She even seemed to be consciously dressing down, and was unable to modify her Queens accent to another more respectable.

After what seemed a precisely timed five minutes of aimless small talk, she went to the core of the matter.

"You have been a member of this faculty for twenty-five years. You must have a suspicion as to who might be capable of composing and distributing the puzzles, not to mention have the ability to carry out this murder."

"We are each talented in a great number of ways," I began with a weak protest, attempting to put off actually providing names. "Composing puzzles? What else is good teaching? Giving answers is poor pedagogy — indeed, none at all. Sending students to the library or back to the dorms not troubled by questions new to them is not teaching; just dictating." I paused to see if she was still with me. Uncertain, I went on.

"Students, readers, scholars, we are all collaborators in a kind of reciprocal exchange. True, you may open doors they want to keep closed. But the teaching begins not when you usher them through but when you go through with them, when their learning advances with your own."

She was looking at me with raised eyebrows. This burst of pedagogical theory was not exactly what she expected. I was, however, secretly pleased with myself, inasmuch as I, contrary to that little lecture, was putting her in the role of the passive opponent. I don't deny there wasn't a small erotic element here. But then, this was not her game. She was playing by other rules.

The coffee arrived. I opened the lid on the silver sugarer and pushed it to her side of the table. She had been eyeing this elegant vessel as if she hadn't the least comprehension of its function. When she saw that it was a replacement for the usual unseemly cup full of the little pink, blue and white paper pockets, three heaping spoons of raw sugar disappeared into her cup. She stirred so rapidly she seemed to be frothing it again. Was caffeine and sugar all that drove this insistent little engine?

"Can you suggest anyone I might talk to? You know, not someone you think a suspect? Anything of that kind?"

Of course, she wanted suspects. I played her just a bit longer.

"You do realize that we are not concerned simply with mental acuity, with someone able only to design verbal puzzles, but a person with the physical capacity to do something like push a vigorous and struggling man out of a partly open window."

"You're talking someone younger. And male."

"That would help to narrow the field--if it were true," I admitted.

"Anyone — ?"

"Here is my suggestion." Back to the rules of *my* game. "Let me mention your request to the Committee. I need to know just how far they would go in making their deliberation public. You understand that the police and the University want to keep control of the flow of information."

There followed another half hour of weightless chatter, during which I was lightly interviewed on my own work. She seemed peculiarly interested in looking for something useful or unexpected in my research, although what I was writing at the time would be far too recondite for *The Times* readership. My last book, *To Persuade or to Prove; That is the Question*, got handsome recognition in the *New York Review of Books*, but was silently shucked by Waterson's employers.

We exchanged cards. Her card stated her position at *The Times*, written in its classic gothic script, but had no personal cell or phone number.

SEVENTEEN

After I called the Committee to order, Nkwame Smith, chair of African Studies, suggested that solving the first clue should be taken as a key to the whole. He read it out loud.

"One letter after a Liberal Arts degree."

We did fast work on it. What is a Liberal Arts degree, but an A.B? What is one after A.B. but *C*?. "Naturellement," said the French Department's Gardolini in her usual world-weary tone. Marguerite (nee Marsha) Gardolini was born in Brooklyn and spent her entire childhood there, including high school. Her frequent use of French phrases and expressions, in an elegant Parisian dialect, seemed meant to soften the rough edges of a Greenpoint background, but had the effect of emphasizing it. No Lucille she.

Clue number two, **Entire entirely re-lettered**, did not yield so easily.

"It couldn't be more obvious," offered the deconstructionist and queer theory scholar, Bobo Winston. "If you re-letter **entire entirely**, you get a word or phrase completely different from the original **entire**. Because there is no specified limit to the letters at stake, what we have here is a conscious application of 'differance.' Mind you, 'differ-ance' is different from 'differ-ence.' 'Differ-ance' is a kind of reader/writer's self-cancellation, ultimately opening the text to any number of inter-pretations, which, of course, is the same as no interpretation at all."

He held his hands out, his fingers forming the shape of a large ball, then worked them around as if as if struggling to contain a miss-ing content.

The Committee's silent fixation on this digital enactment was bro-ken only when Alfie asked, "And the answer, Bobo?"

Bobo scowled as if it were a mild offense to be required to explain.

"Nothing," he said finally, in an ecstatic whisper. Then again, barely audible, "Nothing."

Harvey Rilling, a suspected but as yet undemonstrated mathematical genius, said, skipping over Bobo Winston's mystical aside, "Because we are asked here to 're-letter' entire, and not to 're-spell' it, we should look for the same word with different letters, that is, a synonym. "Wouldn't *whole* do?"

"So would 'complete,'" someone suggested. There were a few nods, meaning: Let's get on with it.

"**Net the wrong way?**" Darius Pennybacker scoffed. "How wrong could anyone net?" His field, art history, we were to understand, offered no wisdom on right or wrong netting. With a fluttering of fingers, he brushed the clue away.

"You miss the point of the clue, Darius," the great physicist/chemist Armand Chernovsky explained (pronouncing the historian's name in the classical mode: Dahrioos.) "We are not challenged here to find kinds of netting, but to look at the word **net** in **the wrong way**. How many **wrong ways** can there be? It is either 'ent' or 'ten.' 'Ent' means nothing (nussing), leaving one option."

"Perfect, Professor," O'Malley interjected. "Carmody, why don't you keep a record on the whiteboard where we can all see it?"

I took a marker and recorded the results in large letters.

C

WHOLE /COMPLETE

TEN

"*C. Whole. Complete. Ten?*" someone asked. "What could that mean? The Committee ignored the question and went directly to the fourth clue.

"Pas d'un, mais il y a sept." Specialist on European philosophy, Percival Calkins, read the words with an exaggerated emphasis on the correct pronunciation of the French, an indirect reminder that he has written acerbic essays on Jean-Paul Sartre. When no one translated the phrase, as if it were necessary, he announced it in English: "There is not one, but there are seven."

"Pas d'un, mais il y a sept ," Marguerite voiced in that melodic Parisian cadence, a subtle cancellation of Professor Calkins's academicism. "C'est n' pas immédiatement lucide. Seven of what? I presume we are to ask. And apparently in French."

"There is no shortage of sevens." South Asian specialist, Samantha Gupta volunteered the usual list, ignoring Marguerite's suggestion that we should be looking for something French. "Seven deadly sins, seven wonders of the ancient world, seven days of the week, seven heavens, seven swans a-swimming, seven sisters as in New England colleges, seven muses, "Seven Brides for Seven Brothers" — the movie with who is it, Danny Kaye?"

"Howard Keel," Alfie said, sounding a bit offended.

"Impressive, Samantha, but keep going," Bobo Winston said. "There is a lot more to seven. Evens is an anagram for seven. But seven is odd, not even." His eyes had brightened. Nothing could stop him. "'Evens' here is not singular, implying there is more than one. Three and a half twos come to seven. One odd and three evens. One and three is four, an even. Four is then plural. An indefinite number of fours. An ur number. 'For' becomes 'four,' 'even' becomes 'ever.' Voila. Forever!"

I looked around. To my relief, no one was listening. "Seven, seven," Gupta repeated, concentrating. "What else? Seven seas."

"Seven continents," someone suggested. "Seven colors of the rainbow," said another.

"Seven musical notes," Darius Pennybacker contributed, unfortunately adding a voiced run up the scale: "Do, re, me, fa, so, la, ti, do." Although the last note was redundant, he held it for a weak operatic finish.

"The seven last words of the Jesus," Bobo said. "Or is ten? I'm not a Catholic."

"The seven hills of Rome," I offered.

"Neutral value of PH," Chernovsky announced, with a touch of scorn for our missing it.

"What's that?"

"Neither acid nor base," was all Armand thought needed to be explained.

What followed was a volley of interpretations twisting and respelling all of the number's possible referents, though none quite as original as Bobo's.

In what was a kind of understatement, Marguerite said we should remember that the clue was written inFrench. "Wouldn't its solution be in French? 'Seven seas,' for example, would be 'sept mers.'"

No one was listening. Then Alfie and I looked at each other at the same time. "Jesus," Alfie said in a loud voice, with a discernible note of alarm. "Put *Whole* with *Mers*. Holmers, as in Nat Holmers? Are we to think it's about him?"

There was an uncomfortable silence. I went to the board. I erased 'complete' and added the solution to clue four.

C

WHOLE

TEN

MERS

"Must be a mistake," Nkwame said. "Makes no sense. Let's keep going. Should explain itself. What about, **Leads confused**?

He looked around the table.

Most of us were still working over the implications of "Holmers." But Nkwame persisted. "How do you confuse lead?"

"There is something going on here," Percival Calkins mused in his bored philosopher's intonation. "A deception is at work. It is not the meaning of the word, as Wittgenstein would have said, but what comes of it. As anyone can see, the desideratum here is the five letters **l, e, a, d,** and **s**."

It appeared that, whatever he meant, the point had escaped us.

"You see? We are meant to confuse them."

"And …?" Alfie asked.

Calkins's empty stare indicated he was not yet done confusing the word or himself.

"How's *deals*?" Marguerite. Gardolini asked with a shrug. "Confusing enough?"

Her solution was so obvious I went straight to the board.

C

WHOLE

TEN

MERS

DEALS

Harvey Rilling went on to the next clue and got it almost at once. **"Half a half of a laugh**. Very funny. Ha ha. So half of that is 'ha' and half of 'ha' is 'h.'"

"Or 'a.'"

Rilling made a face. "Possible. But what's to say it's one or the other?"

"What don't I put up both?" No one objected.

C
WHOLE
TEN
MERS
DEALS
H/A

Alfie's face had frozen. He was staring at his copy of the puzzle. But, like Hamlet with his book, he was not reading.

I waited for Harvey Rilling to continue into the next clue, **Scattered hits**. But he did nothing more than shake his head. Then he bit his lip, and went no farther.

Samantha Gupta had no hesitation. "Scatter **h i t s** and what do you get? We're not talking steaks or perfume here. I say 'shit.' She looked around.

"Now I get it," Rilling said. "But it could be 'this' just as well."

C
WHOLE
TEN
MERS
DEALS
H/A
THIS/SHIT

"Get what?" Nkwame Smith asked Rilling.

"An over active imagination," Alfie muttered.

The next clue, by general agreement, was to be solved in the same manner. **Mixing feet with a fin** evidently has to do with an altered combination of letters. But which letters? The obvious choice was **feet** and **fin**. In other words, it is a simple anagram. A quick scratching of pens produced the only possible answer. I recorded it.

C

WHOLE

TEN

MERS

DEALS

H/A

THIS

FIFTEEN

Before we tried to fit this new word into sequence with the seven previous clues, Darius Pennybacker turned to me to ask, "Didn't you say several people got the next one, **That's twisted opposite?** I think you said the answer was *shit*, as in respelling the word 'this,' which is of course not 'that.'"

"Yes," I agreed, "we have *shit* in a previous clue, but as an alternative to *this*. Now we have *this* as an alternative to *shit*. I say the Puzzler doesn't give two shits." Eye rolling and groans passed around the table. Cerebral fatigue was settling in. I wrote both words in both places on the assumption that the final arrangement would be obvious.

I reported that so many correctly solved the last clue — **Remove the beginning of one, and remove one at the end of one?** — that we were excused from making our own attempt. As it happened, no one on the Committee got it themselves. I gave them a hint. "**One** in this case, is not clue number **one**, but the word **one** itself. So, you remove the beginning — an **o** — and you are left with ne. Then you remove **one at the end of one**, that is, **e**, and you are left with an *n*."

71

C
WHOLE
TEN
MERS
DEALS
H/A
THIS/SHIT
FIFTEEN
SHIT/THIS
N

EIGHTEEN

The door suddenly opened with an urgent push. I looked up. Lucille was standing there, holding out a large manila envelope.

"Professor Carmody," she said in a slightly breathless voice. "This is obviously meant for you."

I stood up to take it.

"Not twenty minutes ago," she said, "someone this under my door. By the time I got to the corridor, I saw a young woman walking rapidly toward the fire exit. I saw her only from behind and recognized nothing about her."

Written across the outside of the envelope were the words:

PLEASE FORWARD TO THE FACULTY COMMITTEE

As I removed the document from the envelope, Lucille turned on one of her stiletto heels and walked out through Iolinda's office. Before she closed the door behind her, she glanced back fleetingly at me. I took a moment to look over the enclosed message, and read it aloud.

To the Committee: While tenured heads bloviate, I have solved the puzzle. Whether you have solved it yourselves is immaterial. You cannot know what I know. The so-called puzzler knows his shit. That dreadful bastard, Holmers, is manufacturing — manufacturing! — crystal meth in his lab.

"Der lieber Gott!" Armand Chernovsky audibly slapped his forehead as if he had suddenly seen the meaning. He stood and shook the puzzle at us as though we should have seen its solution all along. "You take out *whole, mers, deals, this,* and *shit,*" he said, flicking at it with the back of his hand, "and here's what you're left with: *C ten H/A fifteen N.* Then you drop the *A,* and this is what you get." He went to the board and wrote out:

$$C10 \ H15 \ N$$

He stared at us as if we knew at once what this chemical formula represented. No one spoke, or moved.

"This," he explained, "is the chemical formula for methamphetamine. Take out the *c, ten, h, fifteen, n* and," he continued his voice rising in a kind of triumph, "what you get is: *Holmers deals this shit.*"

The puzzle was solved. But the anonymous message I was holding in my hand did not end there. I continued reading it aloud.

And yes the puzzler is right. Holmers is selling this shit. How do I know? I am one of his dealers! Whether I am a student is not relevant. You do not know my name. Don't even try to find out. None of your business. But it is the cops' business. I am willing to make a deposition. I can testify that I have been blackmailed into selling. You don't need to know how he did that — he meaning Prof Speedo, as we call him. (If you didn't figure out long ago that he is a heavy user, you're fucking idiots). What you need to know is don't go to Lt Roche. I sent him absolute proof. He never answered, wouldn't even talk to me. Screw him. Go straight to narcotics. They've got their suspicions about Holmers anyway. And do not, I stress, do not, go to the administration with this info. Never mind why. Don't delay. Good luck. I'll be cheering from the sidelines. Or booing.

NINETEEN

It might not only be the ten members of the Committee who had correctly decoded the puzzle. It occurred to several of us at once that Holmers himself might have solved it.

We needed proof. Was Holmers really selling "this shit"? Or was he being defamed — a strong possibility, given his characteristic abrasiveness. The anonymous messenger claimed she had proof. What kind of proof could that be? The student dealer was our link.

"Lucille!" Marguerite Gardolini called out. "Maybe she could add a detail or two on this mysterious woman."

Lucille answered after the first ring. I framed the request to sound a tad Oxonian.

"It'll take a coupla hours, Socko," she said and hung up without another word. Her response sounded like verbal nose thumbing.

I heard nothing directly from Lucille, but by early evening the mystery meth dealer had been identified, contacted, and accompanied to the narcotics division where she made a deposition. A detective called to request me to be at the southwest corner of the Square by five A.M. the next day when I would be met by two plain-clothed narcotics agents. We would then relocate to the opposite corner of the Square and the building where the Department of Anthropology has their laboratory. I am to follow their directions and I am to speak of this to no one. Say nothing especially to campus security officers or members of the city PD. This was an exclusive action of the narcotics division. I could only assume I was to be a witness to whatever was about to happen.

I must admit here that although I was relieved that the proper authorities were in command, something was disturbing me. How did Lucille so easily and quickly identify a fleeing young woman whom she saw only from behind and did not recognize? She not only named her; she *accompanied* her to the appropriate police office. Was there more to her role in this affair than appeared?

A cold rain arrived the next morning, displacing the clear skies and unseasonable warmth of the past few days. It was still dark when I positioned myself at the corner of the Square, a full quarter-mile across the Square. Two figures appeared, from different directions, one wearing a Levi jacket, the other a hoodie. They flashed their IDs so deftly, they could have been brushing away cigarette ash. They said nothing and paid no further attention to me as we strolled toward the northeast corner.

A weak light struggled through one of the windows on the fifth floor of the building. It went out and appeared in another. Someone was evidently at work in the lab. If it were Holmers, would he flee and stay ahead of the pursuing law officers? Or has he already destroyed the evidence?

Ten plain-clothed officers had gathered at the entrance to the building, making no attempt to conceal their presence. Three were women. The group moved as a unit, abruptly and with business-like concentration. One stood at the bottom of the emergency stairs, a possible exit route. Two more stood at the main entrance. The others took the elevators.

Unmarked sedans with tinted windows were parked at each corner of the Square and the entering streets. Two fire-trucks closed in on both sides of the Square. If the killer had been present, the odds were definitely on the side of the small army of the city's enforcement personnel.

I was asked to accompany them through the building though to stay in the background in case there was violence but to be on hand if they need me to I.D. Holmers.

After reaching the fifth floor, they formed a semicircle around the entrance to the lab. There was the ritual heavy knocking, then loud shouting: "Open up. This is the police."

The effort was greeted with silence. They knocked once more. It was a substantial steel door, not standard University stock.

The first explosion came almost immediately after the door was pried from its hinges. As the police took momentary shelter in case it was gunfire, I could hear the wild smashing of equipment. It seemed as if the entire space was being reduced to shards of glass and plastic. There were several more but smaller explosions. They were violent chemical reactions, but so far there were no flames. Nonetheless, the rooms began to fill with smoke, along with the fumes of chemicals that had a searing effect the lungs.

The lead officer paused at the door. "Professor Holmers, do not destroy more evidence. It will only make things, more difficult for you.

Let us take you to safety."

Sliding close to the wall, holding a handkerchief over my nose and mouth, I came around a corner with a full view of the lab. Holmers was whacking at the large collection of vials, beakers, and labeled bottles. It took a moment to realize that what he had in hand was, of all things, a squash racquet which he was swinging in a powerful series of fore- and backhands. He was as careless here as I knew he was in the squash court, causing shards of glass and chemical beakers to fly in all directions. His hands and arms were already badly bleeding. His facial expression suggested one of his demonic masks an expression focused on destruction, even self-destruction. In what seemed like seconds he had cleared the main tables, then, stumbling through the fractured glass covering the floor, he took a key from his pocket and opened the door to a heavy metal cabinet.

At that second he looked in my direction giving me a sudden accusatory smile. Because of the smoke, I could not make out exactly what he took from the cabinet. Whatever it was, he held it close to his chest. I could, however, see the hypodermic needle in his other hand. His use of it was practiced and swift. The man knew his veins. He dropped the needle and turned back toward me, a wobbling finger pointed savagely in my direction. The addict's gleam in his eyes, as if backlit from behind the notorious bush over his brow, was all that needed to be said. Slipping on the sudsy sheen of chemicals, he fell backwards into the laboratory trash covering the floor.

A small object had rolled out of his hand. It was a squash ball, the old-fashioned, hard type. I picked it up, careful the police didn't notice, and dropped it in my pocket. I was not sure of its function, though I could guess.

Suddenly masked firefighters in rubber coats carrying enormous backpacks of oxygen and fire retardant were surrounding me. The sight of Holmers' body, bloody and twisted in the wreckage, stopped them but only briefly. They opened the valves on their hoses and sprayed him and the area around him with a thick and expanding foam until his body, and much of the rest of the lab, was hidden under it.

"What if he's still alive?" I asked the firefighter standing next to me.

"Too late," he said, without pausing. "If this place goes, the whole fucking Square goes with it."

Coming up behind him were firefighters pulling a giant hose in from the hallway. They opened the nozzles at once. The force of the water drove the remaining equipment off the tables, across the floor and into corners, then blew out the windows. The horrific possibility of a fire had been averted. I backed out of the laboratory.

Before I reached the elevator, I caught sight, through the smoke and chemical haze, of a familiar figure. Deborah Waterson was talking with a tall man who from where I stood appeared to be in uniform. He was listening closely to what she was shouting to him over the clamor, and nodding at her in what seemed to be an attitude of pained attention. Then I recognized him.

What was Waterson doing there? Who authorized her presence? Why was Lieutenant Roche listening so closely? And for that matter, why was Roche there at all? He had hardly been seen on campus since the opening days of the Dean's investigation. Somehow both he and the reporter knew in advance what was about to happen. The suspicion that there was a connection between the two was hard to suppress.

I had no time to put my troubling thoughts in order. All that really mattered was that Nathanael Holmers was dead. He was his own killer.

Or was he?

FALL
SEMESTER
MIDTERMS

TWENTY

If the University community's reaction to the first murder slowed in a few days to a murmur, the second was electrifying. It was universally agreed that the Puzzler (now regularly referred to as such) might well have it in for the entire University. We were dealing with someone of considerable macabre talents. How did the Puzzler divine Holmer's well-concealed behavior? Did Ridley's apparent suicide have similarly dark implications? These questions merged with another topic of frequent speculation: who among us had the profile and the skills of the Puzzler? In Holmers' case, it could have been the work of one of his graduate assistants. Of course, there was also Lucille.

One amusing consequence of Lucille's faux English pose was that, like many of her so-called fellow citizens, she was an avid hiker, drawn to the kind of rocky slopes and steep inclines one might find in England's famed Lake District, or the Cornwall coast, or the Cotswolds. I could attest to the fact the woman was fit, with tight muscular legs and with alluringly carved thighs. (Forty-three years old? It was hard to believe. Why did she insist on this number?) Within a couple of hours from the city, mostly unknown to its residents, lies a ring of rugged hills and naked rock faces that rival some of the finest walking challenges in her putative homeland. Not long after we had become lovers, she introduced me to Mount Skunamunk, an isolated massif an hour and a half to the north of the city.

After some two hours of scrambling up a trail of loose stone, we reached the highest point on the mountain, a bald crown known prosaically as the Megaliths, a jagged assembly of huge boulders rising up out of a ring of stunted pine. From this point, one has a view of the city some fifty miles to the south and the stark cliffs of the Shawngunk range an equal distance to the north. Although there was no reason to think that another human being was to be found anywhere within miles, the site felt dangerously exposed. I was astonished therefore when Lucille, seated next to me, said simply, "Here."

The invitation was hardly unwelcome. Watching her from behind the full length of the ascent, several of my usual fantasies had taken firm hold. But the invitation was also perplexing. She was motionless and looking at me with an expression I could not interpret, giving no sign as to what was meant with the single word, "Here." Since she was not initiating anything, what exactly was she expecting of me? Was this a sexual matter? If not, what else? Overriding my hesitation, I soon discovered she was as willing as ever. It was far more than what I had imagined over the two hours of the climb up.

When we had retrieved our clothing from where it had been thrown, and pulled it right side out, she stepped back and looked at me as from a distance.

"That was a Two," she said in an uninflected voice. "Only a Two."

"Two? Two what?"

It was then that she taught me what I would later think of as the Game of Tens (of all things). It was a matter of stages, each one higher, more perfect than what came before. A stage, she said, always ended with what she called a Moment.

"A Moment? Oh, that." I would have used a word with a less ambiguous physiological referent. "Why is one Moment any better than another? What does a Two have that a One doesn't?"

"A One you can do alone. There is no need for an other."

"A Two, then?"

"There is another, but only for one's use."

When I had no response, she went on almost as if I were not there.

"A Three," she said, "is where the response of the other is of equal importance. Their separate Moments are identical."

"And simultaneous?"

"Well, yes," she answered. "That's assumed. For most, this is thought to be perfection, but they're wrong. It is here that anxiety enters. 'Now that we are acting together,' they ask themselves, 'is the intensity of the Moment sufficient?'"

"Is it ever?"

"No, of course not." She came toward me, as if to speak more directly, and more intimately. "And because of that, the anxiety is only heightened and we realize we are unknowns to each other."

"That's Five?"

"Four and Five. They are hard to distinguish."

"What happens at Six?" I was beginning to feel anxious myself.

"Six," she said in a stronger voice. "Everything changes. The Moment now takes on a power of its own, independent of what we may wish or do. There is no calling it forth, no arranging for it, and no clear image of what it will be when it comes, as it inevitably will. Six is the stage of Waiting, of being helpless before an unrelenting force."

What, I asked myself, is this woman talking about? The words were delivered as in a lecture. Uneasily, I framed the question she must have expected. "Waiting? That's all? Then what happens in Seven?"

She now sat on a flat patch of rock and seemed to be drifting off into her own thoughts. Then she lay back and looked up at scratchy traces of cloud. There was a long pause.

"Ah, Seven," she began in a stage whisper. "In Seven, the Waiting itself takes a new life. As the anticipation magnifies," she continued, her voice rising, "the Moment seems to have preceded itself and is already present, but extended in time, more a state than a terminus. It's at Seven that we are astonished to learn that the Moment has taken Waiting into itself. The Waiting and the Moment are one. Yes, one."

These last words were uttered with a sigh. Then, before I could respond, she sat up and looked out at the surrounding forest as if it were an audience to be addressed.

"Now, Eight! When we understand that the Waiting and the Moment are one, Eight comes at once. And quickly. It comes of its own initiative, in its own time, and without warning. For this reason, Eight can arrive with or without physical contact, when we are next to each other or are separated by great distances of space or time."

She looked over at me with a curious smile, as if expecting me to be surprised by this last declaration. I was. I put the next question with some fear of its possible answers.

"You mean we can be in a Moment of highest intensity with each other while in different places and at different times?"

Her smile broadened. She nodded very slowly. "Yes, that is exactly what I said."

"And Nine?" She asked the question for me. "The final transformation. The Moment does not come, it does not act on its own, in fact, and it no longer exists as itself. We ourselves have become the Moment."

"We have …?"

"We are its incarnation," she went on as if dictating to a disciple, "its avatar, a living paradox, the merging of the material with the immaterial, the boundless combined with human earthiness. Together, we can now say there is no Moment and never was, for we are all that it could ever have been."

As I lay on the rough composite surface of the rock, staring at threads of high-altitude cloud, I began to wonder if Lucille were truly sane. At the beginning, it was still possible to have some experiential grasp of what she was describing. But as she went on with these abstractions, they seemed to lose touch with anything familiar. It was somewhere around stage Five that my credulity, if not my comprehension, began to weaken. Then, I realized that while I was lost in the herringbone pattern of the unusual cirrostratus fibratus forming above us, she had stopped talking, maybe minutes before, maybe an hour. I sat up.

"That's only Nine."

"Yes."

"Isn't there a Ten?"

"Yes."

"What happens at Ten?"

She brought her face close to mine. We were all but touching. I had the sensation that the next words came as much on my breath as on hers. "You die."

"Die? And you?"

"We both die."

TWENTY-ONE

The third puzzle was published twenty-five days after the death of Nathanael Holmers. Although the ten-question format was repeated, it obviously called for a different analytic approach, this time distinctly literary. I called for a preliminary meeting of the Committee late on the same day.

PUZZLE # 3.1

1. COME, O CHILDREN, AND _ _ _ _ _ _ _ _ . I WILL TEACH YOU THE FEAR OF THE LORD. [PS 34:10]

2. I WISH THE _ _ _ _ _ _ _ _ _ _ WOULD COME, ROBERT JORDAN SAID, I WISH SO VERY MUCH THEY WOULD COME.

3. DON'T MAKE ME _ _ _ _ _ _ _ _ _ _ SOPHIE HEARD HERSELF PLEAD IN A WHISPER.

4. IT WAS HERE THAT HIMMELSTOSS GAVE TJADEN HIS

_ _ _ _ _ _ _ _ _ _ .

5. _ _ _ _ _ _ _ _ _ _ THE RIVER A GOLDEN RAY OF SUN CAME THROUGH THE HOSTS OF LEADEN RAIN CLOUDS.

6. THEY ARE CARRYING OUT ORDERS, COLONEL LANSER SAID. THEY ARE DOING

NO _ _ _ _ _ _ _ _ _ _ .

7. A BILLION TIMES TOLD LOVELIER, MORE DANGER-

OUS, _ _ _ _ _ _ _ _ _ _ , MY CHEVALIER.

8. A _ _ _ _ _ _ _ _ _ _ HIS BURNISHED CARRIAGE DROVE BOLDLY TO A ROSE

9. HAPPY ARE MEN WHO BEFORE THEY ARE _ _ _ _ _ _ _ _ _ _ CAN LET THEIR VEINS RUN COLD.

10. KNOW THIS OF A TRUTH, SAID SIEGFRIED, IN SLAYING ME YE HAVE SLAIN

_ _ _ _ _ _ _ _ _ _ .

The University, the media, and now a growing national audience had been holding its breath. Before the day was out, the campus was over ran with cops, reporters, and a virtual army of onlookers. Students were terrified and they were thrilled. They spoke in a high pitch and moved at a charged pace. *The Times* reproduced the puzzle in its entirety, taking up a full quarter page in the Metropolitan section. The TV evening news had invited in experts to comment on the likelihood that this latest puzzle could be solved ahead of the threatened killing.

When we were all seated, it was Alfie who opened the discussion.

"Look. Before we dig in," he said, glancing around the table. "Consider this: a single email showed up on the screens of every faculty member and every student, even the mass media, including the student newspaper — if the rag deserves to be so called."

"We don't have time for your critique of student journalism, Alf."

"Well, you better have time for this. Someone is breaking into the system — overriding any codes or blocked accesses. We've got a real talent here, boys and girls."

"We've been hacked. What else is new?" someone said to an indifferent chorus of nods and "mms."

"Okay, hacked, if you insist. But think again. This is no twisted high school dropout genius who knows how to fiddle with character-less numbers, but someone who knows the University, as you might say, from the inside. That can only mean that he knows all our ugly little secrets and moreover knows how to shake them out for the public's mounting amusement."

We were listening.

"I'm talking some twisted member of our esteemed faculty. I say we give up any thought it could have been a student. It has to be one of us who knows the rest of us goddamned well. He got our attention by throwing Ridley out the window, but by exposing Holmers went straight to one of the most hidden and sordid corners of the institution, a thriving commercial enterprise none of us dreamed existed."

Someone broke the weighted silence by observing, "So we have a double task here. Not only solving puzzles, but also snooping into private lives to head off more scandal. Well, I for one am not playing Columbo."

"The cops don't know shit about the University or how to investigate it," Alfie responded. "My learned colleagues, we gotta use our brains, but also our noses. Academe's crania, but also its armpits and crotches, if you please. Unless we take the Puzzler seriously, we've got eight more mangled surprises." He held up his copy of the puzzle. "So who's the unsuspected malefactor behind this one?"

The rest of us glanced over the ten obscure clues with a new kind of attention.

Kwame Smith sat up. "Let's first settle the matter of access. How difficult is it to break into the University database?"

"It's really not that complicated," Darius Pennybacker said, with the implication that any fool could figure it out.

A short fellow, apparently sensitive to the appearance of his slight frame, he wore his expensive tweed jackets a size too large, making him seem even smaller. Darius saw himself as a natural competitor of mine. Being an art historian, with degrees from several distinguished institutions, and specializing in the influence of Hellenic sculpture on the decidedly more vulgar Roman heroic monuments, he made no effort to conceal his resentment over my uninvited and uncredentialed intrusion into his discipline by photographing rare illuminations for no other reason than to use them as illustrations in undergraduate classrooms. That I was an appointed University Professor and therefore encouraged to make a home in as many disciplines as I wish, only added to his disaffection.

Now, in his role as chair of the faculty's premier ethics panel, Darius maintained a vigilance over a wide range of collegial behavior. How the Winged Victory of Samothrace was related to professorial sexual exploitation of students was not immediately clear. Also, he must have been aware that the student who was currently filing a case against a colleague of Darius' — a recognized expert in Low Country ceramic medallions of the early eighteenth century — happened to have been in my class as well. This must have caused a degree of unease. It made sense that the complainant was sheltering herself behind his expressed morality as protection against social opprobrium for her role as revealer. In my class, she was a B to B- student. In his, she was a straight A, though I admit I did not know her nearly as well.

"Access is child's play," Pennybacker went on. "Any graduate student, especially if he's Asian and involved in computer-based research, can read our emails as easily as we can."

"Ethnocentric sexism aside," snarled Samantha Gupta, "let's leave the IT issue with the police and get back to work."

During this discussion, Iolinda appeared several times with printouts of the emails, tweets, press releases, and suggested solutions that were constantly coming through her computer and addressed to the Committee — amounting to hundreds of individual messages.

At the conclusion of that day's deliberations I said with a nod at the growing stack. " We owe it to the community to at least glance at each of these suggestions. My thought is that we divide these up, go through them singly, and reconvene by noon tomorrow." I waited. "Agreed?"

No one answered but within minutes the material was distributed and the room emptied. I took my own assignment and left. Only when I reached the door of my office did I notice that Alfie had followed me there.

TWENTY-TWO

"Carmody," he said without explanation, and without an excuse for the interruption, "there's something about these puzzles that's getting to me."

"I've noticed. Come in. Sit down."

"This ain't Blacksburg," he said. "It ain't Austin either. Or Penn State. Or Columbine. Or Newtown. Or Umpqua. Or Charleston for that matter."

He could have gone on with the long list of massacres at public schools, post offices, resorts, army headquarters, churches, crowded streets, movie theaters, summer camps and conferences.

"Every one of these," he said in explanation, "was the work of a single nut, usually hauling a full armory of guns and grenades. Not one of these acts made any sense outside the twisted mental interior of these sad fucks. They were all loners, mind you, and all guys."

"You've blown in here to tell me we're not dealing with a nut?"

"This killer is a mental case, all right, but unfortunately for us, he's mental in both senses, fucking crazy and fucking brilliant."

"Your view, then, is that we're not concerned with this bastard's particular mental illness, but with his ideas."

"Carmody, you can read. 'The first to go is the most recent of ten.' Ten words. Ten threatened murders. Two we already know. There are eight to go, eight targeted doofuses walking around here unaware they've got no more than a few months among the living. The only way we're going to catch this guy is to get ahead of his mind."

"I'm reminded of that little 'γνφθι ϛεαυτον' pinned to the end of the first puzzle."

"Quoting Socrates," Alfie said, staring at his hands. "How do you think '*know thyself*' fits in?"

"Well, it's in quotation marks," I went on. "The Puzzler is quoting himself, speaking directly at us. No need to give the remark another meaning."

"So?"

"You know better than I that γνφθι ϛεαυτον can be variously translated."

"Yeah, sure." He shrugged, as if it were obvious. "'Wake up, fella!' 'Dude, what do you think your doing?' 'Hey, buddy, time to take a good look at yourself.'" He paused. "You remember how Socrates puts it in the *Phaedrus*?"

"Not exactly."

"Well, after saying nothing is more important to know than yourself, he admits to Phaedrus that he does *not* know himself, therefore why should he bother with learning anything else. Until you know yourself, he told the young man, all other knowledge is irrelevant."

Alfie drifted into a reflective mood.

"So when this guy," he continued, "— our Puzzler guy — appends the γνφθι ϛεαυτον, he's hitting us with the plainest but maybe scariest of all messages: you, the administrators and professors of this higher learning outfit, *are living unexamined lives.*"

The implications were multiplying. "You mean," I volunteered, "we are not to explore his thinking but our own?"

"Go on."

"His γνφθι ϛεαυτον is telling us not to examine what *he's* doing but what *we're* doing. What really needs solving is our own thinking. That's where the true puzzle is to be found."

Alfie was silent for a moment. "Which makes us and not him responsible for the killing?"

"In his sick mind, yes."

"I don't know, Carmody. I think I'll go look for a certain idiot I used to know, one Alfred X. O'Malley." Then he was gone.

TWENTY-THREE

I wondered: When the Puzzler puts the γνφθι ϛεαυτον in quotation marks, perhaps he isn't just quoting Socrates — perhaps *he is Socrates speaking*? And perhaps The Puzzler is a puzzle to himself.

Looking out in the direction of the Square, I let myself mull over the implications.

We know Socrates chiefly through his dialogues with fellow Athenians, as remembered by Plato, one of his students. Plato leaves a vivid account of Socrates' trial and death. He was charged with a mortal crime: corrupting the minds of the youth of Athens. His guilt was decided by a narrow majority of the five hundred members of the jury. They were correct to find him guilty; he was not innocent of the crime with which he was charged, a crime still found on the legal books of most of the world's governments. The Law mandated the penalty: death by poisoning, in this case a potion of hemlock. (On the question of the punishment, the Athenian jury was almost unanimous.)

Suppose the jury of his peers had judged the troublesome philosopher to be harmless to the citizens of Athens, an itinerant jokester, which in many ways he was. (A contemporary, Aristophanes, caricatured him in his comic drama, *The Clouds*, as a blundering fool who makes his entrance in a gas-filled balloon, kept aloft by his own airy nonsense.) Had they dismissed his case, we would never have known of the man or his manner of thinking.

Other than the drama of his trial and poisoning, there are few reasons for remembering Socrates, and remembering him with what often seems to be worshipful regard. He was a person of no substance, of no political importance, apparently homeless and famously ugly. His personal history contains nothing of note beyond his career as a common soldier, having displayed a modest degree of bravery in battle. There is no evidence he was even literate. To this day there is nothing we can call a Socratic doctrine, no system of Socratic thought, only a simple method of inquiry into the thought of others. We can say little more than that his was a mind on the loose. He was a terror to the citizens of his native city for no other cause than that he was a thinker whose profoundest thought was that, if he were unable to understand himself, he could understand nothing else.

Socrates himself was, of course, quite aware how easily he could be forgotten. His rich friends offered to bribe the jailor. He refused. Why, he must have calculated, should anyone remember a sneak, a willing participant in a corrupt and petty scheme to avoid punishment, much less a clownish prankster embarrassing to the civilized rulers of Athens? He seized our attention, and kept it, by being executed for nothing other than the radical ignorance that is the vital core of his teaching. His options were reduced to two: *Hemlock? or Oblivion?*

In identifying with Socrates, the Puzzler must see his assault on the University as a perfect parallel with the ironist's rattling of Athenian self-satisfaction. The Puzzler must be well aware, as we all are, that if the real Socrates were to appear unannounced before, say, the secretary of the philosophy department, he would hardly be ushered straight into the chairman's office, much less signed on as a professor of Greek thought. More likely, this aging veteran of several wars — this this illiterate, unbathed, and sandaled miscreant — would be swiftly bused to one of the city's homeless shelters, one with a full complement of psychiatric services. Consider the fact that what began in those casual encounters on the stone summit of the Acropolis has exploded over the twenty-five centuries since into a vast network of academies, schools, colleges, universities, research institutions, and an ineradicable climate of the critical examination of all things physical and spiritual — altogether the most transforming force in the whole history of human civilization. To get the attention of the modern university, "our" Socrates can succeed at his brand of intellectual terrorism only by a series of extreme and shocking acts — all of them requiring an encyclopedic grasp of modern knowledge and a masterful command of the latest instruments of electronic manipulation.

There is an embarrassing slip that Plato allows into his narrative. Moments before he receives the chalice of hemlock, Socrates jests with his friends. Jests! When they ask how he wants to be buried (after a long unresolved discussion of immortality in which he argues for the possibility of a disembodied soul), he says, "Just try to catch me!" To put it quite simply, by Plato's account, *Socrates goes out laughing.* It is that laughter that we hear throughout the Dialogues, a carefree dismissal of the weightiness and finality of thought. Socratic irony is a phenomenon of many shapes. In the final scene of his life, an hour or two before the end of day, the irony is especially rich, since it is

Plato who is caught in the web even as he spins it: it is he who relates Socrates' joke, but *it is he who doesn't get it*. Plato is not amused and not amusing, there is no laughter in his ponderous non-Socratic writings. It is almost as if Plato wrote the Socratic dialogues, the most brilliant portrait ever drawn of a true teacher, then never read them. We learn from the rest of his life that he did not want to be a philosopher at all, but a philosopher-*king*. The irony is complete. The jest Plato reports is a joke on Plato himself.

"Our" Socrates was every measure the comic who haunted Plato. As with the Athenian, until we solve the larger puzzle of his work, we did not get the jest. But now the terms have escalated. For Socrates the joke was on Plato and all that Plato came to represent in Athenian society. For the Puzzler, the joke was on us — that is to say, on the university and all that it has come to stand for in contemporary Western civilization. For us, too, the irony was complete. What we regard with the greatest seriousness is in fact laughable, an amusement. Once we invert the irony, once we have seen who we are and what we are doing, the Puzzler seemed to be promising, we all go out laughing.

TWENTY-FOUR

The Committee's meeting was nothing like those called around the first two deaths. We were now in ominous territory. We were no longer playing sophisticated word-games. We were now the ones being played.

The solution to this last puzzle seemed much the simplest of the three. One clear advantage was that the answers could at least be verified by examining the works from which they were taken. From the beginning, there was wide agreement among correspondents and members of the Committee as to how the blanks were to be filled in.

But there were also common errors. Most readers did not understand that one word, and one word only, would solve each of the clues. No multiples or phrases fit any of the blanks. The great bulk of responses were no more than wild guesses. And many answers were meant to be derisive and/or comical.

On two of the clues — four and eight — there were few submissions and it seemed likely even they were incorrect. As for us, the Committee found the solutions to four and eight difficult. But before we could get to them, we dutifully went through the pile.

Starting with number one, **Come, o children, and _____, I will teach you the fear of the lord,** we tossed out such wise-ass entries as "take your seats," "behave yourselves," "you have been away long enough," "bring your mom and dad," and, "don't just stand there." There were a number of close calls, or direct quotes from a variety of translations: "Hark," "behold," "be still," "hear what I have to tell you," "look unto the Lord," and "now is the time." More than half, however, got the correct answer: *listen.* A surprising number put their finger on the actual source of the quote: Psalm 34.

I wish the _____ would come, Robert Jordan said, I will so very much they would come was a different matter. Even though the name, Robert Jordan, pointed right at *For Whom the Bell Tolls* as the origin of the quote, found near the end of the book, there was a flood of suggestions, many of them outright tasteless, even perverted, and many just nonsensical. The more disgusting favorites were variations on "frigid women" and "the guys with the booze." Somewhat fancifully, such answers as "jugglers and clowns," "dancing elephants," and "the evening news reports" were typical. Only a handful supplied the exact word: *bastards.* Several correspondents could not stop with the answer and submitted comments on Hemingway's style, the subject of the book, and its historical context. One person declared "the whole volume a piece of crap that twists history into ideological pablum." (What derision Hemingway could have injected here: a four-way mixed metphor!)

Crude and prurient remarks were not limited to clue number two. Apparently oblivious to the horror of the setting from which **Don't make me _____ Sophie heard herself plead in a whisper** ... is lifted, answers included "do it right in front of all these people," "now, there's time later," "eat that sauerkraut," and "sit out here in the rain."

Nkwame Smith snapped, as if resenting the foolishness, "Look, the name "Sophie" gives us the title of the book, one of the most disturbing novels of the Holocaust literature. The answer to the clue is obvious. The hint is in the title itself." Nkwame didn't bother even to state the indicated word, as only an idiot would miss it.

As I mentioned, the fourth clue, **It was here that Himmelstoss gave Tjaden his _____** , was not solved accurately by readers or by members of the Committee. This didn't prevent a long list of possibles including: "Walking papers," "underwear back," "you know what," "salary check," "opinion of weak-kneed liberals," "comeuppance." and "own toothbrush," topped thc list.

Answers to _____ **the river a golden ray of sun came through the hosts of leaden rain clouds** were almost universally correct: *Over.* Only one writer, however, recognized it as the last sentence in Stephen Crane's *Red Badge of Courage.*

Number six; **they are carrying out orders, Colonel Lanser said. They are doing no _____,** stumped everyone but fans of John

Steinbeck, who recognized it as coming from his *The Moon is Down*. Colonel Lanser is a major character in the story and since it is an uncommon name, a simple internet search led most of the readers right to the book. Finding the actual quote was a bit time consuming but they listed it correctly as *harm*. There were compatible solutions such as "danger to anyone." There were also the usual jokers, writing in "more KP duty," "somersaults on the parade ground," and "more drugs."

Seven and eight — **A billion times told lovelier, more dangerous, _____ my chevalier** and: **A _____ his burnished carriage drove boldly to a rose** — brought out dedicated fans of Gerard Manley Hopkins and Emily Dickinson. At least a dozen said they had memorized Hopkins' poem, "The Windhover," when they were students and never forgot it. Some went on to provide professional level theological analyses, reading the work as a brilliant gloss on the incarnation and the crucifixion. Not surprisingly, everyone who identified the missing word, *bee*, in Dickinson's poem — fifteen or twenty in all — identified himself or herself as female. This selection from the poem, #1339 in the Johnson edition, was characteristic of her work as a whole: nearly unintelligible, until, that is, you untangle the odd word placement and grammar. And when you do, one woman wrote, "The mind is not big enough to hold the meanings of any one poem."

The ninth — **happy are men who before they are _____ can let their veins run cold** — is easily recognized as a war poem, and an angry one at that. Wilfred Owen wrote this line near the end of the Great War, after witnessing the senseless carnage of a conflict whose causes were opaque, especially to the soldiers who fought in it. And in fact Owen was himself a victim of this grand and pointless venture, outrageously named as, "The War to End all Wars." Most readers, even those who could not identify the poem or the writer, got a correct answer, or something close to it, as *killed*.

Siegfried is of course killed in the middle of the *Nibelungen Lied*, or Song of the Niebelungs, another ironically labeled history: **know ye this of a truth, said Siegfried, in slaying me ye have slain** _____. The jokesters overlooked this one, or found it difficult to lampoon. The solutions were mostly reasonable, and uninspired: "the greatest warrior of them all," "the beloved husband of Brunhilde," and "your own last hope for victory." The semantic balance of the line makes the final word obvious: *yourselves*.

Alfie had tallied the answers on the white board. We had consensus on eight of the ten:

LISTEN

BASTARDS

CHOOSE

OVER

HARM

O

BEE

KILLED

YOURSELVES

To a person, we agreed that there was a threat here, and that its meaning was dire. It was now only three days from the end of the month. It was critical to get it right. Just one blank remained, the fourth: **It was here that Himmelstoss gave Tjadin his** _____. We took a break. Some remained in the room, a few went back to their offices to get messages.

TWENTY-FIVE

When we reconvened, only Armand Chernovsky was missing. We started with a full sense of the threat facing us, but still there was no suggestion as to what this clue might mean. Suddenly Armand entered, pushing the door open with his foot. He was holding up a book opened to a page held in place by his thumb. "Ich habe es gefunden," he said in his excitement. "I found it. *Im Westen nichts Neues.*"

"*All Quiet on the Western Front,*" Bobo Winston said, practically shouting. "How could I have missed it? Himmelstoss, is one of its most memorable characters. Not a particularly pleasant fellow."

Ignoring Winston, Armand went on, "Ich wiederhole, in German, 'Hier hat Himmelstoss Tjaden erzogen.'"

"Erzogen, as in the past tense of erziehen?" Bobo asked. "Train? Educate? Raise?"

"Ja. Yes. I translate, 'Here did Himmelstoss educate Tjaden.'"

Bobo looked a little confused. "Could we read it, 'gave Tjaden his education?' That would fit smoothly into the sentence structure of the English translation."

"Bestimmt. Definitely."

"So, that's it," Bobo continued, and dictated the words to me.

LISTEN
BASTARDS
CHOOSE
EDUCATION
OVER
HARM
O
BEE

KILLED
YOURSELVES

Several of the committee members read off the list: *"Listen bas-tards, choose education over harm, O be killed yourselves. O?"*

There was a brief discussion about punctuation, and a small debate as to whether the sixth words should be read as *Oh* or *Or*. We decided that the meaning was clear either way. With *Oh*, the last phrase is an imprecation, with *Or* it is a threat. In both cases, it was alarming. Finally, it was agreed that we read it as *Listen, bastards, choose education over harm, or be killed yourselves.*

"Now what?" Gardolini asked. Suddenly there was a multitude of questions. Who are the "bastards" being addressed? What exactly is meant by "education?" Is it a reference to all institutions of learning, or to this University in particular? What kind of harm is implied — physical, political, societal, military? Or something else altogether? As for being killed, how specifically is the word being used? Should we expect a murder similar to the first two? If so, of one person, or, given the plural of "bastards," many? Is this the familiar threat of terrorism, or is it something more figurative, psychological, or ideological?

Which member, or members, of the faculty had been involved in something so corrupt or despicable as to deserve death? Assuming that the answer to all of these mysteries lay in the words of the puzzle in full, we began to look for patterns. The first observation was that all of these examples are related somehow to war or violence. A problem with this interpretation first rose with Hopkins' poem, which was, after all, subtitled "To Christ our Lord." The dominating vocabulary of the text sounds like the opposite of violence: "daylight's dauphin," "the mastery of the thing," "brute beauty," a "heart in hiding stirred for a bird." But the last line with the metaphor of embers that "Fall, gall themselves, and gash gold-vermillion," changes everything. This too is a poem of violence. Since vermillion, the color of blood, is the work's final word, we are reminded that at the center of this vision of beauty there is suffering and dismemberment, and that triumph does not come before, but after, death.

"Emily's bee visiting roses," Pennybacker said with some disdain, "is not much in the way of violence."

"Professor Pennybacker!" Samantha Gupta said in loud protest. "Don't you see this is not a sweet little lovey-dovey poem? It is, sir, a description of nothing less than rape. The rose opens, the bee — he! — enters, then leaves her — her! — not with 'rapture' but with 'humility,' which in Emily's vernacular means the same as humiliation." She looked around at the Committee with a severe expression. "Rape and murder, tell me these aren't universal elements of warfare."

No one dared to question Gupta on this. After a polite silence, we were prepared to move on. But where? Marguerite spoke first. "War and violence. This can't refer to something on the campus. There's plenty of intellectual brutality, sure, but so severe that it calls for murder?"

"Football," Alfie offered, "is violent, but because it is voluntarily administered and voluntarily experienced — no one, remember, is forced to play the game — does it deserve our moral scorn?"

Samantha immediately replied, "I have a twelve year-old son, Alfie, who is not only coerced but physically assaulted by his classmates because he will not play football. Perhaps football is not as voluntary as you think!"

The level of passion in these last several remarks threatened a discussion that would lead us away from the puzzle itself. I decided to cut it off.

"Who's dead?" I asked.

TWENTY-SIX

The question had its effect, but slowly, like a high-speed motor running down when the plug is pulled. The resulting silence was complete.

"Dead?" Percy Calkins asked with a vague expression.

"Someone's scheduled to die," I said. "And if we can't figure out *who*, they're dead."

A few members picked up the document under study and stared at it with no visible comprehension. Others looked off, embarrassed or annoyed at being stymied. The work of the Committee had gone nowhere. The solution to the puzzle was as enigmatic as the puzzle itself.

"Lucille!" Alfie said in a raised voice, looking over my shoulder.

I turned to find her standing in the doorway. Her appearance was classic Lucille: a Bergdorf Goodman silk scarf tossed casually but elegantly over one shoulder. She was wearing shoes so new they could have been purchased for the occasion. They were Manolos as far as I could tell from where I was sitting. I could see the Committee looked a bit thrown off. What was she doing here? As on her previous visit, she gave no indication that she thought she was intruding. Indeed, she came in as if she had been begged to attend. She glanced over the gathering with a faintly sweet smile, the kind you might direct at a stranger's child. She was holding a large manila envelope against her breast. She came around behind me.

"A few minute ago I received a document on my office computer — breaking through the firewall, I must add — with instructions to print it out for the Committee," she said in flawless Proto-Oxonian. "I thought you should see it without delay."

She opened the envelope and removed what looked like a dozen pages. She set one at my place on the table, not touching me, no doubt intentionally. Then, as if in a slow ballet, she squared the page in front of each member of the Committee. The uninterrupted flow of her movement around the room worked a spell. No one bothered to look at the page lying in front of him or her.

She left. Her smile hadn't changed. It could have been glued on. In any case, it was perfect, just as her painted lips were perfect: no smudge, no worn spots, the lipstick following precisely the natural shape of her mouth. As she neither touched nor looked at me, I felt as if I had evaporated. But, like everything else with Lucille, it had a double meaning. Had she indicated my existence in any way, it would have meant that my connection with her had been severed without emotional remainder. As it was, she was not only ignoring me, she was making an effort to ignore me; in other words, not ignoring me at all. She was not exactly inviting me to return to where we were. It was obvious why. Playing that song backward was impossible. My only hope was that I still possessed a bit of power over the interiorities of that remarkable and infuriating woman.

Knowing she would not exchange the gaze, I watched through the open door (why didn't she close it?) as she made her way down the long corridor of faculty offices. Before she reached the exit at the far end, a figure emerged from an office and stepped into her path. Raimundo Guttierez. What happened next only I could have properly interpreted. It came at me like a hammer on a wound. As he sidestepped to let her pass, she lightly brushed the sleeve of his Patagonia anorak without directly looking at him. It was not accidental but a subtly executed gesture. Any passerby would have noticed nothing. There was no exchange of words, nor did she alter her pace. He only nodded and returned to his office while she disappeared at the end of the corridor.

At once questions multiplied. Was this an arranged encounter? Why did she do this knowing it was in my full view? What did it have to do with the unexplained appearance of the new document? Most disturbing to me was that what just occurred was what I could identify as a Stage Four exchange. Has she caught this ambiguous Latino in her game of Tens? If so, could she use him as a hapless tool in her own designs?

I recalled a certain exchange of my own with her. One day, in a moment of crazed passion, I admitted that I virtually floated, serenely, on a current of fantasies about a life together, just the two of us. She laughed, sweetly, as she had that day on Mount Skunamunk and put a finger over my lips. "Remember, my learned fool," she said in a barely audible whisper, "who owns your fantasies, eats your soul." There were tooth marks on Guttierez's soul. Could she already have guessed the secret in his past, something I would learn only much later.

"What is this?" I heard Samantha say. She was leaning over the document that Lucille had placed before her. The question brought us back. Some raised it to get a better view; others placed it squarely in front of themselves.

PUZZLE # 3.2

1. COME, O CHILDREN, AND LISTEN.

I WILL TEACH YOU THE FER OF THE LORD. [PS 34:10]

2. I WISH THE BASTARDS WOULD COME,

ROBERT JORDAN SAID, I WISH SO VERY MUCH THY WOULD COME.

3. DON'T MAKE ME CHOOSE,

SHE HEARD HERSEF PLEAD IN A WHISPER.

4. IT WAS HERE THAT HIMMELSTOSS

GAVE TJAEND HIS EUCATION.

5. OVER THE RIVER A GOLDE RAY OF SUN CAME

THROUGH THE HOSTS OF LEADEN RAIN CLOUDS.

6. THEY'RE CARRYING OUT ODERS, COLONEL LANSER SAID.

THEY ARE DOING NO HARM.

7. A BILLION TIMES TOLD LOVELIER,

MORE DANGEOUS, O, MY CHEVALIER.

8. A BEE HIS BURNISHD CARRIAGE DROVE BOLDLY TO A ROSE.

9. HAPPY ARE MEN WHO BEFORE THEY ARE

KILLED CAN LET THEIR VEIN RUN COLD.

10. NOW THIS OF A TRUTH, SAID SIEGFRIED,

IN SLAYING ME YE HAVE SLAIN YOURSELVES.

"It's like getting the answers to the exam you have just passed," Alfie said, a bit annoyed. "What's the point of Lucille bringing this in?"

"It may not be so simple," I suggested. "Perhaps it is worth closer study. Take some time with it."

"Shit, there's even a misspelling in the first answer," Marguerite complained.

"Well, there's another one down here," Bobo Winston said, pointing to the clue at the bottom of the page.

"They're all over the place," Calkins groaned dismissively.

"Hold on a minute." Alfie held up his hand. "There's more to this. You notice there is a mistake in every clue, but only one to a clue. Maybe this is telling us something."

"Well, make a list." Rilling already noted the missing letters in the margin of the document.

"Read them out," Alfie asked him.

"The first is the *a* left out of 'fear'. Next is, oh yes, the *e* that should be in 'they.'"

I went to the board and wrote out the letters as they were identified. The list read:

1. FE/R = A
2. TH/Y = E
3. HERSE/F = L
4. TJA/EN = D
5. GOLDE/ = N
6. /RE = A
7. DANGE/OUS = R
8. BURNISH/D = E
9. VEIN/ = S
10. /NOW = K

"*A, E, L, D, N, A, R, E, S, K.*" Several committee members read the words out loud.

"I suppose it's an anagram," Bobo said. "Let's see. *Desk* something? *Learn?*' But then we have an *a* left over. Maybe it's *Learn a desk.*"

"I've got it," Darius said with typical confidence. *Send a Laker.* Now just how we could use a Laker, that's the next question."

"Darius," snarled Samantha, "the letters spell other words as well. How about, *Ed ranks ale?* Or, *Ades rankle?*"

"*Ales darken,*" was the next suggestion. After that, "*Sales drank.*"

I wrote those five on the board.

> LEARN A DESK.
> SEND A LAKER.
> ED RANKS ALE.
> ADES RANKLE.
> ALES DARKEN.
> SALES DRANK.

There was a wild scribbling and crossing out of letters, accompanied by mumbles and test pronunciations. The list grew rapidly, especially after it was suggested that a *K* could stand in for a *C*. Several of them were a reach and several were nonsensical.

> CANDLES ARE.
> SANDAL REEK.
> A KLAN SENDS.
> E DRANK ALES.
> ANKLES DARE.
> SCREEN A LAD.
> AND ELKS ARE.

LEND A SCARE.
CLEAN READS.
DEALER SANK.
READ ANKLES.

"There's something odd about the first and last clues in the puzzle," Alfie said, "Why would the list begin with the Psalms end with the Niebelungenlied? They are the only non-modern references, as if calling attention to themselves. Like it starts Hebraic and ends Germanic. Am I overstating this?"

Nobody commented, just continued to read over the listed phrases.

Alfie scribbled a few letters, crossed out one, and added another. "Jesus!" He jumped to his feet so quickly his chair tumbled backward. "Holy shit! What the fuck! Speak of Nazis!"

He had our attention.

"Look what it also spells," he said with the same alarmed tone. He went to the board and wrote in large letters, *ALEKSANDER*, then turned to the group. "Let's get moving. There's almost no time left."

"Who's Aleksander?"

"Aleksander who?"

"Someone's name?"

"Aleksander Krauss," Alfie announced, "the computer guy who has the D.o.D. project on the tenth floor of Applied Math."

TWENTY-SEVEN

Having several full days' grace, the key authorities were able to set in place extensive security arrangements. Jack Lister deftly coordinated the relevant forces, spending the largest part of his time with the U.S. military since it was they who had commissioned Aleksander Krauss's research into the missile defense system

What seemed to be a full battalion of Army Rangers arrived in green military vehicles, lights flashing, and swept through the Institute, emptying the building and placing guards at every possible entrance or exit. It was assumed that for his protection Krauss had been moved to an unannounced location but the federal government was alarmed that his laboratory was equally vulnerable to attack.

The strong military presence immediately attracted the press who, by the morning of the next day, had moved in with their boom mikes, rolling cameras, and klieg lights. The Rangers' snappy caps, scary weapons, and muscled torsos showing through their green uniforms made exceptionally good TV and Internet subjects. Videos and taped interviews with faculty, students, and administration, as well as with the military were spread across the evening news.

At the center of the mêlée were the imposing figures of Police Lieutenant Thomas Roche and President Jack Lister, rising what seemed half a foot above the surrounding crowd. Together they provided the media with a detailed summary of the measures being taken to assure the safety of the University's staff and faculty. Roche was especially impressive. It was the first time I had seen him in uniform. The visor of his hat was pulled down just enough to darken his eyes, giving his face a confident look of masculine authority, especially when framed by a two-dimensional TV screen in full color.

The media made high drama of the time element. If this anticipated event were anything like the previous two, it would occur by midnight, exactly seven days since the puzzle first appeared and the last day of the month. In fact, given several days of lead-time and the high audience expectations, the media designed their coverage to roll out like a full-length film. There was a simulated count down; a non-stop voice-over narrative by a familiar TV personality; and powerful lights illuminating the neighborhood to make it resemble an enormous stage set.

The Square proved to be a living made-for-movies spectacle. A classic urban space, nearly ten acres in size, it serves as both campus and park. A patchwork of lawns, gardens and paths, and a veritable arboretum of giant trees — some approaching two centuries in age — surround a large open space with a fountain and reflecting pool, an ideal open air theater for jugglers, acrobats, steel drum bands, orange clad monks, bobbing saxophonists, drug dealers, unicyclists, and always a small population of the bearded and tattered survivors of the 70's counterculture. On the north edge of the Square is a monumental marble arch celebrating the country's first President, an excellent frame for capturing scenes of the human carnival for immediate broadcast.

In one memorable sequence, a young man with a body so sleekly muscular it could have been carved by Praxiteles was caught by the camera performing a series of balletic dips, sweeps, and spins — on roller skates. He would execute a backward leap, a full grand jeté, his legs flying out in a perfect split, then turn, all in the same motion, and return to earth, finishing in a spin of increasing velocity. The performer was memorable not only for his remarkable skill, but also for his tightly-fitting satin tank-top and pink tutu.

A predictable media favorite was footage that opened on a shirtless and barefoot guru standing at the edge of the reflecting pool, holding his hands out in a salute to the cosmos. Wrapped around his hips was something resembling a Gandhian dhoti, though more Vermont than Varanasi. A small crowd watched with amused disbelief as he began distending his stomach then sucking it back up into the cavity of his chest. One could only imagine a large round object violently bouncing through his midsection. Down, it took the shape of a seven-month pregnancy; up, so little remained of his intestinal region that you expected to discern the outline of his spinal column. Up, down, up, down. The process was slowly increasing in rhythm, suggesting the rapid spinning and pumping of kundalini yoga. In the last frame he returned to his original pose, greeting the universe while his belly settled into its normal location. The performance ended with a sudden segue to a water fight in the reflecting pool among a handful of loosely clad female students.

In the background, of course, were visual reminders of a severe police and military presence, giving the (false) impression that riot control vehicles, Humvees, unmarked SUV's with dark windows, a fire captain's personal sedan, and ambulances from several urban hospitals virtually surrounded the Square and all University buildings. The voice-over actor's deep timbre assured viewers that the impending peril had been addressed and neutralized.

One can well understand the disappointment, therefore, when in the seconds after midnight on November 30, nothing happened, nor in the next hour. By four o'clock in the morning, the cameras were turned off, the lights dimmed, most of the reporters left, and the soldiers stood around in small groups smoking and looking bored. Even by noon of that day, there was not a hint of trouble. The disappointment of the media slowly turned to resentment. There was a wide feeling that they were being manipulated, although exactly by whom it was not clear.

A second day passed. Still nothing.

TWENTY-EIGHT

On the third day, there was an apparently insignificant report from the soldiers on duty on the tenth floor of the Institute. One of them, while patrolling the length of the hallway outside Krauss's laboratory. This solider noticed, that the lab's main door had taken on a reflective sheen, almost mirror-like. Curious, he ran his finger across it. He thought he detected a thin film of moisture. At first, he made little of it. But like the other Rangers, he had been instructed to take note of every detail, no matter how small. He reported this to his Lieutenant who then passed it on to the General.

Moisture on a door? That hardly sounds like terrorism, the dutiful warrior thought, but better we look into it. He confirmed the soldier's finding, and raised the matter with members of the Institute faculty. They too were somewhat dismissive, but they had long since learned to draw no conclusions about the secret work lying behind that door. Moreover, there was no one in the entire building beside Krauss who knew the laboratory's entrance code. One of the embedded army officers decided it might be better to contact Krauss, which he did through the General, who alone knew the location of the professor.

There followed a strange procession of three black SUVs winding through the city to the Institute. Five or six figures climbed out of each of the cars, all of them looking remarkably alike, all in combat readiness, including helmets with face masks, jack boots, and shields. It was only because of what was about to happen that we later learned Krauss had been part of this detail. He was dressed as an Army Ranger, obscuring his identity (perhaps satisfying a hidden fantasy), and protecting him against hostile action. He was conducted upstairs, taking the elevator with several armed Rangers, and went straight to the solid metal door that sealed the facility against any possible incursion.

He asked all military personnel to remove themselves to the ends of the corridor. He took no chance that anyone might be close enough to catch the series of numbers he pressed into his smartphone. He stroked the door with his finger. He stood there without moving except to draw closer to the door, his nose almost touching. He was evidently baffled as to the source of the moisture. The door after all was designed to prevent either water or air to be exchanged with any outside source. So it could not have been some sort of leak from within, but condensation only on the outside. But from what source? He entered the code.

At the last number of the code the door blew open and the massive explosion that followed was not fire or dynamite. A huge fist of water shot out of the laboratory with enough force to destroy an army tank. It was not a spilling forth as if emptying a container; it was a directed sluice, a blast as if from a ferocious opened fire hydrant, or a whitewater torrent, a liquid tornado, the outlet tunnel of the Hoover Dam. Some actually thought it was a building collapse and not water at all. It blew across the corridor more like a giant hammer or piston.

In the confusion, all sight and trace of Aleksander Krauss was lost. A deafening crash overwhelmed the plans; by the time the brain registered the relevant data, water had blasted its way down the corridor, sweeping soldiers and riot cops down the stairs, now a virtual waterfall.

Water cascaded down the stairwells to the first floor and the building exits, left a number of soldiers and graduate students in a sodden huddle in the building lobby. But Krauss was not among them. Two rangers were assigned to make their way back up to the tenth floor. Krauss's corpse was found buried under a heap of office furniture, trash baskets, and unidentifiable detritus two floors below in an eddy of the receding water, his helmet still securely in place. In recreating the event, the speculation was that when the door shot open it hit the mathematician with enough force to propel his body to the end of the corridor. The body was strangely flattened by the impact, as if he had fallen under a massive steamroller. To make it even stranger, the surging water had cleansed the corpse of its blood, giving it a pale, ghostly appearance. As the EMT team transferred the body to the ambulance, the plastic cover slipped back, revealing the blanched remains of his crushed face, described by one of the tabloids as resembling a "flattened vanilla custard donut."

Before the ambulance door was slammed shut, I saw Deborah Waterson standing silently at one corner of the crowd. Unlike the others, she paid no attention to the action of the EMT's, but was looking around from one face to another as though there was something deeply troubling her. I thought it could be rage that I saw in her face. I left before we made eye contact. I followed the line of her gaze until it stopped at a tall figure approaching from the opposite side of the growing mass of onlookers. For the briefest moment, I was sure I saw the Lieutenant nod in her direction.

FALL

SEMESTER

FINALS

TWENTY-NINE

The next day Lister called a meeting of the faculty's best computer minds, inviting me in what seemed an afterthought. He entered his conference room dressed as always in a crisply starched shirt and an expensive, casual sport coat of an Ivy cut, with the mandatory leather elbow patches. He took his place at the head of the large antique table, his "pirate's desk," and looked over the group with an uncharacteristically exhausted gaze.

"Let's get to work. How did this fucker do it?"

There followed a discussion that sped along at such an expert level that Lister frequently held it up and begged for an explanation in layman's language. The consensus was that the perpetrator carried off the amazing feat entirely by cyber-manipulation. That person, or persons, must also have had an intimate familiarity with the operation of a large array of inter-connected computers, and have known of the high level of heat they generate. The sophisticated air conditioning for the tenth floor of the Institute was exactly calibrated to the wide variations in the temperature levels of the programs underway. If there was a point of entrance into the engineering, it had to be in the way the sprinkling system was coordinated with the thermostat. The University's electrical usage records presented a convincing coda: the power supply to the laboratory's air conditioning units went dead exactly at midnight on the specified day.

As with Holmers's execution, there was the thought that Krauss's grizzly end could have been carried off by a student. Essentially everyone enrolled in the Institute for Applied Mathematics had the technological skills to manipulate the climate system of the building. But contrary to the Holmers episode, there was no comparable motivation among the young mathematicians for revenge.

The destruction of the computers was so thorough there was no way of recovering the stored data. It was generally agreed that most of the work, four years of it, was lost forever. This is what exercised the DoD most inasmuch as it endangered the entire nation by exposing it to the Iranians and North Koreans. Every piece of the affected equipment would need to be completely destroyed, making it useless to any hostile agents who might come into possession of its detritus.

A young FBI agent made an important discovery during the final stage of deconstruction. A MacBookAir, not connected to the massive room-sized units appeared to have been spared contact with the water; perhaps it had been hidden in a space of its own, sealed off from the rest of the operation. The agent's analysis of its contents yielded a long list of numbers that had no mathematically interesting connection to each other or to anything else he could find. It looked as if the contents had been garbled by the event. But he dutifully printed out the roster and confidentially invited several of the Institute's computer wizards to help him interpret the mess. It was a full three days of analysis before they were able to make sense of them. Each number, they found, was the access code to a bank account of dozens of shell companies. But which bank or banks, and where? Further investigation led them to locations spread across the globe — from Venezuela to Uzbekistan extending s far as Lebanon, Syria, Iran, Yemen, Panama, and Indonesia. Each account established in these countries was payable mostly in Iranian rials. And only to the private Swiss account of one "Sandler X. Raucous." Suddenly the entire project took on a dramatically different meaning.

At a subsequent press conference in Washington, the Attorney General of the United States took questions on the discovery of the accounts and his estimation of the harm that had already been inflicted on American interests around the world. In response to a reporter's question, he said that for a spy who has penetrated this deeply into the bowels of national defense, the crime would be punishable by a number of concurrent life sentences, but the death penalty would have been demanded by the department of Justice.

THIRTY

The immediate media coverage of Professor Krauss's demise was so intense — print, video, radio, social media — that only those hiding from the law or lying comatose in an ICU ward could have missed it. The count-down drama at the Institute, the dauntingly sinuous bodies of Navy Seals, crashing against walls and railings as they were carried down ten stories to the building's ground floor — how could one find footage more startling and beguiling? The stairways of the Institute had been converted to something like arroyos in a freakish rainstorm.

A seething rage grew among the military and police detachments for being tricked by this unknown and perverse manipulator of the fates of innocent victims, all the more infuriating in the face of the warnings they had received.

The parents of students were in a category of their own. Several thousand emails lighted up dormitory laptops with the demand that their darlings exeunt the campus pronto. One rarely passed an undergraduate dormitory without witnessing a now familiar scene: a family car, typically a late model SUV, packed to the roof with the usual student clothing and equipment, while the parents nervously waited for their offspring to finish their goodbyes so they could escape the city and reach the tranquil suburbs and safety.

Student Affairs added nine therapists to their counseling staff.

Still, it is fair to say that the jocular element never completely left student discourse. As one quipster put it in a guest column in the student Square Journal, "So, you're kvetching, the University doesn't have a football team? You're asking yourselves, Why can't we be like Ole Miss? They have a stadium full of a 100,000 screeching fans while all we have is a fountain with hippies in it. But what we really got, friends, is worth Ole Miss squared. They have to cheer athletes who never lived in Mississippi and don't give a flying ____ for the whole ____ state. We got deans flapping out windows, professors stoned out of their twisted minds, drowned computer geniuses with faces like squashed vanilla donuts. Rah, rah, rah."

There wasn't a lot of laughter among the trustees. These three executions were tragedies whose true losses could be measured in dollars — millions of dollars. Who is going to contribute a hard-earned hedge fund fortune to an institution of higher learning not learned enough even to discover who is killing off its own human assets? The trustees were convinced that this brazen eliminator was a member of the faculty and was receiving a six figure salary for a few hours of work a week. For all the board knew, its resident violent criminal might be protected under the University's tenure system.

While some classes seemed to have thinned out after the third execution, not a few professors noticed new faces in their classrooms, a decade older than their teenage classmates, miniature telephones hanging from their ears, and dressed in adult styles that would draw guffaws in the dorms. There were also occasional groups of uniformed officers checking student ID's in the corridors, on the sidewalks, and even in the library reading rooms.

The media continued to storm the campus, especially dirt-sniffing reporters for the tabloids. A kind of competition developed among students (and, sure, some faculty) to rise to the popularity level of reality TV by offering 24/7 accounts of suspicious signs and behavior. Several students were obvious shoo-ins for a future in the viewing media.

THIRTY-ONE

The tragedy at the Institute for Applied Mathematics had another meaning for many of the faculty. The heavy investment of the government in academic proceedings could hardly be missed. A handful of leftish professors submitted a petition to Jack Lister demanding to know why the University was so deeply involved in military planning and what other research projects might be currently funded by the Department of Defense.

Lister hid the blaze of his anger behind a bland refusal to discuss the issue, releasing instead a statement written in the purest administrationese.

Memo: to the University faculty and students
From: Executive Administration
Re: Inquiries into funding for research.
The University is the recipient of public funds in a wide array of studies and research as part of its responsibility as a prominent and legitimate organization.

A widely distributed poster, printed in black and red, announced the creation of the Radical Faculty Caucus on DoD Manipulation of the University. Raimundo Guttierez was the near unanimous choice to chair the group. His characteristic, easily triggered temper, was a perfect match for the ardor of this protesting body. His public performances were brilliant. He had the unexpected gift of deftly eliciting the hormonal exuberance of students, the resentment of underpaid graduate instructors, and the reckless energies of mostly untenured faculty, and focusing them on precise issues.

It didn't hurt that Raimundo sometimes addressed the crowd as *mi muchachas y muchachos,* or *niñas y niños.* The Spanish accent, along with the slant of his politics, bore the strong (if artificial) hint that in another setting he would risk being among the *desaparecidos.* The fact that he played so loosely with the uncertain prospects of his own future at the University only added sheen to his heroic mantle.

As an orator, he was a master. As a writer, on the other hand, Raimundo had for too long been poisoned with the scholarly habit of presenting one's own views by showing how they are superior to discredited others, then citing a blizzard of supporting opinions. The Caucus's publications were on the whole, intellectually numbing.

Raimundo and the Caucus were aided by the creation of another faculty group: senior professors and tenured associate professors, joined by a verbal throng mostly from the student body of the School of Commerce. The Committee of Sobriety, as they called themselves, selected the perfect public voice: Leonard Gold. Lenny's ironic oddness proved to be, as he would love to have heard, eighteen carat.

Lenny had the studied appearance of a 'seventies pinko, complete with a moderately successful Afro, torn denim jeans barely hanging on his snake-thin hips, and unlaced Keds. So long as he kept his mouth shut on his atheism and sexual orientation, he qualified as an authentic Jeremiah of the angry right. He was no equal to Raimundo for flashy rhetoric and evangelistic fervor, but his unchecked rush to the edge of the politically possible kept his chorus of hundreds in full voice. A signal metaphor was his repeated reference to the (current) government as a slimy organism of grasping fingers: reaching first into your pocket, then between your bed sheets, around your tongue, into your ears, and on to the remaining physical orifices.

Like true believers everywhere, both sides had become experts on each other's views, often more articulate on what they opposed than on what they advanced. Lenny used bigger words, and a good bit of undiluted conceptual material, drawn from his field — economic and business history. Also typical of extreme believers, Lenny and Raimundo were in acute need of each other, attached like lovers in a *folie á deux*. Where one appeared, the other was soon to follow. Whatever new angle emerged in the ideology of one, his antagonist was obliged to produce a 180-degree-reversed version of it. On one side, the government was picking your pocket; on the other, the corporations were corrupting your mind. Charges of a military takeover were met with accusations of selling out to the enemy. Taxing the rich guaranteed soaring unemployment. A respect for life on one end was disrespect for a woman's right to control her own body on the other. It was a rehearsal, in other words, of the same oppositional ideas that have been entertaining the American public during a recent campaign for the White House.

THIRTY-TWO

One cold day crossing the Square, not far from the fold-up lectern that Raimundo's acolytes assembled for his performances, I stopped to listen. After all, as the chief rhetorician on campus, I could hardly ignore a public exercise of that art by students and colleagues.

Raimundo was wearing his alpine down parka, a tightly rolled rappelling rope causing a bulge in a lower pocket. Was that loose strip of fabric hanging from his pocket the headscarf he wore when hiking?

That bit of color reminded me that our lives had a small but pleasant overlap. We were both outdoorsmen, to use an antique term, he far more experienced than I. Because of that discrepancy, I rarely joined him in even local expeditions. But we were in frequent conversation on the subject, and sometimes exchanged hiking equipment. At some point in his life, he had been extensively trained in the use of survival techniques, able to find water in deserts and follow animal tracks in otherwise impenetrable rain forests. He was an adventurer, a trekker, and above all a climber.

I never really advanced beyond a beginner level in climbing but when I was younger and in condition for it, I always found the sheer face of a rock cliff irresistible, if for nothing else than my fantasy of being one of those half naked death-defiers hanging from the tips of their fingers over an abyss while smiling up at the camera. Raimundo was an authentic member of that tribe. In my occasional conversations with him, I learned that his fantasies ran to geologic extremes. For him, K-2 was a priapic marvel of nature.

Raimundo had just opened his diatribe by engaging in the obligatory ritual of shouting down any suspected "others" in his audience, patently trolling for an angry response in equal volume. Pat on cue, a faithful squadron of School of Commerce hecklers entered stage right, setting off the desired volley of scripted words: corruption, distortion, mendacity, exploitation, distribution (of wealth, that is), violation, and insurrection. Then it occurred.

THIRTY-THREE

Without a break in his verbal stream, without so much as a catch in his breath, Raimundo looked backwards over his shoulder in the direction of the Administration Building. It was not much more than a glimmering shadow. I could make a confident guess as to what she was wearing. It was the Akris tweed with just the suggestion of shoulder pads and her salmon blouse that buttoned up the neck. But it was not her elegant fashion that had Raimundo's attention. She was his Anna Purna.

Raimundo and Lucille had come much further than I expected. The undisturbed surface of Raimundo's action was an essential strategy in the Game of Tens. It was a skill difficult to acquire. I estimated they had already achieved the moment at a full Five. At the beginning of my months with Lucille, I thought I could hasten my ascent up those levels by pouring out a large vocabulary of romantic terminology — variations on the word of love in a dozen languages, fresh superlatives for describing passion, unusual adjectives to go with ecstasy, poetic images for parts of the body, and arousing episodes in classic mythology. I was dismayed that Lucille's reaction to this verbal effulgence was, frankly, no reaction at all. It wasn't until I had reached Four that I knew why. It was on a day when she was unusually, and wonderfully, aggressive. I was a mere toy, an object on strings, a wired mechanism in her hands. Near the higher slopes of this adventure, she asked me a surprising question.

"Were you at the greengrocer today?"

I was completely baffled. In fact, I scarcely had enough breath to answer. "Wh...? What?" was all I could manage.

"Was the lettuce fresh? Are the new grapefruit in?"

The even voice in which she spoke these words was so extraordinarily out of place with what was actually happening, I hardly knew how to respond. She was still in perfect English, (not a syllable of New Jersey.) And given the level she had just reached and the impending arrival of a new Moment, I could not imagine how she could even hear me.

"What was the price of peaches?" She was relentless.

I was now angry. "Yes, I was at the fucking supermarket today. Or the goddamned 'greengrocer.' What the fuck does it matter?"

Suddenly she was doing remarkable things with her hands, some of them completely new. I had never known of such movements, not from experience and not from my wide reading of erotica. Then a doubt began to form. Maybe they weren't new. Maybe it was only that my responses were new. I began to think I was ascending to another number. Five? My next action utterly astonished me.

"They had a sale on carrots," I said.

"Did you purchase any?"

"No," I said, then used a word that came to have long trails of meaning. "I got the broccoli instead." This was the end of my speaking. From here on out, there weren't words I was conscious enough to utter.

Lucille offered no explanation of all of this until the next day, and even then it was not a full elucidation of the perplexing event. I only began to understand when she spoke the key word.

"Broccoli."

I looked at her for a long time, trying to make sense of what she had just said. There were depths here I couldn't divine.

"Broccoli?"

"Yes, broccoli."

She was smiling, but it was her office smile, the generic token every visitor to the Dean's office received. While others experienced it as warm, I knew it as a slick cover hiding giant malevolencies and, yes, whole labyrinths of interiority still unvisited. Knowing no other suitable term, I call it "broccoliana."

Lucille was not particularly of a philosophical turn of mind. Her mental throughways were composed mostly of metaphors.

"Look: the flames of hell right under where you're walking," was one of them. "What are those rock things they find in streams out there in Wyoming?" she once asked me, and then answered it herself. "Geodes."

"Oh, geodes."

"So ordinary as to cause no one to notice, almost as if they aren't there at all. Then break them open," she made a sudden move with her whole body, "and they are beautiful. Rare. Blazing colors. And full of very sharp and dangerous needle points."

I was getting my first lesson in broccoliana: not knowing the treasures are there is what makes them precious.

I never perfected the art of broccoliana, but I became acceptably adept at it. I could, for instance, describe to Lucille in a flat voice how I walked from my apartment, crossed the street, and on my way to the next corner fell behind the pigeon woman who was dribbling a trail of seed the length of the block. The sound of the pigeons' wings, wads of identifiable trash in the gutter, the sanitation department truck picking up the large plastic bags of recyclables, the gray sky, a temperature around 58° — all of this uninflected detail went into constructing the outer shell, the bland surface, that provided a thin membrane for the cyclonic tumult, hidden to any observer. Concentrating on these trivialities, acutely aware they were trivialities, magnified their opposite to a near onset of madness.

Soon I realized that I was spending a large amount of the day searching the quotidian for hollow detail: conversation with a student about her B exam grade; a bald prophet in the Square passing out empty sheets of paper, saying only "Blah, blah, blah" to each person who accepted one; a bicycle speeding down the avenue toward the Square, its peddler leaning dangerously over the handlebars while his passenger, a girl sitting on the seat behind him, her arms and legs spread wide, singing the familiar aria from the third act of *The Daughter of the Regiment* — it all worked.

Nothing revealed Lucille's broccoliana as effectively as her car. One day early in our relationship she suggested a drive in the country. I was surprised she even owned a car, but not as surprised as I was when I was introduced to this object. We found it in a dark corner of the faculty parking garage. I recognized it, just barely, as a Karmann-Ghia, a sports car from the early Seventies, when Volkswagon ceased production of the model. That Lucille, of all people, with her closets full of Marc Jacobs, Stella McCartney, and Christian Louboutin, would even admit to owning this thing was frankly shocking. It looked reasonably intact, but the metal exterior, scratched and dented here and there, was sufficiently aged as to be colorless.

Lucille slid under the wheel while I climbed in on the other side, careful to keep my tender parts protected from the exposed springs in the seat. She asked me to find the "wire" in the glove compartment. I combed through this wretched little space and found only a piece of stiff insulated cable, bare on each end. She looked over at me for a pregnant second, and then attached both ends of the wire to small hooks beneath the steering wheel. "That's it," she said and gave the cable a vigorous jerk. There was a violent trembling and an ear-deafening roar as the engine came to life. I think I was yelling something at Lucille, like, Jump out before it's too late. But she was giving me one of her unique smiles, the one that melted all inhibitions. Even then I was capable of no more than, "What the fuck is happening?"

Her response was quite unexpected. She told me to lean over the back of my seat and lift up the ragged cushion of the seat behind us. It wasn't a seat at all but a hinged cover that sprang upward. What lay there in its elegant nest was the gleaming creation of mad automotive geniuses, a sculpted body of steel and aluminum so pure it seemed to have a light of its own.

"Corvair Spyder," I heard Lucille say.

"What?"

"Engine from a Corvair model called a Spyder. Flat six-piston engine, two carbs, four turbochargers, rack-and-pinion steering, five forward gears, Jag X15 drive train, air-cooled, one hundred fifty-four CID, 275 HP, runs smoothest at 115 to 125."

"Jesus, Lucille, how do you know all of this?"

"Listen, bustah, dontcha know I'm from Joisey? Dontcha?" She gave me a violent shove on the shoulder. "Dontcha?"

It wasn't until we reached the upper end of East River Drive that I could breathe somewhat normally. Not completely normally since Lucille's default speed is around eight-five. Sustaining this level required a stunning series of dart-like moves around inferior machines to keep a track of open highway ahead of her.

Somewhere on the thruway, Lucille asked, "What do you hear right now?"

"Hear? The sound of air splitting and whistling over the roof of the car."

"That's good. Go on."

"The tires humming on the asphalt. The engine."

"What about the engine?"

"It has the tiresome drone of a tuba, all on one note."

After a mile or so, she asked, "What about the explosions?"

"What explosions?"

"Thousands of them every second, each loud enough to deafen you for life." She looked at me to see if I got it. I didn't. "The auto engineers are paid to hide them from you. They trick you into thinking it's all tuba when it's lightning strike, howitzer, volcano, blitzkrieg, all of it every second — many times every second. The hammering of it, its violent revolutions and its vast array of moving parts, all locked into each other with flawless precision. In ten seconds your ear drums are gone."

I got it. Her shabby little car was the fragile shell that was hiding a frenzy of high-octane violence. And as for Lucille herself, that afternoon the frenzy was, well, let me say only that it lived up to its 275 horsepower, unmuffled. A perfect metaphor for my life with Lucille through these several months. An unbroken series of Sixes and Sevens.

THIRTY-FOUR

When I had heard enough of the twisted rhetoric in Raimundo's spirited exchange with Lenny Gold that cold day in the Square, I headed back to my office, passing the Administration Building. I noticed a small group standing at the entrance staring at what appeared to be a half dozen copies of a broadside someone had taped to the double glass doors. It was not difficult to guess what had captured their attention. I managed to get close enough to read it.

PUZZLE #4

1. CONFESSION

2. ALL THAT IS WRITTEN IN THIS CHAPTER

3. IS EITHER TIED DOWN WITH TWINE OR SEALED WITH A RIVET

4. TO PROTECT IT AGAINST WATERS, AND ITS TWIN, TORNADOS

5. BY GOOD FORTUNE, TODAY THE PLACE IS CHARY WITH SLOBS AND HOBOES.

6. BUT COME MONDAY THEY ARE BENT ON INVASION.

7. HOWEVER, THERE IS EVERY REASON TO GO ON TO WONDER

8. BECAUSE, FOOLS AS THEY ARE, LOSSES WILL PROVE ONLY A GAIN FOR TORIES.

9. THEREFORE THE EXCESSES OF THE INVADER WILL RESULT ONLY IN HIS DEATH.

10. WE CAN CELEBRATE WITH THE JOY OF A LITTLER DOG.

The puzzle was so different from its predecessors it could have had a different author. These differences were beginning to support the nascent theory that there was a group behind the murders.

Alfie and I agreed to assemble the Committee at once.

Just before we convened I received an email from Deborah Waterson. She was under great pressure from her handlers at *The Times* to stay ahead of this one, she said. Would I give her a few minutes in my office? Fine, I replied. But I would have to make it short since a meeting was about to commence.

"I'll be frank with you," she said. "We feel edged out here. The tabloids are feeding on the gore, the ghastly detail of the murders. Surely, that's not the angle we want. As an alumna, I want the nation to see the University at its best. Our aim is not to exploit the situation but to help our citizens come to terms with it."

"Admirable in the extreme. By all means, proceed."

"What my chief is asking for is a closer exposure to the process of solving the puzzles."

"Meaning?"

"Let me cover the deliberations of the Committee, you know, be there when you meet? I could come with you right now. You would have full right of approval before I print one syllable."

Full right up approval? Reporters never ask for this. What is she after? I asked myself.

"I'll ask and get back to you at a later date."

"I am on your side."

"Deborah, I notice your name has not been on the articles to date."

"Oh, that's because so far I have been sending in the material but someone in house has been assigned to do the final writing."

"I also searched through the enrollment history at the registrar,

135

and could not find your name in any of my course registers."

She laughed. "That's because I got married right after graduation. I took that loser's name. Then we split." She looked straight at me with an empty expression. "Then I married again. I have a weakness for losers."

"What was your name as a student?"

She told me without hesitating. I didn't bother to check with the registrar later because there was no way of knowing whether she was in fact the person she named. She was clever enough to find the name of at least one woman student who had enrolled and completed my course some fifteen years earlier.

"If you get closer to the case, if you were to get an exclusive, what would that mean for you?"

"For me personally. Nothing."

"Would you get the by-line?"

"Well, naturally yes. But this isn't about credit."

"I will let you know." But I had already decided.

THIRTY-FIVE

"The first thing you notice about this puzzle," Nkwame Smith said as we took our places, "is that for the first time it has an obvious title: **Confession**. Not an anagram or scrambled sentence. But what that means..." His voice died.

"I take it as one of the clues in the puzzle," Alfie offered. "You notice immediately following it — the second clue — **all that is written in this chapter** is numbered two and not one, as if **confession** is clue number one. So even though the word makes sense by itself, it has a meaning not obvious on the first reading."

At that point, the discussion set off at a sprint, one voice interrupting another.

"It means the murderer is telling you who he is."

"Or who they are."

"Why does it have to be the murderer speaking?"

"Who else?"

"The victim?"

Marguerite Gardolini laughed. "You mean it's the dead talking?"

The remark had a brief quieting effect, as if we realized, not for the first time, that what we were up to was not some kind of parlor game.

"I have an idea," Chernovsky said, rather soberly. "Smith is right that the unscrambled word 'confession' draws attention to itself. But before we try to figure out what is to be confessed, look at the word itself. What just hit me is that it has ten letters. Ten again. And of course ten clues. If we include the word, '**confession**.'"

There was a lot of nodding.

"Could this mean the answer to each clue is ten letters?"

"Some of the clues are less than ten words long."

"One has thirteen."

"Any anagrams here?"

"Good question. If there are anagrams, that means that the words to be unscrambled are ten letters long themselves."

"But there's not a single word of ten letters on the whole page. I get a couple of nines. That's all. **Therefore** and **celebrate**."

Silence.

"Let's not get ahead of ourselves here," Darius Pennybacker said. "We haven't asked whether the whole sentences are scrambled, like the first and second puzzles."

"Darius," Samantha responded, "the first and second puzzles were hardly like each other, and the third was something else altogether. What we are dealing with here is an original. We have to think differently to catch up with him."

Pennybacker stared at her, and said nothing.

"Back to the suggestion that each of the answers is likely to be ten letters," I said. "But if no single word is…"

"You just answered your own question." Alfie cut me off. "No single word. Bunch of dopes here. Two or more words, then."

Harvey Rilling was bending down over the second clue. "Hmm, strange." He read out the clue. "**All that is written in this chapter.**" After studying it briefly, he said, "No two words add up to ten letters. Wait, yes. The first and the last. **All** and **chapter.**" He held up his hand. "Wrong. **All** and **written.**"

"Start with **all** and **chapter**," I suggested. "A hunch says it's more promising." There were no objections.

We started scribbling letters.

"I've got it!" Bobo Winston lifted the page as if he were showing something to students. "Path caller."

"Path caller? What the hell sense does that make?"

"How about, 'larch plate?'"

"Or, 'clap leather?'"

"Too many letters."

"'Clap lather,' then."

I listed the suggestions on the white board. As I did, several more were added.

CAPE THRALL.
PARCEL LATH.
CLEAR PLATH.

"We don't have it. We're out of letters."

"Aha!" Percival Calkins entered the discussion for the first time. "'All that crap.'"

"Too many t's," it was immediately pointed out. There was general agreement that the phrase, though one letter truncated, made more sense than the alternatives already on the board. "Could be dialect.," was one opinion. It also had an interesting resonance with the heading of the puzzle. There was a motion to hold it tentatively, to see if it made sense, as we got deeper into the solution of the whole. I put the word up, right under *confession*, but gave it a conventional spelling.

CONFESSION
ALL THAT CRAP

There was a collective mumbling as each of us played with the words and their unscrambling, in no particular order.

"Take the sixth clue," Marguerite said. "**But come Monday they are bent on invasion.** Only a couple word combos make ten. **An invasion**, and **bent Monday**. So we obviously have to respell one of the two. I take **bent Monday**. Anyone for the other?"

"I get 'aviaries' out of the first but that leaves me with two n's unaccounted for."

"'Nova anners,'" someone said, crossing it out.

"Let's go to Monday bent. I see a 'not,' and an 'an.'"

"That's it, Marguerite said. "'And not by me!"

I added it to the list.

AND NOT BY ME

"I'm looking at clue number eight," Alfie said. "**Because, fools as they are, losses will prove only a gain for tories.** A quick read here turns up two words that add up to ten letters have the feel of an anagram: **gain** and **tories**. Not that I see that much in them. Oh, yes, I've got an 'organ,' an 'ore,' and, well, 'grain.'"

"I get 'origin' out of this," someone said.

"'Origin'? That leaves 'stae.' Could it be 'ate origins?'"

"I've got it," Nkwami said. "'Originates.' Yes?"

General agreement. I recorded it.

ORIGINATES

"I'm still on the second clue," Samantha Gupta said. "**Is either tied down with twine or sealed with a rivet.** I see two possibles here. **Sealed with**, or **twine rivet.** Take the second, and I get, 'Wet inviter,' 'review tint,' twin verite.'"

"'View tinter.'"

"Ha!" Gupta all but shouted. "'I've written.'"

Nods around the table.

I'VE WRITTEN

"There's a very odd phrase at the end of the last clue." Chernovsky reentered the discussion. "**We can celebrate with the joy of a littler dog.** What could '**littler dog**' mean in the context of this sentence. Nonsensical, really." He looked down at a scattering of letters written into most of the spaces on his copy of the puzzle, most of them crossed out. "There are only two words I can make out of this. 'Litter' and 'gold.' Of course, 'toted grill' and 'rotted gill' are possible but they make about as much sense as 'litter and gold."

Alfie gave me his knowing glance across the table. I thought I knew why but hesitated to say anything until we had completed the list. No one had anything to add to Chernovsky's conclusion, except a reversal of the words.

GOLD LITTER

Bobo Winston brought us back by declaring his favorite among the clues. "The fifth. **By good fortune, today the place is chary with slobs and hoboes.** It's got **place, chary, slobs,** and **hoboes.** Great words, but all I can say is that 'hoboes' is out of the picture. It doesn't add up to ten with anything."

"**Place** and **chary. Place** and **slobs. Chary** and **slobs.**" Several people were talking as if to themselves. There was a furious scratching of pens.

"Well, well. How do you like this, friends?" Marguerite had the sly look of a winner. She had written a bold pair of words on her puzzle. "I mean, what are we, the ten of us sitting here?" She looked around the table.

"A bunch of idiots."

"Complicit in the murder of colleagues."

"Take the word, 'by" out of **chary** and **slobs,**" she said.

There was a pause.

"Oh, shit," Calkins said, quite out of character. "'Scholars.'"

"That's it," Alfie announced as if the matter were now closed.

BY SCHOLARS

"Three to go," I reminded them. "Keep going, people."

Gupta had the first question. "I have been counting letters in that long one. Is it the ninth? Yes. The ninth. **Therefore the excesses of the invader will result only in his death.** The only suggestive combination I get adding to ten letters is **in his death.** There seem more possibilities there than will result. But as I look at the first combination, a couple options show up at once. 'Head in shit,' is one of them. Sort of jumps out at you. Agreed?"

"Stinks," Alfie said. "I say wipe it off. Try something else."

"In this head!" someone called out.

"Better," Alfie said.

There was a reluctant assent, as if the others were embarrassed not to have seen either of the two possible solutions. I thought the choice was clear, and appended the result.

IN THIS HEAD

"I've solved clue number seven, **However, there is every reason to go on to wonder,**" Professor Darius Pennymaker announced in his best stentorian manner. "On the principle that we can combine only whole words, there is self-evidently only one sequence that works: **on to wonder.**" That it was self-evident to rest of us was doubtful. "You've got only three possibilities, and two of those are nonsensical: 'torn wooden' and 'rood went on.' A slight redistribution results in the correct answer: 'not one word.'"

No one seemed moved to differ.

NOT ONE WORD

"So what's left?" I looked from face to face. There were satisfied grins for the progress so far, but no rush to do number four: **To protect it against waters, and its twin, tornados.**

Not an easy challenge. The letter count principle was applied by several of us, agreeing that **waters, twin,** and **its twin** were what we had to deal with. **And its twin** had no takers. **Waters, twin** looked more promising. I wrote these ten letters on the board and waited for directions. With a number of cross outs and replacements, there was a clear choice. I added it to the list, backed off a couple steps, and read through the solutions.

ALL THE CRAP.
AND NOT BY ME.
ORIGINATES.

I'VE WRITTEN.
BY SCHOLARS.
GOLD LITTER.
IN THIS HEAD.
NOT ONE WORD.
WAS WRITTEN.

All of this following the opening word, *Confession.*

Even though there was little argument about whether the anagrams had been correctly decoded, we were baffled by the sequence as it occurs in the puzzle. There was a suggestion that we could try organizing the phrases into a sentence, or at least several sentences. About five more minutes we had arrived at what we thought was being confessed. It was a smooth flow of words and made excellent sense.

CONFESSION:
ALL THE CRAP
I'VE WRITTEN
WAS WRITTEN
BY SCHOLARS
AND NOT BY ME
NOT ONE WORD
ORIGINATES
IN THIS HEAD.
GOLD LITTER.

It made excellent sense, except that the confessor remained unnamed, and then there was the sticky matter of the last two words. Alfie jumped up and headed for the door. "I had a sudden idea," he said without explanation. "I'll be back in a minute." He gave me another glance as he left the room. We waited.

THIRTY-SIX

"Look at this," he said, coming back through the door. He flipped open his MacBook. "Just look at this." He pushed the computer around so we could see the screen. "I'm typing in the words *Goldlitter. com*. Now, Enter." From where I was sitting what came up was not quite readable, though I could see that it was all typescript, roughly resembling a puzzle. Those close enough to make out the writing were soon reacting with gasps and shocked expressions.

"The bastard."

"What a shit."

"Why am I not surprised?"

"What do we do now?"

"First, let's see the whole text."

"Those of you who have your computers, stand by. I will email it to you. Take the time to read it carefully. We'll reconvene in fifteen minutes. Okay?" He looked over at me for approval.

"Fine."

This is what appeared on our screens.

MEMO
from Leonard Gold
to the whole fucking academic community,
but especially to you idiots in the School of Commerce,
along with the dolts in Economics and Political Science.
How could you be so stupid as not to see
what I have been getting away with
all these years?
Read and weep tears of shame

for not having grasped how you were duped.
I quote:

1.

What we have here is the problem of *catallaxy*. To have a proper understanding of this important feature of the market, it is essential to realize that an economy is not just one thing, but a vast accumulation of systems of exchange, all mostly independent of each other. The question is whether there is any control over the catallaxy. Does it have a spontaneous order or must it have one governmentally imposed. The major problem is the intellectual defense of this order. It is a system that is unlikely to secure automatic support, especially as its reliance on spontaneity and adaptive evolution seems strangely out of tune with modern thinking which sees virtually all political and economic order as a result of conscious direction and control. **Also, undeniably, the catallactic process seems to throw up phenomena, which, superficially at least, appear to be in conflict with the main tenets of the liberal credo.**

A full half — are you reading me here, my brilliant colleagues? — a full half (half!) of this essay under my name is quoted from other writers. You might think of it as "Gold and Bold." You will further note that it is in a refereed journal and therefore a trick on the whole ham-headed profession. So, you missed the source like everyone else? I'll give you a hint. Check out: Norman P. Barry, Hayek's Social and Economic Philosophy, *p. 50. You never read this guy? And you're supervising doctoral dissertations?*

2.

Okay, I'll lob you an easy one:

How do we define the word "liberalism?" In popular usage the term slides through a number of loosely conceived meanings. In its simplest sense, it implies a reduction, or even a total elimination, of external

145

control. This only takes us so far. Absolute liberalism is essentially the destruction of community, or so say some critics. **The challenge from the so-called communitarian critics of liberalism has had a substantial impact on contemporary liberal theory. It has persuaded some that, if liberalism is defensible, it can only be so for existing liberal societies, which should endorse the practices and values of their own traditions.** To a significant extent it has also persuaded Rawls to re-present his own theory of justice as a response to certain important features of the modern world — notably, its pluralism and religious diversity.

This was purloined from none other than the distinguished scholar, known personally to most of you: Chandran Kukathas, "Hayek and Liberalism," The Cambridge Companion to Hayek, 2006, p 1975. Embarrassing. And an insult to Chandran.

Reminder: Gold is bold.

3.

Guess where I got this, geniuses. How you never caught it is a mystery explained only by your own empty, arrogant claim to have read everything.

"It is important not to confuse fixed capital — that which banks and the very rich have placed in reserve — with the net revenue of a society. The net revenue is composed of four parts — **money, provisions, materials, and finished work.** The last three of these are regularly placed either in the fixed capital of the society, or in their stock reserved for immediate consumption. Whatever portion of those consumable goods is not employed in maintaining the former, that is fixed capital, **goes all to the latter** which is **reserved for immediate consumption, and makes a part of the revenue of a society.** Maintaining those three parts of the circulating capital, therefore, withdraws no portion of the annual produce from the net revenue of the society,

besides what is necessary for maintaining the fixed capital.
Adam Smith. *The Wealth of Nations*, Book II, chapter II, p. 394.
Ever heard of the dude?

4.

How I fooled you with this one, O intellectual elite, scions of liberal political philosophy!

If we were to look for a single term — whether that be a concept or an abbreviated theory — that captures the heart of liberalism, it would have to be "spontaneity." Any sort of predatory coercion in economic activity has an ascertainable monetary value when the agent of that coercion resorts to an expansionary economic practice, similar to that first observed in nineteenth century British monetary policy, during the early period of the conquest of India. The monetary value in that instance can be calculated by dividing the results of the coerced subject (that is, the quantity of disposable wealth) according to the resources spent in the act of coercion itself, where a factor of seven is at the high end and one at the other. (Zero is not applicable here because it would imply no activity at all.)

This, you Masters of the Financial Universe, occurs in my article, "Spontaneity: a Redefinition," Journal of Socioeconomic Theory, 1999. *It is distinguished by the fact that it is intentionally and utterly incoherent. Try it out yourselves and see how thoroughly you were hoodwinked.*

5.

You certifiable ~~idiots~~ conservatives: feast on the truth.

"The degree of the durability of physical property is directly related to fixed capital. How rapidly the objects of production wear out or become otherwise useless, has a direct and measurable impact on fixed capital. Durability is of course a temporal term — objects decay at different rates. **But it is in no way simply this physical property** of durability, which leads them to function as fixed capital. In metal works, the raw material is just as durable as the machines with which it is processed, and more durable in fact than many components of these machines — leather, wood, plastic, etc. But the metal serving as raw material does not form any the less a part of the circulating capital. This distinction rather arises from the role that it plays in the production process, in one case as object of labor, in the other as means of labor.

Ha!

Marx, *Capital*, II, *298*

6.

That the range of your ignorance of Smith and Marx knows no rational bounds is indubitably established in overlooking this article, into which I carefully tucked in words of the master.

"*Adam Smith was the first of the great economic* and political theorists to argue that the creation of wealth provided a moral basis for commercial society. The earning and expenditure of wealth was no longer considered a dangerous excess to personal and public life, it was urged as the basis of civilization itself. To maximize the creation of wealth there had to be a 'system of liberty' that more than encouraged it—defended and promoted it. **What is new in Smith is that a system of liberty' would not only stabilize domestic prices and stimulate trade, it would also permit the inherent self-regulating features of a national economy to function.** The 'system of liberty' is not simply a charter for the removal of tariffs and duties, both internally and externally; it proposes that the interaction of individuals, if untrammelled by excessive rules and regulations, would result in an optimum increase of national wealth which was at the same time self-regulating and stable."

You get it yet? Consult: The Wealth of Nations, *p. 27*

7.

Okay, you hotshot lefties, especially those of you who refereed this article of mine for The Business Ethics Quarterly. Since you so love to quote this fool, how did you happen to think the following came from the golden fingers of your colleague, L. Gold? In this case, it is not Gold and Bold, but Gold and Bold. (Ha, ha.)

I repeat that I am not dealing with the complete set of cases, which determine the volume of output. For this would have led me an endlessly long journey into the theory of short-period supply and a long way from monetary theory; — though I agree that it will probably be difficult in future to prevent monetary theory and the theory of short-period supply from running together.

Purloined straight from Satan himself: Collected Writings of John Maynard Keynes, *Volume XIII, page 145.*

8.

This is a sweetener for those of you whose egos were wounded by failing to identify the subject of discussions One and Two, vide supra. Here is another chance to disprove a portion of your stupidity.

My own view of the algebra of multifaceted relatedness is that there is always a necessity to isolate the individual foci of societal relations in the large. We then discover what was hidden in the presupposed but unexamined capital relations. The "emergence" of "new" patterns as a result of the increase in the number elements between which simple relations exist, means that this larger structure as a whole will possess certain general or abstract features which will recur independently of the particular values of the individual data, so long as the general structure (as described, e.g., by an algebraic equation) is preserved. Such "wholes," defined in terms of certain properties of their structure, will constitute distinctive objects of explanation for a theory, even though such a theory may be merely a particular way of fitting together statements about the relation between individual elements.

All right, suckers, tear your hair out. This is straight out of Friedrich himself. Studies in Philosophy, Politics, and Economics, *p. 26.*

9.

This, I confess is my favorite. Not one scholar in the entire goddam field caught me on this one. Try to see why.

The major problem is the intellectual defense of this order. The challenge from the so-called communitarian critics of liberalism has had a substantial impact on contemporary liberal theory. Maintaining those three parts of the circulating capital, therefore, withdraws no portion of the annual produce from the net revenue of the society. The monetary value in that instance can be calculated by dividing the results of the coerced subject (that is, the quantity of disposable wealth) according to the resources spent in the act of coercion itself. The interaction of individuals, if untrammelled by excessive rules and regulations, would result in an optimum increase of national wealth, which was at the same time self-regulating and stable.

The entire essay is a collection of sentences from the above quotations. Even the Neanderthals among you should have seen how they were being played with. Nice going.

10.

The following is stolen without variation from an article dated several years before this one. Guess where I got it!

If we were to look for a single term — whether that be a concept or an abbreviated theory — that captures the heart of liberalism, it would have to be "spontaneity." Any sort of predatory coercion in economic activity has an ascertainable monetary value when the agent of that coercion resorts to an expansionary economic practice, similar to that first observed in nineteenth century British monetary policy, during the early period of the conquest of India. The monetary value in that instance can be calculated by dividing the results of the coerced subject (that is, the quantity of disposable wealth) according to the resources spent in the act of coercion itself, where a factor of seven is at the high end and one at the other. (All at activity no imply would it because here applicable not is Zero.)

If you haven't figured out the joke played on you, it is that the author from whom this text was stolen is the author of the stolen text. I so enjoyed the attention it got in The Journal of Socioeconomic Theory, it seemed a waste not to faithfully copy and insert it into The Annals of Economic Research. You can be assured that it still is completely incoherent. (Hint: You might check out the final sentence, which for some reason was overlooked by the shit-for-brains proofreader — after I proofread it, of course, adjusting it for the backward brains of the School of Commerce.)

THIRTY-SEVEN

It was a somber group of senior faculty from the School of Commerce that gathered the next day in the office of President Lister. Lenny was invited but nobody feigned surprise when he chose not to attend. He had posted a blistering attack on the false claims made by the anonymous Puzzler, denying he had created this web page, and vowing to attack its source with every available legal device. It took only two hours, however, for a graduate student to confirm the accuracy of the charges of plagiarism as illustrated in *Goldlitter.com*. The meeting with

Lister was brief. He listened for a minute or two then slammed the table. "I'm sacking the fucker. Meeting adjourned."

The notoriety of the revelation ricocheted through every pocket of academia, including admissions of sloppy editing in each of the scholarly journals that had published Lenny. But in the larger world, the response was somewhat different. The hero of right wing talk radio could not be so shamed, however true or false the accusations. It was repeated frequently on every channel and wavelength that Gold could not have been the author of this web page, and that some politically offended left-winger invented the whole thing. Lenny made it sound as if the termination of his career at the University had been an act of charity and that shortly he would receive a job with a salary commensurate with his true value. Not a week passed before an unidentified source reported that a certain reclusive billionaire had anonymously signed him on as head of a wilderness think tank, tripling his University salary, complete with an office building containing a pool, a fitness center, and ten research assistants, all with special high tech security, in the town of Wasilla, Alaska. With terrific fanfare, Lenny took off for his next celebrity incarnation.

SPRING
SEMESTER

THIRTY-EIGHT

"No body!" Jack Lister announced in a near shout. "You got that Carmody? No body!"

I pictured him holding the phone like he was broadcasting to the whole Square.

"Yet," I dared.

"Listen, that skinny dude, Gold, he's up there, wherever 'there' is, stretched out on a giant water bed under sun lamps counting his thousands while nubile Mädchen are dancing around him in the altogether, and ..."

"Nubile Mädchen aren't exactly his flavor."

"Nubile Jugend. Who cares? The point, Carmody, couldn't be clearer. The guy made out big. They got him in an armed fortress. No one's gonna get near him. You know those right-wingers, they're all gun nuts. The place bristles with Uzis and 30/30s. A polar bear makes a funny move, it's seal food."

"Look, Jack ..."

"Carmody, what I'm saying is that so far as Gold is concerned the news has gone silent. The two-day memory range of viewers has passed, no one even recognizes his name. You know what that means for us, Carmody? For the first time in three months, you can flip the pages, surf the channels, stir the tabloids, and find not a single word aimed our way."

"Jack, you're telling me this for a reason. Just say it."

"I got an idea. Get over here."

As I have indicated, what Jack calls an idea is what the rest of us would consider a fully developed plan, already decided. And this one was a doozie.

He sat back, propped his feet on a corner of his pirate desk, and looked at me, obviously creating a bit of theatrical tension. Sitting that way, he was plenty of theater himself. He seemed to be extending himself half across his office.

"Carmody, how's your math?"

"Passable. I factor polynomials to put myself to sleep."

"Stay awake for a moment. You remember the number on the base of the monument in Founders' Court?"

"I do."

"Subtract it from the present year — the *new* year, now that we're two days into it."

I did the calculation and began to suspect what he was up to. "One fifty even," I said.

He swung his feet to the floor and gave the desk a booming flat-hand slap. "The University at One Hundred Fifty!" He hit the desk again. "Whadda ya think?"

I thought for a moment. "You mean, as in a celebration?"

"That's it! Yes! We'll call it *'The University at One Hundred Fifty: a Celebration.'*"

"A celebration of — ?"

He looked up at the ceiling. I could hear his teeth grinding. The idea was apparently not as well worked through as I expected.

"A Celebration of the American Mind. We'll make it an awards cere-mony. Give a prize to some major mental giant."

"You mean, like a renowned professor or scholar?"

"Professor! Scholar! Hell, no." Jack look offended. "It's for what I call a great 'public intellectual.' Look, Carmody, nobody knows better than you how the quality of our social, political, and cultural discourse is in the toilet. An original, articulate idea, delivered in a mode of speech, free of clichés, garbled metaphors and grammatical sloppiness is about as rare as a coherent deconstructionist."

He sat up and leaned toward me to get as close as that great piece of furniture allowed.

"Carmody, I've had it down to here," he grabbed his crotch, "with the way our names — the University's, mine, and, my honored rhetorician, yours too — has been smeared across the screen and print media like so much dog poop. We need to step forward with a bold new idea, show the newsmakers we're still a class act, that we still stand shoulder to shoulder with the world's great centers of learning."

He sat back and stared at the ceiling again as if his new audience was looking down at him from somewhere on high.

"We'll set it up in the library atrium. Couldn't be more dramatic with its twelve-story ceiling. Place is wired like a giant sound studio already. Shit! It'll be great theater. And celebrities! Let's make it fifty — fifty luminaries of American Kultur. Damn!" he yelled out again and hammered his desk with the fist of his left hand, like he had just hit a match-winning squash shot. "Two can play this game. The media smear us with bad news, we manipulate them with good news."

"You have a date for it?"

"Of course." He paused a moment. "What'll it take us — seven, eight months to prepare? Publicity. Select an honoree. Invites to celebrities. Set up the library. Middle of the summer. July. Make it the third week of July."

The discussion was over. As I left his office I had no doubt that by the next morning there would be a text message to the University community detailing the Ceremony along with a full cannonade of press releases and announcements to the public. I admit that I was irresistibly buoyed by his enthusiasm, thinking the plan just might work, especially if the ebb in the carnage would hold.

There were also marginal factors that made the idea of a sesquicentenary Celebration seem reasonable and timely. For one thing, the new year was opening with all its usual rosy promises. The religious holidays had passed with trumpeted commercial excess; the stock market hit a high for the year; student enrollment had dipped but not without a meek surge in transfer student applications (this is where all the fun is); and alumni contributions showed a deceptive lift as donors found they had to write off more than anticipated. Without a spray of brain matter on the sidewalk outside Administration, a charred suicide in the Anthro lab, and a famed mathematician with a flattened donut for a face, it was easy to convince ourselves that the worst was behind us — in spite of our exiled Professor of Political Economy.

Of course, for all the turmoil the Puzzler had cost the University, there still was a University. Registration went on, classes met, study areas in the libraries were filled by noon, the science labs were occupied from nine to six, faculty committees convened, toilets were scrubbed, hallways were mopped, trash was collected, pizza and burgers with fries remained the top requests in university cafeterias, tenure decisions were made and challenged, the dormitories erupted nightly with the help of the usual substances.

Celebrating the University's one hundred and fifty years as a major American institution found particularly strong and immediate support from the faculty. As Lister was careful to explain, the honorees will not necessarily be professors or even attached to universities. Each is to be selected for his or her role as an especially articulate public figure, someone who has made a discernible intellectual impact on conversation in the public square. This, the faculty reasoned, puts the University in the powerful role of being the arbiter for what passes as informed and critical thinking in the population at large. By bestowing prestige, many calculated, they would greatly enhance their own.

And then, there was Jack's masterful manipulation of the community's expectations. In addition to the press releases and the promised formation of faculty and student government committees, he hinted at the growing list of attending celebrities — whose identities he coyly refused to reveal. It thrilled students, and more members of the faculty than would like to admit, to anticipate a visiting throng of film idols, industrial moguls, and financial wizards — the types whose faces regularly appeared on the magazine covers at supermarket checkouts.

THIRTY-NINE

I was in my office after hours when I received a call from Marguerite Gardolini.

"You know what that bastard has done now?" she began.

"Which bastard exactly?"

"That rich shit-head bastard, Pennybacker."

"No, I don't know what he's done but I have a feeling you're going to tell me."

"He's now got a woman student to place charges against Judy Schlager. You know, in Philosophy."

"He got a student to place charges? As in, he's using her to make charges of his own?"

"Exactly."

"Is there some relationship between you and Schlager that's got him aroused? I don't mean intimate relations."

"Yes, well, we're friends, more or less, occasionally more. But I see no other connection. Unless he's out to make some kind of moral clean sweep — his morals, his sweep."

"And, like you, Schlager has initiated nothing."

"Of course not. Neither of us would dream of having anything with a student. Well, all right, I might dream of it. Dreaming isn't against the regulations surely. But that line is never crossed. What do we do with this son of a bitch?"

I thought for a moment. "For now you must content yourself with dreaming of revenge."

"If we could figure out who the Puzzler is, maybe we could add Pennybacker to his list. I've got a few suggestions as to how he could do it."

"Let's hope we never hear from the Puzzler again, Marguerite. Maybe he's bored with his success."

"Oh, how fondly I recall the boredom around here before the Puzzler made his entrance," she said. "Speaking of boredom, you'll be at the installation ceremony for Evgeny Klonska? Isn't it sometime next week?"

Jesus, I thought to myself, I had forgotten. I penciled it in.

"Can't imagine anything more asphyxiating," I admitted.

"As a University Professor we will expect you on the dais looking properly stuffy in your academic robe and hood, but paying rapt attention."

"As long as I don't have to look the jerk in the face."

FORTY

Guttierez had borrowed my gown and hood for the last commencement six months ago. He had almost no visible tokens of his education in what he suggested indirectly was the University of Barcelona. There was no diploma on the wall, no collective photographs of his class or department. No surprise then he didn't have any of the commencement regalia. I thought it time to retrieve them. I knocked at his office.

"Carmody!" He backed away from his doorway with a mock bow, making space for me to enter. He was holding a phone to his ear. Nodding toward a chair facing his desk, he soon resumed his conversation in impossibly rapid bursts of Spanish. As if he had forgotten I was there (and that I understood Spanish), he stood at the window looking down at the Square. I was always impressed by the size of his library. The works were mostly in Spanish, of course, though I did notice that the political material was chiefly in English. Novels, poetry, and literary essays were jammed on top of each other, and showed heavy use.

Fascinated, I found a copy of the great early twentieth century writer, Blasco Ibanez, the 1919 publication of his famous *La Catedral*. In fact, he had Ibanez' two volume *Obras Completas*. Fascinated, I pulled it out to check the date and publisher. Inside the cover, my eye caught a name written in the dressy, schooled manner that I recognized as Raimundo's hand, but the name was of a different person altogether, a Felix Cisneros. On a high shelf he had a number of volumes from the *Classicos Castellanos*. I was intrigued to find Fray Luis De León's *De los Nombres de Christo (CC vol 33)*. Was there a trace of piety in Raimundo's background? After all, Miguel de Unamuno's notorious *La Agonia del Christianismo* (banned by the Vatican) was on the same shelf next to his widely influential work *Del Sentimiento Tragico de la Vida*, and a favorite of mine. However, he also owned the deliciously naughty, comic tale of Cesar Gonzalez-Ruano, *Afrodisio Aguado*. I slowly came to realize that each of these volumes bore the same owner's name. Felix Cisneros. Who was Felix Cisneros? The name meant nothing to me, though it seemed to be someone of importance to Guttierez. Guttierez himself?

"Carmody, forgive me, I was talking to an old friend in Guatemala. Childhood friend, you know. Old times and all. How can I help you?

FORTY-ONE

It was now the middle of January. The second term was well underway. I was still in the stage of making sure the books for my University course have been placed on reserve, and double-checking with the University bookstore to see if they were fully stocked. But I hadn't completed making electronic copies of the relevant selection from the classics. It would require a few more afternoons with the IT lab's state-of-the-art equipment.

When I came out of the elevator into the reception area of the IT lab, a small group of computer geeks were forming a half circle around the bulletin board. I edged in to where I had a clear view:

PUZZLE #5

1. UIF EFTL QMBZIQVTF

2. SGD LZFHBHZM NE SNDR

3. VJG RTKEG QH BCTCVJWUTC

4. RCL RM JGDR MDD

5. XTVLGH GRZQ WR JHURQLQLPR

6. X PQOXTZYBOOV LSBO QEB BADB

7. UJQQVLPI KPVQ USCEG.

8. RFC YPR MD PGBGLE KP VCPFGO

9. OBUVSFT GJDLMF HJGU

10. TNCDQ SGD OHMJ STST

"Okay," one of the students said, "so it's separate words on each line. But is each line a full sentence?"

"There's no way we can answer questions like that. Gotta figure the formula for each word."

"Anagrams, or whatever you call them?"

"Spelled backwards?"

"Maybe it's sheer gibberish to throw us off."

I headed back to the faculty office aware of the twist of anxiety in my midsection. Alfie already had a copy of Puzzle 5. He and Iolinda were on the phone trying to arrange a meeting. Most of the members were sensitive to the University's and the public's loss of confidence in our abilities — just as they were themselves. Such criticism as there has been is unfair, of course. We are hardly the only active group on the case. The police are far better equipped and trained to find the killer. Besides, our responsibility has more to do with identifying the next victim. Still, from the Committee's point of view, what had been an honor and a recognition of high intelligence has now come to be drudgery with small hop of success. Nonetheless, each of the members fell in and agreed to our next rendezvous with the Puzzler.

#5 was unlike any of the Puzzler's previous efforts. There was no obvious avenue into the logic of its creation. As I studied it, I felt the letters had taken up a wild dance as if defying us to join their mad doings. I pushed it away, and after a few more moments of reflective speculation, I returned to Iolinda's desk where she and Alfie were busy looking through a folder of emails, mostly from students and faculty who had seen the new puzzle on their computer screens. A quick look through the heap revealed that the preferred solutions were as confusing as the puzzle itself.

The Committee convened at the appointed hour. Our members had ceased showing off to one another. It was all too evident that had any one of us half the acumen we attributed to ourselves, the three corpses would not have found their graves. There was no small talk or gossip. We had three days til the end of the month. We settled down like graduate students about to take their final exams.

There was an early breakthrough. Armand Chernovsky had the ninth line. He said it was immediately obvious to him that if we go backwards one letter from each one on that line, we'll see that it forms a series of words. Calculating out loud, he wrote the letters on the white board.

O = n
B = a
U = t
V = u
S = r
F = e
T = s
G = f
J = i
D = c
L = k
M = (l)
H = g
J = i
G = f
U = t.

NATURE'S FICKLE GIFT

Several people repeated the words over and over as if by pronouncing in different ways it would start to make sense. We agreed that "natures" should have an apostrophe. Beyond that, nothing sounded hopeful. No one wanted to take it as an anagram.

"I've got clue number one," Darius announced with considerable enthusiasm, and wrote it on the board just below Chernovsky's *natures fickle gift* while Armand was standing there concentrating on his own words.

UIF EFTL BT QMBZIQVTF

"It's the same as Armand's," Darius said. "Each letter in in the clue is one ahead of the letter intended. And that gives you, let's see, *t h e* as the first word." He hesitated briefly before the next word, then proceeded uncertainly. "E is *D*, F is *E*, T is *S*, and I is *K. Desk!* Now the next word. **B T** gives us *as*. And after that, **Q** gives us *p*, **M** gets an *l*. That means...let me figure this out." He wrote out the rest in silence: *a-y-h-o-u-s-e.* He squinted at the words as if they had some kind of dangerous meaning, and said nothing more. When Darius returned to his seat, I transcribed the result.

THE DESK AS PLAYHOUSE.

None of the others seemed to have any interest in the peculiar phrase, instead going ahead to the rest of the clues.

"That same analysis does not work on mine," Bobo said. "I have line number four." We looked down at the clue: **RCL RM JGDR MDD.**

"It doesn't work with mine either," said someone else.

"One letter ahead, one letter behind," Alfie said. "Maybe it's not always one, plus and minus. Let's look for other respellings. Try two ahead and two behind."

From here on it went quite rapidly. The lettering scheme, we discovered, had an order of its own, alternating a plus with a minus, then a progressive increase and a corresponding decrease in the number of jumped over letters. I wrote it out.

Minus one.

Plus one.

Minus two.

Plus two.

Minus three.

Plus three.

Minus two.

Plus two.

Minus one.

Plus one.

Each member of the Committee was able to decode his or her lines without difficulty. I filled in the list with the added phrases:

UIF EFTL QMBZIQVTF (- 1)
THE DESK AS PLAYHOUSE.
SGD IZFHBHZM NE SNDR (+1)
THE MAGICIAN OF TOES.
VJG RTKEG QH BCTCVJWUTC (-2)
THE PRICE OF ZARATHUSTRA.
RCL RM JGDR MDD (+2)
TEN TO LIFT OFF.
XTVLGH GRZQ WR JHURQLQLPR (-3)
UPSIDE DOWN TO GERONIMO.
X PQOXTZYBOOV LSBO QEB BAD B (+3)

A STRAWBERRY OVER THE EDGE.
UJQQVLPI KPVQ USCEG (-2)
SHOOTING INTO SPACE.
RFC YPR MD PGBGLE KP VCPFG
O (+2)
THE ART OF RIDING IN TANDEM.
OBUVSFT GJDLMF HJGU (-1)
NATURES FICKLE GIFT.
TNCDQ SGD OHMJ STST (+1)
UNDER THE PINK TUTU.

There was a period of silence as we looked over the list with some grateful relief. Might we be in time to intercept the next impending event?

Our collective elation was short-lived. While we had successfully decoded its scrambled letters, the roster on the white board made no sense at all. Not one line had a recognizable referent. We found ourselves with as much of a mystery now as we had encountered at the beginning. More than ever, we were aware that the immediate solution only left another mystery. The key to the solution to the puzzle was itself a puzzle. Every case so far required a *double* solution, this one perhaps more than the others.

We needed to break through the opacity of this strange mélange of words. Bobo Winston, avid deconstructionist and specialist in queer theory spoke as if it were a special test of his analytical skills. "Notice the use of the following words: off, down, over, into, in, under. To begin with they are all spatial concepts. You go down *to* something, or *over* something, and so on. So what we have here is a missing area, not named or directly pointed to in these words. Shall we call it a realm, or an arena, which acts as an attraction to the author? This unnamed locus has a power, which is working through the entire list. The use of the term, 'space' in the seventh line seems to present itself as a hint, especially with the use of the word, 'shooting,' which has the sense of propulsion or destruction."

"I'm caught by the two names among the clues," Samantha Gupta volunteered, emphatically ignoring Bobo's enthusiastic offering. "Zarathustra and Geronimo. If I remember my Nietzsche, Zarathustra is a Christ figure whose ultimate failure is foretold. And Geronimo the failed leader of some Indian tribe, I don't know which. Two outsiders who are also sources of wisdom." She trailed off, seeing that this line of thought was going nowhere.

"Do I read these lines correctly as being iambic?" Calkins asked. No one answered.

"Incongruity, that's what strikes me," Marguerite Gardolini said in a tone of reflective intensity. "In almost every line are at least two elements that have nothing to do with each other in the *quotidienne* as we experience it. Desk and playhouse. Magician and toes. Money and a prophet. Well, maybe that's not quite true of the others." She dropped it.

Armand mumbled something that sounded like, "*Durchschnittliche Alltäglichkeit*," then out-loud, "Sorry. 'Average everydayness.'"

"Frankly," Alfie said with a long sigh of resignation, "no light's coming through the cracks in this fucking document. Excuse me for saying it, but none of us has made one helpful observation."

He looked around the group, from one to the other. It was then that I noticed that Darius Pennybacker was missing.

We had essentially become the most talked about institution of higher learning in the world. But, as President Lister declared with tiresome repetition, the more the publicity mounted the more we could measure the University's losses in numerical amounts. The Director of Admissions, Binky McAllison, let it be known that the pile of applications for the coming academic year was now showing significant shrinkage from foreign countries as well. There was considerable doubt, she admitted, that if we accepted every applicant we could fill the freshman class.

FORTY-TWO

Alfie entered my office without a knock:

"Pennybacker has not shown up anywhere. Iolinda has been trying to reach him by phone, email, twitter, and messages pushed under his door,"

"Has he met his classes?"

"No. Neither of them."

"That's odd. Darius doesn't like to miss a performance."

"Iolinda has a key to his office. There may be a clue to his whereabouts."

"It's missing, the envelope with an encrypted number on it, the one that only Iolinda and Pennybacker could identify--it's there. But there's no key in it."

"Darius probably took it and forgot to replace it. I've done that myself. Alfie, you're getting ahead of yourself. There's no reason at the moment to think it would have been anyone other than Darius who retrieved the key."

"We need an explanation for his absence and our lack of access to his office."

"Agreed. If he doesn't appear by the end of the day, we'll force the door."

Black SUV's seemed everywhere. The police formed what was nearly an arm-in-arm chain around the Square. The undercover squad was so expanded the student body looked as if it had grown a decade older. Cameramen speaking a variety of languages were stationing themselves at different places around the campus, just as uncertain as the rest of us where the action would occur.

Deborah Waterson called me several times during the day. I sensed in her imploring voice there was very little she would not give to be the first to know of the fifth death.

FORTY-THREE

Independent Study is an arrangement many students seek with the University's most prominent scholars. Sessions are focused entirely on the work and ego of the student. Typically, students expect high praise for each turn of phrase and the consequent revelation of their genius. In their imaginations — rarely in reality — they foresee knocking back a snifter of a particularly good brandy in wood paneled rooms. But few would imagine the scene as it was revealed on YouTube later that day a few minutes before midnight. In the first 24 hours, more than seven million viewers would have downloaded it.

Scene One.

The film opens modestly in a typical academic office. The first scenes offer stills of the space from different angles. To anyone familiar with the process, it was clear that there were three separate cameras, all obviously activated by remote control. They would also recognize from the quality of the tape that the cameras were of the CCTV variety used in apartment lobbies, banks, and convenience stores. Once installed, they were all but invisible, except to the trained eye.

A figure enters left. We see him from behind. Facing downstage, he takes his place behind the desk, opens a drawer, and removes a file. The surface of the desk is completely free of objects. Once the figure had seated himself, we can see the unusual size of this remarkable piece of furniture, as much as eight feet in length. He opens the file and studies its contents. There is a knock at the door. He goes to open the door. A student enters. He returns to his desk. The figure behind the desk, now in full view of one of the three cameras, is that of our own Savanorola, Darius Pennybacker.

The student sits facing him across the desk. The film editor artificially smudges the student's face on the tape and masks her voice. From the initial discussion, we know, in spite of the poor sound quality, that she is here to protest the grade of B-, endangering her application to law school. It is the worst grade she has ever received. She's willing to undertake any extra work to improve it. In a low, somewhat avuncular voice (not masked), the Professor assures her the grade might conceivably be improved. What follows is unfortunately too obscured to hear the conversation in full, without more sophisticated transcription equipment. The viewer sees only that the woman virtually leap to her feet and with a muffled cry of disgust leave the office. The tape goes to another camera, this one facing the desk from the opposite side of the room. The Professor is looking in the direction of the door. Because in a tape of this nature it is impossible to focus on detail, we only notice gradually that emerging over the edge of the desk is what seems to be a large blanched strawberry. As it continues to rise, it seems to be riding atop a giant spear of pinkish asparagus.

When the Professor stands, it is immediately apparent to the audience that nature has been extremely generous to the gentleman, this in spite of the fact that in every other way he is a small man. He pauses to admire himself, almost as if he were in full display for the viewer, then starts in the direction of the window. The camera switches to a head on view. As he moves, the object of note, now pointing about 50 degrees upward, swings from right to left and back again as if on a lubricated hinge. We next see him, face pressed to the glass, searching for something outside and below the window. He takes a quick breath. The viewer can only assume that the fleeing student comes into view.

The Professor reaches for the student's paper, still on the desk, and rolls it into a large tube. Although it is now just below the range of the camera, we can make out that he is fitting the tube in place. There is an erratic movement of his head and a vibration in the soft skin of his face. We sense that, still out of the camera's eye, there is a rapidly accelerating action. We begin to hear a low groan. Perspiration is now visible on the subject's face. The facial trembling increases, along with the groaning now at a higher pitch. At the top of the scale, there is a sudden expulsion of breath and the articulation of a single word. On replaying this sequence, we reached consensus on the identification of that word. "Geronimo."

He walks back to the desk. From this perspective we see that he still has the student's term paper in his hand. He straddles the wastebasket, unrolls the paper, studies it briefly, wads it in a pounding motion, and lets it drop. He readjusts his clothing and sits at the desk as before.

Scene Two

This episode closely resembles the first, except that it is a male student across the desk from the Professor, facing upstage. As the film editor cuts to the camera located behind the Professor, we see with some relief that the face of the young man, as with the female student, has been effectively obscured. On this tape, after the young man reveals that he has come to challenge his grade, the Professor begins his offer, similar to that made to the young woman in Scene One. In this case, however, the student is slow to awaken to what is being offered. We see the impact when he finally understands. After he bursts from the office, the film follows the action, quite much like what occurs at the end of Scene One.

Scene Three

Apparently taken another day, film #3 begins quite like the first. A woman student enters and takes her place. This time, however, the face is not obscured. She is clearly recognizable as one of the two women who brought the case against Marguerite and her friend. The student's manner with the Professor is quite different than that of the first, more intimate and relaxed. There is empty banter. Then an exchange of shrugs, as if they are saying, Might as well get to it. Quickly removed, their clothes are laid across the surface of the desk and arranged as a sort of rough mattress. As soon as both are positioned, the pace changes abruptly from the casual to the athletic, especially on the part of the student. Still, there is a disappointing conventionality on this part of the tape, at least until the countdown begins.

The Professor calls out a Ten, shortly afterward the student echoes it. Her Nine, however, comes before his Nine. Judging from his heightened labor, it is now evident he is trying to catch up. They are struggling for a joint chorus in the numbers. Eight is nearly simultaneous. At Seven a small gap appears. Then at Six, the student surges ahead, seeming to have lost control. The Professor displays alarm and increases velocity. But there is no slowing the student. She gets all the way to One while he is still back on Four, working for Three. However, not to be selfish (in a section of the tape that becomes a favorite on YouTube) she doesn't stop with the first One but has another, then another, about a dozen Ones altogether, until he finally arrives at a One of his own.

Scene Four

Not every scene has the desk as its primary prop, but here, to considerable acclaim, it serves a function certainly not a regular practice in faculty offices. At the opening, the Professor is giving instructions to someone, apparently off stage. All three cameras, in sequence, show no second person in the room. Only because of the muffled response to these words, do we learn that the voice comes from underneath the desk. Although too faint for positive identification, it has a distinct similarity to that of the woman in Scene Three.

After issuing several commands, the Professor takes the posture of meditation, staring at the wall, both hands resting on the surface of the desk. Judging from the absence of facial expression, he could be in an advanced yogic state. Presently a hand reaches up over the edge of the desk with an article of clothing. It is a woman's hand. Then another article. This continues until the last possible piece is lying on the desk. The phone rings, its intrusive noise startling to the viewer.

The Professor breaks out of concentration and enters into animated conversation with the calling party. From the detectable words, we know that this party is a woman. We recognize a mildly southern accent. The talk narrows itself to a description of what is happening below, the area he calls the playhouse. Occasionally he receives instructions from the caller, which he passes on to the playhouse. He reports the completion of this assignment and receives another. In a slight shift we discover that the occupant of the playhouse is now giving instructions to be passed on to the caller. Obvious to the viewer is that Darius is the subject of the instructions exchanged between the unseen women. There is little surprise, but considerable entertainment, when he grips the desk with both hands and stares directly into the camera (unaware it is staring back, of course) as if he is bracing himself for the approaching tsunami. The action steadily accelerates until he springs up and slaps the desk with a triumphant "Bonsai!"

Scene Five

Tape #5 features the second student, recognizable as Marguerite's other accuser. It begins with the same placement of garments. The initial activity is predictable to the point of yawning, until we begin to perceive something unexpected. Nature might have been generous with the Professor, but as we know, nature is not always reliable. In fact, it is now withholding its blessings altogether. This occasions a memorable performance. Positioning himself at the foot of the desk, he stands patiently while the student, still lying on her back under the desk, exhibits an uncanny ability to manipulate her toes. These amazing digits have an octopus-like talent for wrapping, crushing, thrashing, nudging, and compressing. The strategy is unsuccessful, despite its lengthy administration, but there is much here for the audience to admire, even emulate.

The two students only twice perform together. It begins when the Professor announces what he calls "the horse show." The students spring at once into action. There is a great deal of stomping and parading as they shed impediments and prepare for harness. The miming here is expert. The Professor, in the role of trainer, generously greases the pair as if rubbing down one animal then the other. One of the women, on hands and knees, stirs nervously in a horse-like motion. The other steps over her into the jockey position.

Scene Six

The race begins. With a vigorous bouncing, they seem to emulate bursting from the gate. Unlike a conventional event, in this case they exchange roles, one takes over as rider, the other as steed. The trainer is on hand to supply another coating of the oily substance when the switch occurs. This is repeated several more times. But now approaching the finish line, the activity rises to a new level. It is enough to say of the outcome of the event that they arrived perfectly together at the finish, each a winner, to the trainer's vigorous applause.

Scene Seven

In the third appearance of the pair, the trainer reveals he is himself quite prepared to join the field. This is largely a repetition of Six. This scene is oilier on the whole and the carpet is now covered with a white sheet. The main difference in this case is that the object is to produce a clear winner. We are not surprised to see that it is the trainer who takes the blue ribbon.

Scene Eight

The camera catches the Professor in his white medical coat. The patient enters, complaining of a large number of ills, each needing its own treatment. As usual, every treatment begins with a diagnosis, requiring a number of exploratory assessments. A program of applications is then discussed and promptly executed. The novelty here is not so much in the relation between the white-coated physician and the under-clothed patient — every school child knows that one — but in the doctor's use of the stethoscope. Not an instrument usually thought of in episodes of this nature, it proves to be ideal for a wide range of both diagnosis and cure. It is not often noted how many areas of the physiognomy need sonic attention. The viewer cannot but wonder what unexploited commercial value for the medical profession lies in the use of this ancient device.

Scene Nine

In some ways, except for Scene Ten, this one showcases the most professional filming and editing of the entire collection. At the opening, there is no student present. When the knock comes and the Professor opens the door, the visitor strides in, looks around, ignoring his host, rearranges some of the furniture, paces off an area in the center of the office, and adjusts himself for the action. A bit of a Houdini, he sheds in a matter of seconds. This occurs so rapidly that the viewer is not quite ready to catch on that we are being presented with an iron-pumping phenom. The muscles of this performer are so beyond normal that they seem to have been riveted on. After a series of rapid warm-ups, these extraordinary features have swelled even more, reaching physique contest levels. The Professor stands, still in coat and tie, staring at this wonder like a small animal stupefied in the presence of its predator. The lifter prepares his employer as if dressing a turkey then begins without a pause. The act consists chiefly in a sequence of lifts, tosses, flips, and swings. The Professor never once touches the floor. After several long minutes of this, the weightlifter seizes Pennybacker by the ankles, lifting him head down almost to the ceiling, perfectly stationed for the concluding event. Though upside down, he was able, and much more rapidly than usual, to sound out a respectable "Lift-off." Then, as a kind of bonus for the audience, he returns the favor to the heavily sweating muscled wonder with vigor. The lifter accepts it with a barely audible low growl. He then dresses as he disrobed in the opening segment of the film. Back under his hoodie, he exits, but not before picking up an envelope by the door.

Scene Ten

The final presentation looks for a moment like the lifter has returned but, with a more direct exposure to the physiognomy, we see it is quite a different person: muscular, certainly, but aesthetically sculpted and not so unnaturally assembled. There is another difference. This visitor, face also obscured, moves with grace, rather like a statue in motion. The most downloaded fraction of this episode comes early. The statue is standing, hands on hips, looking out the window at something distant. The Professor drops into a prayer position, as if at a *prie dieu*, and begins his part of the drama. We switch to a third camera, this time aiming from the sidewall. We now see the duo in profile, head to foot. Except that the Professor's head is not visible, having disappeared under the pink tutu. In one famous re-editing of this segment, the unknown filmmaker accompanied the rise and fall of the tutu with a skillfully edited selection from the Rap classic, Sistah ZT's *Up From Below*.

Still, the best is yet to come. After the Professor completes this task, he arranges the dancer like he was a manikin, having him lean forward with his hands resting on the bookcase. What follows is largely out of the camera's range. The editors could have selected a view from the other wall, but chose this camera for a good reason. As it happens, the very shelf where the young man has placed his hands is where the camera was attached. His face fills the screen. Then, a broad smile forms on his perfect face. There is a silent laugh when he discovers the camera. He winks into it. And while Darius is still hard at it — well, sort of hard — the dancer begins looking over the books. He removes one and casually thumbs through it, stops at a certain passage, and reads it transfixed, seeming not to notice as the professor drops to the floor, his head hanging in shame at his failure. The editors cut at this point. We segue to the dancer, the tutu now tucked out of sight into his street clothes, as he shows the book to Darius, now seated behind the desk. There is a brief exchange. Darius nods his approval. The dancer reaches for the envelope the Professor had laid on a corner of the desk. Before pocketing it, he removes a ten-dollar bill and hands it to the Professor. "For Zarathustra," he says. Just as the dancer reaches the door, he looks in the direction of the camera and gives it a thumbs-up. The film ends.

(The payoff from this performance for the dancer was extraordinary. Choosing to call himself Antoine de la Grandville, he was recruited immediately into the renowned Mark Morris Dance Company. His first performance on the big stage at City Center was covered by all of the major dance critics. Although he was recognized as a member of the corps in several numbers early in the program, the grand moment did not come until the final scene. The tension was magnified by his nonappearance at the first entrance of the dancers. Even into the middle of the piece, with anticipation at feverish height, there was no sign of M. de la Grandville. And then as if out of a cannon he spun wildly to the middle of the stage — dressed as every member of the audience had hoped. They exploded with applause, blanketing out even the over-amplified tape of Stravinsky's "Firebird," and continued undiminished to the end of the entire performance. The name, Antoine de la Grandville, has taken its place in the history of ballet.)

FORTY-FOUR

"Carmody." Alfie was on the line. "Pennybacker's cell is dead. His Mercedes is still in the faculty garage."

"Call Maintenance, Iolinda, please."

The maintenance crew found that the locks were so cleverly attached that the door could not be simply pried off its hinges. Instead, they were forced to use an enormous hand drill fitted with a diamond bit. After nearly half an hour, the three men ground through the last of the locks. The heavy steel door dropped inward.

We were dazzled by the elegance of the space. Although we had all seen it on our computer screens, we were not ready for the reality of what confronted us. What we noticed first about the naked body stretched out at our feet, even before marveling at the little man's now famous equipment, was the oddly serene look on his face. He was stretched out on the floor as if he were in a restorative yoga pose. We all backed away, feeling we had intruded on something painfully intimate. This, in spite of the fact that there was little about Darius' secret life we did not know.

What also remained was an explanation for his death. In the police's search of the room, they found no empty bottles, hypodermic needles, or signs of stashed medications. The office showed no signs of being disturbed. It was clearly not the site of a life-or-death struggle. Pennybacker's clothes had been thrown into a loose pile, but no marks of violence were detected anywhere on his naked body. In other words, there were no early data pointing at either murder or suicide. Pennybacker was, so far as any of us knew, in excellent health. Yet the man was dead.

EARLY MIDTERMS
SPRING SEMESTER

FORTY-FIVE

If I thought that another tragedy would surely dim Jack's commitment to the Sesquicentenary Ceremony, then I had misjudged his passion for the idea.

It started with a typical phone call. "Carmody, get over here."

There were four other people in his office, all of them standing, except for Jack. No one seemed to notice when I entered. Sidney Snelling, Director of Alumni Affairs, was leaning over the desk toward Jack who, in spite of Sidney's high volume delivery, was pushed back, feet on the the desk, studying his nails.

"Jack, this whole Ceremony crap is not going over. You know what I am hearing from alumni, especially the givers? And the bigger the givers, the nastier they are?"

"I know what you're hearing, Sid. I'm getting the same shit."

"I've got a stack of letters on my desk — every one of them from someone pissed over these goddam murders and asking how the fuck can we let it all go on."

Jack nodded and made a gesture that said, "So what else is new?"

Binky McAllison, Director of Admissions was next to her, hands on her hips, piped up.

"You know the bags of applications that gets dumped on my desk every morning, Jack? Yesterday the mail guy just stood in the door and shook an empty bag at me. That's what's new!"

Jack dropped his feet from the desk, sat up:

"We have a choice," Jack said, suddenly changing to a reflective mode. "We can act like a wounded institution, defamed and defeated by a single, twisted psychopath. Or we can act like what we are — the premier university in the world's greatest city. Either we win the world's scorn or we have their unqualified admiration. They're against us or for us, there's no in-between. So, folks, rise above it. Promote that Ceremony like it matters not just for us but for the whole fucking refined world. Either we go down in flames or we soar to greatness. That's our choice, friends: Oblivion. Or glory."

Jack dropped back into his chair, arms folded, and looked at each of us. No one spoke. He turned to me.

"Professor Carmody," he said as if in a formal introduction, "honored rhetorician, faithful chair of the Faculty Committee on the Puzzler Murders." He paused. "Professor? What's our choice?"

"Oblivion?" I managed to say the word without choking. "Never."

Jack made a grand sweeping motion, like a killer squash shot, directing us to the door.

"That's it, guys. Bust ass."

The meeting was over.

FORTY-SIX

On a blustery day of cold rain, about the second week of February, at the height of Spring Semester midterms, I was walking across the Square, preoccupied with these matters, when I heard a cheerful, "Bon jour, Carmody."

It took me more than a moment to recognize the face of Raimundo Guttierez, all but hidden in the hood of his down parka.

"'Dias, Guttierez. What's all this?" Under his arm was a large pack, obviously full of equipment.

"Ice on the Gunks is great this year. We're headed out for the weekend."

We? Can it be that Lucille has cheapened her standards by ice climbing with this maniac? On Skunemunk, I remember the hours of scrambling up mostly shattered rock — and I ready to recline in a yoga pose. Our Lucille was not inclined towards passivity. She had gone to the edge at once. There she stood, her toes virtually over the precipice, looking out over miles of farmland and villages. She held her arms back, a signal for me to seize her from behind. For a terrifying moment, with her hands pressed tight over mine, she rocked back and forth, causing us to lean forward, inches from plunging the hundreds of feet below us.

It is a fixed principle in the art of climbing that one knows at all times the location of the next step or handhold, regardless of the angle or the surface of the rock, and especially that of the climbing companion. As she bound me there, wobbling perilously, I was for the first time as a climber utterly under the control of another, and in this case, another well beyond the range of her competence.

"You can never trust me," she told me once, "because if you can, my precious metaphysician, it is only because your fingers have closed around me. And closed, I am no longer interesting to you. Then who would I be?"

I could only assume that Raimundo had gone beyond me with Lucille. It is one thing to be locked in her arms at the edge of a precipice; it is another to be roped together on a vertical wall of ice where she can be trusted even less. And be that much more interesting to her guileless partner.

He put a firm hand on my shoulder. "We'll get you out there one of these days. Keep your pitons sharp."

"Not before warm weather, you won't."

"Sounds like a promise to me."

"Viel Glück, Raimundo."

"Arri V, amigo."

Oblivious to the severity of the elements, I continued through the Square. Would she be so reckless as to attempt to scale a sheet of ice, endangering the life of an untenured associate professor of Middle Eastern Studies and the veritable Seneca of liberal politics? Well, yes. Recklessness in one form or another was her given métier.

Did the connection between these two have a more ominous interpretation? Raimundo and Lucille certainly had the skill to triangulate the hapless Dean Ridley out his window — while the upright and honorable Lucille claimed ignorance of the event. Her claim that she had heard nothing like a violent struggle had not really been challenged.

In the five murders to date there had been no sign of a killer at the crime scenes. Each seemed to have been an event without a perpetrator. How Pennybacker lay dead as the consequence of an unseen but skilled manipulator, how Lenny Gold (fate unknown) seemed to have been exiled to the deserted Alaskan wilderness, how Aleksander Krauss was killed by a blast of water in full view of Army Rangers, how Holmers was trapped in a laboratory made so secure that there no escape, how Ridley was silently thrown from his office with no witnesses—all of this suggested a coordination among conspirators. Or at least two.

FORTY-SEVEN

Iolinda waved me over out of the elevator.

"The President called a few minutes ago," she said in a voice that had the feel of a warning. "He said I should tell you to check your email, before you do anything else. I don't think it's particularly good news."

"Thanks, Io."

What appeared on the screen was an email sent directly to Lister which he then forwarded to me. I could see by the date and time on the document that he bounced it to me less than a minute after he received it.

Dear President Lister:

I am the Director of the Arctic Foundation for a Free America. You will recall that your distinguished professor, Leonard Gold, was appointed as Senior Research Fellow at the Foundation. He arrived here four weeks ago and was inducted into our circle of Fellows a day later.

Before assuming his duties, he asked for a brief leave to drive into the surrounding country to take in a bit of our magnificent scenery. We recommended that he do so. We did explain to him that the weather in the area was a bit iffy, and recommended he rent a Land Rover adapted for travel in ice and snow.

He left in said vehicle seventeen days ago. We have had no communication from him since that time. A flyover of search copters has found no trace of the vehicle.

I am writing in the hope that you or one of your colleagues

would have heard from Professor Gold, or might divulge the number of one of his unlisted phones. Your assistance would be most appreciated.

Sincerely,

Admiral Josephus Edmund Bainbridge III (Ret.)

Jack attached no comment.

FORTY-EIGHT

There were not more than 150 persons present for Klonska's installment ceremony, mostly younger faculty and students. I recognized members of the Physics, Mathematics, and Chemistry Departments. Representation of the Liberal Arts departments was thin. The students appeared to be mostly graduate students from Physics and the other sciences. The few reporters were easy to identify. They were the only ones with notebooks. No one else felt it necessary to remember whatever Klonska was about to say, or, I suppose, even try to understand it. In addition to Klonska, Jack Lister, and the Chairman of the Board of Trustees, there were eight of us on the stage, only some wearing the heavy bronze medallion conferred in earlier ceremonies.

Jack adjusted the microphone and began: "The University Board of Trustees is honored to present this award to one of the most celebrated members of the faculty."

He looked back at Klonska to get his attention for the introductory remarks. Klonska was staring at the floor, looking like he would rather be anywhere else.

"Professor Evgeny Klonska has boldly introduced a theory into the field of physics that has excited a great deal of interest both inside the academy and out." Lister made no attempt to hide the fact that he was reading straight off a prepared text. "He is number forty-eight in Time Magazine's list of the World's One Hundred Most Influential People. Some theologians have said that he provides the most hopeful connection between science and religion since Thomas Aquinas' adaptation of Aristotle transmitted through the work of the Islamic scholar, Averroes. Calling into question the orthodox scientific view of creation as the Big Bang, he challenges Einstein's contribution to understanding what scholars refer to as the Singularity."

I could see the gazes of audience members fading away. It was time for Jack to give it up.

"Professor Klonska's theory that all of time is contained in a single moment has won him fans in a number of fields — even poetry where it has become a pregnant metaphor for much of the meaning of life."

From my perspective on the stage, I could see that he had completed two of the index cards and was now staring down at the third. He turned it over, paused, then tossed it aside and made a signal to Klonska, asking him to come to the lectern. Then he introduced the Board Chairman. Still saying nothing, this gentleman held up the medallion for the audience to see, like he was proclaiming the winner of a boxing match, then awkwardly lifted the blue and white satin ribbon over Klonska's head. Klonska did not appear to realize this was happening. When the medallion dropped into place just over his sternum, the Chairman put out his hand. Klonska stared down for a moment as if deciding what to do with it. He then reached for it in a move that resembled stealing an orange at an outdoor market, giving the man's paw a single shake, and dropping it.

With a sweep of the arm that could be taken as something of a theatrical bow, Lister invited Klonska to respond to his induction into the University's highest academic order. Klonska stepped to the lectern without any indication he thought the applause was for him. There was no printed text lying on the lectern, and there was none in his hand. What was coming was evidently extemporaneous.

With that famous look where his stare, when aimed at your face, seems focused on something distant, he said, "I did not introduce a theory. I have not added to our knowledge of physical reality. My work is not concerned with the field of physics. It is cosmology."

I looked at Jack. He peered at me over the rim of his glasses, his eyebrows raised.

"I am not number forty-eight, but forty-seven on Time Magazine's list. There is no connection between my work and religion. The science with which Thomas Aquinas concerned himself was so primitive there is no relation to the present. It is a misreading of the history of thought to call Averroes a scientist. And he didn't transmit Aristotle. That had been done long before. The orthodox view of the origin of the universe is a rejection of the Big Bang. I do not challenge Einstein. I reject only sixty-five percent of his thought. Time is not contained in a single moment. A moment is a phenomenon of time. It is nonsensical to say that time is contained in itself. Einstein contributed nothing to the present understanding of the so-called Big Bang, another fiction."

Jack was leaning back and staring at the ceiling. His legs seemed to stretch halfway across the stage.

"Nontranscendental Simultaneity." Klonska announced the title of his address like it was the first two words of a sentence, and it practically was. What followed was an hour-long recitation of facts and explanations which, I must frankly admit, when carefully followed, made remarkably good sense regardless of its being true or false.

Evgeny was in some sense, the intellectual opposite of Leonard Gold, now at the wheel of his Land Rover somewhere in the Arctic Circle. Lenny was an evangelist for right-wing political fundamentalism. The public's attention in Lenny's case was drawn not by his intelligence, but by his partisan fervor and the quotable one-liners that found immediate purchase on conservative talk radio. Klonska's status was that of a public intellectual. His work was rich with provocative ideas that generated discussions among the nation's best thinkers. Lenny's pronouncements were meant to sting. Klonska's thundered.

Listening as closely to the lecture as my afternoon slowdown permitted, I picked up a confusing element that recurred several times in this verbal cascade. Three times he used the phrase: Codex I, II, and IV. It was unclear whether he was referring to a document or some identified organization. Arcane that they were, these letters stuck. They required interpretation. I got the impression he was intentionally confusing us, as if he were drawing our attention to something we were guaranteed not to understand.

As Klonska sped on there was no indication that he was aware of an audience, or that he was lecturing to anyone but himself. When his voice stopped and he turned to retire to his place on the stage, the captive crowd did not exactly pile into the exits, but they absented themselves as rapidly as decorum would allow. It took several vigorous shakes of the Board Chairman's slumping shoulder to bring him back to consciousness.

FORTY-NINE

Deborah was standing at the door of the auditorium as I left.

"Boy, do I have questions." A bag had been thrown over her shoulder. I could see a chaos of scribbled words on the open page of her reporter's notebook. "I am so entirely lost and I have to send in seven paragraphs in an hour. Do you have time for coffee?"

The Café Rossetti was filled mostly with students scrolling through their messages, a few professors in intense conversation with each other, hands locked over their foreheads, and the usual handful of emerging screen writers typing out their futures on laptops.

Deborah threw her bag onto the table. As before, she got her usual latte grande and treated it to four spoons of unrefined sugar.

"Start from the beginning. What the hell does 'nontranscendental simultaneity' mean?"

I hesitated. Klonska's intellectual acrobatics were obviously not the actual object of her curiosity.

"Start with the term 'non-transcendental.' Crudely put, the universe cannot be based on anything outside the universe. This has a strange consequence. Namely, everything we postulate about the universe — whether the whole or a part — has a question mark buried in it. Quite simply, we cannot arrive at the truth of *anything* by our own calculation."

"Oh, my." She shook her head as if insects surrounded it. "What about the other part? Simul …?"

"Klonska reasons like this. There is no point in time when the universe began, because time itself began with the universe. That means there was not a beginning *back then*, because the beginning was not *in time*. Instead, it is happening *now*. Everything that has ever occurred is occurring now; separate from us by no time at all. Because the beginning is at no time and in no space, it is always and everywhere. This is what Klonska means by 'simultaneity.'"

"Thank God I don't have to write the headline for my piece. Why does everyone get so worked up over Klonska?"

"Klonska's notoriety owed his bold objections to both the Big Bang theory of the origin of the universe, and to string theory, one of the most popular explanations of creation among cosmologists at the moment. The Big Bang — that is, the notion that everything that exists began at a precise moment — has proved an inadequate metaphor for describing the origin of it all. To make it very simple, the reason the Big Bang doesn't bang loud enough — sorry for that — is that it cannot be described by quantum theory. At the heart of quantum theory is the odd fact that the action of electrons and other primitive participants in subatomic reality is unpredictable. One might even say it's accidental."

By now Deborah was loading up on her second latte grande. I was a bit dismayed when I saw that we had covered only the first few scratchings on her clipboard.

"You mean," she asked, somehow determined to keep this going, "the universe exists by chance? Without anything causing it?"

"Something like that. But that creates a dilemma. How can you explain something that has no laws of its own? It is not good enough for most scientific minds to say, 'Oh, so that's it, is it? We exist just because we happen to exist? Nothing came before all of this?' So a number of bright minds have proposed the existence of alternative universes essentially coexisting with our own. Some contain us unaware in a dimension, or many dimensions, unimaginable to us, some of them infinitely small. Ask how many of these alternative universes there are, and you get answers from about seven to billions."

I looked around the coffee shop. I didn't notice among the clientele a whole lot of concern about the intellectual failure of the Big Bang as an explanation. Sitting close enough to hear everything said was a small, strangely built man whose face was vaguely familiar

"Put simply, Klonska rejects this analysis because it leads necessarily to an infinite regression, and therefore has no capacity to explain anything. He is no happier with Einstein, who argued that space bends as it approaches the speed of light. In fact, that is the way classical physics understands the phenomenon of gravity. The so-called orthodox view is that space doesn't bend enough to explain the odd behavior of galaxies. That is the same as saying there is some missing gravity. Therefore there must be a massive amount of unseen matter out there sucking what we can actually see back into otherwise inexplicable shapes."

I could tell the little man was listening by his awkward but unmoving posture, partly leaning on the table and partly falling away from it, yet very careful not to look in our direction. The way he was twisting himself suggested he might be adept at contortion.

"Klonska denies this. He argues that the curvature of space is so extreme that there is no need for what is called 'dark matter.' In fact, the curvature is perfect insofar as it completes itself, thus forming a whole. That means that every view into this self-enclosed universe, if extended to its limit, ends with the viewers themselves viewing the universe. They are looking into their own looking."

"What will the average Times reader be expected to take away from all this?"

"It's actually very simple. Because all time is no time, and all space is no space, and it is all in a constant state of creation and destruction, and all this happens even as we gaze into the great Nothing, you are…" I waited to make sure I had her complete concentration.

"Yes?"

"You are the very eye of God."

She stared at me like I was mad. "You think that I could write this up for Times and not lose my job?"

"But you're not going to write this up, Deborah. Because you weren't assigned to write up Klonska's talk."

"Don't be absurd!"

"Who is the absurd one here?"

I gave her a small conspiratorial smile. "Ask the real question."

"Who Is the Puzzler?"

"You don't know?" I answered.

"Maybe," she said. "I think I do. What if I do? "

"To name the suspected killer may prove the greatest mistake. Once we believe we have a genuine suspect, our perception is distorted, and we could miss more revealing clues. Thereby overlooking the real killer altogether."

"And therefore could ourselves be killed?"

"We are all equally in danger. You'll notice that the victims have little or nothing in common, and that there seems to be no pattern in the sequence of murders. You could be next. Or I could."

"There is no telling?"

"Oh, there is a great deal of telling. It is perhaps a rhetorical masterpiece. The Puzzler throws bombs — call them word bombs. The campus is covered in an explosion of language.

"For once, dear Deborah, the world is listening to academia! The whole world is tuned in to our university as it never does to our academic jabber. How many millions of academic papers would need to be written before their readership added up to that of the Puzzler's treatise? The Puzzler's readership it would seem far outstrips *The Times*."

"You are at such an advantage over everyone else as the University Professor of Rhetoric."

"No, my hapless dear alumna reporter, the activity of teaching rhetoric is itself rhetorically deadening. The Puzzler need not know the least shred of that subject. His language is a work of sheer poetry. The puzzles are dismaying at first, but provocative enough that we need to replace them with words of our own. That's what a puzzle is, after all: a collection of words or symbols that do not say what they appear to say."

She seemed to be studying the features of my face like there was something unsaid in it.

This whole conversation has been a collection of words that do not say what they appear to say. Wouldn't you agree, Professor?

I stared at her for a full five seconds, not taking my eyes off hers.

"Possibly. Very possibly."

FIFTY

When I returned to my office, a large envelope was on my desk. There was no name on it, neither sender nor addressee. It was not sealed.

PUZZLE # 6

1. "SPECTRAL ANISOTROPY OF THE CMB RADIATION."
(MARCH, 2006)

2. "ENUMERATING INFLATION BY TEMPORAL QUANTITIES."
(SEPTEMBER, 2003)

3. "SINGULARITY: ITS NONLINEAR REPRESENTATION
IN QUANTUM PICTURES." (MAY, 2011)

4. "INTERACTION WITH GRAVITATIONAL ANTENNAS:
A REASSESSMENT." (NOVEMBER, 2008)

5. "SCALAR-FACTOR DUALITY AND THE PRE-BIG BANG SCENARIO."
(JULY, 2004)

6. EXPECTED RELIC GRAVITONS FROM INFLATION." (AUGUST, 2010)

7. "UNIVERSE VS MULTIVERSE: A SURVEY OF THE ISSUES AT STAKE." (MAY, 2005)

8. "LEPTON, QUARK, AND NEUTRINO MASSES IN HORAVA-WRITTEN INSPIRED
MODELS" (JANUARY, 2007)

9. "VARIABLES IN ASSEMBLING CURVED BACKGROUNDS AND
CONFORMAL ANOMALIES IN STRING THEORY." (SEPTEMBER, 2009)

10. "JUSTIFYING IRREGULAR AND NON-SELF-DUAL SOLUTIONS IN THE CLASSICAL
PHYSICAL MODEL." (NOVEMBER 2002)

I glanced over the page. It felt as if a deep pocket of technical terms had been emptied onto the page and scattered about until the words came to resemble sentences. The dates added no guide to any meanings hidden in the mess of letters. This was a puzzle of a whole new variety.

The phone rang.

"Carmody, thanks for picking up." It was Justine Secour, the chair at Physics.

"You've seen the puzzle, Justine?"

"It is all physics jargon, and very familiar to me. Extremely familiar. This is a series of essays by Evgeny Klonska, actually the first ten pieces he's written since coming to the department seven years ago, but not arranged according to dates of publication."

I thought of Lenny Gold, of course. "Please, not another case of plagiarmism among the faculty."

" No, they're all clean, all original. And they're damned good. He's takingonthemajorityviewofthecosmologycrowd,stringtheorysection."

"Why do you think he's being targeted ?"

" It's not just Klonska, it's the whole department. We are his acolytes, his clones. If he's attacked, it's a nuclear blow to the whole department — hell, to the whole field."

" He's targeted right after the installation ceremony."

She hesitated. "Maybe the ceremony was the trigger? Somebody passed over for the honor? "

"If academic jealousy justified murder, Justine, there would be a funeral every day. Who could possibly want Klonksa dead?"

She did not answer immediately. I had the impression that she was loathe to say what she actually suspected. Then she answered with a single word.

"Christians."

FIFTY-ONE

Unlike previous publications there were few volunteered solutions from elsewhere in the University or the public. Either the language or subject matter were so specialized that most readers left the solution to the few academics comfortable with such terminology. The Committee made it clear that they had hit a wall. I suggested that since the Puzzler knew he was dealing in arcana, there might be something hiding in full view that any amateur could grasp.

"Time is not our friend here, as it never is," I said, "but take a day to do a little creative playing with the words and letters, and leave their scientific content to the side. Tomorrow morning at ten."

Iolinda got my attention. She was holding up the phone and whispered, "the President."

As usual, Jack went straight to the matter. "What are you going to do about this, Carmody? Our University is turning into a graveyard."

"Jack, as I've mentioned to you more than once, you have appointed us to this Committee, but we serve voluntarily. Beyond our generosity with time and the disruption of our teaching schedules, we have no intrinsic obligation to do anything about it. I don't think any one of us would mind being replaced. "

He evidently expected that answer, and ignored it. "I got a call here from Cedric Silverstone, the Shakespeare guy at English. He had a suggestion. Turns out a friend of his from way back, high school or worse, has a son who's currently a sophomore at the University and who's the national Scrabble champion. The lad is a near genius at puzzles, word games, trivia, and who cares what else. Families are still close enough that the youngster knows Silverstone as Uncle Cedric. His name is — I have it here — Phil Azarian."

"A sophomore?"

"Okay, Carmody. Maybe you'd prefer hearing this memo from the National Science Foundation saying they are reassessing the projects they have been supporting for years."

I arranged for Phil Azarian to present himself to the Committee the following day. They took the announcement with visible relief, as if we had just invited the Times Puzzle Master into our graduate seminar room.

I met Phil as he stepped off the elevator. Except for the fact that he was a white guy with dreads, his physical appearance was so ordinary as to be forgettable, although I doubt that anyone on the Committee will forget what happened over the next hour and three quarters.

"I can't be late," he said to me as if in a greeting.

"You're not late, Phil. In fact, it's still two minutes to three."

"I don't mean here, man. I can't be late for Anger Management. Five O, not a second later."

"Anger Management?"

"Yeah. It's a group, meets at Student Health. You're late to a meeting, it's 'cause you're pissed at having to take Anger Management and everyone yells at you when you come in 'cause they're pissed you're late. Part of the treatment."

"That's fine. We'll make sure you get there in plenty of time. I am Professor Carmody, by the way." He nodded, like he already knew. "I assume you've studied the puzzle?"

"You got a copy?"

"Here."

He held the page at arm's length, squinted, twisted his mouth and then went completely motionless for about ten seconds. I don't even think his eyes moved. He half turned toward me. "Let's go. I can't be late, man."

FIFTY-TWO

I offered Phil my chair at the head of the table. He ignored the offer and casually dropped the puzzle on the table. Without seeming to acknowledge the presence of other human beings in the room, he began.

"Rule One: Look at the whole thing. No analyzing, no guessing, no memorizing; hints aren't like lint; you don't roll them up in a ball. Just scoop the whole thing up in your field of vision."

Phil paused and looked around like he was a bit annoyed. Several of us got the point that we were to do this scooping and looking now. One by one, we picked up our copy of the puzzle and stared at it.

"The whole thing," he repeated. "Very important. That's why we call it the Cosmic Rule."

" Are you looking or are you staring? Because I didn't come here to solve your puzzle. I came to 'help with the process.' I speak the rules. You apply the rules. You get your answer. Hey!" He looked at his cell phone. "I only got an hour and a half, so we better get our butts moving. Or somebody's gonna get somebody very angry."

No one responded, wondering how to look at a whole page without even reading it.

"What if we start with a sentence?" Harvey Rilling dared.

"Who's stopping you? Go ahead. Go!"

"Let's take the first clue." Harvey hesitated as if unsure how to pronounce the words. "**Spectral anisotropy of the CMB radiation. I** don't know what one word in that sentence is referring to."

Azarian made a soft puffing sound. "You're are obsessing about definitions. The guy knows we got no idea of the substance here, and he like doesn't care because it's not important. So, it's like there's a more or less familiar word here we're supposed to work on. You know, take it as an anagram."

Alfie shook his head. "Can you explain that?"

" You got a Rule for it, the Varied Vowel Rule. You want a word that's got enough vowels to begin with, and then you can't have all the same vowels. Not too many repetitions, because," he paused, "*identifying* them can make you feel *unusually idiotic*. Ha, ha."

That none of us were amused made no impression.

" Look at these words. **Anisotropy** has two o's. That's not bad but not great. Then you got **radiation**. Two i's. Difficult to deal with. Finally, you got **spectral**. Only two vowels here but there's letters that definitely like each other."

"Like each other?" someone asked.

"They kiss and make up. **P** goes good with **r, t,** and **c**. **S**, that goes with anything. That's the Compatibility Rule. So here you have **alp crest, lap crest** and **let's crap**. There's also particles."

"Particles? There's no i in **spectral**."

"That's because you're ignoringThe Missing Letter Rule. Not everybody spells right. How do we know this jokester didn't just forget an i somewhere? Or trick us into thinking it wasn't hiding like behind the clue? Okay go down the page. There's like one word in each clue that fits all the rules, especially the Varied Vowel."

He waited. Another puffing sound. He gave his dreads a shake.

"All right," Samantha Gupta said, "I'll make a guess. How's **temporal**?"

"Like I said, man, it's your puzzle. You like **temporal**? You got **temporal**."

"I'll take **pictures** in the third clue," Nkwame Smith volunteered.

Phil responded with an ambiguous nod.

I went to the board and recorded the first three suggestions. In a few minutes we had our list.

1. [**Spectral**] anisotropy of the CMB radiation
2. Enumerating inflation by [**temporal**] quantities.
3. Singularity: its nonlinear representation in quantum [**pictures.**]
4. Interaction with gravitational antennas: a [**reassessment.**]
5. Scalar-factor duality and the pre-big bang [**scenario.**]
6. Expected relic [**gravitons**] from inflation.
7. Universe vs multiverse: a survey of the issues at [**stake.**]
8. Lepton, quark, and neutrino masses in horava-written [**inspired**] models.
9. Variables in [**assembling**] curved backgrounds and conformal anomalies in string theory.
10. Justifying irregular and non-self-dual solutions in the classical [**physical**] model.

"As you can see," he said in something of a bored tone, "pretty much all these words can take the Varied Vowel Rule. Anyone like give temporal a shot?"

We stared at the word.

"**Am petrol?**" Percival Calkins suggested.

"No good. That says nothing. Here you got **patrol me, mop later**, and **late romp**. This guy's not gonna give us letters that don't work."

What followed was a kind of storm of suggested words and phrases from our list. The Committee was acting like a grade school class, everyone with a hand up and calling out answers. Azarian stood to the side and let the enthusiasm take its course.

I did what I could to organize the proposed words into an organized scheme.

Spectral

Alp crest. Lap crest. Let's crap. Particles.

Temporal

Patrol me. Mop later. Late romp.

Pictures

Cue strip. Rite cups. Cure tips. Ripe cuts. Piecrust.

Several hands went up when we got to the fourth clue. "Reassessment," Alfie objected, "has four esses. I don't see a single possible combination."

"That's because you're not following the Esses Rule," Phil said. "You get two esses together, they read like one."

Reassessment

Seen stream. Steer names. Smear teens. Name trees

scenario

Airs once. Econ airs. Croanies. Nice oars.
Car noise. Air scone.

"That's not how you spell cronies," Samantha objected.

"This puzzler dude," Phil said with a bit of disdain, whether for us or the Puzzler one couldn't say. "How can I help it that misspells a word?"

gravitons

Raving to. Avon grit. Roving at.

stake

Takes. Skate. Steak. Astek.

inspired.

Sin pride. Ride pins. Rid spine. Rids pine.
Nip rides.

assembling

> *Blames gin. Glib names. Bang limes. Gambles in.*
> *Nimble gas. Sing blame.*

physical

> *Play hics. Achy lips. Hip clays. Clips hay.*
> *Lays chips. Clay ship.*

Stunned. That is probably the correct word for the Committee's glaring at the board. Several tried to speak but gave it up. Finally, I asked, "Phil, what's next?"

"Well," Azarian said in a loud voice, "you cross out the ones you don't want."

"Is there a rule here?" Armand Chernovsky asked.

Phil looked at his cell phone and winced. "Naturally. It's called the Contiguity Rule. You look for what should be next to what."

The Committee's confusion was only too obvious.

"Phil," Alfie suggested, "why don't you just show us how that rule works?"

"How it works? Yeah." He grabbed the marker, still in my hand, and went to the white board. Without hesitating, he eliminated three of the offered solutions.

Spectral

Alp crest. Lap crest. Let's crap. Particles.

He looked down at us. There was no response, not even a sign of comprehension. He turned back to the board and, without a comment, proceeded through the entire list, slashing at the rejected words with what I took to be desperate haste.

Temporal

~~Patrol me.~~ Mop later. ~~Late romp.~~

Pictures

~~Cue strip. Rite cups. Cure tips.~~ Ripe cuts. ~~Piecrust.~~

Reassessment

~~Seen stream. Steer names.~~ Smear teens. ~~Name trees.~~

Scenario

~~Airs once. Econ airs.~~ Croanies. ~~Nice oars.~~
~~Car noise. Air scone.~~

Gravitons

Raving to. ~~Avon grit. Roving at.~~

stake

Takes. ~~Skate. Steak. Astek.~~

Inspired

Sin pride. ~~Ride pins. Rid spine. Rids pine. Nip rides.~~

Assembling

~~Blames gin. Glib names. Bang limes. Gambles in.~~
~~Nimble gas.~~ Sing blame.

Physical

~~Play hics.~~ Achy lips. ~~Hip clays. Clips hay.~~
~~Lays chips. Clay ship.~~

I erased the rejections and listed the survivors.

> *Let's crap.*
>
> *Mop later.*
>
> *Ripe cuts.*
>
> *Smear teens.*

Cronies.

Takes

Raving to.

Sin pride.

Sing blame.

Achy lips.

When I turned from the board and looked at Phil for the first time since this last gallop, he was trembling ever so slightly. Although the room was minimally heated, he was sweating.

Percival Calkins slid his chair back from the table, as if he were finished with this session. "What in the name of sweet Jesus are we to do with this?"

Marguerite Gardolini is a more measured voice, asked, "Now are we to make a sentence of these words, or just what?"

"Here, you got the Missing Article Rule." He studied the list for no more than a few seconds. "There's **of, the, by, a, it, with, from**, and **and** that go with this puzzle. That's three prepositions, two articles, and a conjunction. The Missing Article Rule says they get a free pass. You use some but not all of them and you got your solution."

"You mean," Nkwame spoke up, "we throw in a few little words and we got our solution?"

"Yeah, that's what I mean."

"Just — throw them in at random."

"Not at random, man. I gave you the Contiguity Rule."

Nkwame wouldn't give up. "These words are contiguous?"

Phil threw up his hands and turned back to the board. This time he paused as long as five seconds. "**It takes the sin of pride**," he began in a paced voice, "**and the ravings of cronies to smear teens' achy lips with ripe cuts and sing blame. Let's crap and mop later.**" He looked at each of the Committee member seated at the table. "That's your solution."

Harvey Rilling hit the table with the flat of his hand. "Just what the fuck does that solve?"

"Solve? I don't know what it solves. It's your solution. It's not mine. That's all I can say."

"All *I* can say," Armand said, rising from his chair, "is that you have come here only to waste our time."

"Waste *your* time?" I could see Phil was struggling not to cross a dangerous inner line. "It's *my* time *you* have wasted. I came in here, gave you the rules. But then what happens? You don't follow them. You missed the first rule, man. The *first rule!*"

"What did we miss?" Samantha asked in a soft voice meant, I suppose to calm the lad.

Phil threw open his hands. "I gave you the Cosmic Rule. The Cosmic Rule says look at the whole thing. Well, you didn't. You missed something that's all over the puzzle. It's in every goddam clue. And you missed it."

He turned to me. " I gotta go. I can't be late."

I took him by the elbow and we walked out to the elevator. I felt like I had to steady him he was shaking so badly. I reassured him that he would get to his Anger Management session in time.

"It takes 195 seconds to walk. A lot will depend on the elevator."

"Why don't you walk down, Phil?"

"Now you're thinking, Professor." And he dashed past the EXIT sign.

I returned to the Committee room not two minutes later.

"Carmody!" Bobo Winston, called out before I even stepped through the door. "This kid is a fucking genius!"

"This is utterly shocking!" Samantha Gupta declared, raising her voice over the others.

"Wait, wait," I begged. "Please explain."

"The dates," Marguerite Gardolini said. "The *dates!*" As if that explained everything.

"They were in every clue."

Alfie held up his hand. " Soon as the kid was out the door, Bobo put the clues in temporal sequence, the order in which they were published. We got the solution in less than sixty seconds."

"What solution?" I asked.

Alfie shoved a copy of the puzzle at me. The new line up of titles wound up as follows:

"Justifying irregular and non-self-dual solutions in the classical physical model." (November 2005)

"Enumerating inflation by temporal quantities." (September, 2006)

"Scalar-factor duality and the pre-big bang scenario." (July, 2007)

"Universe vs multiverse: a survey of the issues at stake." (May, 2008)

"Spectral anisotropy of the CMB radiation." (March, 2009)

"Lepton, quark, and neutrino masses in horava-written inspired models" (January, 2010)

"Interaction with gravitational antennas: a reassessment." (November, 2011)

"Variables in assembling curved backgrounds and conformal anomalies in string theory." (September, 2012)

"Expected relic gravitons from inflation." (August, 2013)

"Singularity: its nonlinear representation in quantum pictures." (May, 2014)

"Is this supposed to mean something?" I said turning the page.

"Remember what the little boy said, Carmody?" Marguerite chided me. "Pay no attention to the meanings. Just look at the arrangement."

I continued staring at the puzzle.

"Carmody, read the first letter in each clue," Marguerite said. "They spell out a pair of words. Who would ever have thought that Time Magazine's mega-atheist could be pegged with *those* two words?"

He waited for my own reading. It came quickly.

JESUS LIVES

I shared their shock. I admitted that my own credulity took a solid hit. This reversed everything we ever thought about Evgeny Klonska.

I called the president.

"Call Secours," Jack barked. "Be here soon as you get her."

FIFTY-FOUR

Professor Secours's secretary said she was chairing a Department meeting in her office and was unavailable.

"Tell her we solved the puzzle."

In less than a minute Secours was on the line. I reported the Committee's discovery.

"Oh, my. Oh, my." she responded to the Committee's discovery., "Who in God's name would ever …?"

"Lister wants us in his office as soon as we can get there."

It was as if we were interrupting a private conversation Jack was having with himself: "Less than a week after I confer the University's most prestigious academic title on the bastard, I'm gonna get kicked around the front pages for honoring some kind of cockamamie Christian?"

"What do you suggest we do here, Justine? You're his chair. You are supposed to be keeping an eye on your people."

"There's not much to suggest," she said. "Evgeny did nothing academically unconscionable. There were no scholarly errors to bring him to a disciplinary body; there were no scholarly errors at all. There's no punitive action available to the University."

"Unless the Puzzler kills him?" Jack fumed. "This will probably be the only one he misses. My luck! But of course, I have to spend the university's budget protecting his ass."

Klonska was under no administrative pressure to leave the University, but we all noticed that he was slowly withdrawing himself. He disdained talking with any of his colleagues, even to the several who worked with him and occasionally coauthored his papers, and even wore an identifiable smirk as he passed them in the hallway. He was frequently absent from his classes. There was no evidence that he was embarrassed, or even angered, by the disclosure of his religious views. Indeed, he may have been pleased for it to be public knowledge. After all, he arranged the titles of his papers precisely to be discovered. Then one day, without informing Justine Secours, or his around-the-clock guard, he was gone.

What went with him was the unsolved meaning of his so-called

Codex I, II, and VI. While, over time, the solution to Puzzle #6 came to be widely known, nobody was able to offer a useful reassembling of the Codex. It was so obscure, in fact, that attempts to solve it were rare. There's a (false) suspicion it is not a puzzle at all.

FIFTY-FIVE

Klonska's fate was the strangest and most symbolically mysterious of any of the Puzzler's victims to date. Less than a month after his departure, it was reported that the church-going citizens of Slovenia were shocked — no, horrified — by the scene that greeted them one Sunday morning as they arrived for early mass at the Greek Orthodox cathedral in the capitol city Ljubjana: a naked and immolated corpse left head down on a large rock at the main entrance to the building. It took a few days for the Slovenian authorities to identify the body as Evgeny Klonska's.

It happened that a renowned orthopedic surgeon was on the staff of the teaching hospital in Ljubjana, attached to the national University and thought to be one of the finest medical institutions of all those in the former Yugoslavian countries. The man's elevated place on the staff was unusual; he was a Muslim. The police, baffled by the strange wounds on the corpse, found with arms akimbo, and most bones broken, turned to this surgeon. His report contained a detailed analysis of the fractures in the victim's feet and hands. Though severe, these injuries were not the cause of death.

Mortality resulted from a stab wound, in the thoracic region of the torso, by a sharp instrument that had penetrated the ribs and went directly to the center of the heart. A good bit of blood had been lost, although none was found in the vicinity of the cathedral, indicating that the killing had been done elsewhere. The final report was a model of accuracy and thoroughness, but it left unaddressed the nature of the crime which was considered a matter for the police.

The police were puzzled about where to begin their investigation. Publishing an artist's rendering of his face led to the identity of the victim. There were eleven responses, all anonymous, each offering Evgeny Klonska's full and correctly spelled name. His name meant a great deal to people elsewhere but drew a blank in all the Ljubjana databases of the country's numerous institutions. They called in a famous forensic specialist from Kosovo where, as it happens, he was busy disinterring the skeletal remains of the men and boys executed in Srbenicia by the Serbians. This gentleman asked to see the corpse immediately.

After a brief scan of the naked body, which included leaning down until his nose was close to the mouth of the victim and inhaling deeply, he nodded silently as if speaking to himself. He pointed to a series of strange lacerations across the forehead. "Crown of thorns." He nodded toward the wound on the torso. "A spear, introduced from below." Nodding at the hands and feet, he said, "Penetration by metal stakes." He invited them to note the odor around the man's mouth. "Vinegar and gall." He looked around at the observers then said, not altering the professional drone of his voice, "The man was crucified." Without another comment, or even a look back at the stunned officials, he exited the morgue and disappeared.

The forensic specialist's diagnosis was confounding, causing not a few to revise their revision of Klonska's thought. Why would the man be crucified, of all possible forms of murder? Nothing is a stronger symbol of Christianity than the crucifixion. It seemed self-evident that Christians would celebrate Klonska as a genuine hero, a man willing to sacrifice his profession and reputation for the advancement of faith. Did they misunderstand what he was about? Or did we? The body was secretly buried without ceremony under an enormous concrete slab, and without any hint to the public of its location.

LATE MIDTERMS
SPRING SEMESTER

FIFTY-SIX

The garish execution of Evgeny Klonska in a remote European country attracted an entirely new set of voices to the national Puzzler coverage. The Southern Baptist Convention, struck the prevailing note when its newsletter assailed the runaway atheism at a major urban university.

"Not only do these secularist scholars teach critical views of the Bible, openly espouse sexual license among students and their professors, and purge any trace of Christian language and practice from all formal events (never invoking the Holy Spirit before faculty meetings, for example), they cruelly cast forth one of the world's most brilliant Christian witnesses (vide Time Magazine) to one of history's most horrifying method of execution."

In addition to a keen and broad command of several academic fields, the Puzzler also had intimate knowledge of the lives of the faculty (his colleagues?) He knew before the rest of us that Holmers was using and dealing powerful substances, that Aleksander was directing millions of government dollars to terrorist regimes, that Lenny was a supremo plagiarist, that Pennybacker was a sexual deviant of epic dimensions, and that Evgeny's atheism was a fundamentalist Christian ruse. Hours and hours were lost to conversations in dormitories, offices, the faculty club, even classrooms concerning the identity of the Puzzler and his singular talents.

Klonska's death left a trail of sharpened and unanswerable questions, but it did not have the broad public impact of Pennybacker's unique demise. The films of Darius's office athletics rocketed him to the highest altitudes of social media. The millions of viewers who caught him on YouTube only hours after the videos were posted, have replayed them countless times since. Now the University was famed not only as a place of death and criminality but also scene of unchecked carnality.

The University's six-month trail of woe had glazed the campus with another kind of celebrity luster. We were all in a perpetual holding pattern — physical, psychological and emotional. Independent movie makers swept the scene from the roofs of rented trucks; The 24-hour dazzle of electronic illumination gave our faces a ghoulish pallor. Many of us wanted to escape to other colleges, other campuses; I myself would never find another position as exalted anywhere else; in a sense I was held hostage by my own success. But many other faculty members were sending out letters, applications; going on job interviews. Our misery had become a boon to other colleges who suddenly could hope to steal our best faculty. We were simultaneously a place of danger but also a curious tourist attraction like the Bronx Zoo.

No matter how great the clouds of foreboding that enveloped our lives, Jack Lister flogged his grand festival into a frenzy of expectation: *The University at 150: a Celebration of the American Mind,* scheduled for mid-July, only three months away. Press releases boasted the deliberations of student and faculty committees. The President's office reported the nominations of Nobel, Pulitzer, and MacArthur winners; politicians and athletic heroes; and naturally the obligatory Hollywood stars. Jack shamelessly dangled the names before the media like bait. Meanwhile the committees met under the pretense of academic euphoria but with an unshakeable angst about a future we could not control.

FIFTY-SEVEN

For Jack, squash seemed to be the one area in his life in which he felt liberated from the mounting challenges to his presidency. The usual pressures on his office, now made infinitely worse thanks to the Puzzler's continuing rampage, apparently gave out at the glass door to the squash court. I could see why. Raised in a once wealthy family, Jack was known to have grown up with an indoor squash court in the Long Island mansion that was his childhood home. To pass through that door no doubt recalled precious memories of a lost part of his youth.

I was no real contest for Jack. He played with prep school finesse, and was essentially indomitable. Being 6'5" tall was not exactly a disadvantage. For most of his opponents, Jack was all left hand, and murderous. With me, he usually played righty, just to give me a meager chance to return those terrifying shots off the back wall.

I don't think I had ever played so poorly against Lister. But it wasn't that something was wrong with my game. It was rather that Jack was firing off one killer shot after another. He broke his usual habit of playing only wrong-handed with me and sometimes switched hands several times in the middle of a point — strictly against the rules. Not that he noticed. He was unusually preoccupied. I could guess why. Gone was the bravado about the Festival.

Today his face bore witness to the pressure of angry trustees, anxious student groups, constant media presence, and a growing but unstated feeling among the faculty that he was losing control of the institution. Somewhat like his squash game, he had become increasingly rash and overreactive, making hasty decisions without consultation, and showing little sign of his characteristically sure leadership. In a couple of games, I scored not at all. When our hour was over, he vanished into the locker room without a word. I remained standing on the court while mentally reviewing another explanation for this exceptional behavior. A new and very different thesis emerged, but one still inchoate enough that I wanted to keep it to myself.

FIFTY-EIGHT

"Professor Carmody." Iolinda was at the door. "Please excuse. *The Times* lady is calling every two minutes."

"Did she say what she wanted?"

"About the new puzzle.""

"I haven't seen it."

"Hold on." Moments later she came into my office, holding out not one but three sheets of printed paper.

I spread them across my desk.

PUZZLE #7

PART I

1. START AT ZERO AND PROCEED TO TWENTY-SIX.

2. SUBTRACT HALF, THEN SUBTRACT TEN FROM THE REMAINDER, AND SQUARE THE RESULT.

3. DOUBLE STEP TWO, DIVIDE BY ONE-THIRD OF STEP TWO AND ADD ALL OF STEP TWO.

4. SUBTRACT TWO-THIRDS OF STEP TWO.

PART II

1. SUBTRACT ONE-THIRD OF STEP TWO IN PART I FROM STEP FOUR IN PART I, MULTIPLY BY ONE-THIRD OF STEP FOUR IN PART I, ADD ONE-THIRD OF STEP TWO IN PART I.

2. SUBTRACT ONE-FIFTH OF STEP THREE IN PART I AND ADD ONE.

3. SUBTRACT THE SQUARE ROOT OF STEP TWO IN PART I, AND ADD ONE-FIFTH OF STEP THREE IN PART I.

4. ADD HALF THE DIFFERENCE BETWEEN STEP ONE AND STEP THREE IN PART II.

PART III

1. SUBTRACT THE SUM OF ONE-HALF OF STEP FOUR IN PART II AND ONE-THIRD OF STEP ONE IN PART II.

2. MULTIPLY BY STEP ONE IN PART III AND SUBTRACT ONE-FIFTH OF STEP FOUR IN PART II.

3. ADD STEP THREE IN PART I AND SUBTRACT STEP ONE IN PART III DOUBLED.

4. ADD ONE-THIRD OF STEP THREE IN PART I.

5. SUBTRACT HALF THE DIFFERENCE BETWEEN STEP ONE AND TWO IN PART III.

PART IV

1. SUBTRACT STEP THREE IN PART I, AND SUBTRACT TWO-THIRDS OF STEP ONE IN PART III.

2. MULTIPLY BY TWO-THIRDS OF STEP THREE IN PART I.

3. ADD STEP THREE OF PART I.

4. SUBTRACT TWO-THIRDS OF STEP THREE IN PART I AND ONE-THIRD OF STEP FIVE IN PART III.

PART V

1. ADD THE DIFFERENCE BETWEEN STEP THREE IN PART I AND STEP ONE IN PART III.

2. SUBTRACT STEP ONE IN PART III DOUBLED .

3. ADD ONE-FIFTH OF STEP TWO IN PART V AND SUBTRACT TWO-THIRDS OF STEP THREE IN PART I.

4. MULTIPLY BY THE DIFFERENCE BETWEEN STEP ONE AND STEP TWO IN PART II.

PART VI

1. SUBTRACT ONE-FIFTH OF STEP FOUR IN PART II.

2. SUBTRACT ONE-HALF OF STEP FOUR IN PART II

3. MULTIPLY BY HALF OF STEP FOUR IN PART II AND ADD STEP ONE IN PART IV.

4. SUBTRACT STEP TWO IN PART IV DOUBLED, AND ADD ONE-HALF OF STEP THREE IN PART V.

5. ADD THE PRODUCT OF STEP TWO IN PART III AND TWO-THIRDS OF STEP ONE IN

PART III.

PART VII (A)

1. SUBTRACT THE PRODUCT OF ONE-THIRD OF STEP ONE IN PART II AND STEP TWO IN PART VI.

2. ADD STEP THREE IN PART II.

3. SUBTRACT ONE-THIRD OF STEP ONE IN PART II.

4. SUBTRACT THE SUM OF ONE-HALF OF STEP ONE IN PART VI AND STEP ONE IN PART VII (A)

PART VII (B)

1. SUBTRACT THE DIFFERENCE BETWEEN STEP THREE IN PART VII(A) AND STEP ONE IN PART VI.

2. SUBTRACT THE DIFFERENCE BETWEEN STEP TWO IN IV AND STEP FOUR IN PART ONE.

3. ADD STEP ONE IN PART II.

4. SUBTRACT THE SUM OF STEP TWO IN PART IV AND STEP TWO IN PART I.

PART VIII

1. MULTIPLY BY THE DIFFERENCE BETWEEN STEP TWO IN PART V AND STEP THREE IN PART VII(A).

2. DIVIDE BY ONE-THIRD OF STEP FOUR IN PART III.

3. ADD HALF OF STEP FIVE IN PART VII(B).

4. MULTIPLY BY THE SQUARE ROOT OF STEP FOUR IN PART V.

PART IX

1. ADD ONE-FIFTH OF STEP THREE IN PART I.

2. SUBTRACT THE SUM OF STEP TWO IN PART IV AND STEP FOUR IN PART I.

3. ADD THE SUM OF STEP THREE IN PART I AND STEP TWO IN PART VI.

4. ADD THREE-QUARTERS OF STEP TWO IN PART IV DOUBLED.

5. SUBTRACT THE DIFFERENCE BETWEEN STEP THREE IN PART VI AND STEP ONE IN PART V.

PART X

1. ADD THE DIFFERENCE BETWEEN STEP ONE IN PART III AND STEP TWO IN PART VI.

2. ADD THE DIFFERENCE BETWEEN ONE-THIRD OF STEP TWO IN PART I AND STEP ONE IN PART III.

3. SUBTRACT STEP TWO IN PART IV.

4. ADD THREE-QUARTERS OF STEP TWO IN PART IV DOUBLED.

"Sound the alarm to the Committee, Iolinda."

"I've done it. You're meeting first thing tomorrow, nine a.m."

"What should I tell *The Times* woman?"

"Oh, Jesus. I'll call her."

FIFTY-EIGHT

"May I ask you a question?" Deborah began without ceremony.

"Shoot."

"When they were destroying Holmers' lab and he had backed into the small closet where he apparently injected himself, I saw you pick something off the floor."

"It was one of these." I took a squash ball from my athletic bag.

She looked at me with a trace of *gotcha* in her face, just enough to let me know that she did see what I had lifted from the wreckage.

"That's an odd thing to pocket in a chemistry lab at a moment like that."

"You would have to understand squash to see why I might do that."

"What does that mean?"

"You notice that it's a particularly hard ball," I explained while she finished off her latte in a pair of aggressive attacks. "Squash is also played with a much softer version. You can almost compress it with your hand. It is the more popular choice currently among the best players. I hate them. And hard balls are increasingly difficult to buy. Holmers played with a hard ball. When I saw this one on the floor, I couldn't resist. His were always the best quality."

She frowned. She started several times to ask a question then stopped.

"By the way, Deborah, what were you doing there, just outside the entrance to Homers' lab? The police kept tight control of the area."

"I was there as a reporter, of course. Why else?"

"You were speaking with Tom Roche."

"Why not? Isn't that what a reporter is supposed to do?"

I waited a moment to give the next question more emphasis. She finished off her coffee but not without breaking her stare.

"Were you reporting to the officer, or was he reporting to you?"

"Don't be so fucking obvious, Carmody. I thought nuance was your trade."

She pushed herself away from the table with two hands, swept up her purse and, without a look back, headed directly to the front door of the faculty club and disappeared.

FIFTY-NINE

I entered the Graduate Seminar Room the next morning to find the full Committee already there, and already unhappy with the task confronting them.

"We are in a land bordered by algorithms and opaque numbers. We are all foreigners here," Bobo echoed the views that caromed around the table.

"Harvey," Marguerite said, "you are the mathematician on the Committee. Lead us through this *cauchemar*."

"*Cauchemar?*"

"Sorry, nightmare."

"My field is analytical geometry. I am no more than an amateur when it comes to plain arithmetic. I'm afraid we're all in this as equal dunces."

"Okay, let's start," Alfie said. "**Start at zero and proceed to twenty-six. Any problem there?**" No response. A few persons shrugged a reluctant agreement. "Carmody, take your position at the board. Put down a twenty-six."

TWENTY-SIX.

"So far, so good, Alfie," Marguerite said. "Now go to the next one."

"**Subtract half, then subtract ten from the remainder, and double the result.** Half of what? Which remainder? Jesus."

"Well," Samantha said. "What's so hard about that? It's got to mean half of step one. Which is twenty-six. So, thirteen."

THIRTEEN.

" I suppose the remainder is what remains from the difference between thirteen and ten."

"Brilliant."

"I'm already lost," Bobo admitted. "Too many implied numbers flying around. Why doesn't he, or they, or *she*, just state the actual amounts?"

"Why doesn't he or she or it just name the victim," I said, concerned to keep the Committee in all-out work mode. "Give us the address where to find the body? It's a puzzle, Bobo, not a public notice."

SIXTY

We were taking a ten minute break when Iolinda found me in the stairwell. "I know I'm not supposed to bother you with public submissions but this one ... I couldn't resist."

She handed me the printout.

It was an email from a Ms. Norma Weiss who identified herself as a fifth grade teacher in P.S. 277 in the Bronx.

"The pupils in my class [not *kids*; I was already beginning to like this woman] have been working on the puzzle. I assigned it to them yesterday for their arithmetic class. Arithmetic is the fifth period of the day on Tuesday. It took them the full period to complete the solution. I told them I would text it to you to see if it was accurate. I can only imagine how busy you must be, but the members of the class would be extremely pleased to hear from you, regardless of their success or failure in completing the assignment."

After the blizzard of proffered solutions from the National Academy of Sciences and the Sorbonne it seemed foolish in the extreme to ask a group of ten-year-old public school pupils for help. I guess it was a hunch that uncluttered minds, capable of sustained attention, were no worse than our own worn and tarnished thinking caps. Also, when are bright ten-year-olds, not yet afflicted with self-consciousness and still free of arrogance, resistible?

"Iolinda, where's P.S. 277? In the Bronx?"

She sighed, and looked away for a moment. "You ever heard the word, 'ghetto'"

"Get the number."

The school secretary answered. I identified myself, briefly explaining why I was calling. "Would it be possible to be connected to Ms. Weiss?"

"No, she's now in class, but there is a teacher's break in an hour. I will see that Ms. Weiss gets the message."

The call came in minutes.

"Hello, Professor Carmody. I assume you're asking for our work on the puzzle."

"Ms. Weiss, could you bring one of your pupils down to the Square and to meet with the Committee."

"Oh … yes. Yes. I'll ask one," she said with a note of surprise. "I'm thinking of Yvonne Thompson." She sounded as if she wanted my approval for the choice. "When were you thinking? Friday during gym period?"

"No, this afternoon."

"This after … ?"

"Take a cab. We will of course reimburse you."

"We don't have cabs in this part of the Bronx. Only car service."

"Fine."

When I returned to the meeting, I quickly saw that the members of the Committee were pushing themselves along, fighting their own resistance, and basically getting nowhere. I announced that at three we were expecting a visitor, an expert at this sort of thing. The silence of their response indicated only resignation.

"Reconvene at three."

They headed for the door like it was time for recess on the playground.

SIXTY-ONE

I found Ms. Weiss and her pupil waiting in the reception room. Iolinda was in solemn discussion with the child over the fading popularity of several favorite rap stars. She looked to be a typical ten-year-old, except for her size. She could have been a nine-year-old faking her age.

"I am Norma Weiss, Professor Carmody, and this is one of our pupils, Yvonne Thompson." The introduction was so comfortably formal, I had nothing more to say than, "Hello, and welcome."

Ms Weiss was formidable. A short, round white woman with unmanageable hair, and attired according to the standard teacher's style, that is, dressing neither up nor down. I could see she would present a dilemma to the Committee. Like most academics, they were uncomfortable in the presence of real teachers.

A college professor's profession has only vaguely to do with the classroom. We are amateurs where this woman is all pro. Standing a few hours a week before large bodies of students, about whom we know all but nothing, and talking as much to ourselves as to them, hardly justifies the title of teacher. This woman spends most of every day with forty young lives, more time than any of us have given to our own children. Teaching is her life. For us it is a distraction. I can't think of a colleague who, if offered the option, would not accept being relieved from teaching altogether, or at least from one course. The highest paid among us (this applies to myself, unfortunately) teach practically not at all.

Observing this small, remarkable woman, I thought of Thorstein Veblen's devastating analysis of the university in his classic, *The Theory of the Leisure Class*. The college faculty is essentially an in-house body of servants of the wealthy who pay them to educate their children. The point of that education is not the extension of one's mental powers, an introduction to new worlds of thought, but a mastery of the skill of convincing others that they live completely at leisure, essentially that they do nothing to make a living. It is therefore important to them that professors themselves are freed of all unpleasant labor — all the better to serve as models for their sons and daughters. This is why it is so simple for us in academe to have a liberal ideology: it is without consequence. We can express it freely only because the rich, and conservative, parents of our students have enough money not to give a damn. We are essentially endowed idlers. *The Theory of the Leisure Class* could have been subtitled, *The Leisure of the Theory Class.*

SIXTY-TWO

Yvonne crossed over to the whiteboard and picked out a marker. She wrote her name in a smooth cursory hand. When she turned to face the Committee, I noticed they were at first mildly shocked to be addressed by a child. It was quickly apparent, however, that this child fit into no one's stereotype of a fifth grader. In a quick scan of the room, I saw that their faces were lit with anticipation.

Yvonne began by a pronunciation of her name in separate syllables, a signal that she was to be properly addressed.

"Ee-vahn," she said in a long, slow voice. "Not Yuh-vahn."

"Do you all have the puzzle on your desks?" she began, arms folded, and waited until each of us had it squared before us on the table."

Her manners and presence were so completely developed and as-

233

sured it was possible to imagine it was Ms. Weiss herself standing in her place.

"We start at the beginning," Yvonne said, turned to the white-board, and, with a thick blue marker recorded the words,

Part I

"Now, open the puzzle to Part One." She held up the puzzle. "That's this one right here."

1. **Start at zero and proceed to twenty-six.**
2. **Subtract half, then subtract ten from the remainder, and square the result.**
3. **Double step two, divide by one-third of step two and add all of step two.**
4. **Subtract two-thirds of step two.**

"Who knows the answer to step one?"

There was a hesitation among the Committee members, as if no one wanted to risk being corrected by the teacher.

"Well," she said, drawing out the word. "it's twenty-six. Right?"

We all nodded. She wrote it on the board.

26

"Now you subtract half from 26, which is…?"

"Thirteen," we said in unison, somewhat sotto voce.

"Good! Keep going. Ten from that is …?"

"Three."

"Three squared?"

"Nine."

"Correct." She turned to the board again.

9

"Anyone want to volunteer Step three?"

Samantha raised her hand, and when called on, said tentatively, "Well, you double nine, that's eighteen. Then you divide by one-third of Step two, which is three, and that gives us six. And when you add half of eighteen, which is nine, to six you get fifteen." Samantha concluded this analysis with what sounded more like a question than an answer.

"Anyone else get that?" Yvonne asked. Hands went up. "Very good, class," she said with authority. By now we had truly become a class. Hers.

15

"Step four. Easy. You can do that on your own. Subtract two-thirds of fifteen. Would anyone like to tell us what they have?"

We looked around at each other. Who would speak first? Alfie, of course. "I get six, that's two-thirds of nine and that subtracted from what — I guess from fifteen."

Yvonne nodded approval and without comment wrote the number, nine, on the board under the others.

Part I.

26

9

15

Nine

For an unexplained reason, she wrote out the final number of Part I, as she would for all that followed.

"Are you ready for Part Two?" She waited. She looked around to make sure we all had it before us.

Part II

1. **Subtract one-third of step two in Part I from step four in Part I, multiply by one-third of step four in Part I, add one-third of step two in Part I.**
2. **Subtract one-fifth of step three in Part I and add one.**
3. **Subtract the square root of step two in part I, and add one-fifth of step three in Part I.**
4. **Add half the difference between step one and step three in Part II.**

"Would you like to start?" She nodded at Marguerite.

Marguerite seemed a bit distracted. She had not so far joined the discussion. She briefly studied the puzzle. "I'll give it a try. One-third of step four in Part I..." She looked up at the numbers on the board. "Nine. Divide that by three. Three. Right?" The number went on the board.

3

"That's part of it. Next? Anyone else?"

Armand jumped in. His puzzle was already full of marks. "It doesn't say what we are supposed to subtract three from. A vague command."

Yvonne shrugged and looked across the top of the class like it was obvious. "Step four in Part One. What's that? Nine. That's what we ended up with in Part One. So what is three from nine?"

"That helps," Armand said. "Then we multiply three by six and that gives us eighteen, and then, let's see, we add to that one-third of, umm, nine, three again, that comes to 21."

This time Yvonne turned to the board and wrote out what appeared to be the formula for step one.

$$9 - (\tfrac{1}{3} \times 9) \times 3 = 18 + (\tfrac{1}{3}\ 9) = 21$$

"Can anyone write their formula for step two?

She rocked her head little to one side then to other as if to silent music. After a bit of collaborative labor, and several corrections, the result was recorded.

$$21 - (\tfrac{1}{5}\ 15) + 1 = 19$$

The empty stares indicated this was not especially helpful. Yvonne, seeing that she had an arithmetically challenged audience, went back to the board, slowly recorded each formula, and provided a running commentary as she proceeded.

$$19 - (\ 15\ )$$

"Now, class, we begin with nineteen because that was the result of step one. One-fifth of fifteen is, what?"

"Three."

"That leaves?"

"Sixteen."

"Correct. Sixteen." She gave the class an encouraging nod. "Next, what is the square root of step four in Part One?"

"Is it three?"

"Good. So this is what we have." She wrote that part of the formula on the board. "Can anyone tell us the result?"

"Nineteen?"

"Correct again." She completed the formula.

$$19 - (\sqrt{9}) + (\tfrac{1}{5}\ 15) = 19$$

There was easy agreement on the formula for step four in Part II.

$$19 + (\ \tfrac{1}{2}\ (21 - 19)) = 20$$

Yvonne then erased the formulas, leaving just the list of numbers.

21
19
19
Twenty

She held up the puzzle, pointed to Part III and looked around at each of our spaces just to make sure.

Part III

1. **subtract the sum of one-half of step four in Part II and one-third of step one in Part II.**
2. **by step one in Part III and subtract one-fifth of step four in Part II.**
3. **Add step three in Part I and subtract step one in Part III doubled.**
4. **Add one-third of step three in Part I.**
5. **Subtract half the difference between step one and step two in Part III.**

With Part Three came a different challenge. Yvonne put us on our own. Working separately, we would calculate the numbers and write out the formulae. While we were at work at it, I looked up at Yvonne. The inner music had apparently increased in volume. Her whole body was moving in rhythmic but subtle waves, first one foot then the other, rocking side to side, throwing out miniature punches, and once even a complete spin.

When she asked for our answers, she had to wait while we double-checked the figures. She circled a finger in the air as a signal to move faster. Samantha volunteered that so far she had three in step one and six in step two.

"Does anybody have different figures?" Yvonne asked. Harvey Rilling said he had five for step two, not six. "The two of you get to-

PhDeath | 238

gether over there," Yvonne said, pointing to a corner of the room, "and correct each other's results."

Before we had completed Part Three, there were several groups grading each other. This continued until Yvonne sensed there was a near consensus. Only one of us held out. Alfie's numbers were different in each step. Without commenting on this slightly failed group effort, Yvonne recorded the next list.

Part III

$$20 - ((\tfrac{1}{2}\ 20) + (\tfrac{1}{3}\ 21)) = 3$$
$$3 \times 3 - (\tfrac{1}{5}\ 20) = 5$$
$$5 + 15 - (3 \times 2) = 14$$
$$14 + (\tfrac{1}{3}\ 15) = 19$$
$$19 - \tfrac{1}{2}(\ 5\text{-}3) = Eighteen$$

"Moving on, then, we will turn to Part Four."

Part IV

1. **Subtract step three in Part I, and subtract two-thirds of step one in Part III.**
2. **Multiply by two-thirds of step three in Part I.**
3. **Add step three of Part I.**
4. **Subtract two-thirds of step three in Part I and one-third of step five in Part III.**

Apparently dissatisfied with our progress, she completed this part without asking for the participation of the class.

$$(18 - 15) - (\tfrac{2}{3}\ 3) = 1$$
$$1 \times (\tfrac{2}{3}\ 15) = 10$$
$$10 + 15 = 25$$
$$25 - (\tfrac{2}{3}\ 15) - (\tfrac{1}{3}\ 18) = Nine$$

Yvonne's speed in computing Part Four had an encouraging effect on the Committee. Parts Five and Six were another collaborative effort with general consensus. Yvonne recorded the results as before.

Part V

1. Add the difference between step three in Part I and step one in part III.
2. Subtract step one in Part III doubled .
3. Add one-fifth of step two in Part V and subtract two-thirds of step three in Part I.
4. Multiply by the difference between step one and step two in Part II.

$$9 + (15 - 3) = 21$$
$$21 - (2x3) = 15$$
$$15 + (\tfrac{1}{5}\ 15) - (\tfrac{2}{3}\ 15) = 8$$
$$8 \times (21\text{-}19) = Sixteen$$

Part VI

1. Subtract one-fifth of step four in Part II.
2. Subtract one-half of step four in Part II
3. multiply by half of step four in Part II and add step one in Part IV.
4. Subtract step two in Part IV doubled, and add one-half of step three in Part V.
5. Add the product of step two in Part III and two-thirds of step one in Part III.

$$16 - (\tfrac{1}{5}\ 20) = 12$$
$$12 - (\tfrac{1}{2}\ 20) = 2$$
$$2 \times (\tfrac{1}{2}\ 20) + 1 = 21$$
$$21 - (2 \times 10) + (\tfrac{1}{2}\ 8) = 5$$
$$5 + (5 \times (\tfrac{2}{3}\ 3)) = Fifteen$$

Before starting on the next Part, a bit of confusion was expressed concerning the fact that we were looking at VII (a) and VII (b). Some wondered if it is one part or two. Another asked how we are to record them when complete. Do they have a significance we haven't perceived? That this meant that the puzzle's clues were eleven in number and not ten, seemed to throw off most of us, so conditioned we were to the dominance of the usual pattern. We turned our attention first to VII(a).

Part VII (A)

1. **Subtract the product of one-third of step one in Part II and step two in Part VI.**
2. **Add step three in Part II.**
3. **Subtract one-third of step one in Part II.**
4. **Subtract the sum of one-half of step one in Part VI and step one in Part VII (a)**

Yvonne stayed out of the discussion, for a reason we did not know until we had complete both (a) and (b). She just started with the first step of Seven (a). This time we were confident enough to complete the formulae without her assistance. Her dance movements approached performance level, so evidently absorbing her that she paid no attention to us. When we were finished she just nodded her approval and transcribed the formulae as we dictated them to her.

$$15 - ((\tfrac{1}{3}\ 21) \times 2) = 1$$
$$1 + 19 = 20$$
$$20 - (\tfrac{1}{3}\ 21) = 13$$
$$13 - (\tfrac{1}{2}\ 12 + 1) = Six$$

Maintaining her silence, we moved on to Part VII(b).

Part VII (B)

1. Subtract the difference between step three in Part VII(a) and step one in Part VI.
2. Subtract the difference between step two in Part IV and step four in Part I.
3. Add step one in Part II.
4. Subtract the sum of step two in Part IV and step two in Part I.

She nodded with approval as we dictated our results to her.

$$6 - (13 - 12) = 5$$
$$5 - (10 - 9) = 4$$
$$4 + 21 = 25$$
$$25 - (10 + 9) = Six$$

Norma Weiss was quite calm through this exhibition of Yvonne's gifts and talents. I expected to catch her looking on at this remarkable show with pride. But what I saw was a much finer human emotion than pride: affection. She was much less impressed by our amazement at Yvonne and how a ten-year-old had transformed a committee of well-published and distinguished academics into a fifth-grade class, than by the experience it manifestly was for her pupil. That the child was flying was a thrill; that she took us with her was merely incidental. I recalled Sartre's apt remark that pride and shame are paired opposites, both to be avoided since they are focused on our assumptions about to how "the other" views what we are doing, rather than on what we are actually doing. Weiss was a woman incapable of shame, and remarkably free of its companion, pride. She loved this child.

Yvonne was now standing facing us with an animated gaze and holding her hands out in a gesture that said, What are you waiting for? Do you still need a teacher? Why have I been wasting my time here? We caught on and without further prompting finished out Parts VIII, IX, and X.

Part VIII

1. **Multiply by the difference between step two in Part V and step three in Part VII(a).**
2. **Divide by one-third of step five in Part III.**
3. **Add half of step four in Part VII(b).**
4. **Multiply by the square root of step four in Part V.**

$$6 \times (15 - 13) = 12$$
$$12 \div (\tfrac{1}{3} / 18) = 2$$
$$2 + (\tfrac{1}{2} \, 6) = 5$$
$$5 \times \sqrt{16} = Twenty$$

Part IX

1. **Add one-fifth of step three in Part I.**
2. **Subtract the sum of step two in Part IV and step four in Part I.**
3. **Add the sum of step three in Part I and step two in Part VI.**
4. **Subtract half of step three in Part II.**
5. **Subtract the difference between step three in Part VI and step one in Part V.**

$$20 + (\tfrac{1}{5} \, 15) = 23$$
$$23 - (10 + 9) = 4$$
$$4 + (15 + 2) = 21$$
$$21 - (\tfrac{1}{3} \, 21) = 14$$
$$14 - (21 - 21) = Fourteen$$

Part X

1. Add the difference between step one in Part III and step two in Part vi.
2. Add the difference between one-third of step two in Part I and step one in Part III.
3. Subtract step two in Part IV.
4. Add three quarters of step two in Part IV doubled.

$$14 + (3 - 2) = 15$$
$$15 + (\tfrac{1}{3} \, 9) - 3 = 15$$
$$15 - 10 = 5$$
$$5 + (\tfrac{3}{4} \, (10 \times 2)) = Twenty$$

Without our quite noticing it, as Yvonne recorded the solutions to each step she had lined them all up — forty-three in all — into tidy columns stressing the final number in each Part.

Part One	Part Four	Part VII(a)	Part Nine
26	1	1	*23*
9	10	20	*4*
15	25	13	*21*
Nine	*Nine*	*Sixteen*	*14*
			Fourteen
Part Two	**Part Five**	**Part VII(b)**	
21	21	5	**Part Ten**
19	15	4	15
19	8	25	15
Twenty	*Sixteen*	6	5
			Twenty
Part Three	**Part Six**	**Part Eight**	
3	12	12	
5	2	2	
14	21	5	
19	5	*Twenty*	
Eighteen	*Fifteen*		

For a full minute no one spoke, stupefied by the surfeit of numbers and no indication as to what they might mean.

"Now what?" Marguerite asked, appearing to direct her question to Yvonne, who was making motions of preparing to leave, having completed her work.

"Now what?" the child repeated.

"What are we to do with all these numbers?"

Yvonne bent down and looked straight into Marguerite's face. "Well?" she asked, as if talking to a puzzled child. "What is the largest number in the puzzle?"

Someone said twenty-five, others twenty-six.

"Twenty-six," Yvonne said. "Well?" She opened her hands as if there were an obvious answer. "Well?" she said again, repeating the gesture.

Chernovsky answered first, though with some hesitation. "Letters of the alphabet, yes?"

"Yes, yes. That's good."

"Yvonne, I think we had better go." Ms Weiss spoke gently from where she was sitting in the corner. "The professors can now do the rest of their work. We have three buses to catch."

"I'm giving you cab money. Follow me." Iolinda reminded her.

"Maybe we can get back in time for Assembly, Ms. Weiss."

Then they were gone.

SIXTY-THREE

The spell of the child's presence did not depart with them.

"Wow," Marguerite said in a quiet voice.

"So," Alfie said after a measured delay, "these numbers represent letters. Can't get simpler than that."

"Child's play when you think about it. I wasn't going to say that to her and pop the child's balloon," yawned Armand.

"Nobody more gallant to little girls than you, Chernovsky," Gupta said with a smile that could be either affection or derision.

"The numbers and letters correspond," he said, ignoring her. "What is more fifth grade than that?"

"Let's get on with it, people," Alfie said. "A is one and twenty-six is Z." Nods all around. We scratched out the letters in their order. "We all know this is supposed to spell something," Percival mused out loud. "But where do we start?"

I suggested that since the murderer broke the letters into parts, he probably wants us to look at them in parts. "Each part seems self-contained, as if it is arranged to produce a single number."

"Possibly, and possibly not," Bobo Winston said, "but at least each final number is stressed. So, give that a shot. Make a list of the last number in each part."

I went back to the whiteboard.

I T R I P O F F T N T

"I trip off TNT?"

"It's an elegant ruse." Samantha said. "Has to be an anagram like so many others we've seen."

"Not so fast," Bobo responded. "The TNT is quite suggestive."

Part One	Part Four	Part VII(a)	Part Nine
26—Z	1—A	1—A	23—W
9—I	10—J	20—T	4—D
15—O	25—Y	13—M	21—U
Nine—I	Nine—I	Six—F	14—N
			Fourteen—N
Part Two	**Part Five**	**Part VII(b)**	
21—U	21—U	5—E	**Part Ten**
19—S	15—O	4—D	15—O
19—S	8—H	25—Y	15—O
Twenty—T	Sixteen—P	Six—F	5—E
			Twenty—T
Part Three	**Part Six**	**Part Eight**	
3—C	12—L	12—L	
5—E	2—B	2—B	
14—N	21—U	5—E	
19—S	5—E	Twenty—T	
Eighteen—R	Fifteen—O		
		Part Nine	
		W	
		D	
		U	
		N	
		N	
		Part Ten	
		O	
		O	
		E	
		T	

"As a murder weapon?"

"Why not?"

"I see the word, 'print,' in those letters," Samantha Gupta said with considerable energy. "What does that leave us? O F F and a second T. And a second N."

"And an I."

"And another I."

"Right. So that's O F F T I I."

"Okay, we've got OFF, OF, and FIT."

"Let's keep in mind that Seven (a) and Seven (b) are both F's. Could be an elision," Alfie said. "You know, the Double Letter Rule." He looked around the table but no one was smiling.

"So, just one F?"

"Then I see FIT and TO."

"FIT TO PRINT!"

"Fit to print what?"

"All the news!" Alfie all but yelled. "'All the news fit to print!' "

"Jesus, Carmody, isn't that reporter you keep talking to, the one we didn't want coming to the Committee, isn't she from *The Times*?"

"But she can't be the next victim; she's not connected to the University in any way. Not faculty. Not admin."

"She claimed she's an alumna." I offered.

"Oh, Christ. Media field day."

"Call *The Times*."

"I'll call my nephew ." Bobo said. " He's an assistant to the assistant at the Book Review."

We sat in silence while Bobo made the call from Iolinda's phone. He was back in less than a minute.

"Elle n'existe pas," was all he said.

A long sigh from Alfie. "Perfect. Now the dead man's a dead woman."

"I say she is the murderer," Armand pronounced with a kind of growl.

Or, what if she's not the murderer but she's about to finger the murderer?

SIXTY-FOUR

The mystery wasn't solved, but it was given an odd spin, when a day later my attention was drawn to a headline on the cover of one of the tabloids: CABBY COPS CORPSE. I would probably not have noticed if Deborah's disappearance hadn't been on my mind. The story, on page four, ran as follows:

> *Longtime residents of the Murray Hill section of Queens, Margo Lissak and Evelynn O'Mara, had the surprise of a lifetime as they sat talking on the steps of Lissak's home on 32nd Avenue near 154th Street. A yellow taxi stopped to a screeching halt halfway down the block. As they watched, the cabby was seen leaping from the car, coming around to the back door on the opposite side.*
>
> *According to their description, the cabby grabbed a young woman and pulled her out of the vehicle and on to the sidewalk. As she lay there, motionless, the cabby began screaming at her in a foreign language. When he caught sight of the two friends, he explained to them in rough words that the woman was drunk. "The [expletive] woman owes me thirty-three seventy-five fare from Manhattan."*
>
> *According to the two witnesses, the woman's purse fell onto the sidewalk*

with her. When he could not get her to respond, the cabby grabbed the woman's wallet from the purse and held it up to show the two friends still seated on the steps of the Lissak home. "He must have wanted us to know he's going to get paid, no matter what," O'Mara explained.

As the cabby was climbing back into his car, he said only, "Thirty-three seventy-five. Without tip," and drove off, with the wallet.

Lissak and O'Mara went to the aid of the young woman and found that they could not rouse her. They called 911 on O'Mara's cell phone.

Officer Marco Villenueva arrived shortly thereafter and determined that the woman was deceased. The woman's wallet was missing, but the officer found a gun in her purse. It was a Smith and Wesson .38 Magnum revolver, Villenueva said. "And fully loaded," he added.

The responding EMT's determined no immediate cause of death. Because her wallet was missing, the identity of the woman remains unknown.

There was no reason to think this scene nineteen miles uptown from our idyllic campus had anything to do with Deborah Waterson. Why would a reporter, after all, carry a gun? And yet the corpse's missing identity made one wonder. Even in death, our journalist/alumna/victim could not be named.

The reaction of University and the media to her disappearance was, well, no reaction. No one made a connection between the cabby's action in Queens and the pseudo-Times-reporter. Her disappearance had not been referred to once by the media. In fact, apart from my several contacts with her and her badgering several members of the Committee for nibbles of inside info, she was essentially an unknown.

What we cannot overlook, however, is that this apparent nonperson was not a nonperson for the Puzzler.

SPRING BREAK
SECOND SEMESTER

SIXTY-FIVE

The high drama of the Puzzler's brutal march through the stunned and hapless University had so focused the community that most of us were unprepared for a certain media-rich intrusion of the outside world. It came in the bumptious form of the national presidential campaign. It was with surprise and even a sense of relief to find one morning that the Square had been lavishly decorated with large poster announcements that two days hence no one less than Senator Bernie Sanders himself would appear with his entourage.

Although the students and citizens in this famous liberal neighborhood of the city could quote the Sanders stump speech word for word, he was bound to arouse the expected horde to near-riot enthusiasm.

The horde was greater than expected. Hours before the gentleman climbed the few steps to a wobbling platform, his splendid silver mop flashing in the morning breeze, the Square was populated end to end with breathless admirers. Thousands of students were among them — but then the greater half of the crowd seemed the age of undergraduates.

Assailing the banks, casting shame on corporate welfare, daring Israel to deal justly with their subject people, promising a respectable minimum wage, and guaranteeing universal health care — all of this was met with such predictable roaring, it seemed almost scripted. When the Senator proposed free tuition for students at every level, the explosive response could be heard avenues away.

Throughout the entire performance, waves of chanting swept through what was quickly becoming a mob. News photographers shoved their way into the mass to get shots of youths wearing politically symbolic clothing and punching the air with homemade signs. Young woman, many with half their faces painted in the campaign's official color, blue, were especially willing camera subjects.

Then he was gone, and with him the media, the procession of limos, and the cheering crowd. Within an hour, the street barriers, even the posters and campaign trash, had been magically removed. Like a severe summer shower, there had been a noisy entrance, a display of electric exuberance, then a sudden exit, leaving no trace of itself beyond a few dark puddles. Some later swore that the Senator's thrilling summons to action ended with the fountain suddenly shooting upward as a kind of aqueous exclamation point. The fountain, however, was still in its winter shut-down.

SIXTY-SIX

"Professor Carmody." Iolinda was at the door as I put my key in the lock.

"Good morning, Iolinda."

She said nothing, but handed me a sheet of paper she had obviously just printed out.

PUZZLE # 8

1. IN THE BEGINNING WAS GOD. WHAT IS THE BEGINNING OF GOD?

2. PRONOUNCE AN END WITHOUT THE END OF END.

3. THAT A IS MISSING AN ITCH.

4. UMM. WHICH LETTER COMES FIRST?

5. YOU GO NORTH A BIT, CIRCLE WEST, COME AROUND TO THE SOUTH UNTIL YOU ARE HEADED EAST, THEN CURVE SOUTH AGAIN, WEST AGAIN, THEN NORTH A BIT.

6. TRY ENCLOSING WITHOUT CLOSING.

7. AN ARTICLE THAT IS ALWAYS FOUND IN GRAFT.

8. WHAT REMAINS WHEN A GENTLEMAN REMOVES A HAT?

9. WHAT RECURS IN KAFKA IS NOT ONLY A.

10. WHAT IS ADDED TO KAFKA WHEN KAFKA IS ADDED TO KAFKA?

I went over it twice. It was the easiest challenge that we had faced to date. Or perhaps I had had too much practice by now. Or perhaps the Puzzler was running out of ingenuity. In any case, The Committee's ego would be boosted by the latest puzzle. A few simple twists of thought and the answers fall in your lap. I had to remind myself that even if the puzzle's answers could be quickly shaken out, the result would still have to be interpreted. In fact, the Committee's failure to stay ahead of the Puzzler was not that we were unable to solve the clues, but that we were slow in discerning their deeper meaning. First the solution, then the solution to the solution.

SIXTY-SEVEN

The phone rang. I picked it up expecting someone from the Committee about our schedule.

"Professor?"

"Yes."

"T. Tommy Spevak here." This was said as though any idiot would know immediately who he was.

"Yes?"

"I am Founder and Chair of Rock 'n Feather Films. Like the rest of the world, Professor, I have been following with keen interest the occurrences happening on your campus."

"Good to know of your concern." I could just as well have used the term, amusement.

"I understand you are the chief investigator here."

"There is no chief. Everyone is deeply committed to finding the mite. Of course, it would have to be edited. My personal favorite is the computer scientist who drowns in his own sprinkler system."

"Mr Spevak, I …"

"First we go to the President of some college, get them all lathered up, and guarantee we will goose up the endowment. Student enrollment? Shit, with an audience big as that? Excuse my diction. But it's hard to be well spoken when you're as excited as we are out here in LA."

"All we want to do is close down this dreadful series of murders. This is no TV series. The reality for us out here is actually real."

"Prof, I left out the most important part. We've been talking out here with a lot of money types — and all agree you're the perfect host. I know you college types are paid okay, but this is better than okay. We're talking actual bucks here. You know, seven pointers. Ha ha. Right now I'll throw in a Jag as a signing bonus. Whadda ya say?"

"Where did you get the idea I could host a TV program? I don't even own a TV set."

"Hey, we've seen you on interviews. We've put together a reel on you You look fabulous on screen, Prof. A natural."

"I have work to do, Mr. Spevak. I am anxious to return to it."

"To what? Beowulf? You're anxious to get back to the Ancient Mariner? You don't get it yet, do ya Prof, but you are hooked. You have tasted the golden rush of the media. Footnotes won't lead you to nirvana anymore. PhDs aren't getting you high anymore. It's like PhDeath."

"As I said, Mr Spevak, I have work to do. Thanks for your interest."

SIXTY-EIGHT

Iolinda stood in the doorway. "While you were on the phone, President Lister called three times. 'Tell Professor Carmody to open his email pronto.'" She gave me a wide-eyed look, shrugged, and left.

I opened my email. The first page was blank but for the following letters, printed at maximum font size (72):

FYEO

For my eyes only? On the next page was a communication sent to Jack by Admiral Josephus Edmund Bainbridge (Ret.), under the logo of the Arctic Foundation for a Free America. I paused before reading it, quite sure the news was woeful, or worse. There was an introductory remark by the Director, Admiral Josephus Edmund Bainbridge (Ret.) himself, expressing his regret at having to pass on the information detailed in the attachment, — an article, he said, **"from the Nome Nugget."** He added, **"the Nugget is Alaska's oldest newspaper,"** as **though this distinction would add gravitas to the attached. "I will wait for instructions concerning the disposition of Professor Gold's remains."**

I clicked on the attachment.

PROFESSOR FOUND FROZEN NEAR DENALI

Ten days ago two native hunters from the Athabaskan village of Omarquit came across a mound of snow that had a familiar shape in a most unlikely place. Al Skybear and Leroy Freeshooter, making their annual winter hunt by snowmobile some 200 miles north of Nome, perceived what they recognized as a snow covered car.

Sweeping away several feet of snow, they found a late model Land Rover. When they opened the door on the driver's side, they discovered a man they guessed to be in his forties, seated upright, eyes aimed directly ahead, both hands fixed on the steering wheel.

They removed the body only to find that it was frozen into a sitting position. At twenty degrees below zero the limbs of a corpse cannot be straightened without breaking them off. They secured the body to the front of their sled, already loaded with caribou carcasses.

On their return to Omarquit, they notified the authorities. Finding the car rental contract in his pocket the police identified the deceased as Professor Leonard Gold of the Arctic Foundation for a Free America, based in Wasilla AK.

The Coroner of the municipality of Nome found no grounds for initiating a criminal investigation. In his opinion the cause of death was severe hypothermia.

Carmody, Jack wrote on the next page, you and I are the only ones in the lower forty-eight privy to this (oh, so tragic) news. I wrote to the Admiral that since Leonard Gold was an avid environmentalist, there could be nothing more appropriate than to dispose of his carbonized remains in the Spring salmon run (now underway), and many thanks for caring, blah, blah, blah.

(I left out my gratitude for the image of the two Athabaskans arriving at their village with the frozen corpse of the Professor of Political Economy riding the front of their sled like a giant hood ornament.)

So now, as our distinguished Rhetorician your only remaining duty is to hit that black oblong plastic button at the upper right hand corner of your keypad with the little white letters saying DELETE. We leave Lenny in the Arctic and get on with more important business.

I knew what business he had in mind. I sent Leonard Gold to TRASH.

SIXTY-NINE

That it was already Spring came as something of a shock. The thin patches of grass edging the walks in the Square were ablaze with daffodils and even some lilies of the valley. Shrubs, without character most of the year, showed themselves to be azaleas and flowering Trivet. One rather ordinary tree was shockingly unfolding its lavender tulip-like blossoms. The air was thick with Frisbees and a dozen indifferently tuned guitars.

Just as the fifth-grader Yvonne had instructed, all of the Committee members had flattened out the puzzles on their desks in preparation for the discussion. Samantha Gupta, as if she had been assigned the role, began.

"Carmody, we have been talking and have come to a decision. To say it straight out, the University, the media, the police, and the public have all exploited us, and we have had enough of it. None of us ever asked to be the final word on these goddamned puzzles, and now we have been held responsible for the failures to prevent the murders. We find ourselves blamed for not being able to do what no one else was able to do."

"And?" I asked.

It was Armand Chernovsky who announced in his definitive stentorian mode, "We quit."

"All of you?" I looked at each member. No one spoke. Several had pushed back their chairs. But there was a pregnant silence. If there had been a decision, there was also indecision. I glanced at Alfie. His expression looked to be somewhere between indifference and impatience.

"It has been merciless, I agree. As the Chair do I feel the public's unjustified outbursts of scorn any less? At whom do they point for the failure of a committee of distinguished faculty, all full professors, to solve even one of the crimes in advance of its announced enactment? They point at me, and by implication you. But we are merely a convenient scapegoat. We were only ten members, now nine; the aggregate contributors to the process numbered in the thousands. Among those thousands we must include the police, the military with their sizable resources, as well as those of the country's intelligence services. Colleagues from the Sorbonne and Oxford have likewise failed. Seven Nobel laureates have submitted suggestions. They have failed no less than have we."

"You've got a point," O'Malley conceded in a low voice.

"The only failure we can absolutely control," I went on, "is the failure to persevere."

Bobo said: "Well, as we're all here, we might as well give it one more shot."

The senior faculty sheepishly took their seats. There was some uncomfortable shifting on chairs.

"Okay," Harvey Rilling said. "Clue number one's obvious in my opinion."

We all looked down at the document.

In a voice of exaggerated indifference he read, "**In the beginning was God, but what is the beginning of god?**"

"And…?" I looked over at him.

"I get a G," he said, without explanation.

"I don't see it," Samantha Gupta declared in a challenging tone.

"Simple." Rilling's reply sounded as if Gupta were in a third grade class in arithmetic. "The first God is capitalized and second isn't."

"So?"

"The first," he said, the energy rising in his voice, "is a name and the second is a noun. We are not asked what begins a person, but what begins a word."

He stopped until he was sure that she got it, signaled by little more than a movement in one eyebrow. I went to the board.

G

"This discussion is useless." Chernovsky jumped back in. "We should just leave. I've had enough."

Several members of the Committee began to close brief cases and reach around for their coats.

"What was the other clue, Harvey," I asked, "that seemed to have a similar answer?"

He took a deep breath. "Maybe number three:"

"What's the letter?"

He glanced down at the puzzle. It seemed for a moment he was about to read the entire clue. Then he went silent.

"You mean," I asked, "the one that goes **That A deserves to have an itch.**

"Yeah. That one."

"What do you get from it?"

No one moved. They seemed to be listening.

"Well, the logic of this question seems to be that there is something the letter A doesn't have, but should have."

"How can a letter have an **itch** anyway?" Bobo Winston apparently saw nothing applicant to queer theory here. "Nonsensical."

"I've got it," said Nkwame Smith in a firm voice. "Simple. If an **A is missing an itch,** well, give it one. Combine **A** with **itch** and what do you get?"

Several said at the same time, "Aitch," without much emphasis.

"There you are," Nkwame said. "**H**" There was some groaning, as if a lame joke had just been offered, but there was no objection when I wrote **H** on the board.

I then resorted to a teacher's old manipulative trick. "Do any of you see a clue that could not have a single letter for a solution?" I waited. There were no annoyed expressions. Several shrugged. As I might have predicted, it was O'Malley who first responded.

"Nah. You got us there, Carmody. Seems there all the same on that score."

Several now put their puzzles back in place and gave the list a casual sweep.

"Not number nine," protested Bobo Winston. He read it out loud with just a touch of scorn. **What recurs in Kafka is not only a.** This troglodyte can't even write a sentence. A, a, a what? Are we supposed to translate back to the German? Ach, ach."

"Pretty clever, I have to say," rejoined Marguerite Gardolini. "My German ain't that good, but, if I recall my freshman class, you don't pronounce the German A with an Ach. An A's an 'Ah,' nicht wahr?"

"People, people." Alfie again. "Read the sentence in either language! The letter A is not the only letter that recurs in Kafka."

This was greeted a silence that suggested embarrassment. No one objected when I posted a **K.**

"How about the next clue?" Bobo growled.

"Same trick, guys," Alfie said. "Do I need to read it back to you?" No one reacted. He read it anyway. "**What is added to Kafka when Kafka is added to Kafka?** When you add one Kafka to another just how many Kafkas do you end up with?" He nodded at me to add the letter. I wrote an **S** to the **G, H,** and **K.**

"Okay, I got the second," Gupta said. "Take the d off end and you get the letters e and n, pronounced together: **N.**"

"I get **U** for four." Harvey said, speaking over Samantha, and pinning his index finger on **Umm. Which letter comes first?**

There was a building energy. Armand Chernovsky was back in his seat.

"**Enclosing without closing?** Easy. Another **N**," Samantha declared as if it were a contest. Several hands went up.

"**What** without **hat** is **W**," Winston all but shouted.

I dared a compliment. "Great." And went to the board, adding **N, U, N, W.**

"Two more." A shameless taunt.

"An **article** in **graft**," several mumbled, their attention fixed. They got the answer in a single voice. "**A**." "Another **A**."

Some of them were studying clue five, tracing its directions in the air or scratching it out with a pen. Percival Calkins seemed to be ahead of the others.

"Percy." I handed him the marker and backed away from the board. He looked confused for a moment, then shrugged and stood near where I had recorded the four previous words. Repeating the directions *sotto voce*, he finished the design and stood back. He rubbed it away and rewrote it to fit with the other letters.

That was all that was needed. A half dozen **S**'s were called out. I completed the list.

G   N   H   U   S   N   A   W   K   S

It was generally assumed that we had another anagram. After a few moments, suggestions started coming in.

"I see 'hawks.'"

"'Gnus.'"

"We also got 'Guns.'"

"How about 'gnus n hawks'? Or, 'guns n hawks?' That's got them all covered."

"But does it mean anything?"

They continued, mostly talking to themselves. "Husks." "Shank." I recorded them in a hasty list as soon as they were yelled out, omitting plurals where redundant in meaning.

HUSK / SHANK / HAWK / GNU / GUN / SWUNG / SWAN / ASS / WUSS / GUSH / HUNK / NU / WAN / SKAG / HUSH / WAS / SHUN / HANK / SAW / HUN / GAWK / NUN

Percival Calkins was the most enthusiastic contributor in this exercise. The tally of his words came roughly to half of all those suggested. He was drawing glances. I remembered that he was known to be an uncompromising advocate of the linguistic school of modern philosophy.

WASH / AUK / GASH / WHA / SKA / SHAG / HAG / UN

No doubt there were more words out to be drawn out from these letters, but we were making no progress toward solving the puzzle. There was, I reminded them, a life at stake.

Alfie O'Malley, brushing away the linguistic sideshow, restored a touch of reality to the discussion. "It's not what we find **in** that collection of letters, it's what we do with all of them at once. There's got to be a word that's got all ten letters, or a combination that catches them all."

The mood in the room shifted into grim reality

"Gunks," O'Malley said, looking at the ceiling and spinning his glasses. "Why is that familiar?"

"Well," Rilling joined in, "that's not much help, since that leaves, what? Wash, maybe. Shaw? But there's an N missing. Wash, Gunks, N. That says nothing."

"Shawn," several whispered. "Gunks shawn."

Marguerite Gardolini almost leapt from her chair. "Shawngunks," she said in a loud voice. "Shawngunks. Isn't that where people go to do rock-climbing? Somewhere up-state?"

"Raimundo Guttierez," I said, slamming my hand on the table. "Why did it take us so long to get to him?"

"What about Raimundo Guttierez?"

"He's our avid climber. Has anyone see him recently?"

I charged out and down the hall to his office where the door was closed and there was no reply to my knocks and calls.

SEVENTY

Iolinda tracked down the number of the National Park Service up-state. When I asked for the Ranger station closest to the Shawngunks, I was informed that because this was private land nothing there is a responsibility of the Park Service. I asked, given the life or death circumstances, whether it might be possible to make a special exception. The operator, apparently located in Washington, expressed sympathy and politely declined. The local police sergeant explained that they were severely undermanned and searching an area that large was quite beyond their capacity, especially when we had no definitive proof that in fact there had been an accident.

"For all you know, your friend's shacked up with a graduate student in Hoboken. We can't call out the helicopters, Professor, without some evidence. No one has reported an unattended car in the lots, or on the roadsides. If anyone had actually found a body, we would already know about it. Just because he climbs in the area doesn't mean he's in the area."

"But all signs point to your region."

"I'm sorry, Professor, but we do not accept crossword puzzles dreamed up by college students as evidence."

Suddenly another voice came on the line. "Do you realize," the voice said, identifying itself as that of the police captain, "that the Gunks are one hundred and fifty miles long, from the Delaware River to the Hudson? Do you realize that there are twelve hundred climbing trails on those goddamn cliffs? "

I called Lister and reported on Guttierez' disappearance and our suspicions. When I told him about the lack of cooperation of all government agencies near the mountains, I could almost hear him chewing on his Mont Blanc until he replied:

"I'll take it from here, Carmody. By the time I'm done with him, that police captain will be twisting in the wind in his Cub Scout uniform five thousand feet up."

The next day I found in my email inbox a copy of Lister's memo to the State Ranger Station. It was a predictable burst of verbal assaults, with a generous use of profanity, on the incompetence and irrelevance of the entire organization from the Department of the Interior down. Attached to the memo was a copy of the reply from the state office:

"Dear President Lister: We are grateful to know of your concern re the policies of this important national service. As an expression of our gratitude, I am sending under separate cover 100 feet of the highest quality nylon climbing rope and a karabiner made of the finest steel. Our instruction is that you find a heavy, preferably immovable object in your office — a solid desk would do — wrap the rope around it twice and firmly secure it with either a double half-hitch or bowline. Remove your

trousers. Fold them carefully on the desk. Take a position on the sill of an open window closest to the desk; drop your underwear, making sure they completely cover your shoes. You will notice that the karabiner has a strong wire gate, sharpened at one end. Thread the gate through the scrotum, staying free of each testicle, snap the karabiner shut, and when ready, carefully dive backwards in a way that makes sure that the rope is not tangled elsewhere in the body. Flapping your arms in a flying motion is recommended. Sincerely yours, Sgt. Bruce MacAfee."

Attached to this memo, was Jack's addressed to me: "Carmody, do you realize that this fucking asshole sounds exactly like the Puzzler? Are you listening, Carmody? Exactly like the Puzzler!"

Apparently it did not occur to Jack that a body falling from this height — ten times that of Dean Ridley's office — could be quite dismembered and spread widely in the pockets and crevasses of the stone face of the cliff. Nor would he, a life-long suburbanite, understand that natural settings this remote are inhabited by creatures who spend their days and nights driven only by hunger.

Rock climbing in the nude is not unheard of but it is admittedly rare. Nonetheless, because no clothes were found, the consensus among the professional and inveterate hikers and climbers familiar with the area was that either the missing gentleman had in fact been unclothed or had disappeared somewhere else. Those of us who have been involved in getting ahead of the Puzzler — that is, members of the Committee and the many thousands of the informed public — are convinced that Raimundo Guttierez did not disappear. He was *disappeared.*

COMMENCEMENT

SEVENTY-ONE

Commencement occurred that spring on a cloudless but strangely humid day. The sun was making small ovens of our black robes. Many doctoral hoods came off before the commencement speaker was finished addressing the inattentive and miserable thousands of degree winners and their parents. The fountain at the center of the Square was mobbed by splashing and screaming graduates, some in advanced stages of undress, all of which made for precious media footage.

In a feat of engineering and architectural skill, an ostentatious dais was erected overnight at the center of the Square, facing the fountain. Resembling a vast Bedouin tent, an expanse of canvas covered the elevated platform where the theatre of degree-granting and speech-giving would fill the scheduled two hours allowed by the city for the event. Facing this creaking edifice were thousands of folding chairs arrayed in a vast semicircle, extending to the surrounding streets in three directions.

Not a person present was unmindful of the possibility that the arrangement made the participants — the students, their parents, the faculty, and honored guests — vulnerable to attack by the killer. It was well known, of course, that because it was close to the end of the month, the time had come for the Puzzler's penultimate strike, the ninth of the expected ten. The wide coverage of the previous eight murders over the academic year guaranteed an especially enlivened and attuned audience.

The size of the crowd so exceeded the anticipated number that the seating area was filled three hours before the event. The sidewalks and streets around the Square were overrun with members of the curious public and those guests unable to get one of the seven thousand tickets distributed through the universities and colleges. Given the charged atmosphere, hawkers and concessionaires had sold out of souvenirs, cold drinks and seat cushions well before the trumpet voluntary that traditionally opens the ceremony.

The FBI agents were in theory invisible but their buttoned drip-dry summer suits, buzz cuts, wrap-around sunglasses, and healthy jogger's glow were all but neon advertisements. What a *coup de theatre* the killer would execute if he could use the commencement stage for his next spectacle.

Lister had been urged by the police to move the exercise inside, but he would not relent: "The day we move the Commencement inside is the day we concede control of the University to the Puzzler. Surrender the public square and we surrender our integrity. That won't happen as long as I'm at the helm of this institution."

Directly behind the raised dais was a seating area for all the celebrants including the University Professors. My seat, properly labeled, was two rows directly behind President Lister. It is a traditional practice at commencement to project the canvas cover above the entire seating area, but this time it was noticeably extended, a protective measure, I assumed, making it more difficult for a sniper to locate his victim from the higher perspectives of the buildings surrounding the Square.

Things were not, in fact, running smoothly. An organizational entropy extended through the entire scene. Student ushers ran from place to place with armloads of folding chairs because the numbered areas had been set up improperly. The musicians were changing locations to open areas where they could actually see the conductor at the foot of the stage. The stage itself was erected at a slightly strange angle, causing the precarious overlapping of floor boards.

The faculty was lined up around a corner of the Square waiting for a signal from someone, anyone, to initiate their solemn march to their seating area which was now filling up with parents unable to find their own places. Many of those places were already taken by somber looking ladies and gentlemen, too old to be students and too young to be parents. About a third of the graduates never seemed to have received their robes and many of those who had were hatless. A hot-dog-and-pretzel cart with a red and yellow awning, broadcasting Zorba like music, had penetrated the center of the Square without being intercepted. With no warning, the fountain shot a column of water a hundred feet into the windy sky, its drifting spray drenching the Schools of Nursing and Dentistry. Someone was not in charge and I knew who it was.

As Jack approached his elevated seat on the dais, I saw him make a visual sweep of the area. His practiced and skillful eye immediately caught what was happening. He paused when he noticed that the seat with Lucille's name prominently attached to the back was unoccupied.

Where was Lucille? She had never missed a commencement if for no other reason than to broadcast her indispensability for the smooth functioning of the year's most consequential event.

Half an hour late the orchestra began to play what seemed like the runner-up entry in a graduate composition competition. As the conductor took a dramatic pause before launching into the next movement, Jack seized the moment and began to speak. "Trustees, Mr. Mayor, distinguished guests, parents and loved ones, let us all give a great hand to the class of two thousand and….." There was an immediate explosion of throaty cheers that easily buried the President's voice. He threw out his arms with a welcoming smile to encourage the roar.

There followed the ritual reading of citations and a bestowal of hoods on a line of aged academic and civic honorees. The first honorary doctorate was bestowed upon a Pulitzer Prize winning poet whom Bobo Winston had nominated. She read a few obscure selections from her collected works, drawing scattered applause. . Then up strode the U.S. senator whom we all knew as a regular on **Meet the Press**. Fully suited under his robe, he was already showing signs of advanced perspiration through the back of that garment, the stain showing on the outsized pseudo-academic hood that Jack had dropped over him minutes earlier.

I was close enough to count the pages of his address — seven and, to my dismay, single-spaced. But, earning the gratitude of thousands, he proved his political skill by deftly removing pages two to six as he proceeded. The language of the dignitary's address was just predictable enough that no one could have guessed that the sentence at the end of the first page dropped a dozen syllables before smoothly gliding on to the middle of page seven and onto a very different subject. The rhetorical segue was worthy of my professorial salute, even my vote.

At the conclusion, the University Professors led the recession off the stage. As I passed Jack, he tugged at the edge of my hood and leaned forward, still smiling broadly to the crowds, but speaking under his breath. "Where the fuck is she?"

The question had an obvious answer and Jack knew it. It was common knowledge that Lucille set her own calendar and it was perfectly reasonable to assume that having made sure all arrangements were in order for commencement — at least those having to do with the College of Liberal Arts — she took one of her legendary leaves, presumably traveling to an undisclosed island or country or even to her own home (which no one, including someone as intimately associated with her as I, had ever seen.) The more interesting question was why Jack himself was so disturbed by her absence, especially since we had survived Commencement without her evident presence.

She was still missing a week later when the ninth puzzle appeared.

person committing these murders. I just happen to chair a University committee, appointed by the President."

"No prob, Prof." He apparently loved using the title. At least he didn't say University Professor. "I got the word on you. They say you are a real pro on these puzzles. You are the chief code cracker. That's what I'm talking about."

"I assure you it's very much a joint effort."

"Sure, sure. I like the modesty. We're gonna keep that. Here's my idea, Prof. You've heard of reality shows."

When I didn't immediately respond he said, "You know, the biggest thing ever on TV. Sponsors through the roof. It's real drama, not something made up."

"Your idea? I'm about to go into a meeting."

"Yeah. It's got to have a real simple title. Like 'Murder on Campus' or 'Death at the Blackboard' or 'The Fatal Degree' or 'Gown and Down.' Or 'Murder as a Liberal Art.'"

"Well, Mr Spevak, I am not ready to advocate the spread of capital crime to other universities."

"Not to worry. We call them 'reality' shows, Prof. There's lots of reality, but nothing's actually real, if you get my drift. We don't actually do any of the murdering of faculty members. We leave that up to the community."

"I hate to disappoint you but it's quite possible there won't be another murder. "

"I like that optimism. But let's say you're even right about that. Still, you've already had some great episodes there. We'll reconstruct them intercut with actual footage. You could get a whole program, a full hour, on each murder. The film of the naked guy in his office with his students and that dancing gay guy, I mean that's box office dyna-

SEVENTY-TWO

PUZZLE #9

1. *IAGO:* THOUGH OTHER THINGS GROW FOUL AGAINST THE SUN,
YET FRUITS THAT BLOSSOM FIRST WILL FIRST BE RIPE.

2. *FALSTAFF :* I WILL STARE HIM OUT OF HIS DULLNESSES;
I WILL AWE HIM WITH MY CUDGEL.

3. *MERCUTIO:* NO 'TIS NOT SO DEEP AS A SEA,
NOR SO WIDE AS A CHURCH DOOR, BUT 'TIS ENOUGH, 'TWILL SERVE.

4. *SONNET:* AH, CHANGE THY THOUGHT, THAT I MAY CHANGE MY MIND:
SHALL HATE BE FAIRER LODG'D THAN GENTLE LOVE?

5. *JULIET:* THY WORDS WOULD BANDY HER TO MY SWEET LOVE,
AND HIS TO ME — BUT OLD FOLKS, MANY FEIGN AS THEY WERE DEAD:
UNWIELDY, SLOW, HEAVY, AND PALE AS LEAD.

6. *NURSE:* O, HE'S AN UNCOMELY GENTLEMAN!
ROMEO'S A DISHELOUT TO HIM.

7. *HAMLET:* I HAVE THOUGHT SOME OF NATURE'S JOURNEYMEN HAD MADE
MEN AND NOT MADE THEM POORLY,
THEY IMITATED HUMANITY SO ABOMINABLY.

8. *DUKE:* REPENT YOU, UNJUST ONE, OF THE SIN YOU CARRY?
JULIETTA: I DO, AND BEAR THE SHAME MOST PATIENTLY.

9. *LADY MACBETH:* AND WHEN GOES DUNCAN HENCE?
MACBETH: TODAY, AS HE PURPOSES.

10. *CHORUS [ROMEO AND JULIET]:* WHAT HERE SHALL HIT
OUR TOIL SHALL STRIVE TO MEND.

A couple quick scans brought up nothing in the way of suggestive patterns, pointed remarks, or conceptual themes. What may at first seem simple — direct quotes from Shakespeare — obviously hides a series of tricks meant to throw us off long enough for the Puzzler to act. I called Bobo Winston at his office in the English Department.

"How are you on the Bard?"

"Hell, it's Cedric Silverstone we want, our leading Bardologist."

"Tell him his next performance is a matinée tomorrow."

SEVENTY-THREE

Professor Silverstone was thoroughly prepared for our session. Before we started, he passed out to each of us a copy of the indicated plays and sonnets: *Romeo and Juliet, Othello, Merry Wives of Windsor, Measure for Measure, Macbeth, Titus Andronicus,* and the *Sonnets,* all individual volumes, from his worn collection of the priceless 1955 Yale University Press edition. We moved our chairs so we could share the separate volumes.

When he saw that we were ready, he dictated to us the title of each play as it occurred in the puzzle, along with the act, scene, and line for the quote. We started at the top, with ***Othello***: **Iago: Though other things grow foul against the sun, yet fruits that blossom first will first be ripe.**

"The third scene of Act Two," Professor Silverstone began, "sets out with alarming intensity Iago's scheme to send Cassio, Othello's lieutenant, to visit Desdemona as though to press a suit of love, or better, lust. It is preceded by one of the most chilling lines in this chilling tragedy. 'I'll pour this pestilence into his ear,' that is, the false sug-gestion that Desdemona, though by an act of kindness, has betrayed him. 'So will I turn her virtue into pitch,' Iago says, 'and out of her own goodness make the net that shall enmesh them all.' He knows the scheme must unfold of its own momentum and is not to be hurried."

Cedric held up the puzzle and read the quoted line with something of an actor's cadence. **"Though other things grow foul against the sun, yet fruits that blossom first will first be ripe."** He put the page down and stared at a distance as if straining at a memory. "No, there is something wrong here. **'Though other things grow foul against the sun… though other things grow foul…grow foul…'** No, read this to me from the text I gave you."

Bobo, also inclined to the stage, read boldly, "Though other things grow fair against…"

"Stop!" Cedric called out as though preventing a dreadful accident. "Foul. Fair. Scandalous! Your Puzzler cannot even accurately copy out a line from Shakespeare. This is an embarrassing slip on his part. So," he said, sounding resigned, "in your copies of the puzzle, cross out 'foul' and enter 'fair.'"

Not knowing exactly what to do with the suggestion, I followed the usual practice and put the word on the board.

FAIR

After a groaning sigh, he ran his finger down the quotes. "Ah, Hamlet, in the seventh line," he said as though he were in need of comfort after that unpleasant moment. He held up the page as before. "I know the passage well." We could have thought we were listening to Hamlet himself. We were riveted.

"I have thought some of nature's journeymen had made men

and not made them poorly, they imitated humanity so abominably."

So commanding was this performance, none of us bothered to follow the text as he spoke. Then the previous expression returned to his face. He whispered the line to himself, concentrating on the words, and repeated them. "Let me see the text," he commanded. I handed him my copy.

He stared at it with a mixture of incredulity and rage. "It's in Act III, scene 2," he announced, "and it's wrong!" He exploded. "It's not 'poorly!'"

This time he stood and held up the book to the proper page but without looking at it he delivered the correct passage in his now more expanded stentorian voice. **"I have thought some of nature's journeymen had made men and not made them well, they imitated humanity so abominably."**

It was not immediately obvious to us what change he had made. When he saw that we were puzzled, he said with some annoyance, "Not **poorly**, but **well**."

I dutifully followed this up by adding the new word.

FAIR

WELL

Soon we were all thumbing through our texts, trying to match the quotes. In moments, Bobo Winston, with his flattened text before him on the table, performed his piece — the passage from **Merry Wives** in the second clue — but with rather less theatrical power than Cedric: "I'm reading from Chapter Two, Scene two, Falstaff speaking: **I will stare him out of his dullnesses; I will awe him with my cudgel.**"

"Yes!" Cedric declaimed. "There's the error. It's not **dullnesses**, but **wits**."

FAIR

WELL

WITS

Alfie then made a typically analytic observation. "You notice that in all three cases, the corrected word is the opposite to the original — or I should say the one falsely inserted. Just look at the words paired: **fair — foul, well — poorly, dullness — wit.**"

"In that case," I proposed, "we could find the altered word in each passage by following the logic of the quote — without even checking the text."

"Go ahead," Alfie said, "you're the rhetorician in the group."

"Well, take the following." I read one of the passages from **Romeo and Juliet,** clue six.

"'O, he's an **uncomely** gentleman! Romeo's a **dishelout** to him.' I assume I am right in reading **dishelout** as **dissolute,** Cedric."

"Precisely."

"Well, in that case, you would not propose an opposing contrast between **dishelout** and **uncomely,** or 'ugly.' The opposite to 'ugly' has to be something like 'comely,' say, or the more common, 'lovely.'"

"It's **'lovely,'**" Marguerite Gardolini said, with her finger on the text.

"Well, that makes four corrections, one in each quote. It makes sense to expect at least one false word in each of the others," I said and went to the board.

FAIR

WELL

WITS

LOVELY

"All right," Alfie said, "let's go to work on the rest. I am drawn to the quote from the Chorus in the opening pages of **Romeo and Juliet. What here shall hit our toil shall strive to mend.** Following Carmody's suggestion, there is something wrong with the logic. How can one "mend" a "hit" with "toil." Indulge me if I read it as it was spoken to the standing audience in the Globe."

No one bothered to interrupt him. He picked up Professor Silverstone's copy.

"What here shall miss our toil shall strive to mend. You know, friends, it's 'hit or miss.'"

"Yes, that's it exactly," Silverstone announced. I added the word.

FARE

WELL

WITS

LOVELY

MISS

"I'll try out Carmody's algorithm," Cedric Silverstone said, "and dig into the eighth clue with lines from **Measure for Measure.** If the Duke's words did not end in a question mark, it makes sense to say, **Repent you, unjust one, of the sin you carry.** But when it is read as a question, the meaning is reversed, as if the Duke is saying, 'Why would you of all people repent, when, in contrast to the others, you alone are **just, or fair?**" A look at the text confirmed Cedric's use of my 'algorithm.'

FAIR

WELL

WITS

LOVELY

MISS

FAIR

The use of this method quickly produced three more corrections. The ninth clue quotes Lady Macbeth: **And when goes [Duncan] hence?** Macbeth answers: **Today, as he purposes.**

"He purposes nothing of the kind," Percy said with a scoffing laugh, looking at his text. "He purposes to go on the **morrow.**"

FAIR

WELL

WITS

LOVELY

MISS

MORROW

The fourth clue, a quote from the Sonnets — **Ah, change thy thought, that I may change my mind: shall hate be fairer lodg'd than gentle love?** — was confusing because it was the first time that a syllable was used in place of the entire word, and because the substitute was not an opposite to the original. It was not **Ah,** but **O.** Without a sufficient explanation, I continued the list.

FAIR

WELL

WITS

LOVELY

MISS

MORROW

O

The fifth clue, a quote from **Romeo and Juliet,** makes no sense on the face of it. Romeo is talking to himself here. He would not have addressed himself as "Thy."? A check of the text led to the correct word: **My.**

This time, I listed the words according to the order of clues.

FAIR

WITS

WELL

O

MY

LOVELY

FAIR

MORROW

MISS

"We're missing a clue," Marguerite announced. "That's only nine words."

"Yes!" Cedric almost jumped from his chair. "Mercutio and his church door. Clue number — three, is it?"

We looked at our copy of the puzzle: **Mercutio: No 'tis not so deep as a sea, nor so wide as a church door, but 'tis enough, 'twill serve.**

Ignoring the printed sheet, Silverstone opened his **Romeo and Juliet** and found the passage at once. He straightened himself and took a breath. **"No 'tis not so deep as a well, nor so wide as a church door, but 'tis enough, 'twill serve."**

"No, Professor," Harvey called out at once, pointing to the puzzle and cautiously daring to correct a senior colleague. "I'm reading, '**sea,**' instead of '**well.**'"

"Aha, that's it then," Silverstone responded. "You've got your word. The playwright would never pair 'sea' and '**church door**' to illustrate a contrast."

"There's a rule for this," Alfie muttered, "the Incomparability Rule." No one laughed. I went to the board and added the indicated word.

WELL

Struck with false confidence by the sequence of **O, My,** and **Lovely,** we thought we were near a conclusion to the puzzle as a whole, especially when Alfie observed that we could read the two occasions of **Fair** phonetically as **Fare**, adding it would then give us what was essentially a complete expression: **Fare well, O my lovely, fare well.**

That left just three simple words to integrate into the sentence: **wits, morrow, and miss.** We all started talking at once, trying a variety of ways of integrating these three words into the other seven. The results were uniformly gibberish.

"I'm sorry, gentlemen," Professor Silverstone announced, with an eye on his watch, "I have no talent for this gibberish. This is for mere word persons, not for anyone serious about the literature." He looked at his watch. "I am due for a PhD oral in fifteen minutes. I should take at least one more glance at the young lady's disaster of a dissertation." He gathered his texts and left.

No sooner did the door close on the august Bardologist than Samantha Gupta jumped to her feet. "Holy shit!" she called out. "Pardon my Dutch, but holy **shit!**"

We waited while she seemed to catch her breath. "Put **miss** and **morrow** and **wits** together and what do we have?"

"Oh, my, god, this is not possible!" Armand barked out.

Several said, speaking over each other, "Morrowitz! Oh, my God. Lucille!"

"Someone check right away," Harvey said as if it were a command. "Who knows her cell?"

"Nobody knows Lucille's cell," said Iolinda.

"I have it. I'll call," said I.

A stunned silence fell over the Committee, as I switched my cell onto speaker. A disembodied voice intoned: "This account holder's answering machine is full. Please try again later."

SEVENTY-FOUR

When I got to Jack's office, he simply stared at me as if he were still trying to fit words to his tumbling thoughts.

"Carmody," he said, grimly, "you knew her better than anyone. I happen to know that. How I know it, none of your business. So tell me, Why her? Why now?"

"If I knew, Jack, believe me, I would be somewhere else."

"I know it seems heartless to be pragmatic at a time like this. But I have more than a Puzzle to crack. I have an institution to nurture."

"Is this a prelude to an unsavory request, Jack? If so, just spit it out."

Jack now leaned in towards me and held me in his gaze not blinking. " I don't want you to think there's anything I wouldn't do to protect Lucille. I've had Tom Roche and his top snoops looking for her since Commencement. But as far as the world knows she's just away. To the outside world, Lucille isn't in danger. She's off on one of her larks. She doesn't report to anybody; isn't answerable to anyone. Mostly we wind up reporting to her."

"I don't see, Jack, how…"

"How does revealing her name now help Lucille? Isn't there some advantage in the Puzzler not knowing we know? "

"In other words, Jack, you want the Committee gagged."

"I wouldn't put it that way, Carmody. I am a great defender of free speech. Look at my record."

"I'm looking at it Jack. How long?"

" Not long. Until the Big Day. Until the Celebration of the American Mind. We're so close, Carmody. We're about to reboot ourselves. I'm not talking about me. I'm talking about this whole crazy family. You're a big part of it. If the tabloids start distracting the public with talk about the possible death of Lucille, were done for."

"Don't you think, Jack, with all due respect, you're exaggerating the difference one celebration could possibly make?"

His mood did a sudden 180°.

"No, Carmody, I do not. Look at these!" He jumped up from his desk and went to a table from which he swept up a handful of papers, and tossed them before me. "Just read. Don't talk. Read!" They were printouts of emails and hand-written notes in a variety of lengths and styles, and languages, all positive replies to Jack's invitation to attend the summer's Main Event, now just two weeks away: *The University at 150: A Celebration of the American Mind.* The senders were triple-A notables of the cultural and intellectual world, or Kultur, as Jack once called it.

"They will call it a real God damn Renaissance!" he announced with child-like glee.

Sure, the Puzzler was still at large, still dangerous, and certain bodies were missing, but the Celebration was where Jack was now directing his prodigious energy. I recalled the charged meeting in his office with the directors of Student Life, the Alumni Office, and Community Relations. "Either we go down in flames," he declared then, "or we soar to greatness. That's our choice, friends: Oblivion. Or glory."

"You're short on industrial and financial might," I ventured after leafing through the acceptances.

"How many fucking public intellectuals you think you can find on the Street? Look, I got Warren Buffett. He's worth twenty of your run-of-the-mill one-percenters."

As he spread press reports, sample posters, bumper stickers, and CD's across his desk, he said, "Catch this. Harry Rosenquist, University trustee, owns theaters on Broadway; he's delivering the latest and best in stage lighting and sound systems. Pete Ostergaard, alumnus, big exec at CNN, he's got the media. I could go on."

Jack was headed for glory. Lucille be damned.

SEVENTY-FIVE

But Lucille didn't stay damned.

The Committee was cool to the idea of delaying the announcement of their results to the police. More than cool. They resented Jack's manipulations, especially after his constant railing at their failure to get ahead of the killer. Finally, we name a victim and we're expected to sit on it. I was at my diplomatic best, staying as far as I could from the term "gag order," which was in fact what I was delivering.

Samantha Gupta, showing more support for my dilemma than I

expected said, "Well, the Big Event could be a pay day for every one of us. The foundation money could start rolling in the next day."

"I'm still waiting to hear from the NEA on two proposals," chimed in Marguerite. "I say humor the guy."

Her appeal won no consenting grumbles, not even a positive nod, but their silence was enough of a concession that I moved to adjourn the meeting.

REGISTRATION
SUMMER SESSION

PhDeath | 292

SEVENTY-SIX

Jack decided to locate the Big Event in the University's largest indoor venue: the library atrium. The first floor, with its handsome pattern of black and white marble, was open to the top of the building — twelve stories above. What Jack saw in this great room was not just an impossibly high ceiling; he saw the perfect theatrical setting for his Grandest Idea. The extravagance of his vision electrified the community out of its lethargy.

The Theater Department in the School of the Arts went to work, making profligate use of theater mogul Harry Rosenquist's abundant provisions. Across the wall at one end of the space, set designers hung a massive lavender-colored curtain from the third floor balcony. The stage, erected at the bottom of the curtain, was wrapped in striped bunting, also in lavender, the University's official color. Several towers of scaffolding, with platforms designed for the sound and lighting technicians, reached into the upper darkness of the great space. Sound booms and crane-like perches for the camera crews crisscrossed several stories above the seating area.

But nothing equaled the eclat of an enormous video screen, provided and installed by the Video and Computer Departments. It extended twenty feet in both directions, and hung behind the stage and the speaker's dais. This was apparently meant to allow for a close-up of each speaker's face as they addressed the crowd. Two monitors were located at each corner of the podium where the speakers could see what the audience was viewing on the large screen. It was the kind of technology one expects at major political events — or the annual stockholders's meeting of large corporations, never at academic gatherings.

A dozen student and alumni committees were at work. Posters were distributed, celebrity acceptances were confirmed, print and visual media were prepped for their roles, press releases appeared in a steady stream, the student-ticket lottery went off without a hitch, proper chairs were rented, seating patterns were laid out, tickets were printed, ushers were trained and fitted with lavender blazers, and an elaborate menu of finger food and spirits was prepared for the concluding reception.

One day while we were going over posters drawn up by the University's marketing department, he suddenly brushed the lot of them off his desk, scattering them half-way across the floor of his office. He sat back, and said, "You know what, Carmody?"

"What?" I looked up at him. If angst has a classical facial image, he was wearing it.

"My neck is getting blisters from the idiots breathing down it."

"Which idiots might those be?"

"You do well to ask, Carmody, because there's quite a selection." He held up his hand, as if to provide a count with his fingers. "One. The alumni. They ain't contributing. Two. The trustees. The bastards haven't been raising money. They're hitting me with a budget shortfall of thirty million. Thirty million! As if this were my doing! As if I'm the fuckin' Puzzler."

"Jack, there's always the endowment."

"Carmody, come on! You know how the game is played. They won't dip into their candy jar for an administration of losers. Those are their nickels to spend, not ours. You know what they're suggesting?"

"Cut backs, no doubt."

"Not cut backs, cut *outs*! Whole departments: like Classics and Arabic Studies. And Philosophy. Slavic Studies."

Jack pulled at another finger. "**Three.** The generals. They're threatening to bring in the CIA, the FBI, the NSA, and for all I know, the OMB, the NIH, and the YWHA."

He bent back his pinkie. "**Four.** The tabloids. Those shits go orgasmic with headlines: *U gets an F; Killer 8, Profs 0; Death Dumbing Down the Docs,* whatever the fuck that means."

He stopped almost mid-sentence and just stared at me with an expression that looked like a plea for help. There was a madness in his eyes. Or maybe it was something else. I stole a look at his fingers. The trembling was noticeable. I immediately thought of the garbanzo beans dancing across Nat Holmers' plate in wild flight from his pursuing fork.

SEVENTY-SEVEN

The University had taken up its preparations in a joyous state of denial. But the same cannot be said for the campus guards, the urban police, and the military. The protective forces were not speculating whether their elusive and infuriating nemesis had backed off into the shadows.

Weeks of deliberation went into deciding where officers, soldiers and guards would be positioned, how they were to be dressed, and camouflaged. Some would mingle in the crowd, trying to look like students and faculty. Local restaurants and coffee shops were alerted that unidentified personnel were to be seated in their establishments where they could overhear conversations. The dormitories were closed to all but enrolled students. Some students went home, but most found ways — staying with friends, sharing hotel rooms and airbnb's — to be close to the drama, especially those who were lucky enough to have their names drawn in the ticket lottery.

It was hard to imagine a crime that would break through this veritable Maginot Line of institutional self-protection.

SEVENTY-EIGHT

Late in the day before the event, I received a sealed envelope from the president. It was delivered by one of his secretaries. Before she put it in my hands, she took pains to show that it was securely glued. Jack had signed his name twice across the area where the flap was attached at the back. "No one knows the content of this envelope except Jack," she explained. "And now you."

She apparently thought I would tear it open at once. I had no such intention.

"What about the members of the Nominating Committee?" I asked.

"Oh," she said, "He asked them to submit ten names. They were not informed which one he chose."

"If, that is, the name was among those they submitted," I volunteered.

She made a one-shoulder shrug. "You know Jack," she said as she left.

I sat at my desk for a few minutes staring at the envelope. When I finally slit it open with the brass blade in my desk, I smiled. I lifted the phone.

"Brilliant," was all I said.

SEVENTY-NINE

The next morning I made my ritual visit to the Café Rossetti, ordered the Americano, and headed toward my customary seat in the corner. It was already occupied by a beefy, fortyish patron who was staring at the headlines of the morning tabloids, spread like a hand of poker cards across his table. The gentleman's presence was surprisingly comforting.

I seated myself at the next table. Before I freed the plastic lid from my coffee container, I scanned **The Times** for a notice of the imminent event. **The Times** editors apparently didn't share Lister's elevated expectation for **The University at 150: A Celebration of the American Mind.** I found only a small piece in the Arts section. No doubt the major story would follow in the morning.

I passed the day in a kind of half-dream state. It was one of those rare occasions where you know that everything had been so meticulously arranged it was as if it had already happened and I was merely floating in its splendid aftermath.

The library atrium was a scene of quiet, professional competence, even serenity. Miles of electric cables were hidden behind the cascades of drapery. The sound engineer tested and retested the electronic equipment. The largest seating area, reaching to the back of the atrium, was reserved for those students who had won the ticket lottery. Some four hundred members of the faculty would be seated on folding chairs directly before the stage. A squarish arrangement of padded chairs, separated from the rest of the audience by a velvet rope, was set aside for the invited celebrities. There was a corresponding area for the press. Police and military would be incognito and interspersed throughout.

"Ah, Professor Carmody, you've come for the walk-through. As

Chair of the Committee, you will be seated here, next to President Lister. He has the big chair behind the podium." She pointed to one of two throne-like pieces of furniture. "The other is for the honoree, our mystery guest. The rest of the stage seating is reserved for the Deans."

"I notice you've kept the center of the room open."

"Yes, the video team likes to get angle shots that include the cool black and white designs in the marble floors."

I made my way through faculty seating to the open center. The atrium was so precisely constructed that if you stood at a certain spot on the marble floor — called by students the "magic square" — your voice would create a repeating echo that could last four to five seconds. I spoke my name. A dozen voices spoke it back to me.

EIGHTY

Returning at 7:30 that evening, I was greeted by a young woman wearing a lavender blazer over an oxford button-down and the school tie. "Professor Carmody! Welcome. I'm your personal usher! You remember me? Jeannie?"

At 7:40 p.m. the giant middle doors of the library swung open. A disciplined cadre of young men and women, dressed in the same lavender blazers, lined up in rows of two, forming a human funnel through which the audience would flow.

The students were the first to be admitted. They had waited for several hours in an orderly queue that spun half-way around the Square. Their exuberant entrance was what one expected at a rock concert or a college basketball championship. They raced for the most advantaged viewing areas on the raised seats in the rear. In five minutes not a vacant spot could be found among them.

7:45 p.m. The faculty, in robes and mortarboards, entered in single file, from a rear entrance to the library. The satin colors of their hoods, incandescent under the stage lights, gave the area the look of an exotic aviary.

7:50. The Traffic Police accompanied the first limousines to the main entrance. The first to be ushered in were University trustees, most of them in black tie.

The ambassadorial invitees made a distinct addition to the theatrical sizzle. A gaunt giant with a carved walking stick and a spray of white feathers woven into his hair led the procession. He was followed by a diminutive Celtic sort nearly hidden under a sash decorated with indecipherable symbols, and a stiff gentleman in a fez. Two African women were so exquisitely and generously covered in bolts of patterned fabric that they seemed to suck all the light from the puny hoods of the awed professors. From among the many others, my eye was most captured by a Papal Legate with what seemed a waxed bald dome, an Emir memorable for his nose, and a red-faced Scot wearing a kilt.

Jeannie indicated it was time for me to be led to my place on the stage. The deans were already seated, five to the left and five to the right of the podium. They were arranged in the order of their college's founding, beginning with Arts and Sciences to my far left. That particular chair was empty, of course, as a sober reminder of the dreadful year now behind us.

The fifty invited celebrities — only two didn't show — provided every bit of the theater Jack had promised the press and the University. As they arrived at the entrance to the library, they greeted each other with ebullient roars and hugs. Just as they were known to the public, they were known even better to each other. A passing citizen could have mistaken them for an extended family discovering favorite relatives long thought dead. The audience had a fine view of this animated group kiss-in through the great glass doors that faced outward on the Square.

But as the social animals they most successfully were, the celebrities knew what was expected of them and spontaneously began to move toward the library, all forty-eight of them, everyone talking, no one listening. The crowd greeted them, as they filed into their designated seating area, with an equivalent enthusiasm. The rock star, Sting, got a standing ovation from the student section. Barbra Streisand, who was rumored to keep an elaborate pied-à-terre nearby elicited a blinding storm of cell phone. But her reception was wildly outclassed by the sudden appearance of Lady Gaga (an alumna) dressed as if she were heading to a costume ball on Mars. For her, there was an eruption of cheering and whooping that challenged the structural integrity of the twelve levels of balconies suspended above the black and white checks in the marble floor.

The faculty, settled into their seating area and to this point sitting with hands folded like the model students they had all been, began to stir. "Isn't that Arianna Huffington?" one was heard to say. "Hello, Harold!" another called out to the professorial icon, Harold Bloom. "Oh, my god," still another gasped, "that can't be …yes! It's Camille Paglia!" "Look, there. I believe that's the spot Ted Kooser." An assistant professor in Economics stepped over the satin rope to get a selfie with the grinning Paul Krugman. A distinguished professor of nutritional science exchanged waves and blown kisses with Michael Pollan.

Bill McKibben, standing alone and staring up into the atrium, was the only celebrity who seemed interested in his surroundings. Jamaica

Kincaid nodded warmly at several friends in the faculty rows. Before taking his seat, Gary Wills traded fist pumps with a handful of young English profs. I recognized Warren Buffett from behind. He was one of those in the small group of the famous unable to separate themselves from Tony Morrison. Henry Kissinger and David Frumm were huddled at the back of the celebrity section talking over each other and staring darkly at the floor. Where was the honoree? Oh, there, listening to Noam Chomsky.

It must be said that not all these luminaries were particular fans of the university or even of The Big Event itself. Some were there because "everyone" would be there. But most attended out of a desire to share in the University's, and thus the city's, deepening sense of loss. It was similar to the grand MTV concerts given after the Tsunami hit Asia. And above all, it was a collective nose-thumbing at the Puzzler whom the Bright and Beautiful People of the World defied ever to strike again.

Just then the president strode through the middle aisle from the back of the library, practically skipping up the three steps up to his place behind the podium. In a J. Press suit, tailored shirt, and a subdued tie, with his height and athlete's carriage, Jack was a commanding presence. The effect was immediate. The celebrities began to look around for their assigned places. Jack waited until they were all settled, then nodded in their direction.

I looked up at the control booth, a large glass cage perilously balanced on the third-floor walkway. Both engineers were trying to get the president's attention and giving spinning finger gestures, the classic speed-up command. He took his damned time and clearly loved doing it. When he finally got to the podium, the video snapped on. Jack's face was on both monitors with a smile that suggested he was greeting himself. The focus was perfect.

EIGHTY-ONE

Before saying a word, Jack held up a square manila-colored envelope where it could be seen from every angle in the atrium, then placed it at the center of the felt surface of the podium next to his signature index card.

Introducing himself by name only, omitting his title, Jack began the ritual ten minutes required at the beginning of every august public event, the part no one later remembers: welcoming those present and the viewing public, thanking contributors, praising planners, and making introductions of the marginally involved. He thanked the deans who had no part in the run-up to the ceremony and who were not consulted on the choice of honoree. He nodded silently at the place not occupied by Oliver Ridley.

The mandatory remarks completed, he looked down at the index card. From where I was sitting I could see that it was covered to the margins with his implausibly cramped hand writing, more than half of it x-ed out. He was pressing down on the card, not, I had to assume, to keep it from flying off, but to hide the trembling of his fingers.

"The goal of **The University at 150: a Ceremony of the American Mind**," he began, his voice steady and convincingly self-assured, "is to begin the healing of our broken and dysfunctional public discourse. There are many who would turn first to a philosopher for this purpose, or a political theorist, an economist, or a scientist. Such worthy figures are distinguished by their mastery of the specialized languages of their fields." Pause. "We looked elsewhere. Our goal was more ambitious. We sought a distinguished public thinker who publishes in none of these fields, not because he has fallen behind them but because he has long been ahead of them. They use language to work their field. We sought persons for whom language is the field they work. To put it as simply as possible, the Deans and I wanted a certain kind of lover, a man or woman in love with language. Another requirement: someone whose voice and whose work are not only well known, but have a welcome place in our most intimate verbal exchanges."

He paused again and looked around the silent, motionless crowd. Lister's theatrical timing was flawless. "Like a Sunday morning conversation around the breakfast table."

A number of heads turned, faces brightened. Some were whispering to their neighbors.

"Because it is language," Jack continued, "and language alone, that separates us from the beasts, we have named someone who has elevated not just our love of words but our very humanity."

He picked up the envelope, turned it over twice, as if to be sure it was still sealed, a bit of fakery everyone knew was fakery. He removed the enclosed card. He studied it for a moment, looked out at audience, studied it again and made a face that reflected both amazement and delight (peeking at the monitors.) "Wow," he said just above a whisper. "Wow." The audience was still as a photograph. But he had played them long enough.

He stepped back from the podium and looked over at celebrity seating, then pointed. "Puzzle Master Will Shortz, will you please stand?"

The celebrities were the first to their feet. The outbursts of approval and praise were so explosive I thought for a moment Shortz was in danger of being crushed. The faculty's shocked cries and hurrahs were a close equal. Those two groups alone were raising the noise to football stadium levels. At least a dozen young women were jumping and screaming. It was a scene of nerd ecstasy, with dozens of rapturous looks that said: Finally, One of Us!

The control room engineers were back at their spinning. One was stabbing his finger in the direction of the big clock on the wall behind them. It was time for Jack to call Mr Shortz to the podium. He ignored them and let the exultations take their natural course. When voices dropped to a conversational level, he returned to the podium and looked over at the honoree.

"Will Shortz, what better setting to bestow this award than this vast house of language?" He made a sweeping gesture at the surrounding structure, then stepped back. "The library, sir, is yours."

He greeted him with one of his famed, smothering hugs and settled into one of the throne-sized chairs.

Although Mr Shortz could not have prepared for this outcome, his opening comments came with such an easy style of address one could imagine the words were speaking themselves. As he thanked the University, the deans and the president, his voice slowly transformed the modern atrium into a warm and accessible space where we were all welcome, even where we all belonged. He segued into our past year and its monthly delivery of inevitable horrors. Among his listeners, there were no wandering eyes, no elbowing or whispering, no sagging heads.

While the University had for months made its case before the world, asking for its patience and sympathy, this was the first time that the world was speaking back. We were a suffering Israel, suddenly hearing the comforting words of a divinely inspired Isaiah.

It was a few seconds before I realized that the monitors had gone blank. Heads were jerking back, looking to the side or up into the interior of the building. There were a lot of charade-like gestures in the control booth. Mr Shortz fell comfortably silent during the technical glitch, as if he were looking at his notes in a studio of National Public Radio.

His equable mood was not matched by the audience. There was a steady rumble of growls and carping. Then an intrigued silence as members of the audience reached over to their neighbors and pointed up at the large screen. From where I sat there appeared to be faint streaks of gray forming against a white background. When I turned to the large screen, I saw they were not streaks of gray at all, but letters taking shape, almost as if they were being typed in from a remote source.

In seconds, the atrium realized what they were looking at.

PUZZLE #10

1. TO BE BALANCED, ESPECIALLY WITH BOTH HANDS ON THE BINOCULαRS, IS A CHALLENGE.

2. WHILE YOUR STUDENTS LEARN THAT YOU HAD Sε CRETLY PLANTED OVERWHELMING EVIDENCE AGAINST EVERY ONE OF THEM.

3. WHEN A MASS OF COMPUTERS AND CONSTANT MILITARY PROTECTION WAS ALL THE MOTIVATION NECESSARY.

4. IT WAS AN INTELLECTUAL COUP THAT GUARANTEES A PLACE FOR YOUR MARBLE BUSτ IN AN ACADEMIC HALL OF FAME.

5. IT'S WHAT ANY OF US WOULD COVER OVER WITH A θ IN FILM OF CON-GEALED SELF-REJECTION.

6. AND INSISTED IT BE KNOWN — BUT KNOWN AS MYςTERY.

7. HOW FOUR HEAPING SPOONFULS TRANSFERRED THE WHOLE OF THE SUBSTANCε.

8. AROUND YOUR SPINNING BODY, THε GOSSAMER MONUMENT.

9. OUR DEATHS ιN THE FORM OF A TRINITY.

10. OF THE MANY MOMENTS, THE TENDEREST PULλS THE VEIL FROM ALL THAT HAS OCCURRED IN THIS HISTORY.

EIGHTY-TWO

Nothing could have altered the atmosphere of the atrium faster or more violently than the mysterious appearance of the final puzzle. The reaction was strongest in the faculty section. Half of them were standing, many were calling out protests, some in the tone of outright threats.

"What the ... ?"

"What are we, called here as witnesses to more carnage?"

"Fix that goddamn thing!"

"Professor Carmody!" A physicist had rushed forward and, shaking a rolled program like a club, roared, "Is this some kind of joke? Who's in charge here? Do something!"

Some of the faculty were leaving their seats, as if a certain but unknown danger had suddenly descended upon us.

In vivid contrast, there was little action in the student section. The students seemed far more amused than alarmed by this rare outpouring of real emotion by their usually buttoned-up professors.

Jack, I noticed, was stirring uncomfortably in his seat, looking in all directions, obviously not sure what he was expected to do in the crisis. The celebrities were mostly quiet but looking about and taking in the whole scene with evident fascination. The control booth was in outright turmoil, shouting, flipping switches, pulling at wires, hammering at their sound and light boards, projecting down at Jack desperate signs of helplessness.

Then I looked at Mr Shortz.

The man was perfectly true to form. He remained at the podium, in the same relaxed posture he had taken minutes earlier. He seemed oblivious to the still mounting cries of protest. On a closer look, I saw that his gaze was fixed on the monitor. He was studying the puzzle!

Of course!

The energy of the protesters quickly bled away. A general restlessness soon followed it. Preparations to leave ceased altogether. Filing back into their rows were the several dozen who had moments before headed for the exits.

Shortz held out his hands, a silent invitation to resume the ceremony, and waited until he had the crowd's complete attention.

"My friends," he said, "neither President Lister nor I has an explanation for this interruption. But an explanation is not necessary. Any computer adept, with moderate hacking skills, could have inserted this item into the electronic program."

He paused, as if to let that particular issue die on its own.

"Far more important is this: I have read through the puzzle and want you to know that these ten clues, when solved, will very likely give us the name of your long-sought tormentor."

A kind of hidden shudder passed from one end of the atrium to the other.

"The tenth puzzle," Shortz continued in the same voice, "the Puzzler's final offering, is nothing less than an act of self-identification. We might even say, self-mortification." He paused again. "How do I know this? From a simple one-syllable word, a word that occurs but once in all of the puzzles and then only in the final clue of the final puzzle: **veil.** The veil is to be pulled away at last."

He hesitated once more as if waiting for the audience to catch the deeper meaning in the word. "You will notice, the letters of 'veil' can be rearranged to spell 'vile' and 'evil.' Looking back over the year, we see how both words apply. Note also that the letters also spell 'live.' I take it that the Puzzler has come in person to accept the consequences of these vile and evil acts."

It occurred to me for the first time that Mr Shortz had stayed informed on every detail of this anguished year-long saga, studying each puzzle and each solution as it was announced. Having done so, he knew the mind of the Puzzler like no one else.

"There is something else here that is found only once in the previous puzzles, the so-called signature at the end of the first," Mr Shortz said, turning back and looking up at the large screen.

"Greek letters," someone called out.

"Yes," Shortz said as if welcoming the contribution.

The screen went blank once more. Then a horizontal row of Greek letters appeared, one by one, until the screen read:

$$\alpha \ \varepsilon \ \tau \ \tau \ \theta \ \varsigma \ \varepsilon \ \varepsilon \ \iota \ \lambda$$

"There are, I assume, many here who are literate in Greek. Do any of you find a word hiding in these scrambled letters?"

There was a snapping open of pens, and soon a number of scribblers were rapidly at work. It wasn't five seconds before the answer came.

"τετελεϛθαι," someone called out in an assured tone from celebrity seating. The voice, I gathered, belonged to Arianna Huffington. The authentic Greek pronunciation gave it away.

"'Tetelesthai,'" Shortz transliterated. "Correct. Anyone …?"

"'It is finished,' last words of Jesus on the cross." This from a Classicist in faculty seating.

"Gospel of John. Chapter 19, verse 30." From celebrity seating again.

"Thank you, Professor Bloom," Shortz responded.

After a reflective moment he asked us to consider why the Puzzler would choose these words to emphasize in this final presentation. Are we dealing with madness here? Quite possibly. But only madness? No, there seems a deeper reason. There has always been a deeper reason. Can it be that what is finished is the Puzzler's part in it, that much is left to do, and has been left to us to complete it?

"We can only speculate," he concluded. "It is likely we will not understand until we have the Puzzler's own explanation.

"I promised you the name of the Puzzler," he said. A new silence took hold of the atrium. "If you look over the content of each of these clues, you find only some make sense. You will recall that the Puzzler is fascinated with numbers, is sometimes indifferent to literal meaning, and obsessed with the number ten — an ancient symbol of perfection."

How can I describe what happened to me at that very moment? I felt utterly run through, as if by the shaft of a new and strange power. It came when I realized that the Puzzle Master already knew the identity of the Puzzler. I call the power strange because it was above all else an attack of joy one I had never believed possible; a brain-scalding fever of ecstasy. The search for the Puzzler was over.

It is finished, yes.

EIGHTY-THREE

I am a poor narrator for the events that followed. Too much happened too fast to be remembered. I do recall the Puzzle Master's instructions. They were simple enough. Unlike solving Puzzle #6, a choking mass of technical terms, by reading down the first letters in each line, Puzzle #10, Mr Shortz explained, yields its secret only by isolating the tenth letter of each of the ten clues.

A hundred index fingers counted out the letters in each line. As if it were an on-air contest, the audience was calling out the letters, occasionally correcting each other, until it was clear they had collectively reached the tenth clue.

The puzzle blinked a few times and vanished from the screen. In its place appeared, one at a time, the ten selected letters:

C
S
O
T
Y
D
A
R
I
M

No one seemed surprised at this transformation. A chorus of voices soon began at once to yell out what words they found in the letters. The first responses were comical, if not silly:

"Ditsy carom."

"It's army, Doc."

"My cars do it."

"A misty cord."

"Coy arts dim."

I heard it clearly. It was a woman's voice, one I easily recognized. It had a rich confusion of feeling in it — incredulity, shock, anger, doubt. And it wasn't particularly loud. "It's Carmody," was all she needed to say to cause one more shift of the atmosphere in that cavernous room.

This was followed by a loaded silence. Then the voices began.

"Say it's not true!"

"It's a joke. A hoax. "

"You, Carmody, you're the killer?"

"Professor Carmody, just tell us it's not you!"

A growing but cold realization that no joke had been made was appearing even on the faces of the loudest of my defenders.

I sat unmoving at my place on the stage, waiting until I knew I had every eye in the house. A perfect silence descended on the stunned audience.

Then I rose, stepped down the three steps onto the marble floor, and slowly threaded a random path through the faculty seating area. I looked at no one but I had the impression that some of them were struggling to breathe. There were sounds of disbelief, scorn, and denial, here and there a sob. When I reached the open space in the center I stopped.

How could they understand that the shock of the crowd was not a shock for me. It was, in fact, the exaltation, exactly as I had planned it. That one of their own, an honored professor, a distinguished scholar, an award winning teacher, and a beloved colleague, could commit such a series of horrific crimes is a difficult conclusion to accept. Even more, I knew what incredulity would greet the disclosure that all nine deaths were elaborately planned and remotely executed with no known killer present, outwitting the concentrated forces of police and military protection — all by a small woman in her middle years.

You may think it an exaggeration, dear reader, that I use the word "exaltation" to describe what I felt in being identified as the Puzzler, the sole killer of nine men and women. Do realize that this moment was deeply rewarding, if for no other reason than that it was years in the making. What is more, I knew the pleasures would not end there.

In fact, they continue in full, even as I write these words and the many words yet to fill these pages, when at last you too will understand that my work is finished, and yours has just begun.

Now I see that you are wondering what happened next as I stood in the atrium of the library.

I made my way to the precise center point of the open area, the magic square. I did this, too, by careful planning. I had long before decided what I would say when reaching this place.

The tenth puzzle, solved, yielded the three simple words often considered the most powerful of any said *by* Jesus: It is finished. I have taken from that same volume the three simple words often considered to be the most powerful of any said *to* Jesus. I waited until there was no whisper to be heard from the crowd, not a whir of machinery anywhere in the building, no electronic signals, no annoying traffic, no steel drum bands in the distance. Then I spoke the words of Judas when Jesus announced he had been betrayed by one of the disciples.

"Is it I?"

The question, may I say, was rhetorical for he had already arranged for the soldiers to take Jesus to what was certain to be his execution. Pausing to emphasize to those present that the time for questions was past, I repeated Judas' remark in its full meaning.

"Yes. It is I."

I waited until I was sure the sound had settled into every space and object. I spoke again.

"It is I." Then I spoke my name. "Evangeline Carmody." As before, the name spoke back from a dozen sources. I heard the joy in each of them.

I looked over at Lieutenant Thomas Roche, not ten feet away, positioned near center of police seating. He was staring down at the floor directly before him. I walked up to him and held out my hands, wrists pressed together. He looked at them, baffled by what he was expected to do. One of the decorated police officers behind him reached over his shoulder and dropped a thin plastic strip into his lap. The Lieutenant picked it up and examined it as if he had never seen such a device. I moved a few inches closer. Finally, he managed to secure the restraining band, still not looking up. I tightened it with my teeth to keep it in place, then took one step, now turning toward Jack Lister, still in his chair behind the podium. He was leaning forward, bent almost to his knees, holding his face in both hands. Both men had just realized what they may have long feared: their lives were in ruins.

It was a full minute or more before a sergeant came from behind and took my arm in a firm grip. As he led me through the crowd, still seated and silent, I caught only a few faces. Alfie O'Malley's expression was a mixture of emotion and bafflement. Rage? A sense of betrayal? An element of disbelief? All of that. It may be too much to say, but as I passed I was convinced I could also read, from the intensity of his gaze, that he understood.

The sergeant tightened his grip on my upper arm and as he pushed me toward the entrance we had come through less than two hours ago. Once outside, he propelled me forward with both hands, as if my exit were increasingly urgent. After a few more steps I was roughly shoved into the rear seat of his cruiser and forced to lie face down on the hard plastic surface provided for perpetrators.

It was not until the cruiser jerked to a start, sirens at their highest pitch, that I could hear Lucille's triumphant cry somewhere in the deeper regions of my imagination: "Tis Carmody!" And again: "Tis Carmody!" In her faux accent, smooth as a punt adrift on the River Cam, the **r** slides away to let my name create a meaning of its own.

EIGHTY-FOUR

Cell #17c, Block III, Unit One

If it is too dark in here even to recognize your friends, you can crowd over to this corner. You notice that there is only one window. Over this way, just above my head. From here you get a glimpse of the gibbous moon, unfortunately in its waning phase. My solemn apologies for cramming all of you into this tiny space. They did not know that I invited you for the night. My cell phone has been taken so I do not know the time, but it should be several hours before daybreak when they appear with the decision, long enough to complete the business that brings all of us here.

I am, you may be sure, grateful for your presence. It was precisely toward this moment that the years of planning were directed. Each of you has every right to know exactly why — and how — you were brought here. It is for me of the greatest importance that you understand this. The reader, too, having come this far in the narrative of these events, deserves the same. I will therefore address you all.

First, I should explain why the number ten recurs so frequently in the unrolling of these events. Some of you know, I am sure, that the number ten is an ancient symbol of perfection. Our mathematics develops from a base of ten; our currency and the measurements of length and weight are multiples of ten; time proceeds in decades and centuries. There are ten digits at the end of our extremities. I planned for ten of us be here in our final moments. We are all here because of ten puzzles of ten clues each. Tens of tens. Perfection squared. Although I did not carry all of it out alone — more on that later — I met the original goal, perfectly. I can assure you that historians of the events will find many more decads than I have listed, Bur for the

315

current purposes, indeed not say more. There other pressing matters.

You may wonder why they did not remove me to the court where I could personally hear the jury foreman announce the vote on my fate. They gave me no explanation. I can only suppose I am considered too dangerous. There is no fear that I might physically harm a member of the jury or the spectators, even the judge. No, the danger lies in what by law I am allowed to say before the court utters its closing words.

They call me mad. Yes. They considered Socrates mad, too, forbidding his address to the jury. And why not? He even admitted to having a demon he consulted for guidance. "Make music," that ghostly presence advised. A philosopher making music with his thought? That is, musing? Yes, that is madness of a kind, but one merging with the comic. I, too, have a demon. I think of it as my demon chorus. It is you, my cellmates. You have provided all the impulse I needed to engage in a musing of my own, a true entertainment. And, to be sure, the court's opinion is quite correct. I am dangerous. But you all know that.

EIGHTY-FIVE

Oliver Ridley, since you are the first of ten, I begin with you. I cannot see your face but I know the question that is written on it. I anticipate your admiration for the efficiency and daring such a violent act requires. Excuse my immodesty, but a woman of an uncertain age physically pushing you from the window of your office without being caught or even suspected is more than noteworthy. Agreed?

The black-throated blue warblers play a basic part in this drama. Let us identify them as the material cause of what follows. (That I am the efficient cause I have just confessed. Naming the final cause will have to wait.) As is usual with these shy beauties, they spend most of their lives at the mid-level of northern forests. With your excellent 8X42's you could easily locate them from the fine viewing location the grand nineteenth century windows of your tenth floor office afford you. By the way, Oliver, it was only when I noticed the Fujinon binoculars on the small table near the open window that I was sure of your death.

On the day before, you recall that as I entered your office, the phone rang and since you thought that Lucille had not yet appeared, you answered it. A short time later, I entered. You then had the choice of talking with me or listening to Holmers' explosive sentiments. Since Holmers intrusion was the more difficult to repel, I was left at the window you had opened to scan the trees for new arrivals. It was impolite on your part, to be sure, but in fact it was a boon to me. It gave me the perfect excuse for my returning the next morning.

The decision that you were to be the first victim had been made, but the conditions for acting on it were not quite complete. Lucille's perfectly timed presence was essential to its success.

As soon as I was certain she was present in her office but not known to you, I appeared with my own binoculars. You were not surprised to find me there. You knew of my own passion as a birder. With a bit of excitement — feigned, to be sure — I reported the existence of the *setophaga caerulescens* at the top of a tree not fifty feet from your window. With a gentle invitation, you followed me to the window. I leaned out a bit. I selected the species because like most warblers they lose their summer plumage after breeding season, and in the case of this bird it is a brilliant color indeed. However, as you well know, one field mark remains — a small white notch at the edge of the wings near the shoulders. We had an excellent viewing perspective and needed only considerable patience for the little devil to turn in just the right way to display the mark.

Did I overdo it by placing the bird close to the building but to the left of the window, where it cannot seen without leaning out at a precarious angle? Perhaps, perhaps. Keeping balance, especially with both hands on the binoculars, was a challenge. I admired your bravery for risking it. Because there was no black-throated blue to be seen, in fact no black-throated blue at all, you remained patient and did not notice that I had come to look over your shoulder. The close contact of our bodies would have been uncomfortably intimate on any other occasion, but the possible sighting of the bird — this bird in particular — made it perfectly natural.

I needed little more than a quick action with the finger tips on your right shoulder. The fall was, I must say, extraordinary. Instead of reaching out in the vain hope of grasping something that could check the fall, you spent most of the trip down in a flapping spin that would have made even the ballet star Antoine de la Grandville envious. It is a pity that I seemed to have been the only audience. The taxi driver saw none of this, only the final impact. Whether by design or accident, landing head first added to the theater of the event by delaying your identification until Lucille could perform her shock scene at the entrance to Administration.

You may be confused as to my motivation. It is true your nasty remarks about me to colleagues were somehow passed on to me. After all, being named University Professor is a greater honor than elevation to a deanship. But that constitutes only a small fraction of my intentions, not the true final cause. It is something else altogether.

In spite of your writing style — only a slight improvement on that of undergraduate sociology majors — you have an admirable skill in manipulating the currently prevailing concepts in your field. You are a responsible and professional researcher, intimate with the popular themes in the journals and conferences. But here the problem begins. You are an observer of ... what, Oliver? Society? And exactly from what perspective? Let us review how you proceed. You first find a lacuna somewhere in the scholarly literature, something overlooked or never thought of by other scholars in your field, and then you construct an investigation of the social behavior of certain members of the public to fill in the gap, in the hope that it will be noticed by your colleagues across the discipline. Your intention is that your readers will not be enlightened and grateful but resentful that you got there first. If you are truly successful, shame and envy will greet your arrival at this naked space. You are not, I am sure you understand, studying society (us) at all, but the lapses, weaknesses, and oversights of your academic colleagues — who are themselves on the hunt for damage to your own work.

What results is a great spiral of published discourse that feeds on itself in a spirit of competition and vengeance. Volumes collect, journals multiply, library shelves sag, vast clouds of data float off somewhere into the electronic ether — all of it driven by a population of intelligent human beings wishing each other ill.

My intention here is not simply, I assure you, to cast scorn on the universal desire for competitive triumph over humiliated losers. It is something more inexcusable. Once vacuumed up into this self-feeding and self–destroying spiral of specialized jabber, engagement with real society has come to be seen as a pointless distraction. The ills of those we share the real world with — that is, true competitors like poverty, hunger, war, racism, and (is there any end to this list?) — are ignored with practiced professional competence. Triumphs in the professoriat are measured by the prestige of the institution that pays you, by the frequency with which your name appears in other scholars' bibliographies, by the size of the audience attending your lecture at a national conference of the discipline ... but not by the depth of your commitment to societal well-being, much less the humanizing enlightenment of your students. What sociology needs, Oliver, is a sociology of itself to show the scope of its disengagement with what it claims to study. What you need to perfect is not your methods observing "them." You need to turn your attention back on itself, to observe the observers, observe yourself. Of course, you are loath to cleanse the mirror that will reflect back your own shame. You have failed at that most elemental of all Socratic challenges: to know thyself. (Remember? γνφθι ςεαυτον.)

At the center of that self-reflecting mirror you would find the shredded remains of the Night School whose wreckage you can claim as your own. The Night School was where the spinning intellectual energies of the academy had their engagement with the world as it really is. It was the magical space where talent met need, where inquisitive minds looked for true engagement with men and women lavishly provisioned with what they hunger for. This, Oliver, was for me the final cause of your undoing. It is a perfect example of the way the University has struggled to rise to its current, impressive level of societal uselessness — an example so perfect it required your sacrifice to seal it in our institutional memory. Your shame has become ours.

If my interest were simply the self-contradictoriness and irrelevance of your discipline, I could have chosen anyone from your department, an especially rich source of candidates. What we are concerned with here is not one academic field among dozens, but all of them together.

We are all, as a university, as a community of intellectuals, as sentient and contemplative animals, so busy with each other that the spiral that has sucked us up becomes a tornado that never touches down, never threatens a single human pattern of behavior. I needed a symbolic event showy enough to force us to look upward and see ourselves from below.

Killing a dean of the college is the very minimum required to wake us to our sublime irrelevance to the ground under us, to urge our return to loamy Kansas from airy Oz. And how more fitting it is that when your wheeling flight touches down, an elite institution of higher learning will go through a series of traumas not found elsewhere in the annals of the trade.

But, you, Professor Oliver Ridley, betray yourself in a most original way. In being a surpassing expert bird watcher, you advertise a contradiction in yourself that your colleagues, and perhaps you as well, have never been alert enough to catch. To reach and sustain an acceptable reputation as a sociologist, you observe and analyze what you *must*. As an amateur ornithologist, you observe and analyze what you *love*. Yes, you have your life list and that can be understood as a competitive attempt at superiority over your birding cohort. But there are all kinds of lists, and all kinds of contests. Why birds?

Not much guessing is necessary. Who is not thrilled by knowing that a being almost half the weight of a quarter can navigate whole continents at night — mastering storms, shifting magnetic fields, predators, and the indifference of our own species — to return to the very neighborhood of its origin? And then to realize this yearly extravaganza has not been repeated over centuries but over a number of millennia, a number so large it seems imaginary. That sly bay-breasted warbler calling to the world from the grand red oak at the corner of the Square, or the elusive slate-gray gnatcatcher working the interior of the same tree, are descendants of millions just like themselves, in a line that stretches back a thousand times farther than the one that begins with Yahweh, or Zeus, or Homo Africanus.

Here, Oliver, at the window, you are another kind of observer whose targeted objects are tiny miracles that defy the best of the sciences to explain how and why they behave as they do. When you leave the window and return to your desk, you use the worst of the sciences to explain how human subjects (us again) behave as they do. This is also why you are so appropriate as the first of ten. As an authority you are all answers, as an amateur all wonder.

And you know it, as Socrates would have been certain to explain. You are not only living against society and your colleagues, but against yourself. And how better can a bird-man fulfill his defining moment than in a wheeling, arm-thrashing flight to the earth?

I had made no effort to conceal my presence in the vicinity of your office. Indeed, I planned it so as to be completely visible. Because it was Wednesday, I knew that Jose Ramirez, the custodian responsible for the tenth floor, would be at his noisy machine cleaning and waxing the floor. I have known Jose for years. Not only do I know the names and ages of his and Camila's children, I had the previous year written a recommendation for his eldest daughter, Ariana, for admission to college. As I stepped out of the elevator and turned toward your office, Jose was only a few feet away. He turned off his machine to announce that Ariana was attending her first class at Brown that very day. We talked for a full ten minutes before he helped me step over his machine, taking my arm so I wouldn't slip on the wet floor, then leading me to your office. Jose was later asked by the police if he noticed any suspicious persons. He answered truthfully, "No." They pressed him.

"Are you sure?" "Sure, I'm sure. Whadda ya think? I don't know what a suspicious individual looks like when I see one?"

EIGHTY-SIX

Nathaniel Holmers, I acknowledge the fact that your distress over the grim scene in the lab had nothing to do with its outcome — your death, that is. Yes, you gave me those hateful looks, but we both know that they came more from envy than from outrage at the exposure of your tidy commercial enterprise. You were envious because I stole from you the role of producer in this concluding drama. I saw quite some time back the self-destruction you were bent on carrying out — but to do so according to your own script. That script had a clever reversal in it. Selling your illicit product only through graduate students, especially those nearing the end of their dissertations, was brilliant. Why would they incriminate the only professor who could pass or fail them in their orals? And once having passed, how could they reveal the scheme without implicating themselves and burying forever any chance at an academic career? This basically left them with one option. Since you were the only one who could identify the culpable students, and since you had made sure there was no independent evidence available to them except for your own testimony, you had intentionally made yourself an irresistible target, an inevitable murder victim. I have no doubt, although there is no evidence to date to prove it, that they had already drawn up plans for your elimination, masked as an accidental drug overdose. How clever. They planned to murder you, not knowing you were setting them up for your own suicide.

Only later in the official investigation would the students discover that you had secretly planted overwhelming evidence against every one of them. You would be dead, according to this script, but your graduate students would go down with you, accused of both trafficking and assassination. What headlines that would have made! What an endlessly studied and revisited atrocity at the very center of one of the nation's premier institutions of higher learning!

This is theatre in its most perfect form, where the staged actions are performed in both senses of the term. The actors who play killers and the killed and are also killers and the killed. The blood on the curtains is not fake stain from the prop locker.

It was apparent to any close observer that you were yourself a heavy user. That energy! Those amazingly versatile facial expressions! But that was only a hunch. One day at the squash courts, when you were dressing up after a game, a ball dropped from your jacket pocket. I picked it up to return to you but noticed as I did that it was a tad too heavy, as if solid in the center, or filled with liquid. A quick glance caught a needle prick in a tiny blot of moisture. So this is how you transport your constant supply of meth! Only a few seconds behind a bolted toilet door, and you're up to full velocity. I can only assume that the ball that dropped from your hand moments before your death carried a different substance. Oh, what we might have discovered in your lab! Cartons of squash balls loaded with both the highest and lowest of chemical assists!

For you, Nat, performance is the seamless union of stage and life. That is your genius and your tragedy. I already knew this from your magnificent collection of masks. In your case, they are not faddish decorations hinting at a rarified taste and frequent travel to strange lands. They came with you from the Moluccans where you report spending those four precious years of your graduate study. They are your masks, rewards of the tribe for your tireless industry in learning their language and for your convincing participation in their rituals. It is not too much to say that they adopted you as one of their own, the *sine qua non* for any aspiring anthropologist.

Masks are by intention deceptions. At once concealing and revealing, they leave the identity of the viewer hidden but also unresolved. Is it the actor's persona looking at you through those eye holes, or is it the actor? Yes, you wore those masks in the day-long ceremonies, knowing just when and how to switch from one to the other. But when you went back to your suspended twig bed in the complete darkness of your small reed house, did you know how to switch to the persona that was exclusively your own?

There is a bigger question: when you set sail from Molucca, genuinely weeping at what you were to lose forever, and resumed your role on the professorial stage, did you find yourself an alien presence in a ragged collection of masked players whom you could see as nothing but masks themselves? A huge cast of personae, not a single person present. And did you not then realize that the Moluccans saw behind the masks they taught you to wear only the mask you brought with you? And that what you thought you were losing as you left, you had lost long before? Those tears go back to your childhood.

You are still that brave little boy growing up in a trailer in northern Wisconsin, the child of savagely abusive alcoholics. You fled the violence and abuse by learning to be fascinated by all things strange, in spite of being ridiculed for your insatiable curiosity. At the age of twenty you dared to explore unguided the rain-forested mountains of Halmachera Island in the Moluccas of Indonesia where you found yourself on a clouded mountainside in the presence of an undiscovered tribe of natives for whom there was no "outside" to their tiny world. Your published work on these people is a model of original anthropological research, so detailed and gracefully written we feel as if we have spent years there ourselves. Never mind that no one else had since found this community nor heard a syllable of the language you were able to translate. Never mind that there is no evidence you ever went there. You performed that most valuable service of the true academic, highlighting the horizon of our acknowledged ignorance.

You perform brilliantly in your persona as a professor, as an intellectual, as a scholar. But who is behind the persona? As your colleague for now more than a decade, I have come to admire your histrionic skill in creating a public identity like none other among us. The masks of Nathaniel Holmers, with their ferocious eyebrows, that drilling stare, and the elastic mouth of a dozen shapes is always an entertainment. That is, an entertainment for us. For you, it is an internal horror. There are times when I want to seize that showpiece of a face and look back into those eyeholes. But I know what you know, that all I will see is someone staring into the eyeholes of my own mask. Here is the sizable difference between you and poor Oliver Ridley, now only a half dozen feet from the asphalt. Oliver and his sociological colleagues are observers of what they deign not to participate in. You observe and participate, but only to discover that what you are looking at is looking back, neither seeing the other, neither seeing themselves.

You did more than look at the world through the squeezed apertures of your masks. You looked at yourself *from inside* those masks. It was the dark peering into the dark. In this you were not only far advanced beyond Oliver and his own, but all of us. We still press our false exteriors tightly over every slip of our mental nakedness, speaking in acquired accents, repeating a small vocabulary of verbal tics, pushing uncombed hair into place, grasping our foreheads in pained cogitation, pushing our hair back again, dressing with designed carelessness so as not to be confused with the working classes, whether rich or poor — all masks that are at best pallid shades of the *real* performers. No Moluccans here. Or Tlingit, or Maori, or Olmecs. How well you have learned from your profession that *no one is there.* No wonder your fantasy ritual is to be killed and to kill in a grand final performance in the contrived, hermetic Moluccan setting of your laboratory. After all, you would only putting away masks after a grand performance.

You, perhaps more than the rest of us, have an intimate familiarity with the Socratic insight that without self-knowledge all other knowledge is irrelevant. The Moluccans were your jury of 500. It was they who first saw that behind the mask that was yourself was another mask and beyond that another — with no end. There is someone there, behind them all — whom no one knows ... not even you.

We ridicule you still. Your addiction to chemicals allows us to write you off as an untethered nut, flooding the minds of our young students with inane nonsense. However, we also overlook the metaphoric nuance here. In your theatre of masks, where the frantic search for a genuine self merely turns up another mask, you do what you must: hasten to catch up with the self that you are, only to catch yourself in pursuit of what is not yet caught. So you escalate the velocity of this chase. It is not a surprise that you would turn to a chemical assist. "Speed," as we refer to it.

What the rest of us fail to understand is that this is only the physical equivalent of the assorted intellectual amphetamines — analytical, economic, mathematical, sociological, theological, political, scientific, philosophical — we use in our own vain pursuit of the false gods we call reality. If we were honest with ourselves we would admit that the quarry forever eludes us. Of course, it is just this insatiability that is the very soul of the thinker. The German philosopher Lessing said that if God offered him the truth in one hand and the eternal search for it in the other, he would choose the latter. Even God would step back.

This is the genius of your trade, Nat, and you have performed it extraordinarily well. With you anthropology achieves a level of ignorance those outside your discipline can only aspire to. Farewell. And god speed.

EIGHTY-SEVEN

Leonard Gold, you are an economist. Why would I need a representative from the "dismal science" to join our little circle here in the darkness? Is there something unique to you and to your field that we can accept as an appropriate token for what has gone so awry in the university? Yes. There is an immediate give-away, and in your case, Lenny, an extravagant self-betrayal. I want it made clear that I admire your mental capacities. To repeatedly treat us to your extravagant claim that the world is a political economy and nothing more is a sign of a mind on fire. The only trouble, Lenny, is that it is not your mind that is burning, but always another's. It's a borrowed fire. To give me a five-minute quote straight out of Friedrich Hayek while jumping from one foot another, not wanting to break your sweat, is a virtuoso performance. You may not have noticed, but I was looking at you in disbelief. Can this guy actually think I would not recognize the old Austrian's fluid nineteenth century unrolling of predictable words?

And did you not notice that my response to you was a straight quotation from Georg Simmel's *The Philosophy of Money*, the chapter titled, "The intrinsic value of money and the measurement of value." Check it out. Pages 131ff.

In truth, I rather expected something like that when I saw you change direction and bolt in my direction. Although we have never had an extended discussion, I have rarely heard you complete a sentence that did not have its origin, as the puzzle puts it, not in your head but in those of other scholars. So, bravo, Leonard Gold. You managed to be an influential thinker without having a thought of your own. I consider you a most useful instrument for general discourse in the academy: a mental funnel, sucking up thoughts in random places and transmitting them as a steady flow through the narrow opening of a canny ideologue's intelligence. Who, after all, would ever bother to spend a few hours with, say, the estimable if irrelevant Josef Schumpeter when the rest of the world has forgotten him? So in you we had a ready catalog of salient nonsense only a wagging finger away.

I will admit that this virtuosic cerebral mimicry rewarded me with several quiet afternoons in the library, confirming my guesses as to the origins of your so-called thinking. It did not require as many hours as I hoped since the scope of your plagiarism was not as broad as I had inferred from your occasional comments. I had expected to be days scanning indexes in standard works. It really narrows down to a dozen thinkers at the most. Naturally, when you temporarily inhabit a big mind — say Marx, or Adam Smith, or John Maynard Keynes (okay, our friends Josef and Georg also) — you have a library of quotes that apply to any possible mental inclination. You want an attack on the unjust distribution of capital? Quote Marx. You want an attack on forced distribution of capital? Quote Marx again. Adam Smith, that elusive Scot, can be made to support any view of your choosing. You found what you wanted, just like the rest of us. But unlike the rest of us you wanted to keep what you found. And you succeeded.

I think your highest achievement, Lenny, is not plagiarizing the giants but plagiarizing yourself. That is an intellectual coup that guarantees a place for your marble bust in the Academic Hall of Fame, were there such. The inscription, carved in stone, would remind us that you have attained the highest of academic distinctions by publishing an essay of your own, which is the copy of the same essay of your own in another volume, which is frequently cited by other scholars who have never read it, and which says nothing at all.

I repeat. I want someone who has mastered economics, that most unscientific of sciences. Because nearly everything we do has economic consequences, the available data for analysis are vast and without bounds. Every personal thought and outward act constitute a factum that must find its place in our conclusions. This is why economic theory can be as thick with conceptual and factual material as quantum mechanics. It is also why, somewhat like quantum mechanics, predicting our economic behavior is close to impossible, while at the same time utterly irresistible.

An economist's explanation of our past behavior is similar to a tour guide showing us the map of the territory we have just exited, its paths and obstructions ending at the boundary of the present. We can see the direction in which they are pointing for us, but ahead lies an unexplored forest or sea or wasteland whose details can only be guessed at. Not helping is the appearance of another guide with a map of the same traversed territory but one so unlike the other we may no longer know what journey we have actually taken. Even the giants of the field are undecided on the causes of the grandest economic calamity in

American history: the Great Depression of the 1930s.

There is a wisdom in this repeated failure. It has to do with the confusion of number and wealth. Economists measure. Their techniques are so mathematically sophisticated as to be cryptic to any but the most finely educated professionals. This encourages the presumption that everything is measurable. Each made or found object, each human act, each idled machine, each cubic inch of earth and water — all of it belongs on a scale of the value of comparable objects, however high or low. And what of a sonnet, a dance step, an explosion of anger, marsh grasses in a breeze? Well, they either have a dollar value or they have no place in economic theory.

I needn't remind you that the word, "economy," derives from the Greek, *oikonomos,* or the proper ordering (*nomos*) of our home (oikos.) To be economic, for the Greeks, was simply to be at home, comfortable in our own space, and safe from the hazards lying beyond our door. To be able to manage the contents of our private life is be assured of everything needed for the full expression of our humanity.

Since at this very moment, Lenny, you are stuck in the ice, out of gas, and freezing to death in your four-wheel-drive Land Rover somewhere in the Alaskan tundra, I will have to speak for you. In fact, I can, *a la* Professor Gold, repeat your very words: "Talk is cheap, bunnies. Stick with bananas!" Of course, you're wrong. Talk is not cheap. Neither is it expensive. It has no cash value at all. But in that inadvertent error, you expose so much of yourself, of the field of economics, and of the academic society in its entirety.

Let's go back to Socrates and the Sophists. You read all that in your freshman Intro to Phil class a generation ago so no need to remind you what they discussed; it's set in permanent print somewhere under that thicket of mock Marxist hair. It's simple, in any case. The

331

Sophists, at least as Plato portrays them, teach "philosophy" to young men. For money. The question Socrates is implicitly asking here is, Why would someone pay to be taught wisdom when it is free for the asking? Answer: Because it is *useful*. It has a monetary value. Think of it like an investment with a handsome pay off.

What these rich young men of Athens are learning is how to use speech to reach a certain end. Call it wealth and power. The Sophists are teaching verbal techniques to outwit the resistances of those who can be manipulated to one's own material advantage. And some of the Sophists were good at it, good enough to become wealthy themselves. Call it the clever use of words to make the rich richer.

And homeless Socrates in his single ragged cloak? What do we learn from him? The answer is a bit surprising, at least it is for us who labor in this elite, high-cost market of useful ideas for a handsome income guaranteed for life. What you learn from Socrates is *how to learn*. Socrates' talk leads to, well, more talk. He has no interest in Truth, as a settled and finished system of thought, only in challenging it. There is a payoff, to be sure: in the process of learning we acquire the gift of teaching others how to learn, and in teaching them expand our own capacity for learning.

Sounds thin? Compare it to the Sophists. For them language is trickery. If used well it has the peculiar character of no longer being necessary. Sophistry is a method of talking designed to end talk. Once successful, you can simply shut up and behold the objects you have just "bought," and about which there is nothing more to say. It is one of the deepest contradictions in our collective existence as sentient beings.

One of the signal triumphs of the university's use of economic methodologies is to internalize Sophistry to a degree not imaginable to the Athenians. We sell the skill of thinking as a commodity more precious than diamonds and oil. Even that sonnet that once looked so completely free has its hand out at the entrance to a classroom where it will be "discussed." Then the page will be turned, and we pass on to another object in an expensive textbook that lines up one forgettable literary tidbit after another. Since when has science actually meant "scientia," a large and generalized knowledge valuable only for its own sake? Wisdom, that is.

As a victim, Lenny, you so perfectly fit the requirements here I could not have invented one more desirable. You are an idea man, as good as they get. So the ideas are not your own, but what does it matter? Your high talent is to come in at the conclusion of someone else's thinking and freeze the result in the classy style of academic convention. One elegant idea after another, a rushing current of thoughts that once were original. It is a stream that seems to have no beginning. But it does have an end. There, in the rare adhesiveness of your gray matter and in the pages of scholarly journals, the ideas of others pile up into a formidable mass that can then be so arranged as to block all attempts at getting through or around it. In a word, Lenny, your incomparable gift to the university is converting ideas to ideology. And what is ideology but the Sophistic attempt to shape the world to our own advantage?

For that reason, Professor Gold, we are not thinkers at all, but servants of the rich, hired to teach their privileged children how to preserve and enlarge their already sizable advantages.

Planning your death was particularly entertaining. You are the perfect model for your own destruction. I was so inspired by your talent at duplication that I chose to do a little myself. Just duping the duper, that's all.

The letter you received from the billionaire underwriter of all things conservative, Charles H. Cox, is one of my most satisfying creations.

His "Dear Professor Gold" letter was more successful than I could have expected. I could detect in your face as you appeared on television (especially when you had shorn away the hairy Marxist subterfuge and looked more like a US Marine Corporal) how thrilled you were to be offered a future of writing endless pages of nonsense and offering trusted clichés to stabilize the unmoored mind of an incipient candidate for the Presidency. I was not sure that in describing a tripling of your salary I hadn't gone a bit too far, but this too had its hoped for effect. The concluding paragraph of the initial letter (*"I, Charles H. Cox, am a busy man and therefore difficult to reach, but rest assured that my staff will follow through with the complete details. Their email addresses are attached. All communication with me will pass through them, and will receive a quick response"*) was successful insurance against your skepticism and suckered you straight into the honey pot. But my proudest moment came with the production of the subsequent letter, which, like Leonard Gold, I am pleased to reproduce here.

My dear Professor:

A brief note to say how honored I am that you have deigned to accept my offer to serve our threatened nation in this hour of its need. When all is said and done, at the end of the day, we are an optimistic people, and going face to face with the naysaying elitist losers on the left is a cherished American tradition.

I am aware that Wasilla, AK, seems to be in the middle of nowhere, but it has in the last several years become the font of political wisdom. It is my hope that you will be only the first of many sages to gather in this Athens of the Arctic. For better or worse, and as far as the eye can see, the labor of you and your future co-execs will move the country forward.

As a token of thanks, I have asked my Director of Affairs for the American Northwest to lay out an itinerary through this great state where the scenery will knock your socks off. So, without further ado, my wishes go out to you and this great nation to bring back our freedoms from the tyranny of our government.

Sincerely yours, Charles H. Cox
(Dictated to, and signed by, Mr Cox's personal secretary.)

Attachment:

Memo to: Mr. Leonard Gold

As per CHC's instructions, fly to Fairbanks AK (change in Seattle). Ticket in your name. Simply provide the agent with a valid credit card and the expense will go directly to your account — which will be promptly reimbursed. Land Rover has been rented in your name (your credit card but all expenses to be reimbursed). Four wheels. Since vehicle is equipped with GPS, you may not need the following directions, but at the risk of repetition: Take Route 3 in direction of Anchorage, 632 mi. Drive along the western border of Denali National Forest. At 284 mi enter gravel road, marked "Park Entrance." Head west 31 mi. to the main lodge. As per CHC's recommendation, find America's #1 scenic vista. Facilities available in Park. Safe driving.

GPS equipment, as you discovered a few months too late, is not capable of making adjustments for violent and rapidly changing weather.

EIGHTY-EIGHT

Aleksander Krauss, there are several excellent reasons you should be invited here with the rest of us in this cramped little cell, straining to find my face in the dark. Worry not. You would only see that I am in awe.

You have been correctly referred to as a figure of surpassing intelligence in your field. Your proposal to the Department of Defense was a model of fundraising mastery, especially since the subtle acknowledgment of your patriotism (including the putative hatred of Islamo-fascists and certain Asians) added a glow of sentimentality irresistible to DoD professionals. Of course, they would grant you millions, and years to spend it. You were justly the envy of your colleagues in The Institute for Applied Mathematics, both for securing this rare largesse and for the highly sophisticated design of your parallel-computing equipment.

But I am also extremely pleased with myself for getting you here. You made only one mistake, one so simple that no brilliant technician would have noticed anyone making it, by overlooking a comically simple electronic connection. I will admit that I learned how to disable the thermostat in your computer installation not by any special skill of my own, but by overhearing a conversation between two geeks in the IT Department, several years before I had all the details of your execution in place. They had no idea what they were revealing, or that they were revealing anything at all. Seated one table away in the Department coffee lounge, talking in loud, animated voices, their concerns hardly sounded invidious. They were simply annoyed at the poor regulation of temperatures in the University's classrooms and offices: overheated in the winter, and in the summer, a constant chill. Strictly speculating, they laid out a plan for entering the computerized control panels that anyone could carry off on their own laptop. Although they did warn each other that to prevent being traced you should use the library facilities for electronic research or the ordinary technology available in every academic office, and never your own equipment.

They were admirably clear in their analysis and deliberate enough that I was able to follow their suggested strategy. I was more amused than instructed, however, because of the casual tenor of the discussion. They parted innocently, without any resolve to act. For no reason I had at the moment, I picked up the napkin on which they had drawn their scheme and tucked it away in my notebook, then storing it out of sight in my desk where it lay for at least three years. I had it on my lap in the library while I followed its instructions. I quickly saw that I had no need to go through the DoD at all, that access into the University climate controls was no more than a half-dozen clicks away through a computer in the reading room of the library. Bright young fellows. Everything worked.

In less than a minute, your life as a counterspy, funneling millions, maybe billions, of the Department of Defense budget to hostile regimes, was over. I must say, it is commendable that you have drained off only a small stream from this torrent of national wealth for your personal use, or rather your family's. Less than three million in US dollars have been so far uncovered in accounts belonging to your wife, daughter and son. Just how much has been secretly routed through to the Lister Family Educational Foundation has yet to determined.

But my unapologetic pleasure in outwitting a computer genius on his own computer was not my only motivation. It was not even the initiating impulse. This University is large, but not so large that your secret project could remain secret. What you and your associates were busy with on the tenth floor of the Institute for Applied Mathematics was successfully hidden from all of us, even from your colleagues. Bravo to that. Constant military protection, however, is harder to disguise. Armed, Special Forces soldiers with snappy berets standing guard at each end of the corridor and at the air-locked entrance to the computer lab are, may I say, impossible to overlook.

You were revealing more than you thought. Those Green Berets and Navy Seals were all we needed. We did not know what you were doing in that hermetic capsule not because you hid it, but because *you* were not doing it. That project was not yours, but the military's.

You were a tool, a mere comma in the process for the generals and senators whose real motivation had nothing to do with national defense. Note which industries were financing the senators on the Armed Service Committee. Note which industries have hired the generals behind the project for seven figures per. These gentlemen had no interest in which flag was served in their sucking up the taxes of working Americans. More than a tool, Aleks, they've played you for a fool. A humiliation for a patriot of your sincerity and passion? Certainly.

And how much better can it be to get back at your keepers by doing a 180° with your love of country. What is patriotism anyway but the inverse of its hostile other? How can you be a patriot without a country to hate, and how can you hate a country that doesn't hate you? Each end of this dyad depends on the other. Choose your hatred, basically a toss up. So you must have been surprised that it was as easy hacking with a coded message into Ayatolla Khomeini's home page as it was for me to hit the "off" button on your air conditioner, and that the rewards were more than sizable. Your military and corporate handlers generously paid your university salary, while the Iranians, Saudis, Yeminis, even Hezbollah were paying you the equivalent annual income of your handlers — combined.

The information you sent them is useless, of course. A missile protection screen, heading off a possible nuclear attack from Tehran and Pyongyang, itself a fantasy of the Ayatolla and Kim Jong-un, has no more reality than an escapist computer game. But who will laugh at those government contracts for private rocket launches of earth-orbiting electronic eyes, easily convertible to highly lucrative commercial uses?

You are a tool, Professor Krauss, but so is the University. In our case — by that I mean the University as a whole — it far exceeds your modest swipe of nickels out of a trillion-dollar budget. Who hires us, after all? And why? Who decides which expensive research project to pursue when there are enormous financial consequences for its outcome? Who decides to underfund the historians, classicists, and the linguists, making certain that their thinking will be as harmless to the present socioeconomic order as Kim Jong-un's fantasies of world domination? How many scholars (any?), and how many millionaires (all?), make up the University's Board of Trustees, essentially the institution's only source of real power?

As you have found, Al, for all the references to nickels and dollars, the issue here is not about money. *It is about the control of knowledge.* Knowledge controlled is not only ignorance, but ignorance that doesn't know it's ignorance. One of the glories of the Western intellectual tradition as it awakens in Socrates' peripatetic questioning, is that it sets the mind free to find its own track, with no markers and no guide. The "errant" scholar (from the old French word, meaning to wander) is the very ideal of this tradition. But wander where? Wherever we come upon the dark edge at the end of all that is familiar, whenever certainty feels hollow, whenever the expected begins to surprise us with its opposite.

You might think this is a picture of a scattered army of scruffy secular mendicants randomly confronting citizens, asking for their definition of justice, or whether they place loyalty to their law-breaking parents above the law itself. It is nothing of the sort. Socrates' most radical insight is that teaching is indistinct from learning.

When the teacher is absent, there is no learner, just as when the learner is absent there is no teaching. When the teacher learns nothing from the student, nothing has been taught. When the learner finds a teacher who listens, both always learn something. This is the portrait of an intense and democratic community of engaged souls whose questioning of each other and whose discoveries are both boundless and unpredictable. For this group, there is no admissions policy; all are welcome. There is no tuition and no tenure. It is the steady conversion of boundary to horizon, trading accepted limits for an expanding field of vision.

If this sounds like a fantasy, our poor doomed Aleksander, it is only because we have, as deeply as you, attached ourselves to what has nothing to do with a life of errancy. We, the tenured and non-tenured faculty, have our own version of the DoD largesse to which we have affixed ourselves, albeit with a dedication more timid than yours. We lack your boldness and ingenuity in hunting up the corrupt version of your Ayatolla. We do no more than to remain certain we are safely fixed in place. Consider the term, "tenure," from the Latin *tenere*, to hold. We are firmly leashed, but not because we have been captured by a ruthless overlord.

We are all here by our own choice. Indeed, we jump into the hands of our holders, even making sure their fingers are firmly pressed on the leash handle. As a body of expensively educated academics, hardly a person among us has not read Rousseau's *de Contrat Social* (in the original) and is therefore familiar with one of the most famous lines in French literature, the first sentence of that slim volume: *L'homme il est né libre, et partout il est dan les fers.* "We were all born free but are now everywhere in chains." Little could that poor romantic have imagined that two centuries later we are in bitter competition with each other to grab those chains for ourselves. For him the "Enterprise University" would seem a jest of cosmic proportions.

It would not have escaped your attention, Al, that most (perhaps all) of the U.S. congressmen who supported your project are evangelical and born-again Christians. Not a few of them have offered a very clear picture of the place to which you will be sent for the rest of eternity. I hope it is of comfort to you that, if you request it, I can provide a simple strategy for controlling the temperature in that particular location. Even hell can be hacked.

EIGHTY-NINE

Darius Pennybacker, I think I made a mistake by obscuring the face of the weightlifter in the original tape starring this performer. It was a brilliant scene, but I robbed the fellow of the fame that blessed Antoine when his segment got to the world. He could have had a full performance schedule. Of course, there is no obscuring the fact that being suspended by the feet while pursuing Lift-off (!) was a technique of your own creation, to my knowledge found nowhere else in the literature of erotica. So, in the end, the admiration of the porn community, and the viewing public in general, is indebted to your imagination.

But the film in all of its segments was more than a merely titillating exposition. It was a triumph of moral clarity. The usual discussion of morality emphasizes what should be done, or which values should be placed highest. The appeal of this discussion is not what most students of morality think. The true emphasis of moral discourse is on what should *not* be done. For that reason, every moral system floats on an oceanic expanse of immorality. Without that ocean, moral indignation loses its very buoyancy. More interesting, and also easily overlooked, is that what is forbidden is vastly larger than what is commanded.

Obedience is a narrow path. Disobedience is an unbounded and exuberant undersea of yet-to-be discovered pleasures, thrills, and dangers. The forbidden is so rich and fruitful that it is where most of us live, though secretly. Freud's id is without boundaries; it is timeless and all inclusive. Every social and personal experience is immediately absorbed into it — and lives there in its raw originality as if it were still occurring. But we pretend not to live there, as if this hidden eternality belongs to someone else. Morality works best when it cloaks its dishonesty from itself. This is the same as to say that the unconscious is in reality no different from the conscious. It is a realm of experience we refuse to enter even as we express it. It is unconscious only because we consciously keep it there. Morality, in other words, is in its heart not only self-contradictory, it is profoundly immoral.

Darius, I can think of no single human phenomenon as authentically moral as what you revealed in these ten films. You were not performing. This was not pornography. This was exactly what it appeared to be: an unrestrained plunge into pleasure without putting yourself in the place of a conscious observer pretending to stand outside it. Pure id. Amazing. I placed the cameras in your office, but there was no camera in your own eye. You were a participant in your own actions — and with complete absorption. Nietzsche spoke up those who return from a rampage of murder and rape with a healthy, even noble, purity of conscience. Nietzsche, however, had it wrong. He could have learned from you. Remarkably, you pushed no one whence they did not long to go. Forcing others to cross over into your boundaries was no part of your pleasure. Those who did not wish to participate in what you offered were respectfully shown to the unlocked door behind them. How could a conscience be purer than that?

Your eager acceptance of the leadership of the Sexual Abuse Committee was a demonstration of this integrity. You made a mockery of the committee and its activities. Not one person admired what you were doing, while falsely denying to themselves that their own deepest desire was to be thoroughly engaged in what you seemed to be scorning. All the while you knew that you were addressing what the rest us cover over with a thin crust of congealed self-rejection.

You may well be asking yourself why, after all this praise, would Carmody induct you into the decad of the doomed. I answer by reminding you how Plato's great dialogue on love, the *Symposium*, opens. Socrates' friend, Phaedrus, comments almost as an aside that the poets have praised every god but one: Eros. In the long conversation that follows, no one seems to have a conception of the god persuasive enough to satisfy the others. Around the mid point of the dialogue it is noticed that Socrates has disappeared.

There is a search. He is found at some distance standing motionless, his expression transfixed, gazing into empty space. When he agrees to return to the group he makes the provocative and oft analyzed remark, "The only thing I understand is the act of love." For the moment wisdom and truth are set aside. Earlier he had even said that wisdom is no more than "a shadow in a dream." Darius, you are our

Phaedrus. You challenge us to ask whether we could make the same Socratic claim.

Your unrestrained worship of Eros pushes us to face the obvious: our students are at the apex in the long arc of their sexuality. We, on the other hand, looking over a room of young and willing bodies, realize we are several decades into commitments we are likely to be tiring of. The age difference between students and their teachers is irrelevant. The classroom sizzles in all directions with libidinal restlessness and longing.

Much of the talk in *The Symposium* is about the love of men for boys, of the aging for the young. Socrates does not disagree but his discourse takes a surprising turn. He introduces the name of a wise woman, Diotima, who had severely questioned him on his ideas of love. Diotima turned the Socratic method on Socrates himself, roughly like this:

Why do you love this boy, Socrates?

For his beauty, he answers.

Is he as beautiful as this one? No.

Is it then a different beauty?

No, the same beauty, just not as much of it.

So it is the beauty you love and not the boy?

Yes.

And the more beauty, the greater the love?

Yes.

Socrates! Beauty can be found anywhere, in flowers, in ideas, in the plays of Euripides, even in those old and near death like me and like you. Look now, Socrates, see how you are loved. The young Alcibiades here can hardly breathe in your presence, only from seeing you!

You know what happens next, Darius. Or, what does not happen. His admirer, Alcibiades, does not throw himself into Socrates arms nor does Socrates run his fingers through the younger man's hair. Beauty, as Diotima revealed, cannot be held in Socrates' embrace or stroked on Alcibiades' boyish head. Beauty is not something that can be touched, or captured, or employed, or measured, or sold, or diminished, or described, or bestowed, or attached to anything but itself, or even denied. What then can we **do** in its presence? Only this: behold it.

Diotima (whom we know nowhere but in the voice of Socrates, perhaps *as* the voice of Socrates) implies that beauty is there to be looked at but only if we do look. It cannot be seen if we do not have the vision for it. But, Diotima, we need to ask, how do we acquire such vision? She does not answer. Socrates does. You must be taught it. Nobody **has** beauty, as we saw. It is only taught if the teaching is itself beautiful. Beauty is the only teacher of beauty. This brings us to an extraordinary conclusion: whenever the god Eros is truly present, the classroom is itself a work of beauty.

This subtle god is not confined to a free-floating emotion or inclination but is always something *between* us, something shared, jointly engaged in. The exposed anatomy of a toad, the metaphors in *The Aeneid,* the emerging shape of an historical epoch are not beautiful in themselves but only in our conversation with each other, our acknowledgment of a bond that holds us together for those moments, a bond we cannot contain or freeze into place. We cannot take it with us, neither can we forget it. Once we have been students of such a teacher of beauty, we are forever lovers of beauty — however modest or grand.

There is a conclusion to be drawn here which the reader may find shocking or outrageous. If we stay with Diotima's vision of Eros as shared beauty, we can only view teaching and learning where Eros is present as the most perfect form of the classroom. This is to say that the perfect classroom is utterly useless to the world, even to its own students. It has no worldly value. Just as Socrates was not useful to the citizens of Athens, refusing, unlike the Sophists, to be paid or even accept disciples, he was worthless to rich men's sons. On the contrary, dangerous. What! Fall in love with wisdom? Waste a life by endless talk?

Darius, you got halfway there. Your exuberant celebration of Eros got the first part exactly right. You succeeded where the rest of us stop with fantasy. And in doing so you profiled that *caesura* with high clarity, showing exactly what it isn't. How can we come from viewing your films without a nascent understanding that the god Eros does not know Endings, Bonsais, Moments, Lift-offs? Worse. Every effort to trap the divine fellow not only fails, it produces a scene of discomforting unloveliness. For illustrating this with your rare talent for novelty, Darius Pennybacker, we can express only our deepest gratitude. You are the very maestro of things repellent and ugly.

It was when I began to understand this that I knew you too were dead. If I may use a woeful cliché, death has a certain finality to it that might seem to bring all our pleasures as well as our misfortunes to a conclusion. It is the ultimate *caesura*. But that is only part of a larger truth, for just as there is a finality, there is also an infinity to death. It alone has all the features of "forevermore" and "endlessness" and "inexhaustibility" — those careless sentiments we apply to ordinary experience. You repeatedly brought yourself and your willing companions to the point where you separated yourselves from infinitude by an opaque film of flesh.

In fact, it was that enormous recklessness that rewarded all of you with a rare and enviable thrill. But, of course, the thrill was merely a theatrical illusion, for each time you turned back at the edge of the everlasting, the thrill yielded to an emptiness that demanded satisfaction by repetition, and by yet more repetition. Although your fantasies were that you could continue these small dramas indefinitely without exhaustion, you knew very well that not far ahead what awaited was insufferable and ineradicable boredom. Therefore, the only solution was to breach that small gap at the boundary of the sublime. My admiration for your daring inspired me to provide a bridge over the gap and reward you with the completion of your insatiable desire.

The only question was a fitting method of doing so. The door was the first clue. It was itself a barrier that left us in the corridor, only able to pass by, not to enter. The door wasn't perfect, of course. It took some concentration, but if I listened carefully and patiently enough I could make out the countdowns and Lift-offs, the Geronimo's, and the Bonsai's. Asking to borrow your Greek New Testament and getting a brief and partial view of the space confirmed my suspicions — or should I say hopes?

You wonder how I got into your office, especially when the only key was in a coded envelope in Iolinda's desk. There is no mystery to it. After finding the exact spelling of the Greek word I was looking for — fittingly, Jesus' last expression on the cross, according to the Gospel of John, τετελεσθαι (or, tetelesthai — note the ten letters in Greek) — I asked Iolinda to return the book. I was able to glance briefly at the number on the envelope as she went through the collection of keys in her safekeeping. The rest you can imagine.

As for the camera, there is little to explain. It is the kind commonly hidden in banks, lobbies, hallways, and traffic intersections — as you know, since you found two and smashed them (providentially overlooking the third.) There were boxes of these items available to IT students and professors. Unobserved, I pocketed the three and later was able to find the appropriate recording equipment and bring it to my office. Obscuring the faces was simplified by adopting the same technique I used in focusing in on details of the paintings I used to illustrate the distinctive styles of their artists. I simply reversed the process.

The weightlifter reacted surprisingly fast. Not twelve hours after the first broadcast, I observed him standing under the partial cover of trees in the Square. His gaze was fixed on the now famed office window. I can only assume he was waiting for you to appear at the entrance to the building. Since this did not happen, he concluded, correctly as we now know, that you had locked yourself in, formulating options for the future. He was not in the future you were planning. But you were evidently in his.

Near midnight, when the offices had emptied and oblivion had taken over the temporary residents of the Square, he approached the building. Anticipating this move, I had opened the main entrance about an hour earlier and was already in my apartment seated at the screen of what the overlooked camera provided when the final scene opened.

It was remarkably brief. The knocking surprised you. You were right to be suspicious. Since this segment had no sound, I can only guess what must have been said through the steel door to your room. A seductive plea? A threat? An apology? No matter, you were persuaded. Although the room was too weakly lighted for the viewer to identify the visitor, we can easily make out the action. The man acted with astonishing speed, first ordering you to disrobe, then to drop to your knees. To my astonishment, even admiration, he was already fully aroused. As the massive arm wrapped around your head, I could almost hear the vise-like press of flesh and your desperate but failed struggle for breath. The brute's timing could not have been more precise. His Geronimo arrived only seconds after your limbs had gone permanently limp. He stretched your body out, as if to admire his work, and left.

Now a sequence guaranteed to be immortal in porn filmdom, you have won the gratitude of millions, most of them introduced for the first time to the fantasy (for some the actuality) of an original way to die, or to kill. Hemlock comes in different substances.

NINETY

Codex I, II, and VI. If you had not mentioned this unnamed group of thinkers twice, **Evgeny Klonska**, I might have let it pass. But I saw that it was of primary importance to you. Merely from the timbre of your voice, I could tell you were not a member of it so much as its servant. It was the master of your thought. I was particularly curious as to why you referred to this body at all. On reflection, I came to believe that it was your duty to the group itself to reveal its existence, but without explaining its work. It is a hidden but powerful force that insists it be known — but known as a mystery — as if there is something to know that cannot be known. But in this case something that *must* be known, something essential to our own existence, but without our being aware of it. I am using the words, "something," and, "it," as if we are dealing with an object here. But this is not how you presented Codex (as its elusive members of that secret congregation refer to themselves.) It is an association, a committee, a collective with its own aims and programs.

It was not until I wrote down these letters and numbers and played with rearranging them did I understand. Codex — which spelled this way, is an iconic document — can also be written Code X, or, an unknown document. Now, I saw, we were dealing with letters and numbers that essentially begged to be read in another, but more revealing sequence. After a few more shifts, what emerged was "Code: III. XVI." It was a shocking "Aha!" moment. The combination 3:16 can only mean the third chapter and sixteenth verse of the Gospel of John: "For God so loved the world, that he gave his own begotten Son, that whosoever believeth in him should not perish, but have everlasting life." The body of thinkers referred to as Codex, regard themselves as nothing less than the true Body of Christ.

I would not have thought so until I learned that your naked body had been found on a large rock by the steps of the cathedral, lying upside down and laid out in the form of the cross. On first hearing, it made sense to assume, as the police and the media did, that you had been murdered, punished perhaps for some unknown violation. Before reflecting on it, I took it as an act of retribution by the true believers of Codex. But then several features stood out. Why upside down? Why on a rock? Suddenly it clicked.

Peter, the most prominent of the disciples of Jesus, is known from tradition (not the New Testament) to have requested that his crucifixion by the Romans be inverted. Moreover, Peter is said in the gospels to be the rock (*petrus*) on which the church will be built, effectively the successor to Jesus, his earthly stand-in, the first bishop of Rome. So, Evgeny, why you begged to be killed upside-down and be left on a rock at the entrance to a cathedral ("seat of the bishop") presents us with a delicious puzzle.

Codex, let us not forget, is every bit as literalist as you. Jesus refers to the cross rarely in his brief year in the public, but in one instance he enjoins his followers to "take up my cross and follow me." In fact, this may be regarded as the clearest, most emphatic command Jesus delivers anywhere in the biblical record. His somewhat baffled disciples mistakenly thought he meant that to follow him was bound to be difficult, a life of hardship and suffering, even unto death. Where they made their mistake is not catching the rhetorical structure of the injunction.

Jesus did not say, "Follow me and take up the cross." Reading the words correctly, we see that taking up the cross **first** is the way of following the Lord. A close reading of the text undoes any suggestion that we are to shoulder the awkward object in question and walk down the road with it, or around the corner, then take a break, lean it against a fig tree, and have a smoke. Crucifixion, therefore, is not an unhappy result of a life of discipleship, it is its very substance. It is not where the Christian life ends, but where it begins. Your death was not a punishment, Evgeny, but a reward for your disciplined faithfulness.

Your entire assignment as a physicist was to demonstrate that the only true explanation of the universe, of existence itself, is found in the Incarnation of God in Jesus Christ. Your rejection of string theory as a means of describing the origin of the universe has the effect of obliterating the whole of theory itself in *any* causal account of what is.

Why is there something rather than nothing? It cannot be that there was something before this that came from yet another something, which had also come from something prior to that. This mad infinite regression has no explanatory value whatsoever. In fact, it employs a corrupt form of teleology — that whatever is caused is also a cause for what follows. It is a bogus cosmogeny. Period.

You are right to ask how I could possibly have discovered on my own your surreptitious Christian faith. It was something of a guess, but I thought the evidence was strong enough to act on. From your famed essay, "Non-transcendental Simultaneity," I detected a fierce but indirectly argued Plotinian view of reality. That this obscure Roman philosopher, Plotinus, would so *secretly* inform the view of a modern physicist was a dead giveaway. There had to be a novel explanation. Then I got it.

The universe cannot be an object to itself without presuming it can view itself from without. To do that is to imply the existence of another universe, therefore back to that irksome infinite regress again. The subtler point concerns time. If time has a beginning, the beginning cannot be dated because there is nothing before it. Therefore every moment is an eternity! Nice work.

This led me, Evgeny, to review all that you have written in recent years. The titles of your papers were dazzlingly obscure, their content well beyond anything intellectually familiar. It was just as I was about to admit my utter ignorance of what you were saying that I saw that, put together, the initial letters in each title form an anagram. Unscrambling them came almost at once. So, one of the world's most celebrated atheists is, in fact, a servant of God, an apostle to unbelievers who are sloppily and falsely confident in the verity of their own thinking. Jesus lives, indeed.

Evgeny, you won your place in this minyan of the damned when I realized that I could credit you with two astounding achievements. The first is the easier to elucidate. You have, to put it directly, erased Socrates from your conception of the university and from the Western humanist tradition altogether. It was the faint but sharp-edged picture of Codex that made this clear. The methodology of this singular body is the very obverse of Socrates'. As Codex has it, there is a body of fact, a circumscribed content of propositions that satisfies all empirical and logical requirements to be considered an established body of Truth. It is a definitive end to wonder. It is where all questions come to die.

You are smart and experienced enough to know that simply to state the Truth in its naked purity will summon up every Socratic challenger within range. You would be scoffed at and ridiculed for apotheosizing yourself as the sole font of all that is to be known. Therefore, the apostolic assignment bestowed on you by Codex had a hidden twist. You were to expose the empty arrogance of the scientific enterprise by presenting yourself as the nonpareil champion of disbelief. You carried out the command deftly.

Not one of your colleagues suspected that you were setting a trap. But what a trap! Your task was not to show the world of hard-minded empiricists that they were mistaken in their theoretical thought, but that they were mistaken in what they thought this hard knowledge really meant. They thought they knew what they believed. They were wrong. You were to show that they did not believe what they said they believed, but the opposite. They completely overlooked the implications of their views. The best thinkers among them are in effect unaware Christians. This is a sleeping scandal that will not register with the public for a generation or more.

When the works of this era are read toward the end of the present century they will be properly interpreted as expressions of unambiguous evangelical orthodoxy. Their accumulated writings will be taken as the Matthew, Mark, Luke, and John of the third millennium. Socrates will look on stupidly, his vulgar mouth as open and silent as it is in the single sculpture we have of him from antiquity.

And as for the god Eros, he makes a brief appearance then vanishes. But for a moment, while he hovered over your work, it was splendid. Your thinking, as I know it from your University lecture and your essays, I do not hesitate to say, is gorgeous. The intricacies of fact and theory, the immense collection of data and its subtle organization into a blizzard of categories interlocked in rational and empirical perfection, the scope of your vision drawing in realms of personal and physical reality we rarely see connected in high theory — all of this is done with such skill that the word, "genius," sometimes seems to apply.

I am aware that the work is not quite finished, that there are gaps to be filled in with more research and analysis. I detect, however, an iron certainty that all there is to know will be captured and all of the leaks will be sealed, that the whole can stand alone as the Truth. But here Eros departs; Socrates is dismissed. At that point your thinking stops and is shoved into place as a block to further inquiry. At first it resembles an enormous basilica full of wondrous works. But as we come to see how firmly its great doors have been bolted, it begins to lose its luster and take the character of a grand museum full of once living ideas. In time, we will begin to see it for what it is: a mausoleum of dead truths, a great featureless mass of outright ugliness.

This brings me to a second achievement greater than the first by several orders of magnitude. If it was courageous to ban Socrates from the academy, it is nothing compared to banning Jesus. I know as I write these words some readers will laugh. Perhaps you also, Evgeny. You, the veiled but fervid believer, the Christian of the century, are greeting the Galilean with the same obloquy as you had the Athenian. Can it be?

First, we compare the two. Both Socrates and Jesus were homeless wanderers, unattached to institutions of any kind, and in continuous dialogue with their followers. Neither wrote down or even dictated a single word. It is not even certain they were literate. Their teachings are impossible to codify. Just as there is nothing we can call Socrat-ism, neither is there Jesus-ism. We know of both only through the reports of those who knew and remembered them, and in the case of Jesus those who did not know him but remembered those who did. Both were executed by official decree as enemies of the people.

But there are several important differences. Socrates was an original. He had no precedent in Greek culture. He had himself little interest in the gods or the rich library of classical literature. His voice and his words were unique to his fellow citizens. Jesus was not original. His voice is resonant with the teachings and the stories of the hundreds who walked those same roads with him.

Stand off to the side for a moment, Evgeny, and look over Jesus' shoulder at the biblical multitude that precedes and surrounds him. Quickly, what do you see?

Poets, liars, adulterers, regicides, talking whirlwinds, prophets, slaves, witches, abductors, angels, mass killers, comforters?

Yes, we can put names to all of these. Others?

Fratricides, poseurs, betrayers, child slayers, healers, tax collectors, lamenters, zealots, peasants, rapists, pharaohs, warriors, giants.

Don't forget a certain giant killer. More?

Orphans, masturbators, ethnic cleansers, pagan queens, snake charmers, lawgivers, behemoths, lying serpents, genital exposers, idolaters, deceivers, drunks, sodomists, singers, seeresses, magicians, mourners, protestors.

Good. You can stop there. There are more, many more, but that is enough to show that no type of human being or human action has been excluded from the vast literary populace that is Jesus' biblical heritage.

In this respect, Jesus and Socrates are to be viewed in the sharpest possible contrast. Socrates comes with wit and irony, Jesus comes with a history. Socrates was in conversation with his friends and sometimes his enemies. Jesus was in conversation with a civilization two thousand years old. We hear in Socrates the talk of a given age. In Jesus we hear the discourse of the ages.

A much bigger difference is that Socrates is so fully and credibly presented by Plato that he is altogether without mystery. There has never been a search for the "historical Socrates." With Jesus the contrast could not be more extreme. On the face of it, the matter seems uncomplicated. Simply read the gospels and draw up a coherent narrative, then attach a summary of his teachings. Evgeny, you are so familiar with the two-thousand-year effort to do this I skip the detail and go at once to the summary.

During his own lifetime Jesus was confounding even to those closest to him. Immediately up on his death there were strongly competing views of the meaning of his life, his teachings, and his ministry. If we were to collect every attempt written over the ensuing two millennia to explain who Jesus *really* was, what he *really* said, and what he *really* did, we would need whole city blocks of towering libraries whose shelves would creak with books in hundreds of languages, not one in full agreement with another, many of them works of great intelligence.

Judging from this literature, tens of thousands of Jesuses must have been walking about Galilee in those several years. The variety is stunning. If they were all gathered into one place, each would consider all the others impostors. To put it abruptly, given that more than a third of the population of the earth is Christian or lives where Christendom is dominant, the best known name of all those ever to have been born of woman is that of Jesus. And yet, that same Jesus is the most variously understood person ever to have dwelt among us. What we know best about Jesus is that he is so defiantly unknown that he comes close to being the Unknown itself.

It is reasonable to ask, if the search for the real Jesus is bound to be fruitless, why anyone would bother. It can only be that what we know of the man from the multitude of false attempts is disturbing or provocative enough to demand yet another. There is something in his hiddenness that we feel compelled to make evident. If I were to describe what that something is, it would only add to the vast list of useless tries. In short, there is a powerful absence here that one can neither ignore nor indisputably identify.

This dilemma would never have arisen were it not for a most ordinary event. Three women, all named Mary, one of them his mother, the day after Jesus died, went to what they thought was his grave, looked under the stone and found the earthen pit empty. We can understand Christianity as centuries-long effort to undo the terrible mystery of the emptied tomb. The desire to discover its original content and the need to find a sufficient seal to close it forever has given rise to a grand explosion of theologies, extensive systems of thought intended to secure the Truth of Christianity for all believers.

You know the history well, Evgeny. First, monastic centers of learning, then the appearance of giants like Augustine, Anselm, and Thomas of Aquinas, later Luther, and Calvin — all of whom created wondrous intellectual schemes, which were meant to close that tomb, but all of which were met with spirited objections, igniting still new systems of thought. The rise of the universities, beginning in the 13th and 14th centuries, was a manifest outgrowth of the Christian intellectual tradition. From the start, theology, considered "the Queen of the Sciences," held the center of the curriculum. Harvard and Yale were founded to provide our young country with an educated clergy. As the universities underwent a steady secularization, theology became a minor element in their curricula.

Today, although almost all of the great universities have it in their histories, none of them would allow the word Christian into the definition of their educational missions. But the deepest impulse of the institutions remains the same, as the mottos of Harvard (*veritas*, truth) and Yale (*lux et veritas*, light and truth) have it. The power of these great currents of thought is attested to in the fact that all of the world's premier institutions of learning have risen in the Western world, that is, the Christian West.

To this day, there are no equivalent bodies outside Europe and North America. Is it too much to say that the passion to establish the Truth is the continuing effort to bury the anonymous tomb's dark unknown under durable monuments of verifiable knowledge? You, Evgeny, know the answer. You are, indeed, as a decorated general in this great campaign, its very best representative: a Christian armed with *veritas* itself.

But something else has been going on in the Christian West. We have just come out of the bloodiest century in the history of the race, nearly all of it in, or initiated in, our portion of the globe. Stand elsewhere in the world and look in our direction. What you will see is recurring warfare among such countries as Holy Mother Russia, Lutheran Germany, Papal Italy, "Christian" America, pious Spain, the orthodox Balkans, Catholic Poland, sacred France, and England with its divinely provided monarchy. Even the regnant ideologies are implicated. The Nazis' Holocaust is a Christian crime. Marx was inspired not only by the great überchristian Hegel but also by his own Methodist utopian father-in-law. (Notice that the Nazis' swastika and the Soviets' hammer and sickle preserve the symbol of the cross.) Mao, parasitizing Marx, starved and killed millions of his own. The century's tally? Two hundred million dead is the usual conservative estimate, all slain by governments, and most of those democratically elected. You and your fellow believers, Klonska, have a lot to explain.

Our time is short, Evgeny. Let me offer an explanation of my own. The tomb is still empty. And always will be. This is not a small emptiness. The young Jew, whose life as a rabbi lasted scarcely more than a single year, is not only the most known, but also the most unknown person, who ever lived. He is an infuriating reminder that under all our certainties there are questions that will not go away, that only grow deeper with each supply of new answers. We see it in you, Evgeny. The extreme passion of your dedication to this particular truth is matched by an extreme terror that you could just as well be wrong. You walk your life across a fragile terrain that only partly hides dark caverns of doubt and unknowing. You walk quickly, and do not look down. Even death you receive as a comfort.

You are a large thinker, Evgeny. There is a good reason why *Time Magazine* would honor you as a "most influential" world citizen: your hubristic assumption that the Truth could be clearly declared and firmly fixed in the human mind for millennia to come. When we think of great minds arriving at great conclusions, you are on our list as well as *Time's*. In other words, you have our admiration because *we all want to be there.*

For that reason, I feel justified in claiming that the Western world's existential panic can be pictured as Evgeny Klonska writ large. You are not a Nazi, or a Marxist, but you share their Christian roots and the dread of the void that comes with them, a legacy of that terrifying young Galilean. The triumphalism of the West, the belief that history ends with us, the absolutism that infects all of our attitudes on race, class, and ethnos — all of this is part of the desperate need to hammer tight the splintering cover on his cenotaph. The irony, of course, is complete. In our flight from this terror we terrorize an entire century. By "Christianizing" a national culture, we deafen it to the multiple cultures of a larger world. In trying to close one tomb, we scrape out others by the hundreds of millions.

Now you can see clearly why you belong in this exclusive gathering. You represent one part of our profession as vividly as no one else. Your indefatigable labor to acquire all that can be known to an inquisitive and rational mind is to be properly emulated by colleagues and students. But there is another part, and it is because you lack this so thoroughly that I immediately identified you as a candidate for the Puzzler. Every teacher, who is truly a teacher, will prize knowledge in every form and amount, but will prize far more *knowing what we do not know*. This is not to assign a value to ignorance as such but to how well we learn to know the scope of our ignorance.

Those who do not know what they do not know will soon be reckless dangers to themselves and others. This can apply to persons of great learning. In fact, it is common among such persons. It is true of you, Evgeny. Once the Truth was secured and the seal was in place, nothing was left but to die. For countless others, nothing is left but to kill.

There is another word for the ignorance that knows itself as ignorance: wonder. Aristotle said that philosophy begins in wonder. I can add only that at its best, philosophy, like all forms of knowledge, also *ends* in wonder. Socrates was accused of letting knowledge drain off into mere words. But what we find in him is that there is no end to the discourse, everything remains yet to be said. From the Galilean, we learn that the tomb remains forever empty.

That you found glory at the entrance to the Slovenian cathedral was at first a surprise. Then I remembered that Ljubjana is a center for research into the Western esoteric tradition — that is, the secret knowledge that is considered the basis of all knowledge. Of course, you would have gone there to spend your last days reading the great pagan philosopher, Plotinus, along with such obscure worthies as Pseudo-Dionysius, Duns Scotus Eriugena, the Jewish and Islamic mystics, Meister Eckhart, and Jakob Boehme.

I also knew that Codex would quickly discover your location and that you would be unprotected from any retributive punishment they chose to apply. I knew it would be extreme. But until I received the description of your naked and tortured body laid out on a rock at the entrance to the cathedral — upside down — I did not gauge the degree to which they judged your assignment a success. How perfect. Triumph and death in a single act. For you the tomb is finally sealed. But it is only yours.

NINETY-ONE

You are smart enough for the profession, **Deborah Waterson**, but you lacked the experience necessary to function successfully in the position to which the agency appointed you. You betrayed yourself and your employer with too many questions that were more like assertions than genuine inquiry. Your performance is still too amateur. It was a blunder to have the yogi — the stomach guy — sit so close to us at the café that he was able to get a tape of the whole conversation. I was briefly thrown off when I saw you talking intimately with police Lieutenant Thomas Roche at the time of Holmers's suicide. I didn't get at first that it was a show intended precisely for me, as if to persuade me that you were yourself a cop. It only worked for a few minutes, until I gave it closer thought and realized that the humbled fellow was listening to you only because you had promised him something irresistible — a full year's salary, say, or a retirement home in the Turks and Caicos. I understood at once that Roche was your access to the mass of data collected by the narcotic detectives on Holmers' thriving business. Your duplicity did have the charm of being double layered. You were pretending to get me to see that you were pretending while concealing the true pretender. It was worth several amusing lunches.

And, then, there was the moment when we met in the café after Klonska's address. Why you threw your bag onto the table with such carelessness was almost risible. You seemed not even to notice that the concealed Smith and Wesson .38 made its telltale thump as it struck the top of the table, not two feet away from where I was sitting; I could even pick out the shape of the weapon's handle as it hit.

Your greatest error, of course, was to let me know that you had discovered who I was. Having no proof, you took the risk of assuming that your hint would cause me to betray myself by a sharpened glance or uncommon gesture. It is not a bad idea in the usual case, but you learned too late that before you knew who I was, I knew who you were. Had you not been in so far over your head with powerful players, it would have been a valuable lesson for you. But it was too late for that.

Nor did you know when we had our final lunch in the faculty club that you were already dead. Clever as you are, you failed to notice why I picked up that squash ball in Holmers' lab. From where you were standing — pretending to pretend to be a cop — you must have observed Holmers killing himself by injection. What you didn't catch was that the ball I picked up fell from his hand immediately after that act. It was, of course, the container for the poison he was all along secretly planning to use for the final scene he had prepared. With practiced skill, it took him no more than a few seconds to push the needle into the ball and then inject it immediately into a vein. After years of addiction the man knew the classic techniques, especially the one that would deliver the poison's effects in less than a minute.

Unfamiliar with the game of squash and its equipment, you could not have known that a feature of the rubber from which this kind of ball is made is that it seals tightly after being penetrated by a small object like a hypodermic needle. Only after a close examination of the ball's surface could I later locate that tiny mark. But knowing where it was, I could, with little more than a gentle squeeze, produce a death-sized dot of its contents. While you, Deborah, were searching my face for a telltale expression, it took only a small but natural movement for me to pass the sugar toward you — with the ball concealed in the palm of my hand. You didn't notice — another indication of your inexperience in the profession — that in making this action my hand passed over your coffee. A quick squeeze, a couple drops, your execution was certain. I was confident in its effectiveness, not only because it killed Holmers in seconds, but as it was later learned, it killed his wife as well. Holmers, as a young anthropologist in the Moluccan Islands, had come across this rare and still unidentified poison, concocted by native hunters. Knowing its chemistry was so uncommon as to be impossible to trace, he kept a supply for future needs.

Unlike an injection, ingesting the poison takes several hours to have an effect. Because Jack Lister knew your true name and your correct address, he learned of your fate that same day, while the University and the investigating police knew only that you had disappeared. He could not reveal to the public that you had died, of *course*, for then he would also reveal his secret use of a highly expensive private detective service to spy on the lives of his faculty. His motivation was simple enough.

By knowing the twisted intimate personal details of wayward professors, he could indirectly let them know what would be exposed if they did not make an anonymous donation to the Lister Family Foundation

It is not publicly known that this apparently benevolent organization is a fund to which Jack had exclusive access. In practice it is little more than a personal bank account hidden by its false title from the IRS. The legal term for this activity is extortion.

Jack's rage was not without good reason. Start with Darius Pennybacker. For several years he had a suspicion of what Darius was up to, chiefly from rumors passed on to him by Lieutenant Roche (for years in Jack's secret employ,) but your investigation was producing nothing definitive. That's why, when you kept asking for an invitation to the Committee, I knew that he had you on Darius' trail, thinking you might find an opening as you got closer to him. When I released the films, what slipped out of Jack's covetous grasp was at the very least Darius's potential bankrolling of a membership for him in a Connecticut country club and an appropriate vehicle for driving there.

Then Holmers. Given the smooth operation of his illicit but enormously successful lab, it promised a larger bounty even than what could be squeezed out of Pennybacker. And this was an ongoing industry that could be surreptitiously shielded by the University — that is, by Jack — indefinitely. The plan was simple. Since Tom Roche had a good deal of material on Holmers and his lab already, he would let Holmers know he was onto his scheme, but protect him from the feds and give him some kind of medical cover for his addiction, while taking a percentage of the cash flow. He must also have promised to let the sad bastard win a game or two. That is why he added you to the case shortly after the publication of Puzzle #2. But none of you ever expected that someone would get there ahead of you. Of course you would be interested in what I picked up in that burning lab. Your assignment was to find a way you could somehow falsely implicate me in Holmer's dangerous business, giving Jack an opening to a counter extortion, possibly blocking me from revealing his plan for a share of Holmers' produce.

But you understand, don't you, that neither of these minor tragedies for Jack ranked with the grandest of them all. Aleksander Krauss's project was a diamond mine that would make a Zimbabwean ruler convulse with envy. The chances Jack took here were extraordinary. I can only admire him for the daring. He was Krauss's cover from the beginning. It was not Aleksander, but Jack, who got the government project to begin with. It took only less than an hour of research on my part to learn that the aide to the congressional committee that made the grant was Jack's roommate at Princeton. When that giant fist of water propelled Krauss down the corridor, Jack knew that his own river of major wealth had run dry. No wonder that your facial expression, while standing in the midst of students at the time of the disaster at the Center for Applied Mathematics, was one of both anger and chagrin. An unknown trickster had just delivered a possibly fatal blow to your reputation as an emerging gangster.

I understand why, after the Aleksander Krauss and Pennybacker disasters you were desperate to get closer to the work of the Committee. You correctly assessed the Puzzler's extraordinary ability to sniff out the University's richest sites of moral and financial rot. You were at this point in acute need of new extortive material. The Committee's immersion in the matter seemed to offer a short cut to these exploitable infections, putting you a step ahead of the Puzzler. Like so many of the rest of us, you underestimated the lithe and balletic footsteps that kept the killer several strides ahead of all pursuers. I admit to sudden pinches of sympathy for your ineptitude and the ill consequences that followed, but nothing more.

What you may not have known, Deborah, is that Jack had strong personal reasons for this secret criminality. His wealthy Long Island family fell into sudden ruin when his father was prosecuted and eventually jailed for a vast investment scheme in which he stole millions from the naïve customers of his firm. Jack was fourteen at the time of his father's suicide (he hanged himself in prison), and had to leave his private school in New Hampshire to spend the next three years in a public high school in the working class community of Massapequa Park, Long Island. By a ferocious struggle, he squeezed out college and graduate degrees from the Ivies. His million dollar salary as president of a major American university and his erstwhile upper-class childhood were not enough to erase the shame. How much more was needed? Jack was darkly aware that there was no end to that treacherous highway. This only magnified his competitive drive. But he needed high class monsters like your outfit to carry off the shakedown. Tom Roche was not up to the challenge on his own.

The lovely irony here is that Jack's use of secret investigations to hold others within his grip has turned back on him, leaving him powerless and broke — and with no means of revealing what has been done to him without revealing what he has been doing to others. Your brilliant move — and I do mean brilliant — is that when the Committee's well went dry, you decided to blackmail Jack himself. By your threatening to expose his own blackmailing scheme, the payoffs to you had basically drained the liquid assets of the Lister Family Foundation. And without a steady flow of extorted income from other sources, Jack cannot continue to pay his debts to your "agency." Only by the most devious accounting tricks can he steal the necessary funds from the University budget — to forward to you.

You have good reason to be baffled by my decision to include you in our cell group. So far, you were the only non-academic. That needs a bit of explaining. You were not on my original list of ten. You took the place of — be ready for a surprise — Jack Lister himself. Once Jack had engaged you and your gangster companions, he was already as good as dead, this was long before Oliver Ridley (since your "firm" had been on the scene for more than a year). Of course, we have yet to hear from the FBI on its complete decoding of the bank account numbers. There are billions of rials, afghanis, rands, dinars, kopeks, and rubles out there, held in Jack's name, waiting to be found hidden in banks in Geneva, the Caymans, Cuba, Malta, Uzbekistan, and even South Africa. Had he been able to get to them before Krauss's fall, he could have paid you off and passed the last years of his life with substantial wealth. Now, no sooner will these handsome sums be revealed than the government will take them as evidence. Jack's career will shift location. He can take comfort in knowing that there is a secure position waiting for him in all-paid government housing well into his retirement years. There is a good chance that Lieutenant Thomas Roche will be a resident in the same unit.

But why you, then? At heart, you and your companions are thieves — damned good ones and expensive — but thieves nonetheless. Every one of your actions at the University has its corresponding place in the criminal and civil codes of the city, the state, and the federal government. Extortion, wire-tapping, money laundering, false identity, impersonating an officer of the law, eavesdropping, carrying a loaded weapon, conspiracy to commit a crime, concealing the criminal activity of others — which makes you an accomplice several times over — this and much more hints at the law-breaking scope of your year at the University. By contrast, very few scholars have a need (or the courage) for outright violations of any criminal code. However — and this is why I have invited you here — we are thieves ourselves, indeed, very high-class members of that profession. In fact, thievery is the animating core of our very existence as a university.

Consider a business that advertises its wares as, let us say, very expensive perfumes in handsomely carved crystal vials. Customers discover when they get home that they have purchased containers from which the contents had been drained. The label and its elegant bottle had convinced them, not to mention the exalted reputation of the shop, that they were buying the real thing. They will feel that they have been robbed, and they have been. In our case, Jack's "Enterprise University" is careful to hire nationally known experts in seductive packaging. Take a quick glance at what the students are offered, and not just by their courses. The dormitories are either converted residential hotels or built in that style, each suite of rooms with a modernized bath and kitchenette. The classrooms are fitted with every possible electronic device and are painted in comforting pastel hues. The student center is a fortress-sized building with cafés, study areas, overstuffed chairs and sofas ideal for napping, spas, meeting rooms for clubs, and a theater with Broadway-quality lighting and sound. The library has been furnished with over two thousand ergonomically designed study chairs. There are several gymnasiums, each with its own pools, weight rooms, Pilates studios, basketball courts, running tracks, and enclosed facilities for everything from squash to yoga. There are renowned scholars in every department — altogether three Nobels, seven MacArthurs, and twelve Pulitzers. You know, Deborah, that this is a hasty abbreviation of the University's attractions; I am just creating an impression.

What you may not know, even after observing us through the full academic calendar, is what students walk away with from this lustrous packaging. That is, what have they actually bought? The answer is simple and obvious. They bought the packaging. Only the packaging. For many of them it was not completely empty. As with customers at the parfumerie, there was an aroma, a small residue of what had once been offered there. We have features that closely resemble a university. There are books to be found. On one floor of the University Bookstore, there are numbered aisles and shelves where assigned texts are stacked. Unassigned works can be found on a higher floor, just behind the hooded sweatshirt display. Except for textbooks, the students' dormitory bookshelves are useful for aloe plants, stuffed animals, and boxes of sugared cereal. By early afternoon nearly every one of the library's ergonomic study chairs is occupied. A careful look at what captures the silent absorption of the students turns up but a meager handful of library's claimed three million volumes. Spread out on the tables before them are the technical texts they are forced to buy at outrageous prices, their pages filled with graphs, colored columns, sentence-long mathematical formulae, and numbered outlines — basically memorization exercises. Occasionally one can overhear an exchange of ideas, usually inpreparation for a test.

Lectures are convenient and undisturbed occasions for texting friends, or wished-for friends. There is a student government whose members and officers are the same as those in the sororities and fraternities. The newsstands surrounding the University do a snappy business in fashion and celebrity magazines. There are short piles of the tabloids and never a copy of *The Times*. The coffee shops in the neighborhood, some of the most atmospheric in the city, have little appeal. The expressionless faces of those few students present are locked onto the glowing twelve square inches of rectangular plastic tablet. There are eight members of the debating society. The Classics Club has twelve but has not met for a year. The poetry magazine is published privately and supported by the poets themselves, the only readers of their semiannual pamphlets. The city's theater district, its concert halls, and museums — envies of the world — could all be transferred to the Mollucan Islands without a single student objection.

The word, "letters," is for most English speakers synonymous with literature. For students the "letters" have been reduced to several powerful abbreviations: SAT, PSAT, ACT, GRE, GMAT, LSAT, and MCAT. Protest marches, political rallies, sit-ins, boycotts, work projects, tutoring programs, anti-poverty action, roused environmental concerns, anti-war demonstrations and the unionizing of adjunct teachers — none of this has any reality for students outside the brief descriptions that can found in history books of the '70s and '80s. We have the aroma of a real university but the stench of a fake.

Deborah, you are staring at me, with no idea what I am talking about. It all comes to this: students are being robbed, along with their parents. They bought a very expensive package labeled *education,* sold to them by one of the world's premier institutions of higher learning. But they went away with nothing but the label — what we sometimes call a degree — for which they paid as much as $250,000 over their four years. It was cold, outright theft. As a professional in the field, you know this is a bit more than a misdemeanor. A quarter million dollar heist is prison-worthy.

Of course, you want to know how the University gets away with it. The art of thievery includes not getting caught, after all. I can see you are curious. They got away with it because for both the students and their parents, *the packaging was all they wanted.* They knew very well what they were buying. A true education was of no value to them, no cash value especially. And the University itself knew this all along. The luxurious shell was developed for those who were shopping for a luxurious shell. In one way of looking at it, they were both — the university and its customers — stealing — from each other. The fraud on one side was selling "education" instead of an education. The fraud on the other was knowingly accepting false goods.

Now, if I may, a comment that will likely not surprise you. The reader may wonder why both parties go through this dance and deception in perfect harmony with each other, and at such an expense. There is no mystery here. Both know the value of packaging — not just to the university and its students, but to the society as a whole. *Having the right package* is the very minimum requirement for success. In the present world, the distribution of social and financial goods is a precisely choreographed shell game. Shell against shell, label against label, brand against brand, a swirling collision of externalities. The university, in submission to the surrounding culture, has induced a tragic shift in its educational mission — instead of bestowing students with the gift of seeing, we teach them skills of being favorably seen; instead of teaching them to question the appearance of the world, we train them to make a profitable appearance of themselves to the world.

Unfortunately, not all labels are equal. A degree from this institution cannot compete with a degree from that one. It is even more important to realize that once packaged by our high-status University, the labeling process has not ended. There is much ahead: the right medical or law school, the right hedge fund, the right marriage, the right academic appointment. Robbed and robbing our way up.

Deborah, you are a crook of the classic variety. There is no irony in your professional career. You know the law, you break it for your own ends. You have no collaborative arrangement with your victims. You win or lose and are done with it. Your crimes have mounted, as I indicated, but they are petty violations compared to our much graver crime. What has been stolen from us, even while we put it up for sale as willing actors in the process — what has been stolen from the entire intellectual tradition of the West — is nothing less than civilization itself.

My one regret is that I did not get you into a squash court. You had a perfect physique for the game and were aggressive and devious enough to make an excellent player — good enough, with the right coaching, to compete with anyone around the University ... except Jack. But then you had already beaten him anyway.

NINETY-TWO

Standing at the base of the cliff, looking upward three hundred feet to the forbidding overhang at its summit, I understood, **Raimundo Guttierez**, the erotic appeal of treacherous ascent. Although this rock expanse was only one of many vertical rock faces in the Shawngunks, no higher than a thirty-story building, and certainly nothing so challenging as the peaks that work their temptation on you, I felt the pull myself. I actually found myself a bit breathless as we stood together attempting to track a possible route to the top.

Through your eyes, I could see the much greater allure of a mountain in all its phallic splendor ... rising violently from the material earth ("mater" from the Latin for mother as you well know), thrusting itself upward, lightly clothed in ripped garments of soil and forest, seductively concealed by sheets of snow and blankets of mist and cloud, then to expose itself in all its rough nakedness, penetrating the very heavens, and without rival. Mountains are the most likely of all natural phenomena to diminish us, to make us feel our mortal smallness — the ultimate shame of male inadequacy. They are therefore to be conquered, subdued, made our own, and, at the very Moment of success, we are to stab the defeated rival with a flag of phallic triumph over the mystical mother, and call the defeated body our own.

In spite of your general social nastiness, Raimundo, you knew I was attracted to you, not for all the showy emblems of masculine bravado, but for the intensity of the need to display it. It was an expression of your anti-male maleness. Your attraction to me was a kind of key. There was something in it that was independent of what I recognized as your servitude to Lucille. It revealed itself in several ways, but chiefly in your persistent invitation to me to join you in a climb. It didn't matter that my talent for the sport, even my interest in it, was far from equal to yours. You sensed that there was something to be had by doing it, but without knowing what that might be. But I did know what could be had by it. There was, however, no putting it into words. Or should I say, there was no putting it into a word? I was eager to take up the invitation.

You seemed a bit puzzled that I would have led you to such a remote site in the Gunks. As I explained at the time, I chose it after carefully studying documents detailing the geology of the cliffs. The spot was not only separated by a considerable distance from the most popular climbing trails farther to the east, but presented a rock face of gentle verticality with a minimum of features — protrusions, crumbling faces, cracks, chimneys — that represent hazards to an amateur climber. As you acknowledged this, I thought with evident relief that it was still something of a challenge for you. According to guidebook, it was ranked 4.15, more than I had previously attempted thus putting me in your professional hands. And the way you looked up at the face above us, you seemed to consider it more than a mere upward stroll, strictly for beginners.

When we had strapped on our harnesses, and you offered me the lead position, I believe you thought you were flattering me, but I recognized a different motivation. Putting me just a few handholds above you for the entire three hundred feet awaiting us allowed you an especially intimate view. Since predicted weather was for clear skies and eventually high temperatures, we were minimally dressed only in shorts and sleeveless shirts. More of me was revealed than hidden.

I thought the first third of the climb, one hundred feet or so, was pure textbook: the ropes correctly tied — I used the bowline, you the butterfly, a prettier knot — the pitons inserted without effort, the wire-hinged karabiners that you prefer properly spaced on the new half-inch rope strong enough to stop both of us at once in a free fall. Frankly, the first two hundred feet were a little boring. From there on up, however, I found it increasingly technical.

It was not until we were twenty-five feet from the top with its menacing overhang that I saw what I hoped I would find. Not two body lengths to my right was a device rarely used in modern climbing: an old angle piton, fitted with a ring that had been hammered into a spidery crack in the rock. It must have been inserted many years earlier, well before the ethic of leaving nothing behind had become *de rigeur* among climbers. Coming closer, I saw how thoroughly it was rusted.

I threaded the rope through the ring, and kept it from slipping with a figure eight knot, then came back to the left another eight to ten feet, creating a short triangle. Because my body shielded it, you could not see how decayed the ring had become. I first made sure there was no slack in the belaying rope between us. Then, when you weren't looking, I gave the rope to the ring a quick tug, all it took to shatter the rusted piton. The triangle of rope between us straightened as you fell, exactly as I calculated. I watched as you dropped about ten feet, then barn-doored away from the face of the cliff, putting any possible hold out of reach. What you didn't see was that I had firmly placed two of your more reliable pitons into the rock just below and to the left of the broken iron. You were safely caught and were able to swing back to a foothold. You gave me a thumbs-up, too stunned and grateful to say anything, not at all suspecting it was a trick.

The overhang was all that remained. You must have sensed my uncertainty, as you took the lead without comment. It was also your chance to show your skill at the sport. It was, I admit, with genuine astonishment that I watched you hang by one hand then the other, nothing but empty space beneath you, inserting a piton at each exchange until you were able to get two fingers over the sharp edge of the rock farthest out, then swing back and forth until you could hook your whole leg over the top. What footage it would have made, especially from below — my perspective.

After you had handed me up, an act of strength and balance in itself, I was grateful you said nothing, and reassured to find that you had slipped into a reflective silence. Now that we had successfully completed the ascent and had no physical challenge ahead of us, you turned inward. You knew that the real danger for you was yet to come. There was no need to hurry it. I could lie there next to you for hours, not an arm's length away, close enough that I could hear you breathe, smell your sweat and even feel the heat of your mostly naked body.

Slowly, while you were lost in erotic reverie, I was in a different reverie of my own, recalling the sequence of events that brought you and me to this place on precisely this first day of June. It all started on the day I went to your office to retrieve my academic robe. Felix Cisneros. Ha. How careless of you to keep these volumes in your library. Although when I first made the discovery, I was less than sure what conclusion to draw. Then you recklessly referred to your friend in Guatemala. Guatemala? As if that weren't enough, you unnecessarily added that he was your childhood friend. What happened to Barcelona in your official history? And your practiced but unconvincing Catalan accent with your rolled r's and an exaggerated lisp?

So, Felix, what followed was little more than an exchange of letters with a certain journalist. You know him well. He was exiled from your country at the height of its failed but violent *revoluccion*. I began by typing your name into my computer — your real name. Very little came up, but there was one striking item, one that apparently escaped the technological laundering of your past. It was in an article in the Guatemalan newspaper, *el Heraldo,* that referred to a certain *Commandante* Cisneros, honored for his "heroic" service to the country in his role as the founder of the commando section of the *la Guardia Civil.* The article was dated June 1, 1988, during the presidency of Óscar Humberto Mejía. No other details were provided, but the article appeared under the name of a certain Vincente Lopez. When I entered his name, I found a brief narrative of a journalist exiled from Guatemala for "damaging the honor of the country." I located the gentleman in Los Angeles where he now works as an investigative reporter for *la Opinión,* a Spanish language journal. I called him.

"I found your Felix Cisneros," I announced early in the call. He was at first suspicious of my intentions and acted as if he did not know to whom I was referring. But as our conversation progressed his credulity grew with it. He finally admitted his astonishment that I had located the mysterious *Commandante,* someone he had been seeking for years. During a succeeding telephone conversation, he provided the following account.

"*Commandante* Cisneros," he said, "he was a good soldier in the army of *Presidente* Humberto Mejía. Very smart. Very strong. *Presidente* Mejía, he calls him 'my theenker,' in English. Because of his ranking and, how you say, *brutalidad*, he was chose by the military court to carry out orders for execution of convicted enemies of the state. *Desaparaciementos*, we call them."

What followed was Vincento's summary of your methods for "disappearing" these guilty and mostly young rebels. Because of the cruelty of these methods, it was painful to keep listening. One technique stood out. "With some, he used helicopter and flew out over the *Golfo*." (As Señor Lopez got deeper into his narrative, his accent grew stronger and he began using more Spanish words.) "When far out enough, not seeing land, he shoves the *criminales y traidores* — they were tied with *cuerdas* — out the door of the copter. But before he does that, he, how shall I say, he waited on their screaming, then opened the *botones* of his *pantalones* and did his sex thing on them, you know, *a mano*. It no matter they are *muchachos o muchachas*. He finish and out they go. Pushed, I want to say."

He concluded by explaining that the *Guardia Civil*, learning the rebels were plotting a gruesome death for the *Commandante*, equivalent to his own methods, rewarded him by expunging his military records and providing the necessary paperwork for a new identity, including a false Spanish passport listing an address in Barcelona. This all came with a handsome payout that financed his study for a doctorate and provided him with a well deserved life of comfort.

What Señor Lopez did not know was that a part of the river of Guatemalan funds was directed straight into the Lister Family Foundation. I learned this only by another brief search, and a confidential disclosure from a colleague at Princeton. *Presidente* Humberto Mejía's youngest son spent two years at Princeton before dismissal for violent behavior while drunk, apparently a constant state. There is no indication he was a friend of Jack's, but they were in the same eating club for one year. This explains, Felix, why you had a unique appointment to the University, a renewable five-year contract that required no department membership or tenure decision. You were with us *gratis* President Lister. Mejía, of course, is long gone. But there was an unbroken transition to a new source. Funds have poured out, as generously as ever, to you and the Foundation. You have been, for six or seven years now, an agent of the CIA, an inside eye on the political activities of a major university in a major city on a Square, a role known only to you and to Jack. Of course, you would present yourself as a an outspoken leader for left-leaning campus protests. How convenient to be admitted into the most active cells of liberal plotting against the University.

Can there be a better reason for your induction into our *casa de los muertos*? You have so successfully created a false persona, the exact opposite of your true self (if you have one; cf. Nat Holmers) that your *desaparición* will serve as an effective exposure of the University's complicity in many of the world's most despicable crimes. Nothing less than a mysterious death combined with a shocking revelation could shake the larger university community — faculty, students, staff, alumni — from its somnolence on this matter. Showing the connection between, let us say, a mild, boring professor of Milton studies and the murderous *jefes* of Colombian drug cartels does tax one's credulity a bit.

The famed *armillaria ostoyae*, an underground fungus, or mushroom, is thought to be the world's largest living organism. A single plant can extend over thousands of acres. Largely invisible, it is detected only where patches of dead trees begin to show in a coniferous forest. The fungus sends out masses of filaments to feed off the nutrients in the root systems of trees, slowly starving them. The finances of a university are fed by a forest of sources much like those of a large bank or corporation. There are thousands of filaments that reach back through tuitions, endowments, contributions, foundation grants, and government-funded programs, each of which has its own mass of filaments in search of new sources of wealth. The same is true of an entire country's economy. No one can say where this dollar or that one originated. Even the giver or the payer cannot say. Every economy, large or small, is a deep and intimate penetration into every living entity within its growing range. That is to say, a national economy is a single fungus.

The fungus is a growing thing. It kills, yes, but if the aggressive exploitation of its biota is over-aggressive, the organism slowly draws back into itself and perishes. It grows or it dies. The university's nutrients depend on its skill at feeding off root systems that are themselves feeding off more distant root systems. It is dedicated, to put it in a phrase, to the starvation of its sources. But the starvation must be carefully paced to guarantee a maximum flow of institutional sustenance. The process is not obvious to the casual observer. Some sources are quite remote and easily overlooked; others are well concealed in their daily ingestion.

How remote? Where do the world's reigning financial enterprises look first to easy sources of funds? The most plentiful and accessible fountains of cash are those plutocracies who have control over vast material resources: oil, coal, precious metals, plutonium, diamonds, rare earths, cocaine. Here nothing more than ordinary graft stands in the way of corporate riches. Of course, there will be intense competition — even between nations — for this ready capital, driving up the pay-offs to brutal regimes to dizzying numbers. But note that the fungal filaments, the life-sucking veins, do not stop when they reach the bank accounts of the warlords, cartels, and thieving autocrats, but extend into the hands and stomachs of the poor from whom everything has been stolen.

We, comfortable in our tenured plenitude, are taking our food from the begging fingers of diarrheic children with distended stomachs and peasants whose land has been taken to feed beef cattle for American fast-food burgers and the heavy guts of their consumers — not directly, of course, because there is nothing direct in the giant fungus. The threads run underground, and in all directions, crossing each other many times, massing in one place then thinning in another. But they leave no one out. We are all connected. We are all complicit.

You know all of this, Commandante Cisneros. In fact, I have heard the same lecture delivered with stunning eclat by your inspired persona, Raimundo Guttierez. Raimundo was especially skilled at painting the dire working conditions in the unsupervised sweatshops of Asia and the American owned *maquilladoras* in Mexico and Central America. And not bad at the spoliation of the oceans, the fouling of the air, the uncontrolled burning of rain forests, and the desertification of vast areas on all continents. Of course, he didn't mean a word of it. But then, anyone in the University can give this very lecture; indeed, so can most educated Americans. And, of course, not one of us means it either.

It is a peculiar characteristic of the *armillaria ostoyae* that on rare occasions it will burst out of the earth as a packed colony of handsome butter-colored mushrooms. There is no hint that they are intimately connected to the network growing into and slowly eating away the forest. So, too, with us. As academics in a world-renowned university, we are a privileged and honored society whose roots inthe exploitation of the earth and its people are nowhere evident — except to us. We are too well educated not to know we are complicit. There is no excuse for feigning innocence as yellow fungi.

And now, *Commandante*, I must raise an issue I have not heard you address. In fact, by every indication you are oblivious to the deeper human crisis you masterfully labored to create. You are, indeed, the very model of this particular assault on the people of the earth. Consider your career. You were recruited by an autocrat whose simple goal was to develop and nourish sources of his own personal wealth, and nothing else. His singular fungal skill was to thread his parasitic veins into the agricultural abundance of his small nation, that is, into the native communities and their centuries of experience in making scant mountain soils fruitful. These remote villagers were forced to do what they could to fight off those thirst-driven tentacles.

Your *Presidente* did what he was forced to do to protect his interests. He raised an army and sent its officers to commando training schools in the US. Soon Indian communities by the hundreds were swept from their hillsides and gardens by forced eviction and mass execution. In a mere two or three years, there poured forth from the purloined hectares truck- and boatloads of sugarcane, bananas, cattle, corn, and even chickens, all of which was sold in *el Norte* at enormous profit, shared by the *Presidente* and his small circle of oligarchs. Your part in this was to suppress the noisy protests to this successful venture by devices of your own imagination. And what an imagination.

What you did not see, absorbed as you were with your killing, Felix, is that there was something worse: by disappearing the Indians and your country's young intellectuals, you killed a multitude of rich and ancient cultures, and with them their music, mythology, healing arts, languages, and folk wisdoms. Your *jefe* knew instinctively this had to be done. His real enemy was not the fragile bodies of the Indians and their children, but the *indifference of high culture to material wealth.*

There is a good reason why Socrates is banned from the Enterprise University. The brilliance of his discourse, still vital after twenty-four centuries, earned not one person a single drachma. How much profit can we squeeze from the *Summa Contra Gentiles or The Critique of Pure Reason or The Tibetan Book of the Dead?* Invert the process. If art does not cash out for its society, can society cash out for beauty? How many millions need we allocate for another *Jupiter Symphony or Don Quixote de la Mancha* or the *Upanishads?* Wealth does not create culture nor does culture create wealth. But wealth can destroy culture.

Presidentes the world over fear artists and free minds. They are right to do so. What doomed the Soviet Union was not its failed military but the failed idea of itself. Plato banned poets from the Republic because, uncontrolled by the state, they could weaken the ideology of the Philosopher King. Islamists bomb schools for girls. The Texas State Board of Education filters students' exposure to the science of evolution. Suppressing ideas outright and executing their advocates is a crude tool, only occasionally successful. But there is a more effective strategy: sell them the state. The soldiers were devastating to your small country, *Commandante,* but the motorbike, marketed to the poor for small monthly installments, was far more destructive. Television, all but free, accelerated its mental death. Alcohol, cheapest state product of all, has spread a gray film over what is left. The only price charged to the poor for all of this was their culture, especially those crafts and arts and unique ways of knowing that had grown from intact traditions, millennia old.

I have called you a model enemy of free culture, Felix, but in all honesty, you are a petty criminal, even a joke, compared to the sleek anti-cultural forces at work through the modern university, especially ours. Pay no attention to the creative artists and scientists within the academic community. We have our theater productions, musical concerts, mathematical prizes, writing seminars, daring chemical experiments, medical research, and even a poetry reading now and then — really nothing more than a colony of mushrooms. Instead follow the filaments as they spider out into the society as a whole in their relentless search for nutrients. Corporate wealth — the university's indispensable life support system — is a place to start. Remember this is not a different web; we are all connected. What we must add here is that the meteoric fortunes accumulating in our own financial oligarchies — in totals that would make your *Presidente* dizzy with incredulity — feast on rotting culture.

The evidence is everywhere. Drive through the suburban commercial rings around any of a hundred of our larger cities and try to detect signs that you are in Denver and not in Atlanta, or in Peoria and not in Greensboro. Try to find a single business flourishing only on its original home site, with an ethos, product, and architecture distinct from the chainstores surrounding it. As in your sad, failed land, *Commandante,* it is not that corporations are buying up America; the corporations themselves are for sale and we are racing each other to leap onto the mounting transurban, interstate, supraregional, international, and global consolidation of anonymous monetary transactions unrelated to any specific source.

The McDonald's, Applebees, Papa Ginos, The Gaps, Hobby Lobbys, Ikeas, and Walmarts emerge like plagues of larvae from former corn fields and ex-industrial urban wasteland, all of it managed from thirty stories up in cities with indistinguishable skyscraper profiles by firms whose interests are not in quarter-pounders, assemble-your-own furniture, and tight jeans, but liquid assets that can flow seamlessly into each other. The streams are currently at flood stage, each one rising as smaller currents are directed into it. We are down to two major airlines, four major banks, three car manufacturers, two computer giants, five clothing chains, two publishing behemoths, and one ubiquitous natural foods retailer. The whole of America is up for sale, and we are buying it with two simple payments: what is left of the dwindling material possessions of the poor and the very poor, and a wide range of what we might once have called genuine American cultures.

The scandal for us as honored professors of institutions of so-called higher learning is that we have been set aside like museum pieces, of little more use to a society than to remind it of a past no one really desires to recover. Placed before lecterns in glassed-in dioramas, costumed and masked like anodyne sages and intellectual errants, our words are taken by students as so many brochured guides to high grades and admission to professional schools. Museums can be grand, also costly both to enter and to maintain. But they are safe. The visitors will not be sent into the streets screaming revolution. Nothing new will escape their gothic keeps. Innovative thinking will quickly solidify into remembered ideas. Museum/universities are elegant display cases of dead cultures. The irony is complete. The modern university kills or it dies.

Of course, as we lay there near the lip of a three-hundred-foot precipice, Felix Cisneros, your mind was a hemisphere away from your history. In fact, you could not have guessed that I had contacted Vincente Lopez. There was, however, the small crack in the cover up of your life as an *ejecutor*. Only that one reference came through. What is more, only Señor Lopez knows that I have properly identified you.

So I was at my leisure in planning your execution. When you took up with Lucille, or better, when Lucille took you up, you practically put the plan in my hand.

Indeed, at that moment, I knew that it was she and she alone who was the mistress of your fantasies. I knew it as we lay there, when, after a long silence, you spoke her name, then nothing more. The dialogue that followed was little more than whispered, as if we were addressing a sacred subject. You went directly to the issue.

"Did you ever reach Ten with her?"

"Yes." This was a lie, of course. I got only to nine at that terrifying moment when she held me perilously close to the precipice. Reaching ten with Lucille was still ahead of me.

"How did it happen?"

I described how we had made our own venture to the Gunks — to a milder spot even if still treacherous — when she lured me to join her at the edge. In my account of the way she held me over that terrifying emptiness, when I was completely in her control and unable to attempt escape without throwing both of us into it, I was not exaggerating. That was precisely what happened.

You thought about this. I could see that you looked confused, for good reason. I had set you up. And it worked.

You looked over at me where I was still lying as if you wanted to say something difficult. You began, "She says — " and hesitated. I gave you that conspiratorial smile, encouraging you to continue. "She says — that when you get to ten you die."

"Yes, you do." I tried to sustain a mystical tone to the conversation.

"But you are right here," you asked, not understanding. "You are still alive."

When I responded with my best feigned, spiritual inflection,

"How do you know?" I realized your puzzlement was complete, but your Latin fascination for the living dead was enough to keep you from outright denial. It was now the time for action.

I stood. You rose and faced me. Touching the buckle of my harness was all I needed to do to show my intention. You pulled yours free and dropped it, as if ordered to do so. You tossed your clothes behind you. You kicked your shoes away. Now, fully exposed, I saw that you were ready. You took hold of yourself, not as the *ejecutor*, not to complete the moment *a mano*, but as the act of a celebrant blessing the sacred vessel before invoking its transcendent powers.

It was now as if I were controlling you with the invisible strings of a puppeteer looking down at his weightless mechanical clown. The comedy begins.

I assume the position of prayer, kneeling in the pose of submission, inches from the lip of the cliff. To you, for whom the manipulative strings are invisible, I appear to be silently imploring you, despite my unworthiness, to grant me the bounty of your passion. At my silent command, you place your feet between my knees, your heels slightly over the edge. Soon you take me with a sudden movement I would not hesitate to call violent. At once, there is a *kenosis*, an emptying of power, and you, unaware, give yourself over completely. I tighten my grip, holding you in place as your body weakens. Now, I alone can keep you from falling. Your trust is absolute. I pull you still closer. I feel the approaching surge. Your fingers grip my back like claws, a sign of the Moment's imminence. I wait several seconds, greet its nascent arrival, and then release you. You know, Felix, *a mano*. From where I am kneeling, I witness the full arc of your descent, just as you must have watched after your violated young and innocent victims spun helplessly to the surface of the *Golfo*, where they died immediately or were too stunned to hold themselves above water. In your case, there was a slight difference. This time the arrival of the Moment for you occurs midflight. Your final cry of fury and ecstasy echoes off rock faces in both directions. In the sunlight, I can discern a silken thread thrown off in your downward spinning, a gossamer monument to your now completed humanity. The echoes cease. The comedy has ended. *"Adios,* Felix Cisneros," I speak into the empty air. Then, as a sign of your achievement, I utter the final word: *"Diez."*

Moving quickly, I gathered the equipment; packed it with your clothes in a trash bag I had folded at the bottom of my backpack, and walked down the long path to where I had parked Lucille's Karmann-Ghia. Once on the thruway, I drove at a leisurely and legal pace into the city and left the car in its usual spot in faculty parking. I pulled the ignition cable free and tossed it into the open glove compartment. On the way to my office, I passed a loading sanitation truck, and held up the bag of your clothes and gear to the driver. He nodded. I threw it into the bin. As I walked away, I heard the smashing and cracking as the great metal jaws chewed its treasures into *nada.* You disappeared as quickly and completely as your *Desaparaciementos.*

NINETY-THREE

Well, dear **Lucille**, you are the final pupil in this seminar of the dead. You, the star student. It was a challenge for me, both terrifying and thrilling, as it always is when you have a student who offers herself to the class as the smartest one present — smarter even than the teacher. And with me, you strove vigorously, coming close. Anyone who claims to be a teacher — that highest of all distinctions — knows the dangers before class starts. Not to learn from your students is a fatal mistake. To be instructed by your students is equally deadly. There is a delicate middle path: To teach learning by way of doing it in the presence of your students, and in a manner that allows them to fully understand what is happening — the highest achievement of our art.

At first you were my teacher, Lucille. I was under your instruction and you knew it. How, I wondered, could I recover? I understood the challenge. The critical reversal was to lead you to comprehend, not how much you were teaching me, but how thoroughly I knew that you were aware of doing so. To stay a short distance ahead was my test. I saw that you considered me your best student ever, as I profoundly desired to be. But I had to show you I saw that **you** saw it this way. Only then was I able to keep ahead of you. The distance was small, but too far for you to reach. Therefore, by allowing you to elevate me to the tenth level, I was drawing you closer to completion. I could become a perfect teacher only when you had become a perfect student. But, it is also true that because of the threat I recognized in your presence, I was *compelled* to become your teacher. I had no choice but to stay ahead. Failing that, you would have eaten my soul.

That is why, on that radiant day atop Mount Skunamunk, when you first explained your Game of Tens, I made sure you knew I understood. For a fleeting instant, you were in my power. So I acted fast. I explained to you what I could have called my own Game of Tens. You waited, motionless, rapt, until I finished. Ten deaths, all violent, all committed at a distance, all preceded by a puzzle, all meant to reveal something about our life in the University, even about life itself, that nothing less than a planned and showy murder can awake us to. The tenth and final death, I concluded, was to be my own. And, since I had been preparing this for some time, years really, nearly everything was in place. A few minor details remained.

You then spoke four words, the most powerful ever said to me. "Take me with you."

It was a whisper so faint it could have been the breeze talking. But as we lay there for hours, not touching, staring outward into the fading afternoon, I needed no further proof. We had not only become lovers, we had become equals. May I say it? The Moment was Socratic.

My plans were long in the making, but when I learned that Oliver Ridley had just been installed as Dean, and that he would therefore move into your office, it was all but decided for me that this would be the year of the Puzzler Murders. Your eagerness to join me in my game confused me somewhat at the very beginning, then I understood. Ridley was moving *into your office*. It has long been your office but not just because your desk was there. Ridley had the title of Dean, but you did the work of the dean, as you did for the several deans preceding him. So what were they doing there — except pretending to do the work a certain woman was actually doing? For three times the salary and a free parking space. But the power was in your hands. It was always in your hands. You knew it and I knew it. The time to act had finally arrived. Of course, you would be eager.

It took considerable calculation to get the timing right. It was essential that you be present without Ridley knowing you were present. We could have coordinated all this by phone, of course, but, you were right, there had to be no record whatsoever. This meant there was a degree of chance we could not eliminate. When I returned the next morning with my binoculars, I had to assume the Dean was already there and you were not, because Jose Ramirez called out to me, his voice hardly audible over the roar of the spinning brushes on his floor-cleaning machine. When he got the thing to run down to a slow moan, I was delighted to learn of his daughter Ariana's first day at Brown. Of course, I had to extend the conversation a bit so Jose would assume I was there on routine business without any pressure to escape his touching expressions of gratitude for my help with Ariana's college applications. I then went straight to Ridley's office.

It was just as I was moving to the window with Ridley, that I had the first clue you were there, Lucille. I saw nothing and I heard nothing. It was your perfume, easily identifiable as the Fragrance de Frédéric Malle, a full ounce of which I had bought you at Bendel months earlier. The scent moved ahead of you like a living cloud. With a covered glance backward, I realized you saw how my hand was lightly touching Oliver's right shoulder. The expression on your face, especially in your eyes, was like none other I had seen there. There was no misinterpreting its meaning. Without taking my eyes from yours, crowding Oliver just enough to throw him off-balance was effortless; at least I remember no resistance.

In a fraction of a second, in no time at all, he was air-bound. You stared for a moment at the empty window, then again at me. A single unspoken word formed on your lips. For neither of us did it need to be said aloud. Fortunately, at that moment, you put your hand out to keep me away from the window, protecting me from any accidental viewer in the Square. I, after all, was not there. I watched the silent calculation in your eyes, as you waited for the proper time to act on your own. How much time elapsed? A minute? Ten? You went to the window and looked down. The animal-like screech was perfect. The crowd looked up but you were gone, in a dash for the elevator. Your performance at the door of the building was, judging from the comments of viewers, a masterpiece, Oscar Award level. Since, according to our plan, I exited the building on the opposite side in the direction of Café Rossetti, I sadly had to miss the show. But the barista drew my double Americano so perfectly, I decided on a second cup, allowing almost two serene hours of musing.

I think the ease in planning and coordinating that first murder surprised both of us. We would work together, but there would be a distribution of labor. I was the Puzzler and the killer. You would be the executive producer. You knew the University like no one else — which persons in the administrative staff were competent and which were fumblers, where the most advanced technology was located and how it could be used, how the President and his staff were likely to react to the ensuing chaos.

Though it can sometimes be a painful thought, I knew that your intimacy with assorted members of the University community earned you an encyclopedia of personal secrets. It was typical that you would have so easily produced evidence for what Holmers was up to during his nighttime visits to the lab. I know it was by way of the student who pushed the condemning document under your office door, and whom you saw only from behind as she disappeared around a corner. Then, by accident, in a conversation with Holmers' secretary, some months after the event, she referred to your appearance in her office in what she described as something of a sexual frenzy, asking about a student — here she slipped into your faux Oxonian accent — "with that patch of extraordinary real estate," giving yourself a slap on your derriere. So it wasn't that you saw her from behind so much as you saw her behind! Yes, I admit, I was too weak to repel a painful clutch of jealousy this casual remark aroused. And why were you on such intimate terms with that secretary? How did she know at once whom you meant?

But our coordinated efforts hardly stopped there. Because you have too often had to field complaints from students and faculty about the capricious rise and fall of the classroom temperatures--hot in the winter, cold in the summer — you were eager to assist me in hacking into the University's air conditioning controls. By your success at publishing the puzzles in so many media, exactly on schedule, without a single clue to their origin, you saved me from fiddling about with technology and publicity tricks mysterious to me. Your idea of appearing at a meeting of the Committee with a "corrected" puzzle, especially dressed and perfumed as you were, nicely muddied any track to a suspect. How you got "Raimundo" to brag about his connection to the CIA I can only imagine, but do not want to know. And what a touch of genius to get Jack to appoint you, as one of the legally mandated directors, to the Lister Family Foundation, unaware I suppose of the talents developed in the years you spent scanning budgets for signs of academic funny business. So, there you sat with full view of the funniest business ever conducted within the administrative walls of the University — Jack's all out campaign to blackmail selected members of his own faculty. Quite enterprising. How amused you must have been when you first perceived the flow of pre-laundered cash into the Foundation books through envelopes hand-delivered by secretaries (all of whom you were "friendly" with, I assume) from Anthropology, Applied Mathematics, and Art History. And then, Deborah Waterson's generous and criminal dipping into this evaporating well must have left you rolling with laughter on the floor of the Karmann-Ghia — where there was a floor.

Your absence at Commencement was a theater piece of exquisite scripting. While it was a palpable reminder of your indispensability to the smooth functioning of the University's most basic functions, it also added credibility to the later assumption that you were the Puzzler's penultimate victim. And, of course, in one sense you were.

But for sheer brilliance nothing comes close to the electronic interruption of the opening ceremony for the *University at 150*. To break into Will Shortz's comments at the most propitious point was a work of technological genius. How fitting that your finest act would also close the curtain on the year's thrilling ten-episode drama, thrilling at least for you and me. Indeed, the very fact that the idea for the sesquicentenary Celebration originated in a meeting of the Lister Family Foundation board — an intimate group consisting of Jack, two of his aged cousins, and you — throws a revealing light on the event's true provenance. What is more, Jack's increasingly meth-propelled brain was of no danger to the event's preparation because he never had a real part in it. From the beginning, all arrangements were in the exquisitely manicured hands of the University's grand mistress of organizational planning. The Puzzler's fate could not have been more successfully settled.

I do claim a bit of theatrical legerdemain for myself in designing and executing the disappearance of the Karmann-Ghia. I am especially pleased to report this because there is no other way you would know of it. You never doubted that your own "execution" was imminent, to be sure, but because I never let slip with the merest hint, you could not have guessed what was coming.

It was about three in the morning when I made my way to the faculty parking garage. With the wrench I brought for the purpose, it took only a few minutes before all of the bolts on the front right wheel were reduced to a single remaining turn. With the screwdriver, also hidden in my purse, I removed the license plate and exchanged it with a Toyota Prius parked on the street several blocks away. I will admit to a kind of surprise when I found in the glove department the passport you had left there after returning from an unexplained journey a few days earlier (causing your absence from Commencement.) It was only a modest surprise, because with you I had long since learned to anticipate the unanticipated. It had a convincing photograph, and your correct name, Lucille Morrowitz, but it gave an address I did not anticipate. So, you did not grow up in New Jersey and acquire a fake accent after all, but in the Knightsbridge district of London (SW7). I admit that cultivating an accent from a raw urban neighborhood in the Garden State is far more accomplished than trading that for an elegant Oxonian cadence with its flattened but imitable vowels. (However, I will also confess to more than a shred of doubt about this passport affair. Was it a plant? Is it authentic? Is that really your name? How many of these do you have? Did you expect me to find it? Did you then know how I was planning your final "demise"? I will never know, and perhaps it is better that I won't.)

Once I found the "key" I got the car started and slowly headed east. The highway was all but abandoned. I drove uptown and back several times until I could select the perfect site. It was there that the highway ran closest to the river and had scant guardrail protection. There was not much to it. I coasted to the slow lane and proceeded at a crawl until the roadway ahead was without a car for a quarter mile or so. As I jumped out I jerked back on that strange little device you called a throttle and watched the tires as they all but caught fire on the pavement. The fishtailing grew increasingly violent until the loosened wheel finally shot free of the axle. The car swerved sharply then flipped, passing through at least two complete airborne rolls before it sailed over the guardrail into the river, leaving the isolated wheel to continue its own wobbling course down the center of the road.

As I walked home, I mused on the perfect ending for our year's labors. It comes as a kind of unholy trinity. Felix Cisneros vanishes into the air, you into the water, and I (oh, I do so hope) into the earth.

I reported, a few pages back, on the meeting I had with Jack Lister fifteen minutes after the Committee solved the ninth puzzle. It was then that he proposed, in the absence of a body, we simply erase your disappearance from pubic comment. That was not the last encounter I had with Jack concerning your non-presence. It was true, as I wrote, that he was relieved he could push ahead with his plans without having to account for your unavailability. The matter, however, was more complicated. His true relief had to do with the fact that you were no longer an active agent, and thus a critical witness, in his grand scheme to pilfer the University's funds. He was, in fact, buoyed by the possibility that the one person who knew what he was up to had exited the scene — whatever the reason. But the reason tormented him.

My second meeting with Lister — not previously described in these pages — was quite different. At this point we were two days away from *The University at 150*. He texted me, requesting I come to his office at once. Even on the tiny screen of my phone, I could detect an air of command in this request. I had no doubt it had to do with the missing Executive Administrative Assistant. But why this urgency I couldn't guess. Perhaps he concluded that I knew something substantive concerning your absence. Of course, I didn't — exactly. And, of course, I never will. I can only know that our lives will forever be dead to each other.

I found him at his desk, his feet on the floor, impulsively tapping his Mont Blanc (same model as Oliver's — your gift?) on the pitted boards of that famed piece of furniture. When I took the chair opposite, he performed his all-time best theatrical pause. He stared at me for fifteen seconds at least. No blinking.

"The ninth puzzle." He spoke the words to sound like an accusation. I did not respond. "Who's *my*?"

"Who's what?" I answered, quite aware what he was after.

"Carmody, you knew Lucille as well as anyone. The puzzle was worded to sound like it was written by a lover." Another pause. "*My beloved Miss Morrowitz,*" he quoted, still without blinking. "Who killed her?"

"What makes you think she was killed? That line could have been written by any admirer, and there were plenty of those, a lot of them students."

"Bullshit, Carmody. You're holding something out on me here."

"Jack, why is this coming up now?"

He turned to an open laptop that I hadn't so far noticed. It was just to the left of his desk blotter, the screen visible to both of us. So I was about to learn why I was summoned.

He hit the space bar on the keyboard. Lieutenant Roche's face filled the screen, obviously a posed department photo.

"Jack, I got great news!" the Lieutenant's recorded voice bounced around the room. Jack had apparently connected his laptop to the speakers of his office radio before my arrival. "We got the broad's car! One of my guys, he's going over accident reports, finds this one entered several weeks ago, round the time of Commencement. Seems a vehicle blows over the guardrail on the East River Drive. The accident's called in by a witness. A woman. Doesn't ID herself. Says this 'thing' (her word) passes her on the opposite side of the highway like a 'fucking rocket' (her word,) swerves, hits the guardrail, goes end over end into the water. The 911 operator, she gets the call, she reports it as probable fatality. My guy — smart, college grad — he has a suspicion, inquires. Vehicle not pulled from water. He orders the river dragged in that section. They find and remove this piece-of-shit driving machine from the river. Model or year cannot be verified. They find a water-logged passport, only partially legible. They could make out the last name. Yep, it's our gal, Morrowitz. What's important is that the way this wreck is crushed, no one can get out through doors or windows. There's no body in the vehicle. None's been reported down river. How the driver survives and gets out is yet to be explained. Coast guard says that area of the river, it's known for these invasive Chinese Snakehead fish. Bodies alive or dead, they last minutes is all. Or, so they say."

Jack hit the off button. He stood and tossed the Mont Blanc onto the desk. I watched its wild off-balance spinning as he took a few quick steps toward the window and looked down at the Square, as if trying to decide what to say next.

"The Lieutenant," he announced as he turned toward me, "doesn't buy the Snakehead fish crap. There's only one rational explanation, he says. There was no body in the wreck when they pulled it up because there was no body in it when it went over the guardrail. Some clever fuck drove to the spot, jumped out, manipulated the throttle external-ly, and aimed it at the river."

He waited to see my reaction. I had none.

"So where does that leave us, Carmody?" Another pause, a full ten seconds. "I'll tell you where. Lucille's either fish bait, or she's out there somewhere playing games with us." He came over to my side of the desk and stood over me, the usual threatening stance. "Come clean, Carmody. What's she up to?"

"I'm confused myself, Jack. Sit down for a moment." I waited. "Let's piece it together. Just what sort of game could she have got us into? You're thinking something to do with *The University at 150*?"

He blinked, nothing more.

"Remember," I continued, "that the Puzzler promised ten deaths?

That they were all carefully planned? Far in advance, years probably? Long before you conceived the Ceremony? Each was carried out with robotic precision. This is presumably the ninth. Why an exception now?"

His non-response was all the response I wanted.

"Jack, the Ceremony is the day after tomorrow. My advice? Stick with the Snakehead fish — for the moment. There may be a better explanation later. But please do this: impose the same gag order on Roche you forced on me and the Committee. Tell him to say nothing of a wreck, and nothing of a missing body. Wait at least until the day after the day after tomorrow. Don't blow the Great Event. It's your finest creation, Jack. It will define the rest of your career."

Jack's face was an artist's dream for a portrait of rage, magnified by an acute awareness of his weakened position — all directed at me. He had already learned from his little spies that we were lovers — thus the 'Who's *my*?' question. He was also beginning to realize that my connection to you was more than romantic and that you might not have not been the supremely competent and loyal servant you present-ed yourself to be. When he learned you were not in that car, and that you might be walking about with evidence that would send him and Roche up for long terms, he was of course frantic to know what I knew. Could there have been a leak of secrets and could I have been their recipient? As the terrifying consequences of this possibility slowly un-folded, he held me in a frozen stare, unable to speak. He was caught in the purest of dilemmas: knowing that simply to ask the question was to reveal his own perfidy. It was our last match, and it was becoming clearer which of us was winning. I have no doubt that President Jack Lister was, of all those present at the revived Academic Hall of Fame opening, the least surprised to learn the identity of the Puzzler.

And now, my lovely Miss Morrowitz, there is just a suggestion of daylight visible from our small window. Soon they will send someone from the court with the jury's decision. By then the cell will be emptied of all shadows. They will find no occupant here but me. Even now the others have vanished and you alone remain. But is it you? Perhaps it is only a shade. However, you would find that surrounding us in the growing light, everyone is still present in another way. As the reader knows, I have left a thorough account of each death and why it was necessary. This, Lucille, is what you would see all about you. The hundreds of pages covering the floor to each corner of the cell are the final testimony of the Puzzler. This page, the one I am holding up for you — Can you see? Well, maybe not — will contain my final words. I was forbidden from speaking in the court, not permitted to be present at my own trial. No matter. It was not necessary. All that need be said is on these pages. Though I was absent, I know how the fool Prosecutor presented my case. This is what he said. Do listen.

"Lady and Gentlemen of the jury," (I believe there was only one woman on the panel.) "I will summarize in a few words the dastardly deeds of our killer now safely locked away in our most secure prison."

Lucille, how I wish you can hear this ham-fisted summing up of our work. It gives me such hope.

"Lady and Gentlemen, nine victims were slain by this cold and calculating monster. One was thrown from a tenth-floor window, another crushed nearly flat under thousands of gallons of pressurized water, yet another frozen to death in a remote corner of the Arctic. An adviser to the President was killed by an exotic poison unknown to science. A distinguished anthropologist was forced to commit suicide. The body of the University's most famous professor was found naked and ghoulishly immolated on the steps of a European cathedral. A prominent classicist was suffocated in a despicably violent sex act. An executive administrative official was eaten alive by invasive Asian fish. Incredibly, another seems to have been dropped from the air into a remote forest, the remains never found."

I picture the Prosecutor here trembling with rage and righteousness — all performance, of course — as he announced: "And the killer not only confessed, she presented details on each case, all the while gloating as if each was a noble achievement! Gloating!"

He completed his address to the jury like this: "Lady and Gentlemen, as you retire to your deliberations, you have it in your authority to add one more body to this nightmarish list. The killer planned for a tenth execution. May her plans be complete. One more death and we can say at last, it is finished."

Lucille, dear, did you hear this? Are you here? No? How it would amuse you! τετελεςθαι!

Ah, the sun. Farewell to you all, then. I hear the heavy sounds of steel doors opening and closing. (I must now write very quickly. A few sentences will suffice.) Keys are making a lively music in the swinging hands of the jailers. There are voices. Some I recognize. The court lawyer appointed to my case. The Warden's voice resembles that of a tour guide, directing attention of the small company this way and that. The Chief Bailiff is among them, but he is silent. It is he who was charged by the judge to announce the verdict. I sense his hesitation. He needn't be anxious. His duty is simple. He has only to utter one of two words: Hemlock, or Oblivion.